Praise for Deidre Knight's *Butterfly Tattoo*

"Love and family come in many forms and wear many faces. Deidre Knight takes the heart on a healing journey of love in BUTTERFLY TATTOO, showing that love truly can heal all things. Lyrical...beautiful...unexpected."
~ *Jill Shavis, USA Today Bestselling Author*

"I can't say enough about Knight's writing. The prose is lyrical, each word deliberately wrought, like fine stitchwork on an enormous piece of embroidery. Every stitch is exquisite."
~ *Sarah Wendell, SmartBitchesTrashyBooks.com*

"I'm a fairly traditional romance reader.... It's hard for me to move outside my comfort zone. But this is a rare and different gem. It is a story I'll treasure and remember. I hope that even if it does not net [Deidre Knight] significant financial rewards that [she'll] keep writing these stories. There is an audience for it. I know there is."
~ *Jane, Dear Author*

"A brilliant exploration of the fluidity of sexuality - and the tenacity of the human spirit."
~ *Michelle Buonfiglio, Romance B(u)y the Book*

"[Ms. Knight] demonstrates that she can pull out all stops and portray heartbreak and healing of broken souls in ways that have me feeling simultaneously drained and exhilarated at the same time."
~ *Ms. Giggles, MrsGiggles.com*

"Deidre Knight does a fantastic job of exploring Michael's grief – the numbness, the fearfulness and the reluctance to begin again. Her portrait of his pain and inner conflict is so real, it will definitely have you in tears at times. But you'll also be uplifted by the warmth of his relationship with his daughter and by the tenderness of his romance with Rebecca. I truly loved these characters and hated to part with them. BUTTERFLY TATTOO is a wonderful, deeply moving story that will stick with you long after you've finished reading it."
~ *Lynn Renoylds, Romance Junkies*

Look for these titles by
Deidre Knight

Now Available:

A Midnight Warriors Story
Parallel Fire

Butterfly Tattoo

Deidre Knight

A Samhain Publishing, Ltd. publication.

Samhain Publishing, Ltd.
577 Mulberry Street, Suite 1520
Macon, GA 31201
www.samhainpublishing.com

Butterfly Tattoo
Copyright © 2009 by Deidre Knight
Print ISBN: 978-1-60504-544-3
Digital ISBN: 978-1-60504-134-6

Editing by Angela James
Cover by Natalie Winters

First Samhain Publishing, Ltd. electronic publication: 2009
First Samhain Publishing, Ltd. print publication: 2009

Dedication

To Ann Leslie Tuttle for having been the very first to believe. Without your encouragement, I might not have persevered. I'll be forever grateful for your kind words and guidance.

To Pamela Harty for having always believed—in me, this book, my abilities, my talent. You are a gift from God in my life.

And to Angela James for being the one: The editor who believed that Michael and Rebecca's story deserved publication. Thank you from the bottom of my heart.

Chapter One: Rebecca

Ben McAllister carried a knife, my name burned into the handle like a cattle brand. Oddly enough, I remember noticing that fact while he was stabbing me with the thing. The police showed me his weapon months later, and that's when I realized it wasn't just my first name—he actually had my picture embossed into it. A kind of stylized representation of me, one that matched the tattoo on his forearm. Rebecca O'Neill as cartoon character, not the professional actress I was at the time.

It seemed, according to the police, that he'd named his knife after me, in true devoted stalker fashion. How nice of Ben. It was a butterfly knife, and I'm convinced that something so destructive shouldn't bear such a beautiful name. Killers are like that, though. They find the poetry in violence.

When you work with writers for a living like I do, life's little details are an herb garden, and you pluck a few ripe things here and there to give away. Right now, sitting in a script meeting, I decide to borrow this tidbit from my own personal history for the greater good of Hollywood. I've been giving notes to a screenwriter for an hour, when this brilliant inspiration comes my way.

"You could have the killer carry a knife," I suggest, arranging my pens on the desk in front of me so I can avoid meeting Kelly's eyes. "A knife with the victim's name on it."

"I'm not sure I know what you mean." She leans forward in her seat. "How can a knife—"

"Imprinted in the handle." I hold up my Montblanc pen to demonstrate, pointing to the company logo. "He could've named the knife after the object of his obsession."

"Hmm." Kelly isn't convinced. Clearly, she hasn't made the connection with my own, well-publicized past—and she hasn't made the connection to this clever idea of mine, either. Kelly's young; too young, which means she's quick to see things in bold colors, not subtle shades.

"You have to realize, if he's been stalking her for such a long time, he's consumed." I dare to lift my eyes upward as I talk. "What better reflection of that than naming his weapon after her."

From beside Kelly, my assistant Trevor expands on the idea, his upper-class British accent automatically lending it more weight. "It's a classical idea, really." He pushes his expensive wire frames up the bridge of his nose as he talks. "Many of the great bandits throughout history named their guns. I believe Billy the Kid's shotgun was Big Betty and Jesse James called his rifle Bertha."

Even though he stares at me earnestly as he talks, I have to avert my eyes to keep from smiling. He's the real writer in our midst, capable of spinning a tale faster than anyone I've ever met.

"Okay, sure." Kelly nods enthusiastically, buying into Trevor's fictitious history lesson. "This gives the killer an almost anti-hero quality."

"That's not really what I was going for." I hold out a staying hand. "Our killer can't be sympathetic. I mean, he's the baddie. He's got to be bad. *Big Bad.* I'm more looking to convey his obsession with the heroine. I think the knife does that job very well."

Ed Bardock, V.P. of Development and my boss, stands by the window, blowing cigarette smoke through the small open casement. But he's listening and paying much closer attention than he lets on. I won't allow him to smoke in my office—not with my asthma—and he refuses to endure a one-hour script meeting without a little nicotine jiving through his bloodstream.

"I'm not sure I buy it," he answers in a gravelly voice. "How come a killer like that goes to so much trouble? He'd stab her, The End."

"But, Ed, he's a stalker." My pulse skitters nervously.

"So?" he insists without meeting my gaze. Dang it, he knows all about Ben and what happened to me. I live with this pain; I should be able to mine it, mold it, and reinterpret it whenever I want.

"Ed, it's real." I lift my eyebrows, tossing my long blonde ponytail back over my shoulder. I make sure my facial scars come into clear view for him, illuminated beneath my desk lamp, a small reminder that I know exactly what I'm talking about.

Seated across my desk, Trevor and Kelly squirm in their seats, but not before blessed Trevor manages to offer me one of his kind smiles. He loves me. That's why he's here in this job—not just because he's got fantastic story instincts, but also because he's the one person in my life who can consistently truss me back together. Even though he'd be happy passing his days at Starbucks sipping lattes, writing and living off his trust fund, he spends them here working at the studio with me.

"So it's real," Ed says finally, extinguishing his cigarette in a Styrofoam cup of cold coffee. "But does it add to the story?"

"I think so," Trevor pipes in. "I think everything Kelly can do to show how this killer's obsession has escalated over time is key to the script."

Then, without meaning to, I leave the room. Not physically, of course, but my mind flutters away. I'm eight feet high, pasted against the ceiling, floating there. Bobbing above them all, listening in. I'm watching *her*, down there; that girl at her desk with the Montblanc pen and the ruined face, lost in a company town, in her remote corner of an oversized studio lot.

This is what it's like to almost die. The way you see yourself below, only there's no warmth to what's happening here right now. All that roaring golden *power*, that love from the other side, it's always missing when I feel like this.

"Rebecca?" Trevor's black eyes grow wide. He takes hold of me, tugs me by my feet back down into my body. I was a balloon, ready to drift away, and he held me tight, tethered me to this world.

Trevor pins me with his dark gaze. "Rebecca, what do you think about the *killer* dying at the *end*?"

I've told him how these anxiety attacks work, the way I feel disembodied, the floating sensation. If I'm lucky, the asthma that I feel tightening my lungs won't overtake me.

"The killer dying," I repeat, my whole body numb. Kelly looks at me, nodding, and I realize it's her idea to change the way we've conceived the whole story. But Ben McAllister didn't die. He's up at Chino serving life plus twenty. And more important, he's *here*; I live with Ben every day, all wound up inside of me like a ball of hard twine.

Ed's BlackBerry rings, and he begins talking, already moving toward my office door. "Go with whatever Rebecca says," he announces loudly, making his way past my desk. "It's her baby. Time to wrap this one up." Then, just like that, we are dismissed from his consciousness.

Kelly tries following in his wake, calling after him. Totally uncool, but she's still a newbie. "Just think about it and let me know," she insists, looking back at me.

But I know exactly what I think of an ending in which the heroine wins, the stalker dies, and everything is wrapped up neatly with a bow. "Too easy," I murmur, staring at my Montblanc. "It doesn't work because it's way too easy."

✧

Reaching into my pocketbook, I retrieve a small medicine bottle of what my mama would call "nerve pills". Anything to stop the out-of-body stuff for a while; I dispense a couple of tablets onto my desk. It's been at least six months since I've needed these, and I say a quick prayer that I won't need them again after today. Coughing, I dig around for my inhaler too.

Trevor leans in my office doorway, slipping his headset back on. "Since when did development hell become worth *that?*" He gestures at my prescription bottle with a concerned expression.

"Since we started nudging up against my past in story meetings."

"Ah, right. The Britney Spears solution," he says. "Perhaps you could add head-shaving to your repertoire as well." He laughs, but then his expression grows more somber. "But tell me, should I be worried?"

"*Worried?*" Such a ludicrous suggestion, even if I did nearly die in his arms three years ago. "Trevor, I am *fine*. Fine, fine, fine. So very fine." And I mean it; the asthma didn't even kick in this time, so something must be improving. "I've been feeling really good lately. Honest."

His dark eyes narrow. "Which must be why your mother's been phoning me weekly to check up on you."

"No, she's just convinced that one day you're going to realize you're straight and decide to marry me."

"Well as your future husband, perhaps you won't mind me saying it's time you got out again. Started dating, making new friends."

"I make friends every day." I kick back in my chair. "After all, this is L.A."

"Talent agents and struggling screenwriters don't count, darling." Then his dark eyes widen with irrepressible excitement. "Look, I know this really cute guy from my writing group—"

"I'm not sure a date with one of *your* friends is the answer, Trevor."

"He's straight, Rebecca!" he cries, not bothering to disguise his frustration. "The fellow just moved here from Boston to sell copiers or ATMs or something useless and industrial like that. Does he *sound* gay to you?"

"Yee-ha. Maybe he'll take me to a trade show."

"Since when did you get picky? Let me fix you up with him." Again, my hand moves to my face, feeling the harsh scar tissue with my fingertips. Of everyone in my life now, only Trevor truly understands. After all, he was there to see the damage firsthand.

"I'll think about it."

"He's a real hottie," he promises, "in that computer salesman sort of way." I'm about to make a dubious remark about his taste in men when the whole room goes black without warning.

From down the corridor, Ed shouts, "Damned electrical department! They've screwed us again." When Ed shouts, it's more like divine thunder, and Trevor snaps to his feet without wasting a moment.

"Happy Monday to me, strapping lads in tool belts on their way," he sings to himself. There goes Trev with his recurring Ty Pennington fantasy again.

His shadowed outline moves past the shuttered bank of windows, toward the hall. Moments later I hear him at his desk, phoning over to the electrical construction department.

After a few minutes of darkness, Ed bellows, "Anybody working on this yet? It isn't brain surgery, *people*! Give me some damn light!"

Light. When all I'm thinking is that I can't read my phone messages without it. Funny, because otherwise I'm never more at peace than I am in the dark.

It seems forever before electrical construction sends somebody over to deal with our crisis. I guess Brad Pitt's latest blockbuster takes precedence over our development staff figuring out the *next* blockbuster for the studio to bankroll. Now, don't get me wrong, I'm not an executive in charge of production or anything; I'll leave that up to Ed and his team. It's just about tracking hot projects and trying to land them for the company. Frankly I'm in it for the reading. Lord knows I'm not looking for a producing credit, since unlike most everyone else in this town, I actually want to stay put in my job, not ascend the power ladder.

I'm on my cell phone, returning a call to a literary agency back east, when a huge shadow lumbers past my desk. I glance up, mid-discussion about the viability of translating a bestseller to the screen, when the shape stops in front of me, hesitating, obviously a man shadow, what with the size factor involved and all. In an effort to remain focused, I spin my chair in the opposite direction, toward the wall, continuing my conversation.

There's quiet mumbling from the stranger, then a flashlight illuminates some control panel on the lower part of my office wall, right beneath the covered windows. "Look, I've got to run, okay?" I say, wrapping up the conversation. "We're in the middle of a blackout here or something." I snap the phone shut, and sit in the dark, perfectly still. Slowly I rotate my chair in his direction, although I'm not sure what to say to a shadowy stranger, not like this. Finally I give it my best effort.

"You must be the electrician," I say, tugging nervously on my ponytail.

"You must be from the South."

"Geez, is it that obvious?" I ask, trying to make out the guy's face as he lifts the flashlight to eye level, tinkering with the control panel.

"Subtle, but the accent's still there." Guess all the dialect coaching in the world won't rid me completely of my Dorian, Georgia roots.

There's the metallic clanking sound of a fuse box or panel opening as he settles on the floor until he's leaning low on his elbows. In fact, from what his flashlight allows me to see, he's now stretched out on his stomach like a cat sunning itself, and I'm mildly curious about a guy who can make himself so at home in my office. "You figuring out the problem?" More enlightened commentary from yours truly as he aims the beam of light into the open electrical panel.

I'm met by silence, until he gives a long sigh. It's an exhausted kind of sound that actually surprises me. "The problem, Ms. O'Neill, is the antiquated wiring system in this building. Been patched and whatnot for about half a century, but what it needs is a complete overhauling."

Ms. O'Neill? How does he know my name?

"Your assistant told me this was your office," he continues, answering my unvoiced question. "Not trying to spook you or anything. Seeing how it's dark in here and all that."

"Now look who sounds southern," I tease, feeling a strange familiarity rise between the two of us. The kind you get talking to someone you're intimate with on the phone late at night—in your bed, well past midnight. Or maybe trading e-mails at three in the morning, when neither of you can sleep.

"Virginia, if that counts."

"Not to a Georgian."

"Reckon not," he says with a throaty laugh. "Might as well be a damned Yankee in your book, right?"

"Great, he mocks me."

"I mock not, Ms. O'Neill. I simply speculate." Okay, it's definite. This guy is flirting with me. A nameless, faceless stranger is right here in my office, flirting with me for all he's worth, and I'm not sure what to make of that. Suddenly, I'm blushing despite the darkness. And I'm running my fingertips along the left side of my face, praying he won't see my freakish scars once the light comes back on.

Then I'm unclasping my ponytail, hurrying before he *does* somehow see the horrible scars on my face. Or that strangely twisted half-smile of mine, because the problem is, I *can't* stop smiling at absolutely everything he says. Next, I shake my hair out, so that it cascades loose along my shoulders and then comb it forward with my fingers. Not only does my hair provide good camouflage, but it's also my most attractive feature these days. Golden, honey-colored and long, with natural highlights. Thick and wavy too. At least there's still one good thing that Ben McAllister didn't manage to steal from me.

His outline is highlighted by thin shafts of light that filter through the blinds, and I can tell he's maybe even six foot three or so. "I've gotta go get something from next door," he announces, brushing off his hands as he rises to his feet. "I'll be back."

I nod nonchalantly—as if he can see anyway—and remain calm despite the way my heart is dancing some kind of wild jig inside my chest. He vanishes into the dark hallway, then a moment later there's the sound of the main door opening and shutting to the parking lot outside. Only then do I realize that I've been holding my breath.

✧

"Look, sweetie, he's not the one," Trevor advises me in the dark. We're sitting in my office—darker than the others in this bungalow because it was once a screening room for daily rushes. In fact, Ed still uses it for that purpose which is why my wooden blinds are drawn closed today, just as they are most of the time.

"Why not?" I ask in an arch tone. After all, Trevor's the one always pushing me to date someone. Anyone at all.

"Because he plays for my team. Gay-dar Central, I assure you, my dear." He taps his fingertips on the window for emphasis. "Ding, ding."

"That guy is not queer."

"Why not? Because he's macho and *manly*?" He laughs, drawing out the last word.

"No, because he..." Flirted with me? I'm not about to tell Trevor my interpretation of events.

"I just thought he seemed straight, that's all."

Trevor places a comforting arm around me. "Sweetie, sometimes we gay men can read a moment, all right? There's kind of a current that passes, a look, if you will. Subtext."

"*That* happened?" I ask, feeling small and defeated. "You heard subtext? It was dark!"

"But our eyes met at the front door of the bungalow." Crap, that's right. With the power off, Trevor had to let him in manually.

"Was he cute?" I ask, even though my hope is fading fast.

"Ah, yes," he nearly growls. "Quite the sexy lad, but taken for sure. It's in the vibe. Clearly off the market, so it's a no-go for me, as well."

So much for my own ability to read a moment, I think, stumbling through the blackness toward my desk chair. That's the last time I decide I'm experiencing an emotional connection with a stranger in the dark. No, that stuff's just reserved for stupid sixties songs, not for me or my bungalow.

I drop into my seat and feel inexplicably tired. Beyond exhausted, really, as I wonder if there's someplace else where I can go until our development meeting, somewhere I can hide before the gay electrician returns.

But I don't leave. My cell phone rings, and it's the New York agent phoning me back about the bestseller, suggesting something of a compromise. Next thing I know we're discussing an offer, and then the strapping electrician lumbers right past me again before I can begin to plot my escape.

Once I'm done with the call, I fold the phone shut and begin straightening the manuscript on my desk into a neat pile. I'm ignoring the shadowy flirt, determined to tune him out as I stand to leave, when he says, "Sounds promising." Why do I immediately think he's talking about far more than the deal he just heard me negotiating?

"What?" I ask, rising to my feet. I have to get out of here before this guy weakens my steely resolve.

"Sounds like you're shutting down the competition, Ms. O'Neill."

I clutch the manuscript against my chest, feeling the need to protect myself.

"I like that killer instinct." He's got a throaty voice that I find very arousing.

Then I nearly snort with laughter because Trevor's just plain wrong. He has to be. This guy keeps striking up conversation with me, expressing interest. I may have been off the market for a long time, but I still know when someone's a kick-ass flirt. And he's flirting, big time.

"Killer instinct, right." I laugh, and it comes out sounding self-deprecating and dismissive. If the lights were on, I'd wave my hand, swatting the notion away with an easy flick of my wrist.

"Well, what would you call it?" he asks genuinely, half-groaning as he maneuvers low on his belly again. He's got the flashlight balanced against his shoulder, and I can see it's a tough juggling act.

"Doing my job. And it's Rebecca, by the way." I step closer and get my first partial look at his face. He's got short spiky hair, dark with a little curl and attitude to it.

"Nice to meet you, Rebecca." As he looks up at me, I find myself staring into an arresting pair of brown eyes. Not that I can see them all that well, mind you, but enough that I'm sure I won't forget them anytime soon. Just gorgeous, with long, fluttery lashes. Eyes like that can melt you on the spot, especially when accompanied by a smoky-toned southern accent, so I vow to proceed with caution.

"Can I hold that for you?" I gesture at his flashlight with a quick toss of my hair, ensuring that my scars are concealed from his line of sight.

"Yeah, that'd be great. Thanks." He smiles as I reach for the light, glancing up at me again, and Lord, it's a beautiful thing.

His fingertips brush against mine, rough, obviously calloused from long-term physical labor. They're large and something about their generous size makes me think of whoever it is he loves. Hands like that can protect you when you need it most; keep harm at a safe distance. Can hold you tight when the nights get long and the devouring nightmares won't keep away.

Now *this* is subtext: the simple brushing of his hand against mine, the resulting cascade of uninvited fantasies. I'm about to ask his name when a soft voice pierces the pregnant silence threading between us.

"Michael, can I have some money for the commissary?" Startled, I turn to find the outline of a young girl standing behind us, right beside my desk. She's about seven or eight years old, nine at most.

"I can't take you there right now, sweetheart." Michael. So he's no longer a stranger or the ponderous specter. He has a name.

"But I can walk over there on my own," she suggests, stepping closer. "I know the way."

"Not by yourself, you can't." Michael's voice has shifted from its semi-charming timbre, and become the authoritarian vise of a parent.

"I can't just sit around and watch the guys wire things," she huffs into the dark. Her voice is early-morning innocent, the kind that smells like dreams and comforters tucked around your face.

"Andrea, I've got to work," he says, kneeling there on the floor. "You know that."

"Are you gonna help me get on the *Evermore* set?"

"Maybe, if I can get you a pass," he explains. "But right now—"

"But you *said!*" she cries, and it's not a harsh sound, just a plaintive, frustrated one.

"I said I'd try. Now, go. Back over to the electrical department."

"So can I walk to the commissary then?"

Long, weary sigh, followed by an exasperated breath. "No. You just heard me say no."

"But it's only around the corner."

"Not by yourself."

"But you said—"

"No, not by yourself!" Only, it comes out more like "yoursailf," as his voice kind of snaps, revealing a whole underbelly of tension in that soft twang of a word. Maybe they've been at this all morning, or maybe they don't get along. It's hard to be sure.

Poor man. He's obviously quite familiar with the "wear 'em down" negotiator tactic because this little kid knows it well. In fact, she belongs in my line of work. Just don't let the agents around here find out about her—she'd make one lethal weapon in the hands of the wrong enemy.

"You know, I was thinking of heading over there," I suggest helpfully. "To the commissary, I mean." I'm not sure why I feel so eager to mediate their crisis, but I don't question my motivation.

"Really?" The girl turns to me, her sweet voice breathy as a sigh.

"Yeah, you know, I was going to go for some breakfast. I could take you. That is, if your..." I hesitate because I'm not sure *what* to call Michael. After all, she's called him by his first name, so he must not be her father.

"Michael," she finally adds after a long, impenetrable silence.

"Well if *Michael* doesn't mind, we could walk over together," I say, still curious about their undefined relationship. Only then does it occur to me that if I were a parent, I'd be suspicious of someone like me, a stranger expressing unsolicited assistance like I am. I try searching Michael's face to see if he's uncomfortable, but the office is just so dark, so sheltered by shadow, even with his flashlight providing scanty illumination.

"You sure?" he asks, a husky-voiced sound of uncertainty, as he rubs a tired hand over his eyes. It's not like he's worried that I can't be trusted, that's not it. Instead, it's almost as if he assumes Andrea's an imposition.

"Of course. It's all dark in here anyway," I explain. "We'll just go get some breakfast and then come back."

"Andie, wait." Michael digs in the pocket of his blue jeans, producing his wallet. "Let me give you some money."

"Oh, no, I'll take care of it," I rush to say. "Don't worry."

"No, really, here." Michael presses a ten-dollar bill into my hand. For a brief, incendiary moment, our fingers brush together, and without even meaning to, I step backwards, embarrassed by the unsought intimacy passing between us again.

I'm not sure if he even notices, because he turns to Andrea, reaching for her hand, but she pulls away sharply, so that he's left just standing there. Grasping for her and something about that image makes me feel unspeakably sad.

"Andrea, please be good for Ms. O'Neill, okay?"

She nods, dutifully clutching a small backpack in her hands like a lifeline. It looks to be some kind of Barbie contraption, fluorescent pink vinyl covered with glittery pictures.

"Thank you," Michael says to me in a fierce near-whisper. "I really appreciate this." His gratitude for such an easy gesture unnerves me in a way I don't fully understand, so I just nod, and without even meaning to, smile at him again. I swear, I can't stop smiling at the man.

"Come on," I say to Andrea, leading her down the hallway lined with countless awards and framed film posters. When we head out the front door, there's an explosion of morning sunlight so startling that I feel like someone has lifted the creaky cover off my sarcophagus. Like dust motes and cobwebs are drifting away from me, toward the piercing light.

Maybe this is what Trevor's been talking about, I think, squinting upward at the clear spring sky. For a fleeting moment, I even wonder if it isn't all some fabulous omen. If maybe the darkness in my life isn't about to finally end.

The little girl has about the most amazing red hair I've ever seen. It's not the garish red of a carrot top, yet far more than a simple auburn. It's like a deep burnished amber color mixed together with ruby jewels. As we walk across the asphalt parking lot, stepping onto the dew-soaked grass of Chaplin Park, sunlight catches bright strands of color in it, sparkling like fairy dust.

The shimmering red color is striking, especially contrasted with her creamy, translucent skin and blue eyes. The importance of skin like that is lost on little people. Not a blemish or a mark. Just purity dusted with golden freckles, like oranges in the snow, across her nose and cheeks. She shoves her hands in her denim overall pockets, tossing me a shy, reserved smile, and I can't help thinking of a china doll. A fragile little thing that I need to protect; no wonder I ache to reach for her small hand and hold it tight within my own.

We come upon several long wardrobe and makeup trailers parked outside Stage 30, marked *Evermore*, and she stares intently.

"So you like that show?" I ask, interrupted when a loud buzzer blasts from within. "That means the camera's rolling, so nobody can go inside." I gesture at the flashing red warning light beside the door, and she nods, obviously familiar with the production process.

At my leading, we dart down a side alley and wind up right in the Bronx—only in Hollywood, I think with a faint smile. Though really, it's only at this particular studio, which has the best re-creation of New York City streets outside of the Big Apple. We're strolling down the deserted avenue when Andrea announces in a quiet voice, "*Evermore's* my favorite show."

"Here, go this way." I tug lightly on her backpack, and then we're heading back between more sound stages. "Really? Your favorite, huh?"

"Do you watch it?"

"No, I never have. Should I?"

She only shrugs, and it's clear that I won't get any further with her on the topic. I make a mental note to check with Trevor for the pertinent details. I know a little, like that the male lead is pretty hot. My good friend Cat Marin read for the show, but they wound up casting someone else—someone I don't particularly like, as a matter of fact—and since we're not in series development, I've always ignored it.

"Michael never gets me on the good shows," she says as we walk toward the commissary. "He forgets stuff too much, so he can never get the passes. My daddy was better about stuff like that."

I'm wondering again about the nature of their relationship when she blurts, "*Evermore* is critically acclaimed." You can tell this child has been raised in the bosom of Hollywood.

I keep a straight face, although it's tough. "Really?"

She nods. "It's a 'revelation', that's what the ads say."

Andrea's got me curious now, and I need to know the facts. After all, it's my job to keep my finger on the pulse of America. You never know where you'll find great stories—sometimes they're right where you're *not* looking. Maybe a lot of things are.

Once we're settled at the cafeteria table, I learn that her full name is Andrea Lauren Richardson. Michael is her stepfather, she says, but then reveals nothing else. So I guess Trevor was at least partially right—he's clearly off the market. She doesn't mention her mother; I want to ask about that, but something stops me, something in the vague way she answers my question about Michael. "I live with him," is all she says, gazing down at her doughnut.

"You going to eat?" I ask after watching her poke at the Krispy Kreme's icing for a while.

"Are *you*?" She points to my own untouched bagel and I feel like my old semi-anorexic tendencies have just been shoved under a microscope.

"Probably."

"Yeah, probably me too."

After a moment I ask, "So how old are you, anyway?"

"Eight."

"Third grade?" I probe, determined to learn more, and she nods in agreement.

I flash momentarily on my own experiences at that age: Girl Scouts, dance classes, and horseback riding. I spent that summer on my parents' farm with nary a concern in my mind. "Second grade's really cool, isn't it?"

She shrugs, frowning slightly. "I guess so."

We fall silent, Andrea's eyes constantly searching the busy commissary. This is the place to come if you want to see weird aliens, vampires, or even plain old character actors here for a meal. It's also a good spot to land spoilers for upcoming television shows if you eavesdrop successfully on the right producers' conversations, but Andrea seems oblivious to all of that. Her auburn eyebrows arch upward, and she cranes her neck, scanning the whole of the room repeatedly.

"Looking for anybody in particular?" I finally ask, but she doesn't answer. She only stares down at the table again, picking at the doughnut some more. "Nobody at all?"

For a moment she opens her mouth to answer, but then snaps it shut again. Instead, a melancholy expression darkens her face as she stares out the tall windows into the spring sunlight. Something's going on inside her mind. I just can't tell what it is.

When she looks back at me, she whispers under her breath, "I have one too."

I think hard, certain I should understand this cryptic statement, but since I don't, I lean close and ask what she means.

"A scar. Only you can't see mine." She gazes up into my eyes with an intense expression, and for a moment I fear she might cry. Then just as quickly she stares back down at her doughnut, silent.

Her remark makes me feel self-conscious, but it's not the usual deep shame that such comments elicit. Maybe that's why I brush back my hair so she can really see the marks along my face and jaw line. She responds to the invitation, peering upward for a closer look, then asks in a small voice, "Do they still hurt?"

"Sometimes. Especially the ones you can't see."

Her clear blue eyes widen in surprise. "How many do you have?"

"A few." I leave out the brutal details about my chest and abdomen because she doesn't need the violent truth about my past. "You?"

"Only one. On my leg." I know she must be burning with as many questions as I am. Dozens instantly speed through my head—like why there's such a sorrowful expression in her eyes. Or what happened to her that left this hidden scar.

We fall silent then, the revelations apparently finished for the moment. I spread cream cheese on my bagel; she gives me a tentative grin and says, "So you *are* eating, huh?"

"Yeah, think I am." Gesturing with my knife I ask, "What about you?"

She reaches for her doughnut and licks some of the warmed chocolate off the top. "Yeah, me too."

Subtext, I think with a smile. That's what my little red-haired friend and I are speaking. Volumes upon volumes of it, without any need for translation at all.

If only grownups felt so safe—and so easy to understand.

Chapter Two: Michael

"So did you have fun on the lot today?" I try to sound bright, but Andrea just stares out the passenger window of our truck, remote as always. "Well, did you?" My voice tightens over the words despite my best intentions.

"You were supposed to call Ms. Inez to watch me today. You knew it was a teacher work day." The disdain in her voice is palpable, thick as the smog hanging over our city like a threat. Even if I didn't know that summer's almost here, I'd see it in the hazy evening sky tonight. It's turned all purplish blue, like a bruise.

"I forgot, sweetheart. You know that."

She heaves a weary sigh. "You always forget," she says. "But Daddy wouldn't. He would've remembered."

"You're right. He would have." She turns to me, her ocean-blue eyes widening in shock at my new strategy. But why *not* admit the truth? I have no illusions. Her daddy would have done a better job at this single parenting drill than I'll ever manage on my own. No wonder Andrea's so bitter. She landed second unit with me, not first, and I'll never be able to close that gap.

"You didn't get me on the *Evermore* set, like you said."

"I said I'd *try*."

"But you didn't."

"It was a closed set!" I cry, blowing my cool, and a thin smile of satisfaction forms on her lips. It's like she lives for this now, to see me lose control. It's what she's always after. Maybe because she needs some kind of reaction from me, anything other than this numbness that has such a stranglehold around my heart.

She says nothing else, just stares out the window of the truck again, outlining an invisible pattern on the dusty pane with her fingertip, something that only she can see. I clutch the steering wheel tensely, the familiar silence smothering us as we edge along the 101 toward home. Long damn way there, too, at least in this kind of traffic. Really need to sell the house and move somewhere closer to the studio, but I can't bring myself to do it. Can't bring myself to let go of Alex that way, not when all of our memories are tied up in that place. Well, maybe not all of them, but certainly most of the significant ones.

Just the thought of leaving our old bungalow on Mariposa Way makes my throat clench painfully. Nothing feels more like home than those eucalyptus trees that shade our tiled rooftop, or the thick jasmine vines knotted around our front steps. I can picture Andrea like it's yesterday, maybe four or five years old, collecting handfuls of those white flowers as a gift for me. *Here, Daddy! I picked them 'cause they're beautiful, just like you!*

We have family history that practically hums all around that house. It's in the crevices of the wooden floorboards, on the craggy paths that lead up the canyon hillside away from the garden, and in the sun-drenched windows of the morning room. Every direction I turn, our life resonates there, and maybe that's because memories have a spiritual life all their own. Where there's been suffering, the dark atmosphere hangs over a place forever, becomes a kind of energy that's imprinted in the air. Like at Auschwitz or Gettysburg, or even Fredericksburg, where I grew up, where the bodies of men once fell by the moment. Ghosts before their bodies had even hit the ground.

But when something's been perfect and beautiful, as our family once was then the emotions linger like the perfume of angels. No wonder all my memories of that house are touched by sweet-scented jasmine.

We moved to Studio City because Alex practiced pediatric oncology at UCLA, so it made sense to live in that neighborhood, an affordable family one closer to the hospital. That was more important than buying a house near the studio, like West Hollywood where I wanted to be. Allie hated my insane hours on the set, wanted me home more, so we fought over that decision. In fact, I remember mouthing off that some of us weren't doctors pulling down a couple hundred grand a year, that some of us really *worked* for a living.

God, the scorching, blue-eyed look I earned for that one. Alex was one of the warmest people I've ever known, but he could pack a feisty temper on occasion. The old stereotypes about redheads were true, I guess, because that day I got a pretty pointed lecture on the rewards of higher education versus those of pissing off my father by joining the army at age eighteen. That was okay, 'cause I also got a damned passionate kiss at the end. Making up was always the sweetest part of Allie's firestorms.

I swear those arguments over buying our first home together were some of the worst we ever had. Looking back, it's easy to see that there were other tensions at play, deeper stresses about commitment and starting a family. About even being a couple in the first place. My fears over *that* issue alone were threatening to separate us like the San

Andreas Fault. Besides, having kids and settling down is already pretty big stuff when you're only in your twenties, even if you're a traditional couple.

Being with Allie scared the crap out of me, all right, because I'd never gone that way before. I'd always been straight as an arrow before him. But I realized even then that love doesn't bother with those kinds of distinctions. It just falls over you like a mystery, and once it does, you're gone for life.

By then I understood, too, that I was with Alex Richardson because I couldn't be anywhere else.

"You missed the exit."

"What?" I blink, staring ahead of me at the car-clogged freeway in disbelief.

"That was our exit back there." Our daughter explains the facts to me with the patient condescension of an eight-year-old.

"Damn."

"Daddy didn't like you cussing in front of me."

"No, you're right, sweetie. He didn't."

Your daddy didn't like a whole lot of my wicked ways, I think, maneuvering into another lane of traffic. Now, thanks to my error, it will be another thirty minutes before we make it home.

Yeah, Memory Lane can be a painful detour, all right. Can take you places you really don't want to go, and then send you scrambling for hours to recover.

Sometimes you never do.

When someone dies, you're left with mountains of memories. At first, you rush headlong at all of them, fists opening greedily, desperate to hold onto your loved one, no matter the cost, but over time, particular snapshots come into focus. They're the ones that surface continually in your dreams and mental drifting, popping up on radar when you least expect them.

For me, I'm haunted by Alex's last trip to New York City. A random memory, really, but I think about him calling me from there last March. It was lunchtime back east, and I was starting my workday at the studio when my cell phone rang. I flipped it open, and Al greeted me with his warm, booming voice. "Can you hear them?"

"Hear what, baby?" I asked softly, turning away so the other guys wouldn't eavesdrop.

"Listen, okay?" He laughed, and there was the sound of blaring horns and traffic through the receiver. I could practically smell the exhaust fumes and late winter snow he'd described in an e-mail earlier that morning. But irritation rankled through my system too, because he'd plowed right into my workday, not even bothering with a decent greeting.

Then I heard them. Chiming bells that rang out in a lovely, melancholy voice. Despite myself, I smiled for a moment. It was such an Alex thing to do, to call me for something like that. Everywhere he went in life he discovered an adventure, found something beautiful to appreciate in the midst of stress and chaos.

But the thing was, I didn't hear those church bells. Not really. I was too self-conscious that the guys might be listening in, and frustrated with Alex for not asking if I was busy, if I could even talk in the first place. When he came back on the line, a little breathless, he said, "They're the bells of St. Patrick's. I'm sitting here on the steps, and I wanted you to hear them too."

"Cool," I mumbled, cautiously watching my boss, a craggy old-school union guy, walk closer. I'd never come out to him about Alex, and I wasn't about to start right then.

"Tomorrow's Ash Wednesday," Alex said. "I think I'm going to try to make a service."

For a moment, I pictured his freckled forehead, a sooty cross marking the center of it like a bull's eye. Something about that somber image made me shiver despite the morning heat.

"You sure you want to do that?" I asked, feeling spooked for reasons I couldn't possibly verbalize, but he only laughed at me, so I rushed to add, "I mean, aren't they already lining up today like it's a Stones concert or something?"

"Now, Michael, don't forget I'm a good Catholic boy," he teased, knowing that I never darkened a church door. Well, except for our commitment service, which was the one time he ever got me to attend an ecclesiastical ceremony. No wonder we could never agree on getting Andrea baptized.

"Yeah, Father Roberto would be proud of you," I mumbled, rubbing my palm over my heart. I couldn't shake the eerie shadow that had fallen over me, the vague sense of dread. "You out of the conference?" I asked, trying to turn the subject in a sunnier direction.

"I'm taking a walk during the lunch break," he said. Suddenly a passing siren blared loudly through the phone, drowning out his words, until I caught the end of some amputated sentence: "...and that I wish you and Andie were here with me."

"Yeah, me too," I half-whispered into the phone, eyeing my boss, but he was busy at his desk now.

"I bought you a present yesterday." I could practically hear the smile in his voice; nobody loved a surprise like my Alex. A terrible pang of guilt nagged at my heart for having been irritable, even if he hadn't known it. He'd been gone for days and I'd begun to miss him a whole damn lot.

"Let's bring Andrea here for her birthday in the fall," he continued. "Wouldn't that be great? To really do the city together, all three of us?"

"Definitely."

"We could take her ice skating at Rockefeller Center." I had a momentary vision of holding Andie's small hand in mine, leading her in an awkward circle around the rink while Alex videoed us together. But then my boss stood from his desk, clipboard in hand, making a beeline right for me.

"Let's talk about it when you get back." I wanted to hurry Al off the phone before my boss realized I was on a personal call. After we said goodbye, I wondered what I'd missed when the siren had silenced his words. It seemed like something critical, something I needed to know. In fact, I almost called him back to ask, but then with the day's usual hectic tension, I forgot about it completely. Never even thought about it again—or about him sitting there on those cold steps, phoning me just to hear the bells. Not until he was dead, and by then I could hardly think of anything else.

God, Alex loved me.

He truly did. I just hadn't learned yet that time is elastic: it stretches and gives, far more graciously than it probably should, and then one day, when you least expect it, something simply ruptures, and your sheltered life is done.

No, I couldn't have imagined then that Alex would be stone dead nearly three months from that very day. Long before the fall or Andrea's birthday arrived, or even before we could accomplish a fraction of our dreams.

Hard to believe that only those cathedral bells would remain, haunting me like the refrain of some long-forgotten hymn from my childhood.

✧

Not sure how long I've been on this sofa, but I must've drifted off because the living room is completely dark except for the glow of the television. My head feels like someone's been pounding a dagger into the center of the thing. A big, gauzy swollen melon of a head, thanks to the five beers I've already tossed back. Thank God it's Friday night.

I feel around on the floor beside the sofa, and find a sixth bottle still open. The ceiling spins a little; the blue, artificial light from the television flickers above me in melancholy shades, like some eerie heavenly host watching to make sure I'm still alive.

My eyes drift closed as the warm beer slides down my throat, cloying, but at least I find some release.

Used to be I'd sit outside on nights like this one. Go out on the deck and inhale the spring night air. Maybe smoke a cigar, read the paper. Wait for Alex to come home from the hospital so we could unwind together over a glass of wine. Used to be I treasured putting Andrea to bed; it was something precious, and if Alex got home in time, we did it together. It always felt like the three of us had really formed a family then. Now I only want to close up shop at night. I can barely focus on her bedtime story anymore, much less enjoy reading it to her.

She knows it too. She knows it, but I don't think she even cares at this point. In fact, I'm pretty sure she'd rather live with anyone else but me.

My eyes drift shut and I imagine that I can hear the garage door opening, Alex home for the night. My heart beats faster in expectation, because through the hazy beer scrim, I half-believe it's a possibility. There'd be the familiar jangle of his keys dropping on the kitchen counter, then maybe Andrea's feet slapping exuberantly across the hardwoods. "Daddy!" she'd cry, flinging herself into his arms. The love of both our lives, come home once again.

Tears sting my eyes; I blink them back and take a long swig of the beer again. Anything to numb the pain. I maneuver the bottle onto the floor carefully, rubbing at my temples, when I'm jolted back to reality by Andrea's whispery voice. "Rebecca has a scar like mine," she says, and my eyes snap wide open.

I've spent a year trying to get to this place with her, to get her to talk about the accident. All my efforts to this point have met with nothing but stony silence.

When I jerk upright on the sofa, planting both feet squarely on the floor, the near-empty bottle of beer clatters over, a sticky puddle forming beneath my socked foot. But I don't even notice, not really. My attention's trained only on her.

She stares at the floor, tugging on the sleeve of her long cotton nightgown self-consciously. She wants to say more; I sense it. God, I want to help her do this, too, but I just don't want to spook her. I don't want to do a thing to chase my little girl away. I regulate my breathing, remembering what our counselor has said: it has to be on her terms, her timetable.

Andrea shifts her weight from foot to foot, looking up at me through her dusty auburn lashes. She's waiting for something.

Very tentatively, I begin to speak. "Tell me about it," I urge with a nod. "About her scar." I know it's a risk to press her, but I need to be closer emotionally.

She takes one step toward me, chewing on her bottom lip. "It's on her face." She touches her cheek with a fingertip and draws a line that reaches the edge of her mouth. "Right here. Didn't you see it?" She scrunches her face into a strange, twisted imitation.

Only now do I realize how little I glimpsed of Rebecca O'Neill. I know she seemed attractive, that something about her got to me. In fact, I spent the rest of the workday trying to shake off that reaction, the way she'd drawn me in. Now I can't believe I missed so much of her story.

"No, it was dark, sweetheart. Tell me."

Andrea stops then, wrapping her small, pale arms around herself in a bear hug. "Her scars still hurt sometimes too. That's what she said."

I fight the urge to reach for her, to try and hold her. Like some hostage negotiator, I'm forced to play observer in my own family, as she edges nearer by the moment. "Like mine does."

My lips part and what I want to say is that I'm sorry. Sorry that my sweet little girl has to hurt at all, that she worries about a scar nobody else can even see. Sorry that her daddy's nearly a year dead and all she has left in this frightening world is me.

But I don't, and before I can figure out what I *should* say next, she's already gone, vanished in a blur of white nightgown and coppery red hair. Then there's the sound of her bedroom door slamming shut, and the whole house gasps in shuddered reaction.

All I can do is bury my face in my hands and wish like hell that Alex were still here with me. Because I don't have a clue how I'll ever keep doing this on my own.

I wake the next morning with a jackhammer pounding straight through the core of my skull. Apparently some crack team of demons is on an expedition to my medulla oblongata, and are causing hell along the way. Bravely, I open one eye in my own version of a recon mission, but the sunny spring morning sends me diving back for my pillow with a muffled groan of agony. God, somebody stop me the next time I decide to drink a twelve-pack of Heineken by myself.

Why is it that the denials and oaths of abstinence always make so much sense in the morning, but nighttime brings the same bottomless swell of loneliness all over again?

I bury my face in the quilt, and fight a tide of nausea that rises high. I hear muted sounds from the living room, and know that Andrea must already be up watching television or playing Wii. But that doesn't explain the homey smells drifting my way, something like eggs and bacon and maybe even fresh-ground coffee.

With another deep groan I roll onto my back, sniffing the air as I rub my eyes. It's got to be my imagination; there can't actually be breakfast cooking in the next room. Then I remember. With all the clarity of a boom lowering, I know that I've screwed up big-time. Marti's here to help with my taxes, exactly like she's supposed to be, and I'm the one who's fallen way off schedule.

I force myself to sit up in bed, the whole room gyrating and pulsating angrily. Staring in the mirror over the dresser, I hardly recognize the guy staring back at me: wiry curls askew, hollow circles under his eyes, pasty complexion shadowed by an outbreak of beard.

I'm pathetic, and I know what dear Marti's going to say the minute she lays eyes on me. "Lord, Warner, you look like hell!"

That's why she's my best friend—and a great ex-girlfriend, at that. Sometimes in the past year I've almost wondered if Alex didn't will her to me by divine act of life choice. Wondered whether the two of them, back in kindergarten and lining up for recess, made a sacred pact even then. That Marti would introduce Alex to his life partner, then watch over that poor guy's lost soul once he'd been left alone at the end of the day.

I'm sure that Alex would tell me to be gentler with her, not so grumpy and difficult. And he'd remind Marti that although I may not talk about it much, I'm lost without him. As for our other best friend? I'm not sure how he'd answer Casey's constant grumbling that I won't go out with our gay friends—that I only want to stay home every weekend. Alex would probably say what he learned the hard way: that it's never a good idea to push me about anything.

"So, Warner, you sleeping in?" I hear from the doorway and literally jump, startled from my somber ruminations.

"Marti, hey." I rake a hand over my disheveled hair in an effort to tame the unruly beast. She peers at me with her clear green eyes, a smile filling her full face. Marti's the yin to my yang, short and squat where I'm tall and rangy.

"No use, my friend." She laughs hoarsely, reaching onto my dresser and tossing me Alex's antique comb. I never use it because it's like some holy relic, an artifact left by my dead lover, but she doesn't know that. I reach for where it rests on the handmade quilt, lifting the silver spine gingerly between my fingertips. She stares for a long moment, and I feel exposed, treating such a commonplace object with undisguised reverence. So I do what I haven't done in nearly twelve months, and use the damn thing.

Of course it catches and knots through my short, unmanageable hair as she settles cross-legged on the bed next to me. "How you feeling?"

"Great."

"Yeah, I can tell." She seizes the comb from my hand. "Faker."

"About what?" I collapse back onto the pillows, and the feel of cool cotton against my cheek instantly soothes me.

"Everything." She leans back with me, crossing her stubby bare feet as she settles on Alex's old side of the bed. "The hangover, the comb, our breakfast date."

"The comb?" I'm pure innocence, and she props her head on one elbow, staring at me.

"That Alex's mother gave him when he went to college," she clicks off easily. "Had been part of her father's set. You haven't used it a single time since he died."

"And you know this because?"

"It had dust on it."

"Damn, girl, you're good."

"No, I'm just a good accountant. It's my job to follow a trail." She reaches for my clammy hand, squeezing it in her warmer one, planting a gentle kiss on my knuckles. "Well, and I also know you very well, my friend."

"Did Alex pay you to do this, Marti?" I sigh. "Did I miss that in the will or something? I mean, you and Casey are tag-teaming these days."

"He's out back, actually. Trying to salvage what's left of your garden."

Casey's a landscape architect who runs several crews around the exclusive parts of the city, and my yard's just a charity project.

"Y'all are relentless lately."

"Because you're starting to get scary, Michael. To all of us." I think of Andrea in the next room and how strained things are. Am I scaring her too? Marti seems to read my thoughts. "Andrea's already had breakfast," she says. "We let you sleep in."

"I appreciate that."

"Seemed like a great idea when I tripped over the pizza box and garbage bag full of empty beer bottles."

I rub my eyes with a repressed groan, wondering if Andrea saw them when she woke.

"Casey took care of them discreetly. But you've got to pull it together, Michael," she admonishes gently.

"Don't worry, this hangover pretty much guarantees that I will."

"I'm not just talking about the drinking, even though I know it's a lot more than last night." It's true, so I don't make any further lame arguments. I simply wait for the rest, because with Marti, there's always more.

"You know Alex wouldn't want you hurting this way," she continues. "Bleeding along like this." I flash on a wounded whale, banking through the water, trailing a ribbon of blood—not quite dead, but not living either. "You do realize that, don't you?" she says, her forehead furrowing into creases of concern.

I turn away from her. "Alex loved life," I say flatly, watching the ceiling fan's soundless rotations and fighting a fresh wave of nausea. I can't do this now, can't have the big talk that she's been bucking for lately.

"Alex loved *you*." She sits up in bed, staring down at me for emphasis. "Okay? We both know how much he loved his family. But he'd want you to get on with living, Michael, not mourn him forever like this."

"Come on, Marti, he hasn't even been gone a year yet."

"But you're getting worse every day."

"What? You don't think that sackcloth and ashes is a sexy look on me?" I joke with a bitter laugh, and earn a terrible Marti-sized scowl in return; it fills her whole moon-shaped face.

"I'm not laughing," she says.

"I can see that."

"Life is for the living, you know." She turns Alex's comb within her hands, gazing at it like some divine instrument of guidance until she taps the silver handle against her lips with a sigh. "Look, Michael, you've got to do whatever it takes," she says soberly. "Because you're fading fast, and if something doesn't change, it'll be more than Alex that we've lost. This grief is going to kill you too."

With that sinister prophecy, she slides off the end of the bed and out of my room without another glance.

Drowsy-eyed, I make my way out of the bedroom, wearing faded jeans and a sloppy T-shirt. The pants are loose on me—yet more physical evidence of the spiritual emaciation that Marti's been talking about. When I enter the living room, Andrea's eyes are laser-locked with the television, on what looks to be *Hannah Montana*.

"Morning, sweet pea," I announce with a smile, but she doesn't bother answering me. I watch her as I move past our leather sofa, where she's sitting, knees tucked neatly inside her cotton nightgown. "Did I hear a 'good morning' there?" I push, sounding a little too much like my old drill sergeant.

Finally, she blinks up at me. "Morning." Nothing more, no hint of our late-night truce. Not even a smile; just a chilly blue-eyed glance.

"That's my girl." Back at my game of appeasement as usual. Marti's in the kitchen, doling out eggs and bacon for me, and I bend low to kiss her cheek, whispering an awkward "thanks" as she presses the plate into my hand.

"We only talking food?" she asks, leaning back against the counter. "Or is life advice included in that murmur of gratitude?"

"Whole enchilada, Ms. Murphy." I hoist myself up onto the bar, lifting the plate close to my chin for ease of consumption. It's the kind of uncouth behavior that Alex used to complain about; something I now do precisely because he's *not* here to gripe anymore. Maybe it's my way of venting some of this subtle anger that's always swashing around inside of me.

"You know, since I'm clearly on a roll here," Marti says, snagging some bacon out of the pan for herself, "would you consider one more piece of advice?"

"I'm guessing I don't have a choice."

She steps much closer to me. Casting a cautious glance in Andrea's direction, she clasps my shoulder conspiratorially. "You need some time to yourself. Time to do something just for you. I could take Andrea home to stay the night. The kids would love to see her, and Dave's planning to cook burgers on the grill."

For a moment, sadness stabs at my heart because Marti and Dave lead a family life that I can only dream of giving Andrea. Hell, it's not a life our daughter's *ever* led, not even when Alex was still alive. I should be grateful for the occasional time she gets at their suburban home, not jealous of the way Andrea worships their whole family, but I can't seem to help myself.

In the living room, Andrea's already looking our way with keen expectation. "Sure," I say, tightlipped without meaning to be. "That'd be great."

"Cool!" Andrea cries, bounding to her feet. "Can I go pack now?"

"Yeah, sweetie, go get your stuff together." I barely have the words out before she's vanished into her room.

Marti's gaze drills into me, telling me that I should just take this break. "Don't feel guilty. You always do, but don't. Go and have some fun, for crying out loud. There's nothing wrong with that."

Fun? I doubt I'm capable of it anymore. I think of Casey and his repeated invitations to hit the movies, get a couple of beers, head out dancing—anything that involves going out with the guys. But the thought of passing through those old haunts without Alex chills me to the core.

"Yeah, I'll do something relaxing." Fix that stupid burned-out light in the hallway, the one I've been ignoring for the past year. Maybe work out in the yard for a while, try to pick up where Casey leaves off today. I see him out there now, bent over, slaving to resurrect the flower garden before it's choked alive by weeds.

Marti slugs me on the shoulder. "Good, because there *will* be a test at the end of the break. And remember what I said about life, okay?" Marti admonishes, an encouraging smile filling her broad face.

"It's for the living?"

She gets the look of a pleased parent, as if I've recited my alphabet correctly. "Right!"

Right. But the thing is I can't help but wonder, like I did last night, if I'm even part of that club anymore.

✧

So much for my revolutionary plan of staying home by myself, because no sooner than I'd set about repairing that hallway light, teetering high on the stepladder, that I remember my un-deposited paycheck, left somewhere on my workbench back at the studio. Yet more evidence of the mental haze I've been wandering around in these days, especially since I count on that weekly check. So without showering, I climb in the truck and hightail it toward Hollywood, knowing that with enough luck I can get the check to the bank before it closes at one.

Money's tight, that's for sure. Not that Al's insurance payout wasn't generous in the extreme, especially since he'd arranged for maximum coverage in an effort to offset the loss of his hefty annual income. But after I paid off the mortgage and tucked the rest in a fund for Andrea, it didn't leave much. Frankly, I'm afraid to touch the rest; guess it's the difference in my background and Allie's. When you come from money you don't worry about it drying up like I always seem to do.

So it's a liquidity issue, not so much a bottom-line one, and that means I need to get that paycheck into the bank pronto. That's what I tell myself, not that being alone scares the living shit out of me, or that I'd rather go tinker with something at my job than perform an electrician's task back home. Not that the empty sounds of my own home, the way it groans and settles when no one else is around, spook the hell out of me these days.

No, it's not any of that, I think, rumbling through the famed archway of my workplace, searching for a few hours of peace.

Being the lowly electrical staff member that I am, I'm supposed to park off studio premises in the massive parking deck. But I risk the illegality of swiping a reserved producer's spot since it's Saturday and I'm not here to stay. Still, I'd rather avoid pointless fines, so I give the parking-lot perimeter a cautious scan, and begin walking briskly toward the soundstage that I call home. I'm lost in thought, outlining plans for domestic progress back at the house, when something makes me look to the far right, across Chaplin Park. There's a woman walking alone, golden ponytail swinging as she moves. Something about that single detail strikes me as graceful, beautiful.

I have to watch her move across the brightly lit lawn. She's small with a killer figure, this woman, wearing loose khakis that can't hide the curves. The clingy white T-shirt outlines a well-muscled body, and I know she may be delicate, but she's not fragile. Tough and strong, that's what she looks to be, with loads of power packed into that slender figure.

I keep walking behind her, slow, and feel guilty for the way I'm tracking her movements. I mean, so far stalking hasn't appeared on my resume of failings, so I wouldn't want to start now. Maybe I'm just puzzled to feel this kind of attraction at all, especially toward a woman. It's been such a long damn time since my mind or body even went that way. Still, my fingers itch a little with the urge to touch that ponytail, imagining how silky it'd feel if I ran my fingers through it. My body itches a little, too, and I realize it's not only her *hair* I'm dreaming of touching now.

Funny, but the thing I keep noticing is how small she is compared to me. Maybe because it's been so many years since I've held anyone in my arms who didn't actually stand taller than me. And maybe because it's been just as many years since I made love to any woman at all.

When she darts up the narrow steps leading to her office building I let loose a quiet groan because I know exactly who that is, half-skipping her way up to the door, ponytail swinging down her back. It's Rebecca O'Neill. And standing there, watching her open the door, I realize I'm in serious, deep, painful shit.

I sure hope Alex is watching over me now, because I may need all the help I can get.

Chapter Three: Rebecca

Stepping into the dark hallway of my building, I'm startled by the unusual Saturday silence. There's an industrial hum from the computers and the copy machine, but otherwise it's eerily peaceful. I'm used to endless chatter from the producers' offices, banter from Trevor and the other assistants as they work the phones. Dead silence in this place is unfamiliar to me, and that probably explains the tight fear coiling suddenly around my heart.

Except this nagging anxiety began on the walk over from my car, when I had the definite sensation of being watched. Correction: of being *followed*. I spent far too long in my survivor support group not to listen to my instincts, even if the warning signals strike a false note. All fear cues must be acknowledged, because if they aren't, it could mean my life. I should have listened to them three years ago. If I had, then things might be very different today.

There's the loud, comforting click of the lock as it fastens into place, and for a moment I stand at the door, practically pressing my nose against the glass pane so I can see the far corner of the building. Nothing's out there—at least nobody threatening that I can see—only a few cars and a golf cart speeding past with a maintenance man behind the wheel. All seems safe, so after a tense moment I release the breath I've been holding inside my chest.

Still, the quiet here unsettles me, so I stride right to Trevor's desk, positioned outside my own office door, because that's where the manuscript I've come looking for should be. I turn on his lamp, thumbing through the orderly stack of envelopes in the center of his desk. These are our most recent submissions, and it only takes a moment to spot the one I'm looking for. Eagerly, I pull it from the pile—in fact, a bit *too* eagerly, because another packet dislodges and careens right to the floor. It must have been hidden on the bottom of the stack—I never saw the dang thing coming. Neither did my poor big toe, which smarts so painfully that I let loose with a few choice expletives, wiggling it inside my strappy sandal.

That's when I spot the familiar logo of The Bourne Agency, and it's no wonder I'm cursing. They're a swanky London firm that boasts some of the U.K.'s best authors, including my *least* favorite English author ever, Julian Kingsley. Frankly, I don't care if he's the second coming of Shakespeare, I'll never like him. Not considering how many times he's hurt my best friend. The very same best friend who saved my life three years ago, so my protective loyalty toward him runs pretty darn deep.

The envelope's already been opened, with a log number printed on the outside in Trevor's proper handwriting. *So he's already handled the materials.* Fresh warning bells sound in my head, this time of a different variety. They're of the "my-friend-is-hiding-something-massive" kind, I think, tugging a thin sheaf of paper from within the packet's confines. Imagine my surprise when I find a proposal emblazoned with none other than Julian Kingsley's cocky-sounding name.

I stare at the cover sheet for twenty, maybe thirty seconds in disbelief. Finally, I reach for the phone, ready to call Trevor and issue stern lectures about the danger of flirting with an ex-boyfriend's latest book. Only I think better of it, wondering if I shouldn't wait and see what he's up to. After all, Julian is Trevor's Achilles heel, the one wound that never fully mends. Something tells me that confronting him head-on about this newfound secret isn't such a good idea. There must be a reason he didn't mention Julian's proposal. Probably because he knows just how worried any of his communications with his former lover always leave me.

Like last summer when I found out they'd been e-mailing sporadically for a few months. Trevor and I got into a screaming match over it, and I wound up crying in the middle of the bar where we'd set up for the night. I knew their past and had reason to be afraid.

"Sweet girl, sweet girl," Trevor shushed me, pulling me into his arms protectively. I don't think any man has ever hated to see me cry like he does. "I'm not doing anything with Julian except trading a few e-mails."

"I don't want him to hurt you anymore," I blubbered loudly, wiping my eyes with the back of my hand. "Not again."

"He won't, all right?" He slipped a soft handkerchief into my hand. "He's sober now, and so far, behaving like a perfect gentleman."

"But you might trust him again," I wailed plaintively, burying my face against his strong shoulder. I was tipsy enough to be oblivious to anyone else, especially those who might be eavesdropping on our conversation. Thank God we were off in Sherman Oaks, away from our usual gossipy Hollywood crowd. "What if you get back together with him?"

"I won't do," he reassured me firmly. "Rebecca, dear, I won't do."

That was last summer, and sitting in the dark now, staring at this mint proposal in my hand—one reported in publishing trades only a few days ago—I can't help but feel the hackles of my old suspicions rising once again. Trevor wouldn't lie to me, not him of all people. Would he?

✧

I despise Julian Kingsley. With the fire of ten blazing furnaces, I truly hate the guy. I'm sitting at my desk, reading the last of his ten-page story synopsis, and it infuriates me that he's this talented. I contemplate phoning Trevor and owning up to my small act of espionage, admitting that his ex-boyfriend is brilliant. But I can't shake the fact that he kept this from me, and for some reason I want to play along for a bit. See if he'll confess that he pulled the materials in-house; see if he passes them to another creative executive here. To Ed Bardock himself, maybe, without giving me a look. What will Trevor do, that is my question.

I can't stand distrusting him like this; he's my rock, the one person besides my mother and father who I would trust with my life. It's like this tiny fissure of suspicion has opened between us, and I already feel it trying to swallow our friendship whole.

But the proposal *is* truly amazing, and I'm actually toying with pursuing the project. Which could theoretically put Julian stateside, right here in Los Angeles, and that scares me on principle. No, I have to be truthful with Trevor, tell him about finding the proposal on his desk, so I reach for my phone receiver.

That's when a loud banging sound jars me right out of my seat. For a moment I do nothing, remembering the earlier sensation of someone following me. My heart thunders, causing my chest to rise in quick panting breaths of fear. Nobody should be knocking on the bungalow door on a Saturday. Nobody.

Carefully, I step away from my desk and into the hallway, and glimpse a large stranger there at the door. He's leaning close, shielding his eyes to look inside; I swallow hard to calm the fear, walking toward the intercom with cautious determination.

"Yes?" I say into the speaker, and the man steps back. He sees me and gives an uncertain wave, then hits the exterior intercom button. I don't recognize him, and that he looks a little rough and slouchy only unsettles me all the more.

"Ms. O'Neill?"

"Yes?" I repeat, more firmly this time. *Who is this man? How does he know me?*

"Um, it's Michael Warner." He sounds vaguely apologetic as he removes a baseball cap and mops his brow. "Sorry to bother you."

That's when I recognize him as the electrician from yesterday. I sigh in relief, and open the door a crack, though not all the way. Although he's not a stranger, I'm still jumpy from the adrenaline rush.

"Sorry, I didn't really think about how much of an intrusion this might be." He gives me a slight smile. God, he may be slouchy today, but he's even more beautiful in the shocking daylight, especially his eyes, which are an unusual golden brown color. He has the kind of intense gaze that penetrates you on the molecular level, and I blink beneath it.

"No problem." I swallow hard. "What's up?"

"Just wondering if the power is working okay? Any more trouble?" Now this seems like a thinly veiled excuse to me. All the feelings from yesterday, the sense that some kind of connection was forming between us, well it all comes rushing back, as I lean my head sideways against the doorframe. Maybe that way he won't notice the scars so much.

"You know, it's going great," I answer brightly, forcing myself *not* to smile at him. Instead I hope he'll see enthusiasm flickering in my eyes, even as I wrap my arms around myself protectively.

"You mind?" He gestures over my shoulder, toward the interior of the building. "You know, if I come in? Just for a second."

Without meaning to, I stare back at him. Maybe because I'm surprised at how direct he's being, or even more likely because I'm getting a really strange vibe from him. Like he's interested in me, but not quite sure how to go about it. I wish I'd gotten a clearer answer about his marital status from Andrea yesterday. As sexy as he is, I'm not down with seeing a married man, and if he *is* married, I'm feeling way too much attraction flickering between us.

"Ms. O'Neill?" The brown eyes narrow a bit, as uncertainty flashes across his face.

"Sure, sure, come on in," I rush to say, opening the door wide. "Where's my southern hospitality when I need it most?"

"Back in Georgia?" he says, shoving his hands deep into his jeans pockets as I fasten the lock back in place.

"Let's hope not." I break into a true smile, and I feel the way the muscles pull at the corners of my mouth. God, why does he light me up this way? And he gives me such a glorious smile in return, one that fills his whole face.

"Sorry for being a little cautious," I say in embarrassment. "It kind of weirds me out being here alone on the weekends, that's all. It's creepy quiet."

"You didn't recognize me?" He seems genuinely surprised, and I don't want to admit that he looks a little more ragged than I pictured him being, wearing old jeans and a faded Harley Davidson shirt. Still, he's undeniably handsome, with those keen brown eyes that transmit so much energy.

"Well, it was dark yesterday, you know." I lead him into my office.

His voice gets softer, fuller. "But I recognized *you*." I don't know how to respond to that, so I nod, my ponytail bobbing rhythmically. I feel him behind me, his presence; am aware of his body and how tall he is, as he shadows me all the way into my office.

"Please, sit down." I make my way to the other side of my desk. Maybe if I stick to my usual professional role, I can regain my composure here. I run a smoothing palm down the front of my khakis as I primly take my seat. Then, folding my hands in front of me, sitting very upright, I meet his magnetic, golden-eyed gaze. Oh, yes, he's too beautiful for me—by many long miles. Plus, he's got to be married.

Surreptitiously, I glance at his hand, but it's obscured behind the stack of manuscripts on my desk. Okay, no answer to the Big Question yet.

"So." I clear my throat. "What're you doing here on a Saturday? Don't tell me you're this dedicated to keeping my lights on." As soon as the double entendre is out of my mouth, I regret its accidental escape. Thank God Michael doesn't even seem to notice.

"Oh," is all he says, like he hadn't thought about it before now. "Just forgot my paycheck, that's all."

He reaches absently for a paperweight on the corner of my desk, moving it from hand to hand, which is when I begin to wonder precisely why he's come to visit me. He looks down at the domed glass, studying the picture within. "Your family?"

I wince because it's an old picture of me, one that predates my attack. No scars, just me—as beautiful, I suppose, as I once used to be. "Yeah, me and my parents."

He squints down at the magnified image, studying it intently. I notice the way the edges of his eyes crinkle into smile lines.

"Horse farm?" He turns the picture toward me, although I know the image by heart.

"I was raised on one, yes." I'm not sure why, but I don't want to reveal anything personal—at least not anything more than he's already gotten out of me. Certainly not that my retired parents live just a few miles away, over in Santa Monica, or that they came here three years ago to nurse me back from the brink.

He returns my paperweight to my desk guiltily, giving it a reassuring pat. Again, I wonder precisely why Michael Warner has come to see me, why he keeps fidgeting this way. I try a new tack. "Andrea is a precious girl. We had a really good time yesterday."

"That's what I heard. Can't tell you how much I appreciate what you did."

"It was nothing."

He looks intensely at me. "No, that's not true. It was really important to her." His voice grows quieter. "And me."

"Well, your stepdaughter was an angel."

"My stepdaughter," he repeats, frowning.

"Well isn't she? That's what she told me."

His whole expression darkens like a storm cloud. "Actually Andrea's why I wanted to see you today. Don't know how to ask this, so I'll just do it." Those words always seem to pave the way for bad news, and I tense immediately. "Did Andie mention her scar?"

I relax again, relieved to know what's on his mind. "A little, yeah."

"What about the accident? Did she talk any about that?"

I shake my head no, and it hurts me the way his face kind of falls. "Oh, okay." He nods thoughtfully, the thick dark brows knitting together into a melancholy scowl. "I had hoped maybe so."

"What happened to her?"

His gaze tracks back to me. "She was in a bad car accident. Something she doesn't talk about much," he admits. "Hasn't talked to anyone about it, honestly. It was pretty traumatic."

"I see." I'm starting to understand now. I'm also starting to understand why it was so hard for him to come to me, the awkwardness in his approach. Without even trying, I apparently did what nobody else has been able to do. "You wanted to know what she said to me."

"That's right, Ms. O'Neill."

"Rebecca."

I see him studying my scars: it's in the slight, unobtrusive way the eyes shift sideways, then dart back again. I see it every day, especially around here. Nobody has the courage to ask, yet they all wonder what happened to leave me looking this way.

Michael rises unexpectedly to his feet, sliding his baseball cap onto his head decisively. "Want to go grab some coffee?"

"Now?"

"I'm going over to Borders on La Cienega. We can get some there." Again the winning smile, accented by a single dimple that I hadn't noticed before, and I completely cave. He's got me in the palm of his hand already, damn it. I can't believe that he's seen the visible scars, but he's just asked me out anyway.

"I'll follow you there."

The trouble is, if I'm not careful, I know I just might follow him anywhere. Oh, please, please, don't be married, Michael Warner.

✧

"Heard this one's interesting." From the shelf, he removes a face-out copy of Julian Kingsley's recent novel *Beautiful, But Me.* What editorial genius thought *that* title was a good idea?

"I don't care for the guy."

He turns to me in clear surprise. "You know him?"

"Well." I sigh, taking the book out of his hand, studying the expensively designed dust jacket, inlaid with gold foil. "Let's just say he broke my best friend's heart."

"Guess she hates him, huh?"

"Actually, *he* doesn't." I flip over the book to reveal Julian's disgustingly perfect author photo on the back of the cover. Another good reason to loathe him: no man should be so absolutely gorgeous. Who knows? Maybe this latest title's directed to the world at large as a form of honest apology.

"Oooh, he does look like a heartbreaker." He gives a strange kind of laugh that I don't quite know how to read. I think of Trevor's first assessment of Michael, that he was gay. Because I can't imagine that most straight guys would describe Julian as a "heartbreaker".

Once again, I cast a covert glance at his ring finger, curious. Only this time I don't like what I see—a silver band glinting beneath the streamlined bookstore lights. "Would your wife think so too?"

"I'm sorry?" The bushy dark eyebrows draw together in genuine confusion.

"Your wife," I repeat firmly, this time gesturing toward his hand. "You are married, right?" I ask, folding my arms across my chest. No guy's going to play me, no sir. "You've got a wedding band on, after all."

He stares down at his hand, extending his fingers as if he's never noticed the ring before, and I'm cool as possible, proud of myself for having been a smart girl, until he answers softly, "Uh, widowed. Actually."

"Oh, God. I'm so sorry," I blurt, feeling embarrassed and sad all at once. Sad because of the dark pain that fills his eyes. It's so obvious, only a fool could miss it.

"No, I'm glad you asked." He picks up another copy of Julian's book absently. "Wouldn't want you to think I was playing around or anything."

"I didn't."

"'Cause I'm not that kind of guy," he presses, offering me a gentle smile. The thing is, I don't know precisely what kind of guy he is. A melancholy one. A beautiful one. My kind of guy... maybe. With that quiet realization, I give my ponytail an anxious tug as he leans close, lowering his voice. "But that doesn't explain what *you're* doing, Rebecca O'Neill."

"Me?"

He gestures toward the floor, at my sandal-clad feet. "You're clearly off the market." I stare down, confused, until I realize he's pointing at my silver toe ring, a series of hearts knit together, circling my second digit. "You're wearing a band, yet you're talking to me in a bookstore." He laughs low and throatily. "Unchaperoned, at that."

"We're downright risqué."

"So that is your ring toe?" he asks, studying me closely. "Like your ring *finger*?"

"Oh, the same general rules apply for feet." I giggle, staring at the floor. "My foot is happily spoken for, thank you very much."

"Who's the lucky guy? He wearing a band inside his loafer? Did the pair of you *run* off to Vegas together?"

"Who says it's a wedding ring?" I tease, avoiding his gaze. "Maybe Foot is only engaged."

"True," he observes. "Foot is very sexy, so I can't blame the guy, but I do think she's worthy of true commitment."

I haven't felt this beautiful in years.

I glance upward shyly. Lord, he's tall too—I hadn't realized just how tall until now, when I find myself craning upward to meet his dark gaze. "Truth is," I say, rising to my full five feet two inches of height. "Toe thinks she's Cinderella, and she's still searching for her glass slipper."

"It's good to dream," he says, but sadness veils his eyes again despite our repartee. I wonder if his wife loved fairy tales. I wonder if she believed in happily-ever-after, like I used to once upon a time.

And I wonder if it's still good for me to dream. Because standing here with Michael Warner, some lost part of me thinks that maybe it is.

"Do you?" I ask, surprising even myself with my directness. "Dream, I mean?"

A scowl forms on his face as he considers my question in silence. Moments spread out, long and eternal, until I wonder if he'll ever reply.

He removes his baseball cap, slapping it again into his palm with a sigh. "I used to, yeah," he answers thoughtfully. "But not anymore." It's all he says, and then he walks away from me, ambling toward the coffee bar, and I'm not sure I've ever seen such heaviness on anyone's shoulders before.

For some reason, watching his retreat makes me recall a bit of wisdom my daddy's always quoted to me. *Hope deferred makes the heart sick.*

Daddy would say we're two virtual strangers with the exact same disease.

Chapter Four: Michael

Standing here naked in my bathroom, hands clenching the edges of the antique porcelain sink, I just can't believe a *woman* is coming to cook dinner for me tonight. To cook *us* dinner, Andrea and me—in less than an hour, matter of fact. *Now what would Mr. Richardson have to say about that?* I laugh to myself, until with an unexpected shiver I get the sensation of being watched. From some cloudless, ethereal world far above, which only makes me feel guilty and found out and impossibly straight.

Except, that's ridiculous. We all know my fate was sealed a solid thirteen years ago by one sloppy, drunken kiss out on a gyrating dance floor. It was just supposed to be a joke, straight Michael tagging along with his queer best friend to one of the biggest gay bars in town. Some joke, all right; except that it turned out to be completely on me. Al kissed me that night, a soft, full thing that seemed to last halfway to forever, and all I can say in retrospect is that I never knew a redhead could taste so sweet. Especially not one of the masculine variety. Oh, I was a goner by midnight all right, because by then I doubt we ever could have stopped what we'd begun.

Toweling off my naked body now, it strikes me as strange that no one's touched me in almost a year. That nobody's held me or kissed me or made love to me in the middle of the night. I flash on the way Alex used to kiss my bare chest, the way he'd nuzzle up close sometimes when I was sleeping, after he'd been on a call at the hospital. How warm the bed would feel when he climbed back in beside me after being away, the scent of him at those times, impossible to describe, and just as impossible to miss when he came back to me.

With that thought comes the familiar ache for my lover, as this deep place inside of me constricts involuntarily for him; my missing heart, beating on alone without him.

Do you dream? she asked yesterday in the bookstore. Such an easy question, with such myriad and complex answers.

Sure, I still dream, but I couldn't tell Rebecca O'Neill that, because then I'd have had to admit that I dream endlessly of Alex. That he's still alive, that he's come home to me at last. And that I dream of Robert Bridges, smug look on his face as he walks out of the Los Angeles courthouse in his expensive suit, flanked by his even more expensive lawyers. He walks out, just like he did on that sunny day last fall, without having to spend one night in jail for killing Al. Oh, I dream all right—poisonous, heartbroken dreams that I wouldn't want to tell anyone about.

Makes sleep something to avoid as much as possible, so it's no wonder I drink myself into oblivion most nights, just to be sure the monsters won't come prowling around again. Standing there in the bookstore yesterday, though, I wanted to talk about the good kind of dreams. I wanted to believe they could still exist; I even felt a little innocent, and I think that's why I had to get away.

Explain to me, then, why I asked her over to the house? Because of Andie, that's what I tell myself. Because somehow Rebecca's gotten behind the fortress, infiltrated the sacred land. Andrea hasn't talked to a soul about that scar. Not Marti, or me, or her counselor, or even her Grandma.

Just Rebecca O'Neill.

One last inspection in the bathroom mirror before Rebecca arrives and I'm looking all right. Clean-shaven, and I've even managed to comb my usually ornery hair into place. In fact, this is fresher than I've looked in days, maybe even weeks. So is my wardrobe: a crisp white polo shirt tucked into a creased pair of denim jeans. The shirt belonged to Allie, and just 'cause he's gone doesn't mean I have to stop raiding his wardrobe. In fact, it makes me feel a tangible connection to him, this soft cotton shirt of his against my body. A shirt I took off him on more than a few plum occasions, as a matter of fact.

Makes me feel a little better about having an attractive, single woman into our home too. Less disloyal, more like I'm keeping him in the center of what we're doing here. Since this is about our daughter, not about some kind of strange attraction that I feel crackling to life. I'm not straight—haven't been in more than a decade—so it doesn't even make sense to me, the way I find myself preening here in front of the mirror tonight. Besides, she's going to know I'm queer within a few seconds of walking in our door; the evidence is all around this place.

Then how come I didn't tell her the truth about my sexuality when she asked about my *wife*? I could have been honest then, when she mentioned my wedding ring. Damn, my ring! I touch my naked hand with a start, panicked to realize I've forgotten to slip the band back on my finger after my shower. Reaching for the soap dish beside the sink, I slide the familiar silver band into my open palm.

Alex put that ring on my hand on a sunny fall day in 1998, in an unorthodox chapel out in Malibu, a little seaside building, all white and gleaming in the sun like a bleached shell. I remember my heart was a gull that day, lifting upward and upward into the azure sky. Our future was wide open. We'd have children and dreams and a life together.

I stare down at the weathered band in my palm's center. It's taken a beating over the years, but it's still beautiful. For a moment, I hesitate. Alex is dead, so maybe it's time to put it away. Maybe I should just drop it into his jewelry box there on our dresser, lay it to rest beside his cufflinks and Rolex, and stop holding on.

Turning the silver ring between my fingertips, I study the inscription on the inside. October 10, 1998. Just a date, a marker back in our personal history, but I'll be damned if I won't still wear his ring. I slip it on my finger and turn off the bathroom light.

Cooking dinner had been her idea, not mine. I just asked if she'd spend some time with Andrea; try to make a further connection. We were sitting there in the coffee shop of the bookstore, me trying to ignore the strange jittery sensation in my chest every time she looked up at me with those moss-green eyes. Her eyes have it, no doubt about that. They're almond-shaped, kind of aquamarine, like jewels that might change colors in the sun. Maybe there's a little magic behind them, because they sure made something strange happen inside of me.

She has a kind of ingrained gesture of touching her scars, although I doubt she even knows she does it. The marks are noticeable, but I'm betting they're not nearly so bad as she thinks they are. That's the problem with Hollywood. Everything's supposed to be idealized perfection. So what's a gorgeous woman like Rebecca to do if she's permanently flawed? Like a chipped vase at Tiffany's, she's been shifted onto the clearance rack. Or at least that's what she probably believes.

Truth is she's still lovely. Yeah, the pale streaking marks along the left side of her face take something from her looks, especially the one that runs the length of her jaw. Takes some getting used to, talking to her and not staring at them. Can't deny that. But her eyes, with those dark lashes, and her face shaped like a heart, well it's been such a long time since a girl's had me feeling this way.

Of course, Alex always insisted that I was bisexual, but it just felt easier to categorize myself as gay. I never have been one for half-measures about anything. He loved ribbing me when we watched movies, though, because while he scoped the boys, I still watched the girls. That didn't freak him out, it just made him laugh. Alex Richardson was nothing if not sure of himself about everything—most of all me.

45

I wonder what he'd tell me now, with this infatuation thing I've got going for Rebecca O'Neill. Would he be jealous, as I stand here in the kitchen, pacing around in my polished loafers and sipping my Heineken? Would he remind me that before him, I'd been with plenty of women, especially back in my army days? I think he'd give me a luscious kiss on the mouth and tell me to just relax. That she's coming to see Andrea anyway, because I asked her to, and that it's not even about me.

Alex is right; this is *not* about me. It's about our daughter, and this stranger who has somehow forged a mysterious link with her. I just hope Andie won't retreat when she discovers this plan of mine. I've been there too many times with her in the past year, on the outside, trying to force my way in. I really can't handle being there again.

Rebecca shows up with bags of groceries from Whole Foods and a load of fresh spices I couldn't possibly identify by name.

"I love to cook," she tells me with a faint grin. She tries to hide her smile most times; I've already caught on to that. Her injuries have affected her mouth, so that the left side doesn't turn up quite right. She tries to hide her face too, always kind of moving the left side away from me, brushing her hair forward. Maybe when I know her better I can tell her to just relax. Funny, 'cause isn't that what Alex would have said to me about tonight?

"Where's Andrea?" She drops the paper bags in the middle of our small kitchen floor, and they thud against the old hardwoods. She glances over the bar, into the den, as I clutch my beer anxiously between both hands like a frat boy at a first mixer.

"She's not here yet," I explain, my voice hitching with blatant nervousness. "Um, she stayed at my friend Marti's house last night, but she'll be back soon."

God, I suddenly feel ridiculous, with my freshly combed hair and neatly pressed shirt, like a refugee from some preppy detention camp.

Rebecca nods, and for a tense moment we stand eyeing each other. I clear my throat. "Look, I really appreciate you coming over like this," I begin. "You know, to be with Andrea. She doesn't have enough women in her life. I mean, there's Marti, but..." How can I explain to Rebecca how she's different than the other women, and not offend her?

She hoists a bag up onto the countertop with a bittersweet laugh. "Michael, I get it." She begins unloading cheeses and spices and meat, and I get the feeling she's avoiding looking at me. "Andrea and I have something important in common. You can just say it." She keeps organizing her ingredients, busying herself too much, like she's trying to defuse a bomb or something.

"Okay, yeah, you and Andrea do have something in common."

"Where are your knives? Cutting board?" she asks matter-of-factly, turning to face me finally. I step close, reaching around her to open the utensil drawer, and as I do, my hand brushes against hers. She reacts, jerks backward a little, and I place a steadying palm on her forearm, feeling tensed muscle beneath my fingertips. Thing is, she's feminine, but she's strong too.

"Just getting it for you," I explain gently, and wonder what exactly haunts her past that's left her this jumpy.

She stares down, nodding, and I see warmth creep into her rose-colored complexion. She's wearing a clingy white T-shirt with khaki pants again—almost exactly what she had on yesterday. Different shoes this time. Another pair of sparkly, open-toed sandals, a mild racy touch in an otherwise conservative wardrobe.

"How's Foot tonight?" I ask, and this time she does look at me. Like she's surprised that I'm picking back up our little flirtation. I lean closer, and staring at her pink painted toenails, whisper, "Out on the town again, huh? Foot really gets around, doesn't she?"

She smiles, a broad, genuine smile, and for once doesn't even bother hiding the quirky way it turns up sideways. "She's advised me to be a good chaperone, but yes, she's out."

"Foot is out?"

"Yes, on the town." She stares at her feet, gesturing. "You know, like you said."

"Hmm, I thought maybe Foot was gay or something. If Foot's *out*."

She rolls her eyes dismissively. "No way. She's totally straight."

I'm not. I almost say it, but I bite back the words, and drain the rest of the Heineken from the bottle instead.

Andrea and Marti come clattering into the house, talking and laughing, and seeing my little girl smiling so easily is like catching air. Like dropping into a mammoth wave, the kind that leaves you unable to breathe at first.

"Hey, sweetheart," I call out, and she looks around, her face clouding with confusion as she spots the meal brewing on the stove. Rebecca's left me stirring the ground beef in a saucepan while she's gone to the bathroom.

"Are you cooking?" Andrea's auburn eyebrows furrow into a dramatic line. It's an expression I've seen on Alex's face countless times—funny how she mirrors him without even trying. It's definitely in the genetics.

"You have a good time with Aunt Marti?" I ask brightly.

Marti, closing the door to the garage behind them, looks surprised. "You're *cooking*, Warner?" she laughs. "Oh, my God. Not you, not really?"

"Uh, actually..." I stall a moment, glancing toward the hallway bathroom. "Well...a friend came to make a good meal for us."

"A friend?" Marti's green eyes widen as undisguised hope flits across her face.

"Who?" Andrea folds her small arms across her chest.

"*Your* new friend," I say, a tad defensively, feeling ganged up on by the women in my life. "Rebecca O'Neill."

For a long moment, Andie stays silent, and I fear this has been a lethal mistake, but then a small smile forms on her face. "Oh." She nods approvingly. "Cool."

Andrea walks toward her bedroom, towing her small suitcase with her, and Marti steps close to me. "I wasn't aware that Andrea had made a new friend," she whispers. "Especially not one who cooks in such style."

At that precise moment, Rebecca enters the kitchen, her gaze moving between us. We snap apart and I give Rebecca a guilty smile. Guilty because I know that Marti knows *me*, which means she's going to sniff out my secret attraction like the devoted bloodhound she can be.

Marti, God love her, doesn't miss a beat, but extends her hand warmly. "Hi, Rebecca, I'm Marti."

"Nice to meet you." Rebecca bobs her head in that way I've noticed she does when things feel a little unclear. "I'm just... making dinner."

"Rebecca works with me at the studio," I interject lamely. "She and Andrea have spent some time together."

"That's great," Marti chirps, then glances at her watch. "Oh, wow, I didn't realize it was this late. Dave'll kill me if I don't turn right around and get home. I'm supposed to do the kids' baths tonight."

"Well, it was great meeting you," Rebecca says, offering a hint of a smile, as she turns to stir the ground beef on the stove.

Marti opens the door, then adds, "Hope I'll see you again, Rebecca," and I could kill her for embarrassing me like that.

In the driveway, Marti clutches my arm. "Warner, why on earth didn't you mention that you'd made friends with Rebecca O'Neill?"

"Why would I?"

"Duh," she says, thumping her forehead with the heel of her palm. "Because she's famous? And she's just, what, over at your house now?"

"She's not famous." I fold my arms over my chest, explaining, "She works at the studio as some film exec or whatever."

"She may be, but she *is* famous, Michael," she explains with forced patience. "God, where have you been? Like under a rock?"

"I've had a lot going on this past year," I growl at her.

"This was a few years ago." She lifts onto her tiptoes to brush a quick hand over my hair, neatening it. "You and Alex are just alike. Did neither one of you ever look at *People* Magazine? Watch television?"

"We worked too much to watch television." I duck away from her habitual straightening of my appearance.

"Alex would've known." Now *that* just ticks me off on principle.

"Tell me what the hell you're talking about," I demand impatiently. "How's she famous?" I'm thinking of our time together in the bookstore yesterday, that nobody gave us a second glance. How much of a celebrity could that make her, really? And what would Allie have known that I've somehow missed?

Marti stares up at the night sky, like maybe someone might swoop down and knock some sense into thickheaded me. "Lord, Warner, what am I going to do with you?"

I step close, staring her down. "If you don't just tell me what the hell you're talking about, I'm going to kick your ass."

"Hello? She was on *About the House*? Does that ring a bell?" she asks in exasperation, and it does sound familiar. I think it was filmed on the lot. Maybe. "Well, she was the star of that show," Marti continues. "For a couple of years, until one day some crazed fan attacked her outside her apartment, stabbing her like, what...ten times? The doctors all said it was a miracle that she even lived."

"Rebecca O'Neill?" I ask dumbly, thinking of the lovely, scarred woman in my kitchen.

"Yes, Rebecca O'Neill. The woman cooking you southwestern whatever-that-is in there. The guy killed her career, even if she did survive," she continues somberly. "It was a real tragedy. I can't believe you've never seen the *E! True Hollywood Story* about it."

I catch sight of Rebecca framed in the kitchen window, the house lights an illuminating backdrop. I don't want her to know I'm out in the driveway, gossiping about her past this way.

As I move to walk back up the driveway, Marti tugs at my arm, whispering, "Be honest, Michael. Is this a date?"

I kick at a loose piece of rock on the driveway, avoiding her probing gaze. "I'm queer, remember?" Marti of all people won't buy that one. After all, we made love more times than I can precisely recall, so she knows damn well that my sexual pendulum has swung both ways.

"It *is* a date!" She clasps her hands together conspiratorially. "Isn't it?"

I groan aloud. "I asked her here because she connected with Andrea."

Marti's black eyebrows form a feathery question mark. "And that's the only reason?"

I see Andie through our living room blinds, walking toward the kitchen. "I'll tell you everything later," I say hurriedly, leaning low to give Marti a peck on the cheek.

She opens the door of her Toyota with a devilish look. "I'm calling you at eleven tonight for details."

"Fine," I grumble irritably. "Eleven."

But what I'm thinking, although I don't say so, is what if somehow that's not late enough?

When I enter the house again, Andrea's standing at the sink with Rebecca, holding a couple of tomatoes in her small hands. Rebecca is patiently explaining about washing the vegetables as she takes a ripe one and positions it squarely on the cutting board. Neither of them knows that I'm watching.

"These are from my mama's garden," she explains to Andrea. "Right off the vine." I hadn't realized her family lived here in L.A., not after seeing that picture of the horse farm.

Rebecca begins to methodically slice the tomato into luscious wedges; I can't explain it, but it's such an earthy scene. The way she's bending over the large wooden cutting board, the one that Alex always used when he cooked his extravagant meals. For nearly a year, we've eaten fast food and cereal and frozen dinners; mealtime has been little more than a chore.

But something about all these spices, and the fresh smells, I don't know what exactly, makes my throat tighten. The way Andrea looks up at her, all those usual defenses that I've grown accustomed to in the past year—they've been completely swept away. It's the face of the daughter I had a year ago. All her innocence restored.

"I watched *Evermore*," Rebecca tells her. "It was on last night. A repeat. I thought I'd check it out, because of you."

"Yeah?" Andrea can hardly contain her excitement—her little voice absolutely quivers with it.

"I liked it. I'm betting Gabriel's your favorite," she says knowingly.

Andrea stays quiet, focusing on washing another tomato. "He's an orphan," she finally replies.

Rebecca reaches for a wedge of cheese and the grater. "Yeah, I did kind of figure that out."

I know what Andrea's going to say next before the words are even out of her mouth. I brace for it and attempt to bolster my waning emotional strength.

My daughter peers up at Rebecca with wide-open, vulnerable eyes. "I'm an orphan too," she confesses softly.

"What about Michael? You've still got him."

Andrea drops her gaze to the cutting board. "But he's not my *dad*. Alex was my daddy."

I know Rebecca must be remembering our conversation from yesterday when I referred to my "wife" by that name.

"Are you telling Miss Rebecca about Daddy?"

I step into the kitchen boldly, making them both jump a bit. I should have held back, let them have this moment, but I can't roll back time, not even these past few seconds.

Andrea stares down at the cutting board, her rust-colored hair hiding her features. Rebecca offers me an apologetic smile, and I wonder if she's starting to piece the puzzle together yet.

Maybe... maybe not.

"Andrea's daddy could cook one helluva meal," I say in an overly bright voice. "Me, well, I'm not so good."

There's an awkward silence, and I hope Andrea will answer or say something about Alex, but instead it's Rebecca who finally speaks. "Then it's a good thing I've come to visit, huh?"

I bend down and kiss the top of Andrea's auburn head. "Really good. We need some home cooking 'round here."

✧

After Andrea's asleep, Rebecca notices our family portrait in the hallway, a photograph taken by Alex's own twin sister, Laurel. We're in the backyard of Grandma Richardson's house in Santa Cruz, the lush green grass a canvas beneath us. Alex and I are sitting together, Andrea just in front. We're all dressed up, a little churchy even, with our neat jackets and ties, Andie in a white sundress. The sun had hunkered low on the horizon that day, creating a golden halo around our trio.

"So that's Alex?" Rebecca's voice is thick, a little choked. She stands beside me, reverently studying my family's picture that hangs before us on the wall.

"We were together for twelve years. Andrea's our daughter."

It's such an easy, offhanded explanation, no matter that it sidesteps all the obvious—and awkward—questions about surrogates and the like. The red hair ties Alex and Andrea together like a birthright; that I'm on the outside is apparent to even the most casual of observers.

"So you're gay."

I feel the weight of Rebecca's expectations, her disappointment about the vibe she must have detected between us.

"Well," I answer, drawing in a breath, "I was with a guy for a long time."

Rebecca shakes her head apologetically, the golden hair shimmering. "It was a stupid question."

"Not stupid," I whisper, turning toward her. "Actually, he's the only guy I've ever been with. Only thing I can say for sure is that I was in love with him."

"You still are."

"Can't get past it, I'm afraid."

This comment must hit home, because she closes her eyes a moment, then quietly asks, "How'd he die?"

"On impact. A drunk driver...head-on collision. Andrea was in the backseat." My voice catches; I hesitate, pressing my eyes shut. "It took them more than an hour to get her out of the car."

"Oh God, Michael." She covers my arm with her warm hand. "Oh, I'm so sorry."

She gets it. She gets it all, and I don't have to color in the pages for her to see what's happened here, to my family. Neither of us speaks, we just stand there in front of the portrait, like we're in the National Gallery or something, trying to decipher an Old Master. But she doesn't move that hand, either; it remains fixed solidly on my arm, tender and true. Somebody is touching me, finally. Someone unexpected.

"He was a beautiful man," she whispers, and I hear surprising tears in her voice as she leans up on her toes studying his image. "Very handsome."

Maybe she's crying for lost youth. Maybe for stolen beauty, her own perhaps—or because a violent stranger can career from nowhere and rob you of so much. Maybe we're crying together, for all that we've both lost.

I'm not sure, but perhaps it explains why I lean low and breathe a silent kiss against her scarred cheek. A chaste one that I hope conveys all the gratitude inside my heart that she's come here tonight.

✧

"You *what?*" Marti whispers into the phone. She doesn't want to wake Dave, who'll be up at five a.m. for his job as a construction foreman. I can actually hear him snoring in the background, but I promised this wrap-up call, so I'm stuck.

"I kissed her," I repeat softly. "Made sense, I guess."

"You're gay, huh, Warner?" She snickers affectionately. "I knew you liked her."

"It's not that way." I sigh. "I mean, the kiss was like a friend kiss. Kind of."

"Friend kiss. Kind of," she repeats. "Good lord, you sound like you're in high school. I bet Alex is laughing his ass off right now," she teases me, but I smart at the thought.

"Marti, I miss him so much," I say. "Y'all don't understand. You can't know what it's like."

There's silence, and I hear the rushed intake of her breath. "Sweetie," she finally says, "I do know how hard it is. But you're here, and he's not."

I'm here, he's not, but it doesn't answer the much bigger question looming in my mind tonight.

What *am* I, precisely, now that he's gone?

Chapter Five: Rebecca

Good thing Trevor's a consummate night owl, because after thirty minutes of driving up and down Sunset, gazing at giant billboards of half-naked men in their Calvins, I realize I can't go home yet. My brain is buzzing too loudly. It's like some hyperactive Beat poet, tossing words at me ninety miles an hour. Gay. Lonely. Widower. Lover. Sexy. Romantic. Beautiful. Strong. Smart. Lost. Lonely. Gay.

Bi?

Warring to be heard over this Ferlinghetti-style energy are my own gnawing insecurities, whispered taunts about my face, my body, my scars. I haven't had a date—not a real one—since my attack three years ago. I haven't wanted one. In fact, I don't think I've even had a genuine crush on a guy since Jake dumped me two weeks after I left the hospital. But this thing with Michael... I'm not sure how to handle what's going on inside of me after tonight. I'm scared and edgy, and only one person can talk me out of my tree when I'm feeling this way.

Cutting the steering wheel right, I turn onto La Brea, digging inside my purse for my cell. The nighttime landscape of L.A. spreads downhill from me, a glittering panorama of city light and dying heat as I cradle the phone against my shoulder.

"Hello, Rebecca," comes the cultured, silken British voice. Of course he knows it's me; he's as devoted as I am to caller I.D.

"You still up?" I turn onto his side street, heading uphill toward the Spanish-style apartment building where he lives. It's an old, moss-encrusted dwelling filled with the kind of moody atmosphere my best friend adores. We both moved away from our once-shared apartment building in West Hollywood after my attack.

"For you, I'm awake at any hour, sweetie."

"I'm right outside your building." I nose my Honda neatly into an empty space along the curb, then double-check that my car doors are locked.

"I'll be right there." Of course he offers to walk me up, since he knows how being out this late unnerves me.

Holding my purse in my lap, I settle in and wait, and as always this late at night, the waiting seems to last a lifetime. I glance anxiously toward Trevor's apartment doorway, then back at the street again. At that precise moment, seemingly choreographed to terrify me, a man materializes from nowhere, right beside my car window. I give a startled yelp, my heart hammering with fear as he brushes past my door, close enough for me to touch his shirt sleeve if the window were lowered more than a crack. Or for him to grab me, just as easily.

But he doesn't look back, and instead continues up the street. It must be a lost dog he's after, judging by the way he whistles and hurries down the palm-lined road.

These are the moments when terror comes shrieking unexpectedly out of my dark past. When I can still find myself held captive by Ben's butterfly knife, shocked by how easily it slashes into my abdomen. My chest. My face. And I can still feel myself dying with every slice of that blade, one eternal second at a time.

I clutch the purse against my breast, shivering uncontrollably. And it's not as though I'm out here in the middle of the night. It's a little past eleven, but I still feel like a victim, buckled and locked into my coffin of a compact car. My lungs pull tight as a drum and I struggle to find air. *Slow down, girl. Slow down.* If I don't, I'll hyperventilate. Then I'll need the rescue inhaler tucked inside my purse, and my fingers do search it out reflexively, even as I try to normalize my breathing. *Stilling, quieting... better.*

But then I begin to shake a little. It starts first in my bones, quickening like wildfire to my extremities. I dig my fingers hard into my thighs, feeling the khaki material of my pants bunch beneath my fingernails. Thankfully, Trevor appears below the awning of his apartment entryway, dressed in pajamas, the streetlight bathing him in bluish shadow. He doesn't wait, but comes right to me, because he knows. Oh, he knows what I live with, all right. And what I remember. That's why he'll always come to me first.

One moment I was outside, in the car, quaking and terrified, and now I'm on Trevor's plush leather sofa, heady scotch curled within my trembling hand. He never goes for wine or anything second-rate, instead he medicates me with the good stuff. The expensive stuff: single malt Glenlivet. Which isn't surprising, since expensive is the only way Mr. Baden-Powell knows.

I blink, swirling the clear liquid in the glass, staring into it like I might find the secrets of the universe shimmering there. My hands haven't stopped their trembling, and Trevor studies the glass's spasmodic movement under my fingertips. He's sitting at his antique secretary desk, one bare foot tucked beneath his leg, looking regal in his cranberry lounging pajamas. Even in the midst of my panic attack,

I still notice how beautiful he is. And how utterly unaware of it. He's atypical Hollywood, that's for sure.

"Better?" He brushes a lazy lock of hair away from his dark eyes.

I can't locate my voice, so instead I offer him a wan smile. My lip trembles, the left side of my mouth rebelling even more than usual. It can't be pretty. The corners of his own mouth turn downward in concern, mirroring my own expression.

"What exactly happened out there?" *You sounded well enough when you rang.* He doesn't add that, thankfully, but we both know the thought's still there. I wasn't fine when I phoned him; I was just doing a great acting job.

"Rebecca?" He calls to me from the end of a tunnel, a penumbra of light circling his familiar face. *Hang on, sweetheart. Hang on for me. The ambulance is on its way...*

"I don't know." I shrug one shoulder in my most disaffected L.A. pose.

"Oh, no, no, no." He shakes a finger slowly. "Thou shalt not lie to me."

"Huh, that's an interesting commandment," I snap, knowing that I'm about to turn the spotlight on him. After all, it's easier for me that way. "Especially coming from you." The fear is morphing, becoming uglier, and it's targeting my friend.

"Yes, well, it's a good decree to memorize, isn't it?" he asks, clearly oblivious to the nuclear buildup in my emotional reactor.

"I'm surprised you're not online." I jab a finger toward his laptop which sits open on his desk. "Shouldn't you be instant-messaging with *Julian* about now?" And now the black eyes do react. They widen slightly, then narrow, until there's barely more than his raven-wing eyebrows pulling into a dark line.

"Since it's seven a.m. in London, actually, no," he answers coolly, closing the laptop beside him.

I lean back against the cushions and study him. "Otherwise?"

"You know that Jules and I stay in touch by e-mail." *Jules.* He used that old pet name just to tick me off.

"Is that how he showed you his latest novel? Or did you actually solicit the proposal from his agent?"

A dark, moody groan rumbles out of Trevor's chest. "Bloody hell, Rebecca, is that what you're on about?"

"You could've just told me." I leap to my feet in accusation. "Or showed it to me. But you hid it." Even though blatant anger shifts in his eyes, I also see compassion. Love. "You made me look stupid," I continue, pacing a bit beside his chair. "Feel stupid! I should've known, but instead I just found it there in the freaking submission pile."

"So you're upset about that novel?" he presses, louder, cocking his head sideways as he stares hard into my eyes. "That is really and truly your issue right now. Julian Kingsley's novel?"

"No." Air almost goes out of the room as my anger deflates, and with it my energy. I drop back onto his sofa hopelessly.

"I didn't think so." Carefully removing his wireframes, he folds them together. "You're in an awful mood. This is toppers even for your worst days."

"You should've shown me the proposal, and I'm still pissed about it."

"Look." He rises from the desk, prying my empty scotch glass out of my hand. "I wasn't being underhanded, all right? I just knew how much you dislike him."

"I've never met him."

Trevor pads into the adjoining dark living room, finds the crystal decanter, and refills my glass. There's the sound of tinkling ice cubes, and I realize he's stocked the bucket just for me. Or someone else? Did Trevor have a date over this evening? Suspicion's hard to shake once it has taken root.

"You can stay the night on the settee," he offers as he returns, tapping my crystal glass with his fingertips significantly. In other words, I can drink myself silly if that's what I want. "But first, I'm going to tell you about Jules and his novel, and then you're going to tell me all that's wrong in your world tonight."

"Absolutely everything." I sigh, sinking back into the dark brown leather sofa, feeling the familiar dips and mounds beneath me. "And I'm sorry for being such a bitch."

"Oh, I doubt you've a bitchy bone in your body." He drops onto the sofa beside me. "You're just complex. Like the rest of us around here, aren't you?"

"My life might be getting a whole lot more complex."

"How's that?"

"I've met someone, unbelievable as that might be."

An elegant black eyebrow shoots upward, questioning as he laughs. "Second thought, let's start with you and wrap with Jules."

I try to think of a good way to frame it, but there simply isn't one. So I just blurt, "It's Heavenly Handyman," feeling foolish already. Especially with the way my extremely gay friend stares at me, clearly dumbfounded.

"The lad from electrical construction?"

"That's the one."

"But he's queer." Not a question or doubt about the facts of the situation.

"Not quite."

"Not *quite*?" He coughs. "I'd say it's a yes or no situation, unless—"

"He's bi."

"Oh, dear Lord, no wonder your humor is foul." He gives me a wry, knowing look. "His sort's to be avoided at all costs. By both our kinds. Enter not the forest of uncertainty, for demons dwelleth there."

I smile back at him, my own expression dreamy and naive. "He's amazing."

"Yes, well that's what we all say, isn't it? Right before it gets bloody confusing as to which way the wind blows."

"Trust me, his sexuality is the least of the issues."

"Really? How's that?"

I wonder if I can describe Michael's deep grief about Andrea and all they've both lost. I doubt it's possible to put words to what I'm feeling—to what I *felt* there with them in that house tonight.

So I close my eyes and think like an actress. It hasn't been so long that I can't call upon my method technique. My memory searches for a quarter-inch of something from their house tonight, something tangible to help me translate the emotion to Trevor.

What I instantly recall is their family portrait, the one hanging in the hallway. A dreamy photograph of the three of them, sitting together in that sun-drenched backyard, bathed in a diaphanous halo of light. Alex so alive and vital, like he might step out of the picture and talk right to me. Shock of deep auburn hair, broad grin, freckled face. Natural good looks. A good *man*, obviously. And then the man beside him too. Strong and handsome, years younger than the one I've met in the past few days. Unlike *my* Michael Warner, that one's not weary and weathered; the whole world still bows at his feet.

Then precious Andrea curled in front of them on the grass. Still a little girl, though that would soon change, because the Andrea in the portrait is as gone as Alex. And Michael. None of those three live on anymore. There are only ghosts, shades of what might have been.

Yes, the portrait is the key. My eyes well with tears again, and I feel the loss as if it were my own. It already *is* my own, in some metaphysical way that I can't pinpoint. My palm finds its way to my chest, and I massage my breastbone, blinking back hot tears.

I picture Andrea's clear blue eyes staring up at me while we cooked together. Maybe she was as insubstantial as the girl from the portrait; maybe Michael worried because he knew the truth. That she'd vanished too.

"He's a father," I say softly. "They had a daughter together."

"They *had*?"

"His partner's dead..." I think of Michael in my office, his hopefulness that Andrea might open up to me. "It's been tough for him, raising her alone. She feels like she can talk to me."

"Of course she can. You're a *woman*, sweetie."

"I am that," I say. "I guess that helps with her opening up."

"How convenient that he's found you," Trevor remarks, and I hear an edge to his voice. "Now that he needs a mother for this girl."

I doubt he even knows what he's said, but it feels like he's punched me full-force in the stomach. All the air sucks right out of my lungs, and my head snaps in his direction. I get it now. There's no attraction. How could there be, when I look like this? What an idiot I am. Michael only wants me because of what I can be to Andrea—not out of any desire for me. Even pure-hearted Trevor can see it from a mile away.

My fingers trace the pattern of scars on the left side of my face. How could it still feel this way after five plastic surgeries?

"I thought maybe there was...something. You know, between us."

"I'm not saying that there isn't," he rushes to assure me, but it's too late. "Not at all. Just that I don't want him latching on to you out of some other kind of need."

"Andrea opened up to me." I rub my tired eyes. "That's really all it is, I'm sure."

Never mind Foot and Cinderella's slipper. Or the way he kissed me there in the hall, something tender and gentle that somehow burned me nonetheless. Never mind that for some inexplicable reason, I do still dream.

"But what will you do about hottie handyman?" He studies me carefully, protectively. "About this attraction?"

"I'm resisting it."

He gives a single, affirming nod. "Good. It's best that way."

Even better would have been avoiding him to begin with, I think, and close my eyes.

An hour later, and I've explained everything, or most of it, at least. Michael's past, that Alex was his only experience with a man. When I got to that part, I was hoping Trev might root a little harder for my team, but he only offered a dubious look, to which I explained that Michael's an upfront guy, and I couldn't imagine him lying about his sexuality. Trevor apologized for his naturally skeptical nature, but I noticed that he didn't apologize for his doubts.

What I didn't admit is that I do know there are secrets in that house. I sense them all around the place, especially around Andrea. Heavy things Michael's not able to tell me yet. I wonder if he ever will be. And I wonder if Alex went to his grave bearing those same mysteries and unspoken truths.

Trevor wonders aloud why Michael didn't just tell me he'd been "married" to a man, and with that, nudges just a little too close to my own reservations. That's when I deftly change the current of conversation, laughing about the occasional duplicity of the gay male—present company excluded, at least ordinarily. "Which makes a perfect segue to Julian's manuscript proposal," I encourage, steering us out of the treacherous waves and into safety.

"Oh, thanks, love. Appreciate that, I truly do."

"You did keep it from me," I remind him with a cheery laugh.

"Only temporarily. I was going to show it to you on Monday." He reaches for the engraved cigarette case on his marble-topped coffee table. "Mind?" He taps one out, and I shake my head as he fingers his familiar black Zippo. Unlike with Ed's chain-smoking, Trevor's fast cigarette won't aggravate my asthma very much.

There's the sound of flint striking metal, the momentary pause of quick inhalation, followed by a soft swoosh as he blows smoke away from me. I watch a silver gray ribbon curl into the lamplight. "Terrible habit. Must quit soon." We both know better, but we also know the comfort that self-deception can bring.

"When you give me permission, I'll become your nag hag."

"Not yet." He waves me off with a slight cough. "Every good boy must have at least one bad habit."

"I thought you already had that covered," I tease, and his dark eyes narrow in confusion. Then he gets it, and there's that wide, open smile of his that I love so much.

"Yes, well Julian *is* bad." He giggles like a girlfriend. "At least we both agree on that point."

"But his proposal is freaking amazing!" I slap my hands together emphatically, feeling generous all of a sudden. All hail scotch whiskey! Then, just as suddenly, I grow somber again. "I don't have to love him to see that."

"It's his best work yet. You should read the chapters..." He takes another long drag on his cigarette. For a moment he stares thoughtfully across the room, at the antique bookcases filled with cracked, leather-bound volumes of classic novels and poetry. Books I know he brought from England, probably from Julian's place. From the flat they once shared during their glory days together.

"He's gone deeper. To places I still wish I could go. That I may never go." He hesitates, and there's a haunted silence that I wish I could fully comprehend. When he finally speaks again, it's in hushed, reverent tones. "He hasn't had a drink in four months, Rebecca. And what it's done for his work almost frightens me. To realize how truly brilliant he is. If only he *will* be. It makes me wish I were something that I'm not," he confesses, glancing sideways at me.

I sit upright, turning to face him. "Trevor, you're a great writer."

But being a great writer isn't really what he's even talking about; we both know that.

"How could someone with a gift like that be so careless with it?"

he reflects, and I understand what he's really asking; the deep, soulful question that he's always pondering about the one man he's ever truly loved.

"Only a fool would take something so precious for granted," I reply meaningfully.

He looks away again, avoiding my probing gaze, and I'm reminded of what I often forget. We all have our scars. Most of mine just happen to be on the outside.

✧

The next morning finds me hurrying across the studio lot, not yet late for a development meeting. Suddenly the stifling heat makes my black fashionista suit seem like an imprudent choice. *Silly, silly Rebecca. Hoping you might see him. It's a great, big studio lot, little girl.*

"Ms. O'Neill." The familiar, husky voice angles right into my thoughts with all the gracelessness of a crowbar.

My head snaps sideways and Michael's just standing there beside a wardrobe trailer. Hands shoved in both pockets, he gives me that eccentric, dimpled grin that's already vying to become a part of me.

"Hi!" I hug the folder full of meeting notes against my chest, and the very first thing I notice is my name. On his shirt, emblazoned across the front: *O'Neill.* So, why would he suddenly be wearing a shirt with my name on it; I can't quite figure that out, and a Ben wannabe wanders into my mental vision for a half-second.

"Are you all right, Rebecca?" The question has me pulling focus back on Michael.

I point toward his shirt, feeling a little accusatory—and stupid for that fact. But Ben's shadow falls over lots of parts of my life. "Your shirt." I point a little harder, making a jabbing gesture. "It says O'Neill."

He gazes downward in confusion, the confident smile slipping a little. "Oh, yeah, like—" He points from the shirt to me, drawing the connection I'd intended.

"Like Rebecca O'Neill," I finish for him, smiling again. Michael isn't Ben and he definitely isn't a stalker.

"Or... like surfer gear. Wet suits and all that." He rubs a palm over his spiky hair with a boyish grin.

"*Ohhh,*" I say. Geez, am I a nitwit? How could I forget the O'Neill brand? "I didn't know you were into surfing."

The smile fades now, and he hesitates before answering. "Alex was a lifelong surfer boy. I just gave it my best shot on his account."

"So you don't surf anymore?" I shift my weight from foot to foot. "I've always thought it would be cool, but haven't ever tried it."

"I could teach you sometime." His eyes brighten again, ever so slightly.

"You really think I could surf?" I scrunch my nose up in curious disbelief. "I'm not too... small? I wouldn't want to wash away or anything."

"Nah, Andrea even surfs some. In some ways it helps to be compact," he says, that southern Virginia drawl popping right on out.

"I've always wished I weren't so small," I admit, brushing at my hair nervously. A strand catches on my thumb ring, and I have to give an extra tug that makes me wince.

"You aren't small." He steps a little closer until he's invading my physical zone. My face warms at the intimacy as he leans low and whispers, "No, Rebecca. You're delicate. Really feminine. And that's a good thing."

The warmth shoots from my face down into my neck. Up into my scalp. I'm burning at his simple compliment. How does he always manage to make me feel so beautiful?

"And that Armani suit." His voice grows even softer, his gaze traveling the length of me appreciatively. "Looks absolutely amazing on you."

"I'm impressed." I fan myself with my folder, trying to get a little breeze going. I'm burning up, and my Irish cheeks have surely stained deep red, like a warning flag on a surfer's beach.

"Impressed...?"

"Oh, just that you've gotta love a guy who knows his designer labels, that's all."

He stares down at his weathered work boots. "Hey, don't forget. I spent twelve years as a doctor's wife." Then the beautiful eyes track upward and lock with mine, and there's humor there. Even he realizes the irony of his remark, with him all decked out in his tool belt and boots. "It's tough duty being a doctor's wife too. Having good fashion sense is part of the job."

"I can see that." I eye his faded surfer shirt and denim blue jeans pointedly.

"Didn't say I had to use it, now." That smoky-voiced southern accent traipses up my backbone, and desire chases right along with it. "Just possess it."

"Maybe I should take you shopping with me someday. You know, for a consultation."

"Happy to oblige you any time."

We fall silent, me scuffing the sole of my new Prada shoe against the asphalt, Michael glancing around. I clear my throat, wishing one of us could come up with something to say. Then all at once, like two shy people thunking foreheads together in an awkward moment, we start talking at the same time.

As if on cue, a golf cart bearing some "suit" talking on his cell phone speeds at us, and we part like Cecil B. DeMille's Red Sea.

"You go," I say once the cart has buzzed by. "Tell me what you were going to say."

"No, you go on." Just my luck, he's chivalrous to the core.

."Lunch? I mean, it's Monday and I like to go out to a nice lunch on Mondays, not do the pitch thing. Still, my job, you know...I need to get out and be seen. Circulate, all that. Which, of course, might not be something you'd like to do—"

"What time?"

"Today?"

Michael grins at me, such a sweet, reassuring thing, and it takes some of the sting out of feeling so painfully awkward and uncool. "Yes, Rebecca, today. I'd like to go with you today." He tugs on the hem of his faded T-shirt. "But I do look a little rough around the edges. Sure that's okay?"

I tell him about a great Chinese place around the corner, a hole in the wall that some of the studio execs frequent on occasion, and even some A-list talent, but it's dark there, so my "doctor's wife" can look as casual as he cares to.

He loves Chinese food, and we set our time and meeting place. Then just when I'm walking away, feeling sassy and pretty as I toss my long hair over my shoulder, he calls after me, "Hey, O'Neill!"

I turn back and find him watching me. "Maybe I did wear the shirt 'cause of you," he admits with a serious expression. "But I'm not scary, I promise. Not any kind of threat."

Oh, Mr. Warner, care to lay any bets on that pledge?

✧

The great thing about the Chinese place is that it's dark. Very dark. And that makes me feel more relaxed with Michael than I have at any point before now. We're in a half-moon-shaped leather booth, and he's seated to my good side, the unscarred version of my profile. So I can relax a little; unless I turn to face him, he's only going to see the best of me.

At first we chitchat about the movie business and the restaurant while I glance around for people I might know. But I really don't want to do the table-hopping and glad-handing routine today. I pull at a torn bit of vinyl on the garish red booth seat, trying to think of something clever to say. Nothing comes to mind, so I study the floor-to-ceiling framed photographs of stars who've dined here over the years, an array of famous people—some living, some dead.

He makes an attempt at conversation. "How'd you get into acting?" he asks, the tone a little tight. That's when I realize that he *knows.*

"I guess you're aware of my past." I won't look at him and keep tugging at the vinyl. "Or probably just a tabloid version of it, like most everyone else."

"Maybe I should've pretended I didn't know."

"Why?" I set my jaw, looking away from him. "What would've been the point?"

"To let you tell me first." There's true-blue honesty in his words and tone, and the nervous pressure inside my chest begins to ease up.

I begin picking the dry noodles out of the basket, tiling them into random patterns, trying to decide how to fix this conversational mess. "I'm not actually a bitch," I tell him after a moment, "but I have been known to play one when I talk about my *past* in TV."

This makes him burst out laughing. Stupid joke, sweet guy. "That's a good one. And you weren't a bitch."

"Nope, pretty bitchy just then, and I'm sorry." I brush the noodles together, wiping the slate clean. "I just don't like talking about my backstory."

"That makes getting to be friends kind of hard, don't you think?"

The noodles become my obsession, as I now begin crisscrossing them into an interlaced design. "Hollywood's about the moment."

"You don't strike me as very Hollywood, Rebecca. You're real. I like that."

I drop my head. "Give me some more time in this town, and I'll fade eventually."

"I don't see that happening."

"My past is harsh, Michael," I answer wearily. "Hard for me to talk about."

"So's mine." He's got a point there, and I think of how he opened up to me last night.

"But mine's been made public for everyone to see," I explain, still avoiding his sensitive gaze, which proves nearly impossible. "If you know I was an actress, then that makes me wonder precisely what all you *do* know. And what you don't. Which version you got, because there are lots of versions floating around out there, you know."

"Marti told me," he confesses, giving me an apologetic smile. "I didn't recognize you or know... anything until last night."

"Marti," I repeat dully, feeling slightly betrayed by this woman I've only barely met.

"Don't blame her. She thought I knew," he rushes to explain. He gives a quiet laugh. "Well, actually she thinks I live under a rock now because I *hadn't* heard of you before."

"Would it help if I said I think so too?" I tease, laughing with him. Then, just like that, the tension ruptures. We're buddies again. More than friends, as he leans a little closer to me and lowers his voice. "Rebecca, all your secrets are safe with me."

Safe. What a concept. The most important word in the world to me, and it's something Michael makes me feel on instinct, even without his reassurances.

"What do you want to know?" I ask. "How I got here? About the guy who came after me? I'll tell you whatever."

"I want to know about you. Just you."

"What is this? *Notting Hill?*" I laugh anxiously.

He frowns. "I'm serious, Rebecca."

Jake wanted to know about me too, that first time he took me out, right after we wrapped the first episode of season two. He was my co-star on *About the House*, and even though I knew his reputation, I thought maybe he'd changed over the hiatus. He certainly convinced me that he had, talking about the power of rehab and finding his "center". For a southern Methodist girl like me, some of his New Age talk didn't really make much sense, but I was just so bowled over by his charisma. And he had it in spades.

"I've heard that question before."

"You suggesting it's a line?" For the first time since I've met Michael Warner, I'm glimpsing a slight temper.

Despite myself, I smile. "No, just that it's not a line that will work on me. If it is a line, I mean."

"Rebecca, I've told you the way it is with me. And I don't confess those things to just anyone."

"Why me?" I ask, really wondering. Thinking of Trevor's suspicious take on my new friendship.

Maybe he'll say because he's been waiting for a girl like me. Or that it's been a long time since anyone made him feel this way. I wait, breath held tight inside my lungs, time literally suspended until he finally answers.

"'Cause I know you've been through things too. But you're still smiling. And beautiful. I want to understand how you do that."

Oh, God. He could've said anything else, but now he's got me. In the palm of his hand, like a baby bird just fallen out of its nest. I'm vulnerable, naked. I can only hope he's gentle.

"Can we wait to talk about my past?" I ask, knowing I'll go anywhere he leads me now.

"Of course."

"It's just, well, it was three years ago last week that this—" I hesitate, then point to my face, "—happened. My attack. I've been feeling kind of freaky about it."

"Anniversaries are tough," he answers knowingly, and it makes me wonder exactly when Alex died. "They make you feel like you're in a time warp."

"Or like it's going to happen all over again," I add, and this clearly hits home, because he nods his head dramatically.

"Yeah, and if I had to go through it all again," he agrees, "it'd probably kill me."

I think of the nine slashes of Ben McAllister's knife. If I had to live through those again, would he aim any better? Or would one or two more targeted thrusts finish me off next time?

"That's why it's the past, Michael," I answer, shivering as I think of Ben languishing in Chino. Thank God he's locked away for the rest of my life and his. "Because it's done with."

"Reckon so," he agrees, and then we both just look away. We look away because the platitudes don't work for either of us. We both know that I'm saying what we *want* to believe, because like some terrible Chinese riddle, the fact is that the past isn't in the past at all. It's vital and breathing and a little bit ravenous, and no matter what else we've lost, it's the one thing we can never truly lose.

Chapter Six: Michael

I've dreaded this day for weeks, maybe even months. Now that it's here, though, it doesn't seem to pack the power that I feared it would. No, today's just an average, unremarkable Saturday. Muggy and hot for late May, with a hazy morning sun that's already making me sweat, but it's bizarre how absurdly normal everything feels. Normal, if Andrea and I weren't driving to Grandma Richardson's to visit the family gravesite and mark the first anniversary of Alex's death. And if I weren't seeing his sister, Laurel, for the first time since we laid him in the ground. There's been lots of water under our bridge since then, Laurel's and mine, none of it good.

Weird to think that it was early morning just like this when Alex stopped into the kitchen on his way out to work and said to me one last time, "Baby, I love you."

What made him turn back that way? Andrea was already in the car, his briefcase was slung over his shoulder, and then just like that, he stopped. We said the words often enough between ourselves, though not usually with him halfway out the door. He made such a point of me hearing that last time; he *wanted* me to know. For the rest of my life, I'll see the smile he gave me as he turned away.

Who would've thought that a single day could change everything so much? It's the time warp thing again, like I told Rebecca. Sometimes it even feels like that movie *Groundhog Day*, with me watching him leave over and over, only there's a different ending every time. How I wish.

Even though it's a somber occasion that's calling us back to his hometown today, I'm still determined to make it a special visit for Andie. That's why we're taking this slightly longish coastal route. It's a beautiful day and I liked the idea of her seeing the ocean for a good part of the drive, and while she's not full of chatty reactions, her face lights up once the beach appears off to the side of the 101. She's always loved the ocean, whether it's up in Santa Cruz or out at Casey's place in Malibu. She's pure beach bum, just like her daddy was.

As we crest a slight hill, dark, shark-like figures appear in the water, a group of them bobbing along on their boards. "Look," I point out. "Surfers."

"But it's so early." She wrinkles her nose as she looks at the dashboard clock. Seven a.m. on a Saturday, not my idea of where I'd be, paddling my way out into the chilly Pacific, squeezed tight into my wetsuit.

"Hey, you know what Daddy always said," I remind her with a grin, and she finishes for me, "The best waves don't ever sleep in!" We both laugh a minute, remembering, and my heart beats a little faster at the pure joy of making her smile.

"Won't be long and we'll be out there too. Casey's planning on us for Fourth of July." We always used to spend summer holidays with Casey at his beach house, but this will be the first time without Alex.

"Well I'm not going to surf." She turns from me, staring out the window of the truck.

"Why not?" I ask, even though I already guessed she wouldn't wear her bathing suit, not with how self-conscious she is about that long scar on her thigh.

She only shrugs, studying the open map that I had given her to track our travel progress over the six-hour drive. From the corner of my eye, I see her taking her fingers and measuring out the distance, then comparing it to the mileage legend. Sizing up the world between her stubby little fingertips. The world's a big place when you're that small: everything seems super-sized compared to what you know.

That's what I'm thinking when out of nowhere she asks, "Were you always gay?"

I almost spit coffee onto the steering wheel of my pickup truck. "Why?" I ask with forced nonchalance.

"Well." She sighs as I watch a pair of sexy, lean guys with surfboards walking along the highway shoulder. "Gretchen Russell's daddy is gay now. At least that's what they say."

Peter Russell. I've met him before at some of the school events, especially back in the preschool days. I remember a good chat we had once at Muffins with Mom. Guess *that* event takes on a whole new meaning in this context. So does the interest he took in Al and me being gay parents.

"What happened to Gretchen's mom?" I ask, after a moment of thoughtful silence.

"She's still her mom."

"No, sweetie. I mean..." I pause, rubbing at my eyes. "Did they divorce? Is that what you're saying?"

She shrugs, silent and won't tell me any more, but I don't think Gretchen Russell and her daddy's conversion to my side is the real issue. Andrea wants to know about me.

"I had some girlfriends, you know," I begin gingerly. "Before Daddy."

She turns to me, her bowtie mouth widening in surprise. "But..." She shakes her head, unable to fathom this new catalog of information.

I can't help but smile at her innocence. Really, it's not that different from a straight married couple, their child's pure belief that both parents sprang forth, fully formed, attached to one another from birth. "You find it hard to believe, huh?"

"Wasn't that weird for Daddy?"

"I'd say it was pretty weird for me."

"Well, what if I turn out gay?" she asks softly, closing the map book and turning toward me on the seat. "'Cause I could, couldn't I?"

I think of how delicate and feminine she is; how even at four years old she began crossing her little legs, still sitting in the car seat. I think of how she fusses over her Barbies, taking infinite care with their sequins and satin. But I also know that's no measure of which way one's sexuality will ultimately swing, not even close. Consider my army airborne days if you think I'm wrong about that. After all, I've jumped out of loads of perfectly good airplanes, and I still went pink triangle.

So I ask, "You know that Daddy and I were really happy together, right?" She looks away, silent, and I sense her shutting down to me just as quickly as she opened. "'Cause we were, sweetheart. We loved each other."

"So?"

"Well, so it's okay, being gay." I glance sideways surreptitiously. "That's what I mean."

I swear I see her roll her eyes at me as she reaches for the radio tuner buttons. What I'm trying to tell her, but I'm doing such a miserable job of it, is that love is what counts. Whatever form it comes to you, even if it sneaks up on a strange, unanticipated night, love is all that matters in this world of ours. Even if you lose that love when you least expect it.

"Andrea, are you even listening to me?" I demand, feeling more forceful and assertive than I usually am with her.

She turns to me, blinking her crystal-blue eyes. "Yeah."

"The important thing is whether you find someone to love. Someone to love *you* as much as we all do."

"Do you like Rebecca? 'Cause if you weren't always gay..." she suggests, winding a long auburn lock around her fingertip thoughtfully. "Well, you might not always be gay *now*, right? Then you might like Rebecca, I mean. Sort of like Gretchen's daddy liking boys."

"Sort of like." I cough, raising my coffee mug to my lips as a way of concealing my face.

"'Cause you could do that," she presses, "like he's gay."

"I could, yeah, conceivably like women again."

"Good, 'cause I like Rebecca." She gazes up at me through her rust-colored lashes. "She's really fun and cool. I totally like her."

"Well, maybe we can get together with her again soon," I offer, thinking of the amazing inroads she's made with my child. Thinking of how I could have spent all afternoon in that Chinese restaurant just talking to her. Looking at her. "Maybe she could come back over again and spend time with us." Like we're a unit, a full package, not that I'm one lonely man who has become infatuated with a beautiful, available woman.

"I'd like that," she agrees.

"Yeah. Me too." Oh, I'd like it, all right. A whole lot more than I care to admit, even to myself just yet.

✧

As we hit the heart of Santa Cruz, my breathing changes. Becomes rapid and a little desperate. It's the thought of seeing Laurel again that's got me all wound up, not just being back here to visit Allie's grave. I've already done that drill a few times in the past year. Been there at Thanksgiving, and again at Christmas. But I haven't seen Laurel, not since a year ago, and I'm not sure what to expect. Still, I shove those dark thoughts aside as we drive up the long, steep hill to the Richardson house.

Or maybe "home place" is a better description of the million-dollar house where my baby grew up. A rambling old Victorian by the sea, it crests the hilltop like the local icon that it is. There's no pretension to it: the mansion boldly crowns this cliffside part of town.

"Wonder if Grandma's roses are blooming yet," Andrea reflects.

She loves her grandma's garden, and it's always been something that binds them together, working in it side by side. Planting seeds and watching them yield life. Nipping the buds off waning pansies. She makes Andrea feel important, and reaches her in a way that I haven't figured out how to do since Al passed. What worries me is the thought that maybe Laurel might find a way to do that too.

Andrea unzips her Barbie backpack, pulling out a large envelope. "I brought this for Aunt Laurel."

"What's in it?" I ask, my voice just a little too bright. As I turn the truck into the pebbled driveway, there's a crunch and spray of rock beneath my tires. I have to skid a bit to slow down on the drive.

"Something I made her in art class." Laurel is a world-class painter, with an exclusive gallery of her own in Santa Fe.

"What kind of project was it?" I stare at the closed front door of the house. So much rests behind that colored Tiffany glass pane, and I'm not sure I'm ready to face it yet.

Andrea takes the envelope in one hand, then reaches eagerly for the door handle with her other, never answering me as she shimmies out onto the driveway. Then, full throttle, she runs across the lush green yard and up the steps, onto the sweeping veranda. She hasn't been this excited since *High School Musical 3* finally came out.

Feeling ancient and slow as hell, I plant my Nikes on the pebbled drive, ready to face what waits.

✧

Time is endless in Ellen Richardson's home. There's the steady ticking of the grandfather clock, the groaning creaks of the one-hundred-year-old hardwoods, the rhythm of the crashing waves down the cliff side. My blood pressure lowers; my heart rate slows. The day lengthens whenever I enter. Why couldn't that eternal spell have worked a number on Alex's life?

Ellen embraces Andrea, leaning her aged shoulders low to really hold her close. She watches me over Andie's head, a faint smile playing on her lips. But I'm already looking around for Laurel, 'cause I don't get why she hasn't joined us in the sweeping hallway for our big entrance.

"Laurel not here?" I ask, curiosity corrosive on my insides. Ellen closes her eyes momentarily—wearily—then opens them again as she stands tall to face me.

"Michael, she wasn't able to get away. She wanted to, but..." Her voice trails off, the explanation obvious. Yeah, I don't buy it for a moment. Laurel's putting off our confrontation yet again. Here I've dreaded seeing her almost as much as the anniversary of Al's death, and she bails without a warning to me? I can't believe it.

Ellen steps close, wrapping her graceful arms around me. "Hello, son." She reaches up to pat my cheek, her charm bracelet tinkling musically.

"I can't believe she didn't come," I blurt, thinking of what today means. No matter what's happened between Laurel and me, we should all be together today. A family.

"She wanted to, darling," she explains as I step away. "You know that."

I doubt it, I'm about to grumble, when Andrea lights up, her gaze falling on a package tied up with a dazzle of ribbons and paper. "Look!" she squeals in excitement. "It's got my name on it."

"From Aunt Laurel, darling."

"What's the occasion?" I can't resist jibing, even though I know Laurel's only assuaging her guilt for skipping out on us today.

Ellen doesn't answer me, but walks to the antique Chinese credenza, where the present rests prominently. "Open it, sweetheart,"

71

she encourages. "A little bird told me that you will love what's inside."

Andrea's eyes sparkle as she tugs on the gathered rainbow ribbons. Her small hands pull and wrestle, but it takes me stepping forward with my pocketknife to get the damn thing open. Guess I'm not completely useless just yet.

"Thanks, Michael," Andrea murmurs, the paper unfolding within her hands.

She squeals, "It's an American Girl doll!" as the package comes into view. "Felicity!"

Felicity, the little redhead doll I'd been thinking of getting her last Christmas, but never did. Just great. Laurel's gone for true bribery now. Proffering expensive gifts, more reminders that she's more thoughtful than I am. Of what a terrible substitute I am for the mother and daddy she should have in her life.

"Great, sweetie," I mumble, wandering away from them and into the adjoining parlor as Andrea chatters with her grandma about how much she's wanted a Felicity doll, how she's looked at the catalog and wished.

Their joyous laughter chases after me, haunting me as I sink heavily into the plush velvet sofa beneath the front window, burying my head in my hands. And I have to wonder—is it really possible that a thirty-nine-year-old man can feel this brittle and worn out? I'm not sure if it's realizing Laurel's never going to fade away, or maybe it's just being back in this house again. All I know is I haven't missed Alex so much in a long damned time.

✧

The cemetery is hot. Way too hot, despite the leafy palm trees scattered throughout the graveyard, offering slight shade from the blistering sun. My shirt's clinging to my back in a terrible, sweaty outline, and I just wish we could head on home. But Andrea's taking her time, quiet and thoughtful, and I can't rush that, no matter how restless I might feel about being here. She's kneeling in the grass, running her open hand over the prickly blades that cover Allie's resting place. Back and forth she swishes her pale hand, letting the grass tickle her palm. Blotting my forehead and neck with a McDonald's napkin from the truck, I notice the freckles sprinkled across her fair shoulders. They're peeping out from beneath the shoulder straps of her flowered sundress, even crawling up the nape of her pale neck. Eventually, if she's not careful, she'll be as covered with them as Alex always was.

Ellen holds fast to my arm, teetering beside me in her high heels. Even at seventy-six years old, when we're trudging out here, in the damp grass, she refuses to give them up.

"My precious boy," Ellen murmurs under her breath, as if she were cradling Alex in her arms. "We miss you so." Tears immediately burn my eyes, and I blink them back, not moving. Not even when she whispers, "And we love you so. Always."

"Grandma? Why do you talk to Daddy whenever we come here?" Andrea doesn't look up, just continues to stare at the monolith atop his burial place, reaching with her fingertips to touch that too. Maybe she needs to know that where he stays is solid, corporeal, even if he is not.

Ellen gazes up at me, the quiet blue eyes filled with emotion. I speak for her. "Sweetheart, don't you?" I ask. "Talk to him whenever we're here? Maybe not out loud, but in your head?"

I can tell she's thinking about the question pretty seriously when she finally whispers, "I talk to him in my dreams. 'Cause that's when he talks to me."

Beside me Ellen shivers, and I do too, despite the heat of the afternoon. I know Andie's speaking metaphorically, but it still spooks me. "What's he say?" I ask, barely suppressing the trembling that tries to invade my voice.

"That he misses us. But that he's happy too. He's in a really good place," she explains reverently, then looks over her shoulder at both of us. "He's not here, you know."

"No, darling, of course not," Ellen agrees.

"That's why I asked, Grandma," she continues. "Just 'cause I know he's not down there." She pats the quiet earth beneath her hand by way of explanation.

"Then where is he?" I squint into the sun. Is he high up in some cloudlike heaven? Staring down at all of us today? "Is he there when you dream at night?"

Andrea laughs like it's the most obvious thing in the world. "Don't you know?" She hasn't laughed this honestly with me in a year, nor smiled so transparently. I even glimpse love in her expression. Ellen releases my arm, as slowly I crouch low beside my daughter.

"No, Andie, tell me. Where'd he go?"

Blue eyes fix me, clear and bright, and I behold the mysteries of my whole universe. "Silly, he's at the beach," she says with a dimpled grin. "Surfing. And the waves are always good!"

The beach. Well, of course. Where else would Alexander Barrett Richardson be? Laughter bubbles up from deep within me, unstoppable, despite the incongruity of being here at my lover's grave.

That's when the miracle happens.

For once, just once, Andrea lets me pull her tight into my arms, and rock her like she's still my baby girl.

✧

After the cemetery visit, Andrea and I retire to the adjoining upstairs guest rooms for a nap. She doesn't even complain about that fact, which I'm pretty certain has a lot to do with the cache of Nancy Drew and Hardy Boys books she discovered in Laurel's old bedroom trunk. Typical Ellen, though—neither room has ever been fully converted to dedicated guest quarters. Both retain some of their childhood charm and character. Laurel's room has an antebellum dollhouse that has fascinated Andrea for years, and Alex's boasts a bunch of surfing and football trophies, as well as tall shelves lined with his favorite books.

But right now, it's the cigar box on his old bed that's holding my attention. Ellen told me she'd pulled together some photographs for me to cart home, but I can't believe she's really willing to part with all these family pictures. She wants Andrea to have them, she explained. And me. "Darling, I have more in this house than I can possibly keep up with," she told me. "You must have them."

Dropping onto the edge of the bed, I thumb through a disheveled heap of photographs and mementos. There's a wrinkled camp award for "good citizenship," a handmade potholder, an old journal. That gives me pause, as I crack it open and realize that Al kept it when he was fourteen years old. From what he told me, I wonder if his first confessions about realizing he was gay might be in those pages. I shove the cloth-bound diary to the bottom of the stack to guard his secrets, and then notice a large picture just beneath.

Gingerly, I pull the framed photo out, and at first I hardly recognize him: he can't be more than twelve years old, riding high atop Casey's shoulders. Overhead he holds some flag like it's an exultant trophy, grinning from ear to ear. He's so small and young and vulnerable that I want to reach into the picture and save him. Save him from anything that might possibly hurt him, and hold him close like I did Andrea earlier.

With a sigh, I roll onto my back and smell his childhood bed. Plaid pillowcase, handmade quilt, it's all a little musty. Like he really has left this world, same as he once left this room. Quiet—impenetrable quiet—blankets me as I prop my head on my elbow, and watch dust motes waft listlessly in a beam of light. Squinting, I look at Al in the picture again. He had no idea what the world held for him then, but he was just wide open, ready for it all, fearless.

Strange, but I almost feel like it's me somehow in that crackled photograph, riding high atop the world. For a minute, I close my eyes, and I'm almost certain that it is.

✧

Not sure how long it is before I wake up, and for a displaced moment, I think it's morning. Blinking back the sleep, I even think it's a year ago, as I scrub a drowsy hand across my face. Then I remember the anniversary and just how much we've all lost.

I slept in this room for days after the funeral. Every now and then, I'd rouse from heavy slumber and gaze through the mottled windowpane into the backyard. I'd spy Andrea with her grandmother, sitting in the garden, or see Laurel coming into the back door, arms filled with brown-paper grocery bags. Whenever I tried to awaken during those days, it felt impossible. Like moving under water in a thick dream; like being drugged. Occasionally I'd stumble downstairs, and Ellen would always kiss me, pointing me straight back to bed. "Sleep, darling. You need rest," she'd chide me.

I had to sleep because I couldn't live. Not with him gone.

But then, after three days of barely eating the sandwiches and fruit they kept delivering to the bedroom on that food tray, I did finally get up. I had to wake because Andrea was still alive—even if I wasn't.

The gratitude I'll feel for their protection during those first days after we buried Alex is something I'll never forget, no matter how much some of the later events with Laurel nearly destroyed me. I try and remember that as I blink back the naptime sleep from my eyes and amble downstairs in search of Ellen. Funny how much today feels like a year ago; the same heat, the same shrouding coolness inside this steamship of a house, the same rhythmic ticking of the antique grandfather clock.

"You're up already?" Ellen asks. She is sitting at the dining-room table sipping tea, a hardback open in front of her.

"What are you reading?"

She examines the novel's spine. "C.S. Lewis." Ugh. God stuff. Not what I need today. Settling across from her, I slide my newly discovered picture of Alex across the table toward her. "You see this one?"

She lifts it eye-level, smiling as she studies it. "That's the summer he grew like a bean stalk," she laughs gently. "At least six inches, I think."

"You know what I noticed about it?" I ask as she hands it back to me, shaking her head. "That he was triumphant. On top of the world. Guess he always was."

"Not always," she answers wistfully. "But most of the time."

Staring down at the image, at the way he's riding high and confident on Casey's shoulders, I say, "Bold as a mountain."

"Bold as life," she agrees. "Some people are born that way, Michael. They come to us for a brief, special purpose. We must accept that it was Alex's way."

I know she's right. Alex, the speedy comet that trailed across my life, then burned out fast. He lived to the fullest, that's for sure. No apologies, no hesitation, he reached for life with both hands and took it. Gusto should have been his middle name.

"It was the same way when he came out to me," she continues. "He was gay, that's how it was, and he hoped I'd still be proud of him."

"And you said?"

"How could I not be proud?"

"You're a great mother."

"I had a great son."

"Well, you won't get any arguments from me about that." I laugh, and our eyes meet. We shared a true love between us; the approach just came from different directions.

She gets a distant look on her face, staring past me at some unseen place. "He went at everything so intently, it was almost as if he knew he'd die young."

"Yeah, maybe some people have a short lifespan coded into their DNA."

I thought about that after he was gone. How fitting it was that he'd made a career of staving off death, of battling it, hand to hand; then, ever the victor in others' lives, he succumbed finally in his own.

"I'm angry when I think of all the people he might have healed," I say. "All the kids he could have saved. That really burns me up."

"I receive letters from the parents, you know," she says. "I had one just last week, from the mother of a thirteen-year-old boy he treated for leukemia. Her son has been in remission for five years now. Totally well. She wanted me to know how thankful she was for Alex."

Slowly, she moves toward the credenza, easing a drawer open. There must be family silver and serving pieces in that thing, because it gives an uneasy groan, but she steadies it, pulling out a thin envelope. Everything Ellen Richardson does is deliberate, purposeful, elegant. Her movements are choreographed poetry. Like the way she runs her palm over the creased paper as she removes it from the envelope, ironing the thin paper with her fingertips as she lifts her reading glasses upward to the bridge of her long nose.

She settles into the chair again and studies the page, her eyes skimming over the words. "Your son gave me back my own son," she begins. "For that I will always be grateful. But we are not alone. I know there are countless others like my family. Your son touched us all."

Family. With that one word, tears fill my eyes. Ellen must sense my reaction, because she pauses, glancing upward at me. "Oh, Michael," she soothes, covering my hand with her own weathered one. "I'm sorry."

She blurs, becomes misty as I blink at the tears. I don't want this woman, the only mother figure in my life, to see me cry. Her bony hand closes around mine, squeezing tight, and the tears won't stop.

Searching for my voice is a useless task; there's only a tight raspy wheeze as I bow my head, dropping it into my palm.

Ellen rises from her chair and stands beside me, her familiar hand circling my tired shoulders. "You loved him so much, I know."

"It's not just that," I manage thickly, glancing up at her. "We were a family."

"You still are, Michael. You and Andrea."

"But he was the glue. He's what held us together."

She strokes my hair, brushing her long fingers through my unruly locks. "It only feels that way right now, dear."

Family. What I hadn't really known before Al, and what it feels like I'll never know again. The one thing I still have here, at Ocean Crescent Drive. "I can't reach her, Ellen. I've tried."

"I think she's better."

"Maybe on the surface."

"She told me Inez is going to keep her this summer." There's no accusation in her words, but I feel heavy guilt descend in the space of a heartbeat. That I have to work, that I can't stay with her myself. That I'm not loaded like the Richardson family used to be, once upon a time, before only the trappings of their fortune remained.

"While I work," I offer lamely, wiping at my eyes with the back of my hand.

Ellen leans down, embracing me, and I catch the faint aroma of hand cream and perfume, tinged with earthy smells from her garden. These scents have been a constant during my thirteen years in her family. "Michael, of course you're working." She laughs, giving my shoulder a squeeze of reassurance. "The world works because it must, but perhaps you could take some time off. A vacation for the two of you might help Andrea to open up." She settles herself regally in the chair beside me again, studying me with her aged blue eyes. Eyes so eerily like my dead lover's that for a careless moment, I'm startled.

"I've been thinking of taking her back east. To meet my father."

Ellen nods, but her mouth turns downward in concern. "Have you spoken to him?" *Lately.* She doesn't say it, but I know that's what she's thinking.

"Nope." The grandfather clock in the foyer sounds the quarter-hour, and the chimes echo through the whole house. The quiet here has always been peaceful, never lonely like at my home when I was growing up, where it was empty and cavernous. The kind of silence that would swallow you whole if you weren't careful.

Ellen draws in a breath. "Does your father know that Alex passed?" Staring down into my tea glass, tinkling the cubes of ice in it, offers me a temporary reprieve until Ellen covers my hand with her own again. "He doesn't know?"

"He doesn't even know that we have a daughter, Ellen," I confess, glancing up at her. Damned if fresh tears aren't a serious threat, but I manage to urge them away.

"You should tell him," she states with a resolute nod of her head. "He's your father and he'd want to know."

"He doesn't want any part of what I had with Alex. He made that painfully clear years ago."

Again, only the sound of the grandfather clock, measuring the silence between us like a metronome. She knows my family history. Knows that my old man had expected me to become a doctor, not hook up with one—one of the male variety at that. Knows that the Reverend Warner had some very choice words to say about my life partner.

Keen blue eyes fix me hard. "You are a father, Michael. You understand what this breach between the two of you must be doing to him."

"Ellen, no. Seriously. He doesn't give a crap, okay?"

"Has he phoned you in the past year?"

"A few times." I shrug. "That's it."

"And you didn't tell him that Alex died?"

I lean back in my chair, expelling a tight breath. "What do you hear from Laurel lately? You told me she'd be here this weekend." I'm turning the tables intentionally, reminding her that both our families have their torn places.

Again, the faint, knowing smile. "She sends her love."

I'll just bet she does.

"Good. Tell her the same from me, okay?"

"Maybe you should call her too?" she suggests in a gentle tone, but that's one area where my emotions absolutely fear to tread. I can't deal with Laurel, not yet, and Ellen knows it. She rises to her feet, stepping slowly toward the large picture window at the back of the dining room. Her heeled shoes tap out a staccato rhythm on the polished hardwoods, marking time between us in even measurements.

Standing at the sun-filled window, she presses a thin hand against her temple, shielding her eyes against the late afternoon light. Andrea's been sitting out there on a giant chunk of rock overlooking the Pacific for more than an hour, her nose poked into a Nancy Drew mystery.

I follow Ellen's gaze, and say, "She loves books."

"Like both of her fathers." She laughs. "What perfect sense that makes."

"At least something in this crazy mess does, huh?"

Ellen turns toward me, absently knotting her long strand of pearls in her hand. "That Andrea would reflect so much of you both? Yes, it makes beautiful sense to me."

The idea of some part of Alex, living on here with me, well it's the only comfort I can take in his death.

"Laurel wants to see her, Michael." The warm eyes are still open, but I'm instantly terrified. Terrified of what happened last year, after Alex's death; that it could happen again. "And you. She misses you."

"No way. I can't."

"You must talk to her some time. She's been afraid to push you, after..." She hesitates, staring away from me. She's searching for a diplomatic phrase.

"After what she *did* to me?" I nearly shout. "That what you mean? Well, good, 'cause she should be afraid." The rage swells up and I just can't stop it. We're talking about Ellen's own child, after all, and no matter how much she loves me I can't help feeling cornered. My first priorities always lie with Andrea, so of course Ellen's are with Laurel. How can she possibly support me? "Ellen, I know she's your daughter, but she was wrong."

She steps close again, never taking her eyes off me. "Michael, I'm not choosing sides, dear," she explains gently. "Just like I never chose between Laurel and Alex."

"Yeah, well you wouldn't, 'cause they were your *children*." I'm on the outside here; I'm always on the outside when it comes to family, so why should this be any different?

"You are my son now. You can't possibly doubt that?"

"I can't forgive Laurel for what she did to me."

"Well, you may not, but at some point, you will have to let her into Andrea's life. At least in some way. Andrea needs her too."

"Why didn't she come today? She could've seen her, that's what we'd planned. I know it wasn't some art dealer that she had to meet with back in Santa Fe."

"She didn't want to push you, Michael. Not today. You may find it hard to believe, but she doesn't want to hurt you."

"Should've thought about that a year ago." My hand has closed around the tea glass in a death grip, and I don't realize how badly I'm shaking until the ice cubes begin to rattle.

Ellen lowers herself into the chair beside me and covers my hand again. "You don't need to be afraid of her. All she wants is a place in Andrea's life."

Anxiety knots its way through my stomach and I feel a wave of instant nausea. It's not just Laurel I fear, that she'll work her way into Andie's life. What worries me most is the thought of her waltzing right in and doing what I can't possibly accomplish—making a connection. And then, the unthinkable will happen: I'll lose this one amazing person who binds me permanently to Alex Richardson and the life we once shared.

Laurel's always waiting there, always has been, just off in the wings.

Ellen looks back at me. "Laurel doesn't want to hurt her,

Michael."

"No, but she doesn't give a damn if she hurts me."

And to that, there is nothing Ellen Richardson can possibly say.

✧

Sunday evening finds us back in L.A. again. The day began with early mass, which I politely declined, even though Ellen did her best to guilt me into attending.

"Michael, darling, God didn't kill Alex," she told me intensely.

"Never said He did," I grunted, and she didn't say another word. She's been hounding me about my unresolved God issues for years, and she never gives up. I've always been her pet spiritual project, and now that Allie's gone, I guess she's stepping up the pressure on behalf of her grandbaby.

So they headed off together, me reclining on the old wicker porch chair with the newspaper, Andrea slipping her small, delicate hand into Ellen's aged one as they began the walk downhill to Alex's childhood church, St. Anthony's. Watching them go, I couldn't fight a tug of remorse. Alex always made sure our daughter got to church—was rigorously faithful about it, as a matter of fact, and I'm certain that he'd want it for her now. Plus, the eagerness in Andrea's face told me everything: church binds her to her daddy in a permanent way. Which makes me wish all the painful history with my *own* father, an Episcopalian minister, wouldn't prevent me from giving her that simple gift each Sunday. But as much as I love her, and as much as I still love Alex, it's just one thing I can't seem to do for either of them.

After they returned, we sipped on iced tea and ate chicken salad sandwiches in the formal dining room, making small talk about plans for the summer. Andrea actually got a little animated about going to Casey's for July Fourth, a nice change from our conversation in the car—but then her face fell when I told her Marti would be bringing her kids. "You guys can swim all weekend," I promised, and she forced a dark smile. Inwardly I groaned, realizing I'd unleashed the demons again. With her, it's like walking a minefield, and I never seem to know when I'm going to misstep.

Maybe Rebecca can talk to her again, get her to open up more about the scar. I don't think it looks that terrible, but I'm not eight years old. And I don't bear a physical memento of Alex's death every day of my life. Not unless you count that butterfly tattoo on my shoulder. Ah, but that's a pure, perfect memory, a reminder of his vivid life. I'll never forget that sheer look of mischief that danced in his eyes the first time he tugged my T-shirt off and discovered the small monarch on my shoulder. I remember that he laughed, a soft rumbling sound, tracing it with his fingertip. Michael Warner, maybe a little softer than he'd always seemed on the outside.

I wonder what Rebecca would think about my tattoo. The thought pops into my head before I can even stop it, and I rub my shoulder like it's just been burned, imagining her mouth kissing it, the way Al always loved to do. Almost like the flutter of a delicate butterfly wing, there's the sensation of feminine lips pressed against my skin, Rebecca O'Neill making love to me, one seductive kiss at a time.

What the hell is wrong with me? Alex deserves better than this. More loyalty. I mean, it's only been a year. Then how come with as much as I miss him, something feels like it's starting to change inside of me? Something irreversible, unstoppable.

I've been down this road before, and I know what it's like to feel the sexual pendulum begin to swing. Which is why that unshakable image of Rebecca O'Neill kissing my back, tumble of blonde hair spilling over my shoulder, lithe body pressed naked against mine tells me one thing.

Baby, that damn pendulum has already swung.

Chapter Seven: Rebecca

And so it's Sunday evening. Which marks one full weekend—and the better part of a week—without a call from Michael Warner. Ever since the Chinese lunch that I've come to term The Debacle, I haven't heard a word from him. I should've told him my entire life story when he asked; I knew then that I'd probably offended him, and this whole non-calling scenario only proves that fact. Now I'll never hear from him again, I think, hoofing it up the steep, winding hill to the garage apartment where I live. My lungs are tight from the three-mile run I've just completed, but at least my body's more relaxed than it was beforehand.

Coming to a stop in front of my garage door, I bend down to stretch, sucking in rattling gasps of air. Despite my asthma, I still run five days a week, but it took a long time to feel comfortable on these secluded side streets of Beverly Hills. I figure that six p.m. on a Sunday evening is about as safe as I'll ever be, though I doubt I'll ever feel perfectly secure anywhere on planet Earth again.

Just yesterday in the grocery store I nearly had one of my panic attacks when I noticed a guy staring at me. He had stringy long hair and beady eyes, and generally creeped me out, so I hurried past him, feigning interest in a row of paperbacks until I sensed that he had moved along. Later, he approached me in the checkout line and told me he watched *About the House* in reruns every day and loved it. "I'm a *really* big *fan*, Rebecca," he told me in an oily voice, black eyes bulging wide. I just smiled and stared at the scorpion tattoo on his forearm.

Once upon a time, I dreamed about being recognized in public like that; thought it would be the benchmark of true success—although, admittedly, scorpion tattoos weren't factored into that plan. Now all I want is complete anonymity. The syndication payments from the show are nice, but I wouldn't mind giving them up—not if it meant watching the series slip below the pop-culture horizon and into permanent obscurity.

Even then, I wonder if it would ever really die, especially

considering the rabid Internet base that still supports it. There's fan fiction, multimedia outlets, and online sites that ask me for interviews every now and then, which I always politely decline. And of course all this ongoing devotion—combined with my self-imposed seclusion—only breeds more Rebecca O'Neill rumors. Theories that I'm actually dead, and the execs covered it up by settling some massive lawsuit with my family.

Precisely how this would benefit the studio, I've never been able to figure out. Sure, some intern in the production office tossed out the countless psycho Ben letters. We heard that in court. But I have no interest in establishing the studio's culpability in my attack—especially after having endured all those court appearances associated with Ben's lengthy trial.

Other rumors: that it was all just a publicity stunt, and I'm perfectly fine, living somewhere off the coast of France. That one sounds fairly appealing to me, but unfortunately someone's always spotting me around town. *Rebecca Sightings*, that's what they call them on the Internet message boards. Like last month when a woman apparently noticed me at my gym, then hightailed it back online to detail my entire workout routine. It's plain unsettling to read a description of my recent weightlifting session as told by someone watching me from across the floor of Gold's. *And then she did four sets of overhead chest flies. She was really working hard! The scars don't actually look as bad as we've been told by our sources...*

Trevor tells me to stop trolling for this stuff, but I can't seem to help myself. I've lived in this town long enough that I can't entirely dismiss the rumor mill, and I guess that extends to the fan community. It's not ego, although I do think it helps to have a healthy one if you want to make it in Hollywood. No, it's morbid curiosity; the insatiable need to know what they're saying about me now that I'm gone. *They.* The masses, the invisible people I can't see, but who are always out there, peering in through the one-way glass at me. Who knows, maybe I want to be sure I'm not slowly cultivating a new Ben McAllister somewhere out in Middle America.

Bending low, I finish a deep stretch of my hamstrings, then reach into my shorts pocket for the garage-door opener. It's the only way into my apartment, and I chose to live here after my recovery for that very reason. No more unsecured front entryway, where anyone might sneak up on me when I least expect it—and where I might just die.

Watching the slow, ruminative rise of the old door, I can practically feel the eyes of my landlady, Mona Malone, studying me from the main house. Mona never leaves her home, at least not very often. Ninety-two years old, she was one of the very late stars of the silent movies, and a legendary beauty at that. Now she spends her time regaling her bridge partners with tales of old Hollywood, and doing a really good imitation of Norma Desmond. I can only hope I'm as sharp and alive at her age, although hopefully not harboring quite so many regrets.

Mona also likes to advise me over her nightly martinis, which she sips poolside. "There are other plastic surgeons, Rebecca darling," she'll counsel. Or, "You should sell your story, if there's someone offering. They won't come around forever, you know."

And there have been offers, believe me. Just imagine. *A Lifetime Original: The Rebecca O'Neill Story.* I don't think so, thank you very much. That's all I'd need to activate the next Ben-wannabe, the one I'm always afraid will emerge from the bushes of my life. When I was a girl back in Georgia, fantasizing about fame, I never once imagined the dark side of the dream. Now I often wonder how many stalkers Gavin de Becker must have. Weird, but I'm sure it's true that the world's greatest stalking expert has his own militant troop of crazies.

I dart into my garage, quickly lowering the door again, watching to be sure no one follows me, and then I jog up the small flight of stairs to my apartment. The phone is ringing, and I can't help the hopeful flutter my heart gives at the sound—the wish that somehow, even now, it might be Michael. Of course he'd have called before the weekend, not waited until Sunday night. My head knows that; it's getting my heart to listen that's the problem. Clearly he misunderstood my hesitancy the other day, must have thought I wasn't interested, when really I was just scared to let him get too close.

As I turn the key in the lock, the ringing ceases, and I sprint to check the caller ID box.

Oh crap.

Not Michael, no. Dang it all if it isn't Jake Slater—even after such a long time, I still know *that* cell phone number by heart.

I lift the receiver, already checking to see if a voice mail has registered, and then the phone rings again, beeping through my call waiting. That's so Jake. Ever the actor, he can never get his voice mail right in a single take.

Clicking over, I answer. I'm already working to project my displeasure with him that he's phoning me after all this time. What is it now, more than a year since we last spoke? Almost three years since he dumped me?

"Uh, Rebecca?" comes the deep, rumbling voice, understandably confused by my cranky tone. Not Jake.

"Yes?" Panicked, I glance down at the caller ID box, which might have been a smart thing to do in the first place. *Alexander Richardson.* Interesting—he hasn't changed the billing name yet.

"It's Michael. Michael Warner?" His throaty voice turns up at the end, a question mark, as if he thinks I might have forgotten him already.

"Sorry. Thought you were someone else."

"You must not like him very much." I hear the smile in his voice; sense him easing into our usual warm repartee, but this time I'm determined to resist his charms. After all, couldn't he have called before now? It's been almost a week, enough time that I'd practically written him off. I don't want to be the B-roll of anyone's love life, not even Beautiful Bisexual Boy.

"So what's going on?" I answer, cool. Making sure he knows I plan to keep this phone call right on track.

Instead, I'm surprised to hear his thoughtful exhalation of breath, and then, "I'm not sure, Rebecca. Wish I were." His voice is quiet, notably heavy, and all my anger evaporates in the face of his honesty.

"Tell me what you mean," I encourage, moving toward the sink to fill my water bottle.

"Oh." He gives an agreeable laugh. "Just been a tough weekend, that's all."

"Well *that* tells me next to nothing." There's silence, and I think I hear birds and a lawnmower in the background on his end. "You're outside."

"Yeah, on the deck. Watching the sun disappear into the hills."

"Okay, but please just tell me you're not going to become That Guy."

"Which guy?"

"The one who calls me whenever he gets a little moody and sad," I tease, hoping to make him laugh.

"Nah, I'm more like the guy who doesn't call for a week."

"Oh, so you're admitting that, Mr. Warner?"

"Yeah, and you were pissed," he says, as I chug deep gulps of water. "Weren't you?"

I wipe my mouth with the back of my hand. "Did you want me to be?"

"Maybe. 'Cause if you were, then I could stop thinking about you so damn much," he answers with a soft chuckle. "But like most of my plans, guess it didn't quite work out that way."

"You know, something tells me you're a very easy man to forgive." And I mean it. He's such a gentle, warm guy that I'm finding it impossible to stay angry.

"I have been thinking about you, Rebecca," he answers. "A lot more than I probably should have been. But it's just hard. Figuring things out right now."

I'm sure it is hard trying to cope without the love of his life, to understand what that means for his family. No wonder this strange dance between the two of us is so baffling to him; it's baffling enough to me.

I want to tell him that he's all I've thought about for the past week. That he's invaded my day thoughts, my night thoughts, my dream thoughts. Instead, I practically whisper into the receiver, "You know, you could tell me why it's been such a hard weekend. Considering that I'd like to forgive you."

"Would you consider coming over?"

"Now?"

"I could give you the long-form explanation that way," he says. "Versus the short form that might only get me a tiny pardon."

"Who's cooking?" I'm already mentally clicking off ingredients for a pasta dish. *Ground turkey, tortellini, cilantro...*

"Domino's," he answers decisively. "So we can be together, not dividing our time with the kitchen."

Why do I get the feeling that Michael Warner is a man rarely prone to backing down from things once he's made up his mind about them? And more importantly, why do I sense that in some crucial way, he might be beginning to make up his mind about me?

Too bad I remembered that dang voice mail from Jake, because otherwise my mood would be dreamy perfect after my phone call from Michael. Unfortunately, I do remember, and listening to Jake's smooth Hollywood voice sours my improved humor just a little.

"Uh, Rebecca, hey. Jake. How are you?" I towel off my face, still dripping with sweat from the run. "It's been too long, you know. I've been thinking about you... bumped into Cat down at The Derby the other night. She says you're doing great." He pauses, and there's the muffled sound of him covering the receiver to talk to someone else. "Yeah, so listen, it's been too long, and we need to do something about that, so call me back. You know the number." Click. Not goodbye or see you later, Rebecca, or anything. Just a dial tone.

Oh, so very, very Jake.

Standing there in the kitchen afterwards, I'm not sure what to feel. My heart rate is wild, and too many old emotions have risen to the surface in the space of a moment, but even worse? Some small part of my heart hopes Jake finally misses me.

And some even smaller part of me also wants to believe that he finally regrets breaking my heart like he did, dumping me flat on my ass two weeks after I left the hospital, my face and career ruined. My body torn and broken, in need of countless months of physical therapy and operations that would never fully do the trick. Now, even three years later, I'm still stunned that he chose that exact moment to drop me because dating me was no longer advantageous to his career. Especially for that booby blonde who was just waiting to slide into *my* leading role on *my* hit prime-time television show. And into my boyfriend's cozy bed.

Huh. Moments like this, and I realize I'm really a Georgia girl—not a savvy jaded California one. Otherwise, there's no accounting for the naive optimism that a single call from Jake Slater can elicit.

Because despite everything I logically know, I can't help it: I still wonder why he's calling, especially after all this time.

✧

Pulling into Michael's driveway, I'm struck again by the beauty of his bungalow. I love the old 1930s style architecture of these houses in Studio City. There's something wonderfully charming about them, something reminiscent of Hansel and Gretel's cottage, or *The Three Little Bears*. Then again, maybe I really did spend too much time in those fairy tales as a child; you can blame my mother the librarian for that.

I approach the house, studying the climbing vines along the steps, when suddenly I notice little Andrea sitting on the stoop, shoulders hunched, just watching me. I give her a warm wave, and she lifts her small hand tentatively in greeting as I walk up the driveway.

"Hey!" I call to her brightly, and she rises to her feet.

"Careful," she admonishes, and I'm not sure what she means until she points down at the walkway beneath my thong sandals, and I come to a dead stop immediately. There's a vibrant design scrawled across the stone steps in pastel chalk. "Wow!" I say, staring at the ground in amazement. "Did you make that?"

She shoves her hands into the pockets of her sundress, shyly nodding her head. "It's a picture of my grandma's house." I cock my head sideways, trying to piece it all together, because the image is divided across a series of steppingstones, strung together like a haphazard jewel necklace.

"Show me what each part is."

With her pale hand, she gestures to one flagstone. "This is her big front porch," she explains softly. "With the rocking chairs and hanging flower baskets. That's her cat, Doldrums." She looks up at me, her blue eyes bright and dancing. "My daddy named him that when he found him."

That tells me so much about Alex's sense of humor that I have to smile myself as I settle on the bottom step and listen as Andrea describes the whole house to me, every detail from the mansard roof to the wedding-cake latticework. It's unbelievable to me that an eight-year-old could be quite so capable with a simple set of sidewalk chalk, and I tell her so.

She stares at the stones, twirling a shiny lock of red hair around her finger. "Well, we were just there, and all. In Santa Cruz, where my grandma lives."

"Santa Cruz?" Michael's "disappearance" over the past week is becoming much more clear to me.

Andrea turns away, reaching for a gray piece of chalk. I'm not sure I hear her right, as she bends over her picture and whispers, "My daddy died yesterday."

My body stiffens and I want to say something. Anything at all, but I'm frozen, afraid of sending her scurrying away. This must be how Michael feels around her all the time. But I get brave. "So you went to your grandma's house," I venture cautiously, and she bobs her head.

"And we went to Daddy's grave yesterday."

"How did that feel?"

She stands, brushing off her hands, and gesturing toward her picture. "Look, all done."

"I'm absolutely impressed. It's beautiful."

"You should see my Aunt Laurel's paintings." She mops her brow as she studies her own handiwork. "They're great. We used to have some, but Michael took them all down after Daddy died." My curiosity piques at that statement, but I'm smart enough not to ask.

I'm also smart enough to realize that she's never going to answer my question about visiting Alex's grave, so instead I suggest, "Let's go find Michael and tell him I'm here, okay?"

She shrugs as if it doesn't matter to her, and slips right past the step where I'm sitting. For a few moments a bridge had formed, but it's retracted just as quickly, which gives me a brief glimpse of one reason Michael stays in so much pain.

Venturing into their home, there's no sign of anyone; only the chilly sensation of air conditioning and late-day shadows. Andrea must have vanished into her bedroom, so I call out, "Michael?" but there's no answer. Wandering through the living room, I spy him sitting on the back deck, staring thoughtfully up into the mountains. *Rough weekend.* Talk about an understatement, I think, seeing exhaustion in his dark features. Then, feeling guilty for staring at him when he's unaware, I urge the sliding glass door open. He glances up with a start, and flashes a dimpled smile as he stands to greet me.

"Didn't expect you so soon," he announces a little too cheerily, and I know that his good humor is forced on my account.

"Oh." I wrap arms around myself. "Is that bad? Sorry."

"No, no, not bad," he rushes, taking a step toward me. "Just lost track of time, I guess."

One glance at his wardrobe and I can see that he showered and dressed for my arrival. He's wearing a short-sleeved polo shirt and nicely pressed khakis this time—the first occasion I've seen him out of blue jeans, and he's absurdly handsome, with his dark looks and boyish smile. His hair's still wet, too, curling slightly where he's combed it along his nape. It's obvious that if he'd let it grow, the curls would get out of hand, and I itch to lift my fingers and stroke the damp hair. To lean up onto my tiptoes and kiss him hello, right on his sandpapery cheek.

"I love your outfit," he remarks, glancing at my sundress and denim jacket getup, one I lingered over nearly forever before walking out the door tonight. "Very Reese Witherspoon, gotta say."

I wave him off dismissively, feeling embarrassed that he's putting the focus on me. "Oh, it is so not." But I'm still smiling inside and out, and he sees it.

He takes another step even closer. "Most people would consider that a compliment, Ms. O'Neill," he says, voice whiskey-deep. "She's blonde, she's hot. You do the math."

Swallowing hard, I shove my hands into my jacket pockets, staring at my sandals. I'm about to joke that I might prefer a Naomi Watts comparison when the side gate to the deck opens unexpectedly, startling me until I realize it's the Domino's guy. "Hey, Jose," Michael greets him warmly, reaching in his back pocket for his wallet. No surprise that my single guy is on a first-name basis with the pizza man.

"Mr. Warner, how you doing?" The deliveryman places the insulated bag on the glass-topped table. "I got two large supremes for you." Larges? He must be planning on leftovers.

Michael turns to me. "I went ahead and ordered. Hope that's okay?"

That's when I notice that familiar, bug-eyed look on Jose's face, who begins stammering, "You're... you're... you're... you're." He's hung, like an old vinyl record skipping on a piece of dusty lint. So I do what I always do in these situations, and smile graciously. "Yes. Yes, I am."

"Wow, man, I thought so!"

Michael watches this entire interchange, a mixed expression of wonder and mild embarrassment on his face as he hustles Jose back out the gate. Once he's gone, Michael begins to laugh, shaking his head. "You get that a lot?"

"Not nearly so much as when my show was on, but yes."

"Andrea says it's in reruns on TNT."

"Oh, God. Please, *please*, do not watch it," I blurt, feeling this bizarre burst of embarrassment at the idea of Michael and Andrea cozying up on their sofa together, watching me frozen in the time warp of syndication. It's a strangely mortifying thought, as if I've just been discovered trying on my mother's bra, or doing something that I shouldn't be. In the rush of a moment I feel exposed, my current life and my former one having collided violently.

"Why not?" He's watching me, confused by my reaction.

"Because it's a stupid show, for one thing," I announce firmly. "And because..." Because why? Because then Michael will know what I *used* to look like, and realize what a disappointment this damaged version really is? My face flushes with instant shame at that thought. "Just don't, okay?" I reach for the pizza box, ready to help. But my hands are trembling slightly from the unexpected emotion of the conversation, and that's when it happens. The stupid muscle in my hand—the one severed by Ben's knife that took so long to heal—gives out on me, sending the pizza flying to the wooden deck floor.

"Dang it!" I cry, as my hand spasms painfully, and I drop to the ground to try and scoop up the pizza. Clutching at my palm, I rub my thumb across the center. "I'm so sorry! God, how stupid!"

"Hey, now. It's okay. No big deal." Michael squats down beside me, reaching for my hand in concern. "What happened?" he asks, trying to get a look at it, but I won't let him, and jerk it back protectively against my chest.

"Just my hand, don't worry about it."

"No, let me see," he presses, still reaching. "Is it all right?" No, it's not all right. It's shaking, and all tightened up on me, something that still happens every now and then. Just one more bit of my broken body that hasn't healed quite right, and probably never will. Ashamed doesn't come close to covering how I feel, cowering like this on the floor of Michael Warner's deck.

"Please," he urges, reaching gingerly for my hand again, and this time, I let him. I let him get a little bit closer than I have until now, as one by one he uncurls my coiled fingers. That's when the silvered scar is revealed, jagged through the center of my palm, like a terrible brand. There's nothing mystical or Harry Potteresque about it, I can assure you.

He massages the thick band of tissue, tracing and rubbing his thumb over the length of the thing, and neither of us says a word. Not until I whisper, "I tried to stop the knife." I extend my other palm in front of my face, demonstrating. "Like that. It severed the muscle and a few nerves in my hand."

He nods, then gently lifts my open palm to his lips and kisses my scar. Not one kiss, but a soft trail of them along the slash mark. Tears fill my eyes, unbidden—unexpected, just like his tender gesture. Because in kissing that scar, I understand that he wishes he could kiss away the pain—all the pain that I've had to live with, ever since that fortuitous day.

The tears blur everything. "I'm sorry I didn't... tell you more. The other day. It's just hard to talk about it, when someone's tried to kill you." Then, I have to laugh at how utterly fantastic that sounds out loud. *Someone tried to kill me.*

"You don't have to talk about it, Rebecca." He closes my smaller hand within his much larger one. "I want to know you, that's all. Like I said."

"I wish you could read my palm," I say, the laughter dying on my lips. "You'd know everything that way."

Staring down, he traces the scar with his fingertip. "It *is* kind of like a life line." I've never thought of it that way, but it certainly puts an ironic spin on my near-death experience. We're not so different, him and me, having gazed pointblank into the jaws of our enemy. That's what I'm thinking when I notice the shiny glint of his commitment ring.

"How was Santa Cruz?"

His whole body reacts as his gaze darts upward to meet mine. I regret the spark of pain in his eyes, but not the question. Now that I understand what this weekend meant to him, I definitely need to know.

Continuing to massage my palm, he asks slowly, "How come you want to know about that?"

"Andrea told me you went to Alex's grave." It's weird to speak of his dead partner by name, in such a personal way, but already I feel like I know him a little—as eerie as that seems.

"It was a year ago yesterday he died," he explains hoarsely.

"Andrea told me that too," I say. "About the anniversary."

"Reckon you'll forgive me now? For not calling and all?" He's trying to joke, but the smile fades on his lips before it even forms.

"Michael, you are so forgiven," I assure him with a sympathetic expression. "I know how hard this weekend must have been."

"Gotten used to going this alone, you know, but meeting you's already playing hell with that idea. Not that I don't understand being alone, 'cause I do," he asserts, moody eyes shimmering. "Just not how I got here so easily."

"Tell me, Michael," I encourage, touching his arm. "Tell me what you mean."

He blows out a heavy breath, looking up into the hills. "Well, Rebecca...one minute you're in traffic, minding your own damned business, just driving home and looking forward to the weekend." Hesitating, he gazes into my palm again, at the scar, tracing his thumb across it as he reflects, "Next, the phone rings and it's all over. It's over because some asshole stopped for drinks near your house, near your family, on an average Friday afternoon when you thought they were safe."

"Oh, Michael, I'm so sorry," I whisper, feeling his pain physically. "You've been through so much."

"Yeah, well that's the thing about life," he says with a sardonic laugh. "It's those average days that get you." He closes my fingers, one by one, until my scar is hidden again, adding, "*You* know about that."

And suddenly I'm thinking of my own average night three years back, when Ben followed me home from the set. I was hurrying up the walkway to my apartment, rushing so I could catch the end of *ER*— ironically enough. It was a taping day, and it had left me bone-weary, which was probably why I never knew what was happening until Ben's knife came down on me, even though I'd seen him loitering outside only the day before. I'd seen him and been frightened enough to consider calling the police, but then decided I was overreacting, and chose to ignore the way he lurked there on my street corner.

That thought drives me back into myself, hard. "Your pizza's ruined," I observe, wiggling my hand out of his. Frantically, I begin scooping the errant toppings back onto our decimated pie: anything rather than meeting his probing gaze. See, I'm more than willing to talk about *his* pain, so long as we don't turn the lens on me. For a moment, he seems taken aback, kind of just blinking at me in stunned silence.

"I'm really sorry about all this mess," I rush to say, and hope he'll know I mean far more than the pizza.

"Nah, we'll make it work." He gathers up wayward pepperoni and sausage and a random onion that's dangling from the box lid. "Five-second rule." He laughs, a little too cheerily, working to cover the sudden wall of awkwardness that's fallen between us.

But I don't quite get the joke, so he explains, "It's a parent thing. With little kids, most everything hits the floor. You just dust it off, and hand it back all over again. We always called it the five-second rule, though I guess this is more like thirty."

What a nice tenet that would be for the rest of life; if something ended badly or didn't work, we could simply declare, "Five-second rule!" and start all over again—well, if only all those "average days" weren't potentially out there lurking over the next hill, ready to change our destiny.

"Maybe we could say that about the past few minutes," I suggest hopefully, rising to my feet. "You know, five-second rule about all the awkward stuff since I got here."

"That'll work," he agrees, though I see wistfulness in his golden eyes. He smiles again, giving me an appreciative once-over, gallantly ignoring my stained dress, as he announces, "Great outfit! Very...Reese Witherspoon."

And this time, smiling so broadly that I feel the numb side of my mouth pull a bit, I answer, "Thanks for the compliment!"

"You know, Rebecca," he says, rising to his feet, "never thought there'd be anything good about this weekend. But you've managed to change that."

I turn to him, surprised, and he gives me a winning smile, one that's quirky and sexy and a little ironic without even meaning to be. When Michael Warner smiles, it reveals a world of intelligence, even when he's silent. His expression changes, becomes curious, and then I realize I'm standing there, pizza stain and all, gaping at him.

"Good," I say, brushing at my dress. "Now if we can just keep all those average days on our side, we'll be doing all right."

✧

Five seconds after sailing through my office door on Monday morning, I'm still feeling a happy buzz from my date with Michael. That is, if it was a date, and I'm not entirely sure on that point. It's the bisexuality thing rearing its ambiguous self again, which always leaves me wondering if maybe our whole deal isn't only friendship. And once I go there mentally, then a host of additional anxieties come popping out from nowhere, so I prefer to be in my happy place, at least temporarily.

We're going to the Dodgers game with his group of friends later this week. This seems like a fairly big deal, to introduce me to his circle—a crowd I know used to knot neatly around Alex and him—but I'll choose not to be intimidated by that fact.

"My friend Casey's got an extra ticket," he explained, standing with me out in the drive last night. "Would you want to come?" Some part of my algebraic mind easily deduced that this "extra ticket" in Casey's season package used to belong to Alex once upon a time, but I just smiled and said I'd love to tag along. Then there was an awkward moment when I sensed that he really wanted to kiss me goodnight, but neither of us could quite seem to make it happen. So we stood there, him scuffing his loafers on the concrete and me chattering too much about the Dodgers. Could we do a better imitation of being thirteen?

It's not even 9:00 a.m. yet, but down the hall I can already hear Ed storming at someone on the telephone. As head of development at our production company, Ed rarely talks quietly. He projects. He furies. He dominates. At least two hundred and seventy-five pounds, and a solid six feet two or more, he's one of the biggest teddy bears of a man I've ever met. His office is filled with so much cigarette smoke that it's more like an incense-filled temple, and my eyes never fail to water whenever I enter.

Grabbing the Julian Kingsley proposal from my desk, I head decisively toward Ed's office, where I wait outside the door for him to notice me. Glancing up from his phone call, he waves me in, saying to someone, "Well, don't call me again until you got it figured out, okay? I'm serious! Yeah, yeah, yeah," he grumbles at the person, and I wonder if it's some arch-nemesis from the corporate side until he says, "I love you too. Bye." His wife. Check.

"Whatcha got?" he asks, leaning so far back that I momentarily fear his swivel desk chair might topple unceremoniously into the award-filled bookcase behind him.

I give a Cheshire Cat smile. "Something that's going to make your Monday very, very happy."

He lifts an eyebrow, goatee turning up at the edges in a devilish grin. I can't help feeling a thrill as I hand him Julian's proposal, the option recommendation on top, knowing I'm about to score major points with my boss.

"You've gotta be fucking kidding me," he declares, fumbling for his pack of Marlboros without looking. "How in hell'd you pull this off?"

Briefly, I wish I could take all the credit, but this is my best friend's moment to shine. "Trevor, actually. He and Julian are old friends." Ed's black eyes lift upward. "Trevor was his assistant back in London. Kept all his correspondence, did research for his early novels."

"Bosom buddies, eh?" Ed assesses caustically, his own particular conclusion about the matter already reached. He flips the pages of the proposal quickly. "Who else has this thing?"

"No one. Our exclusive ends today."

"What's it gonna take?"

Chewing my lip, I contemplate the figures I've been mentally crunching since Saturday. "Near as I can tell, *Beautiful, But Me* closed at a ceiling of almost a million. Just ballpark."

Ed whistles loudly. "Damn, that's a lot of money." He drags on his cigarette for a contemplative moment, the Marlboro temple filling with a little more hazy smoke. "Ah, hell. Do it. I don't want this one to get away. Start low, work your way up. Who you dealing with? TMA?"

"His literary agent's in England, but yes, they're co-agenting the film side."

"Do it. Tell me when it's closed."

This stuns me; the other times I've optioned properties, Ed has been a control freak, obsessively watching over all my movements. "Are you sure?" I'm unclear about his motives, and feeling skittish about being offered this sudden freedom on such a big deal. He waves me off with his cigarette, leafing back through the proposal, this time ready to give it his true attention. "Yeah, yeah. You run with this one, babe. I trust you. Show me what you can do."

Okay. This absolutely reeks of a power moment. He just lent me his knee, and hoisted me up the corporate ladder by a few critical rungs. And Ed can do that; he's got enough muscle to make me if he so chooses. Raking a hand through his disheveled hair—it never ceases to amaze me that a slob like Ed can wield such a mighty saber—he glances up. "O'Neill, is there a problem?"

"No, not at all." I shake my head. "I'll get right on it."

Is it my imagination, I wonder, stumbling like a zombie out of his office, or has my whole life just taken a fairly surreal direction? As if everything that was on a disastrous, or at least mediocre, course for so long is now completely going my way.

Only problem is that the heroine of *every* movie always has a sunshiny, riding-high moment like this one—right before the end of Act One, when her entire world goes to hell in a hand basket.

Still, I think I'll keep walking on sunshine, thank you very much. I've had enough freaking trauma and rain to last all three acts.

Chapter Eight: Michael

"I don't know why we have to keep coming here," Andrea whines as we step into the small Burbank office where we meet our therapist once a month. The receptionist closes the door behind us with a hushed promise of the doctor's imminent arrival, leaving us in silence.

"How come we do?" My daughter stares up at me like she half-expects a reprieve, a look I pointedly ignore. We don't have a choice about being here today, and it's not like I'm wild about it either. But I do want a breakthrough with her, which means I'm willing to put up with almost anything to get to that.

"So why, Michael?" Her breathy voice grows more impatient. "Why do we have to come?"

"Because it's good for us," I explain wearily, searching for a way to rationalize dragging her here despite how useless it often seems. "Kind of like spinach. Not all that tasty, but it makes us stronger."

The corners of her mouth turn downward into a scowl, forming what Alex always termed her "disagreeable face".

"Spinach is yucky," she announces, obviously missing my point as she flops on the sofa. "Totally yucky."

I close my eyes, rubbing the bridge of my nose to subdue my tension headache. "Like exercise, then."

Maintenance, that's what Dr. Weinberger calls it. I just call it a joke: no matter how often we come, we never seem to make much progress. Honestly? I think maybe he gave up on us after the first six months. He tells me to be patient, but I never have been much good at that game.

Dropping onto the sofa beside her, I grab *Variety* off the coffee table, and slap it nervously against my knee. Andrea opens a copy of *Highlights*, flipping right to the picture puzzle. She traces her fingertip diligently over the page, searching out clandestine candlesticks and slices of bread. Too bad she can't locate our good doctor. No sign of him yet, which means we're left to our own anxious devices; perhaps time alone together in purgatory is part of Weinberger's grand plan.

"I don't like it here," Andrea complains, not looking up from the magazine.

Trying to be the adult, I ask, "Why not?"

Through auburn lashes she pins me with an I-can't-believe-you're-such-a-dork gaze.

"Maybe he'll have more of those rings," I suggest, resorting to blatant bribery. "You know, those sparkly ones you like so much."

She sighs, rolling her eyes intolerantly. "Michael, those are baby rings."

"You didn't think so last fall." When we first started coming here, she collected them weekly, tucking them into her jewelry box like captured treasure.

"I'm a lot older now, Michael."

"Well, then maybe I'll buy you an ice cream after."

"We're going to the Dodgers game after. *Remember?*"

"Of course I remember," I snap irritably, even though for a moment I did forget that I have something approximating a date later tonight. "I'll buy you an ice cream there, okay? At Dodger Stadium."

She smiles, the brilliant sun unexpectedly brightening the dark sea of our moment together. "Hey! Maybe Rebecca will take me to get it!"

And there it is again, when I least expect it. Rebecca O'Neill, the Rosetta Stone to my daughter's troubled hieroglyphs.

✧

"School's out in a few weeks, right?" Dr. Weinberger asks.

He looks to Andrea, but she just stares into her lap, toying with the zipper of her Barbie backpack, making it clear that I'd better answer. "Yes, that's correct. End of the month."

"Any great plans this summer, Andrea?" Weinberger rubs his fingers over his salt-and-pepper goatee.

Andrea answers with more lap staring, then gives an indifferent shrug.

I answer for her again. "Thinking of a road trip." I cut my eyes sideways to gauge my daughter's reaction. "Back East. Maybe."

"Excellent," Weinberger says, nodding. "To see your father?"

"He's ministering at a church in Texas," I say, avoiding eye contact. "Thought I might take Andrea to see him. So he can meet her."

"And what does your father say about this plan?" he asks.

"Haven't laid it on ole George just yet." Weinberger smiles in understanding because he knows that my father and I are permanently on the outs.

Andrea surprises me by speaking up. "He won't like me 'cause he didn't like Daddy."

"He'll love you."

"But he never liked Daddy," she argues. "And everybody liked Daddy."

"Andie, sweetheart, that's a different story, okay? A whole other situation. He just didn't understand Daddy."

"Why not?"

My stomach clenches, my whole body flexing with coiled fury. *Because he's a cold-hearted, judgmental bastard who wouldn't know goodness if it jumped up and bit him on the ass?* Fortunately, I manage to keep quiet and count silently to ten.

Still, I'm not sure how to answer her question; after all, Andrea knows little of my father, little of how his emotional distance mapped out my youth and defined it. Finally, I settle on this: "Some people in this world don't understand love, sweetie. Not like we do in our family, okay?"

"I think what your father is saying, Andrea," our counselor clarifies, "is that sometimes there are issues for gay couples."

"But Michael might not always be gay," she pipes up, helping. "He told me so. So maybe now his daddy will be okay with me." Her innocent hopefulness as she glances back and forth between us makes my heart twist inside me.

"I don't think it's quite that simple," I explain with a cough, ignoring the curious expression on my psychiatrist's face. "But I know he'll love *you*. I do know that."

"But how do you know?"

"Because I do." Because you're pure and precious and I won't let him hurt you, not like he did me.

"That's not a real answer," she counters with all the saucy muster of an eight-year-old.

"He'll be meeting his granddaughter," I explain gently. "And think of how much Grandma Richardson loves you."

She presses her stubby fingers into her eyes, closing them, and I wonder what I've said to bring out her avoidance maneuver. The Eyeball Gouge is something that we see here frequently at sessions; whenever she gets uncomfortable or upset she blocks us out this way.

"Andrea, is that hard for you?" Dr. Weinberger asks, tapping his pencil against his notepad. "Talking about your grandparents?"

She sucks in a quiet breath, dropping her hands so that she stares right at him. "Michael's father isn't really my grandfather. That's all."

"Families are defined in lots of ways, Andrea. You come from an unconventional one, but I'm reminded of something that Michael said during one of your very first sessions here. 'Family,' he told me, 'is wherever we find it.'"

The words are a battle cry, summoning some lost spirit in me, the urge to fight for my family. That's the only possible explanation for me blurting, "Why don't you call me Daddy anymore?"

The minute the words are out, I know I've pushed too hard. I'd know it even if our doctor weren't piercing me with his steely gaze; even if I didn't see the way my daughter's face flushes with angry blotches that always betray her emotions.

"Michael, Andrea may not be ready to answer that question yet."

"Can we be done now?" She snaps to her feet so fast that the pink backpack clatters to the floor noisily.

"Your session isn't over, Andrea," Weinberger admonishes as she drops to her knees, scooping up the spilled Barbie detritus. "There are twenty more minutes left today."

Over her shoulder, she tosses me an angry blue-eyed look, an accusatory gaze I've come to know well over the past year.

"I miss you, baby doll," I murmur, searching her face. "I miss being Daddy, that's all."

"But you're Michael," she says firmly. "That's who you have to be."

"*Have* to?" I ask, confused, and her pale eyes widen. I think she's said more than she intended. "I used to be Daddy."

With an eerie calm, she announces, "I can't call you that anymore, Michael." Then, without even pausing, she turns to Dr. Weinberger and announces, "We're going to the Dodgers game tonight."

She begins raking Barbie clothing into her bag, focusing all her attention on the task as though nothing has transpired. Clearly our moment has passed, and there will be no further connection. My throat goes tight as she chatters with forced cheeriness about going to the game, about the Dodgers lineup, and whether we have any hope of making the playoffs this season. Like me, she's a true-blue fan of the Boys of Summer. At least I've passed on one crucial trait. Still, that doesn't make my heart ache any less. In fact, it aches all the more for having come so painfully close to getting some answers out of her, only to fail yet again.

"And I get to have ice cream with Michael's new girlfriend," she adds conclusively, zipping up her backpack.

I'm betting she tossed that one in just to screw with me. Yeah, one look from our doctor, and I know I'll hear about *that* comment during my individual session at the end of the week.

"She's not my girlfriend," I grumble, wishing like hell that this headache would subside. "Rebecca's a friend."

"But you said you like her." She settles neatly on the sofa again, hands folded in her lap.

"Right now she's still just a friend."

My psychiatrist scribbles something on his notepad. Maybe his *gay* patient taking up with a woman might not be memorable enough otherwise, but somehow I doubt that. Judging by the expression on his face, I'm guessing he finds this turn of events pretty damn notable.

But I don't even care, because there's only one burning issue in my mind, something that's been eating at me for a year now—ever since Andie left the hospital.

It was just two days after the accident, and we were heading to Santa Cruz to bury Alex. As I wheeled her out to Marti's car, parked along the curb at patient checkout, she looked up at me and asked for a Coke. I remember noticing that her skin looked translucent, she was still so pale. A single blue vein on her temple stood out, and for a moment, standing there in the blinding late May sun, I thought it was a bruise, and lifted a finger to brush a coppery strand out of the way.

That's the first time she ever called me Michael.

"Can I please have a Coke, Michael?" she asked dully.

"Of course. I'll go back in and get you one," I promised numbly, leaning low to kiss her cheek, but she turned away from me, so that my lips grazed her braid instead. I knew that she'd turned away on purpose, and I could deal with that. But nothing had prepared me— nothing possibly could have—for my sudden demotion from Daddy to virtual stranger. To a man I'd never known in relation to my child: a man named Michael.

Standing helplessly beside the car door, a thin rivulet of sweat rolled down beneath my shirt collar, and although I itched to blot it away, I didn't. Instead, I thought of Katie Hathaway, a girl I loved in high school; the only girl I think I ever truly loved. When she dumped me after Basic Training, she left me standing in a Greyhound bus station in Columbia, South Carolina, my whole body nervous and damp beneath my crisp, impressive uniform that I'd thought she would like so much. Katie took a bus for seven hours just to tell me goodbye, then got on the very next one back to Virginia.

Andrea never spoke again that whole day, not all the way home from the hospital, not on the drive to Santa Cruz, where we were heading to bury Alex. She just stared out the window beside me, silent. I kept cursing myself for feeling so helpless—and swearing that she'd only made a slip, calling me by my first name that way. If I'd had any idea then that I would spend the next year aching to hear her call me Daddy again, I think it would have broken what little was left of my heart.

"Michael, any last questions?" our therapist asks, and I get the idea that this isn't the first time he's asked me that. Must've drifted so deep into my head that I missed it the first time.

Just one question, but I won't voice it out loud, not now. So I shake my head, and he rises from his desk, reminding me of my Friday appointment.

Yeah, I have a burning issue all right, Dr. Weinberger. I wish someone would tell me why it is, with Allie gone and the father count reduced by one, that I can't be Daddy to my little girl anymore.

Chapter Nine: Rebecca

My radio's blaring before I'm even off the lot: Elton John, the perfect party music for my Wednesday afternoon. The sunroof's cranked back, the smoggy late spring air making me feel younger than I have in forever as my hair blows loose and wild and free. *I* feel free. Speeding a little too fast through the studio gate, the security guard shakes his head at me, grinning disapprovingly at the blurring blonde banshee with "Bennie and the Jets" booming through her open windows.

Pulling onto Melrose, my cell phone vibrates against my hip. It's Cat Marino, my good girlfriend and former co-star on *About the House*. We played spunky fellow soccer moms for thirty minutes every Tuesday night on our predictable sitcom. You know the kind. Big problems, easy thirty-minute solutions, the antithesis of my own life.

"You're seeing someone." I open my mouth to protest, turning down my radio, but Cat cuts me off. "I know it. I know it, because I also know that Jake called you the other night, and if you haven't called *me* to dish about that, then there's only one answer." She draws a breath. "You're seeing someone. So no denials, because I know."

Laughing in disbelief, not only at what she "knows", but also at how much she assumes, I ask, "So are you and Jake in league now?"

"No freaking *way*," she exclaims loudly into the phone, forcing it away from my ear. "It's a protection racket, my friend. Me protecting you from Jake. I'm running interference."

"Okay, then tell me why's he calling?"

"Well." Again I hear her suck in a preparatory breath, and know she's about to unleash a stream of rapid-fire, Spanish-accented sentences. "Apparently Darcy dumped him? So now he's gone all nostalgic on us, thinking about the good old days and all that, when the only thing he's really nostalgic about is his pitiful career. Gone, gone, hasta la vista, baby!"

"Darcy dumped him?" I'll admit that this gives me a little thrill of triumph, imagining Jake on the receiving end of his own treatment.

"Well he did that pilot, you know? The one for NBC where he played that future cop?"

"Yeah." I remember how depressed I felt, reading about it in *Variety* last summer. "Slater Cops a Good One," the campy headline read.

"Darcy says he took it really harsh when the show didn't get picked up. That he's been drifting ever since. No good calls, no auditions, nada."

"Wow, I wonder what it's like to be me?"

"Forget Jake," she says, remembering herself and her mission. "I want to know who you're seeing."

"Well," I begin tentatively. "There is this one guy."

"Name? Name? I need a name."

"He's someone I met down at the lot."

"What show?" Cat asks.

"He's not on a show," I explain. "He's over in the electrical construction department. For the whole studio."

"Oh," she answers in a flat tone, not bothering to hide her disappointment that Michael's not part of the Hollywood glamour train. "But has he been on a show? Or worked on any good features?"

I name a big sitcom that Michael told me he worked on for a few years as a lighting tech, and also tick off several A-list directors he's worked under as a gaffer, though that was all before fatherhood took him off the prime-time circuit.

"Okay, cool, cool." Cat sounds relieved that Michael's film pedigree is respectable enough. She wants me with a decent guy, like any best friend, but deep down she still wants me with someone from our artificial universe. That she doesn't notice any inconsistency in that tells you plenty about my dear friend.

"I'm seeing him tonight, actually." I lower my voice for no particular reason. "We're going to the Dodgers game."

"Uh-huh. So he's one of *those* guys."

"Which guys?"

"The macho, gotta take you to a sports arena kind of guys."

I laugh. If only she knew what kind of guy Michael *really* is, she'd let loose a spattering of Spanish expletives guaranteed to permanently damage my hearing. Or even more likely, she'd tell me she finds it a freaking turn-on when a guy swings both ways, then gossip about five other people she's heard might be bisexual too. Obviously, Cat can be a loose cannon sometimes, and I don't want anything getting back to Jake, so I keep the rest of Michael's story to myself for now.

"So how'd you know Jake phoned me?" I ask, wondering where their paths crossed again after the recent run-in at The Derby.

"Well, that's the other thing I'm calling about," she answers, serious, and my heart palpitates in anticipation of whatever's coming next. "And I'll say straight up I don't like it. But you should know."

"Okay."

"He e-mailed me last night. Wanted to know why you haven't been returning his calls."

"*Call*," I clarify. "He called once." Everything expands at a geometric rate in Jake's universe.

"He wants to see you, but, Rebecca, don't do it. Stay away from him, okay? He thinks I'll rep him in the deal or something, but you know he's always been crazy. That's the only way he can't realize what a total loser he is."

"Come on, Cat. He's not that bad," I say, feeling surprisingly defensive on the snake's behalf. "I wasn't totally stupid to be with him."

"Stupid is as stupid does, but I love you anyway." Yep, Cat knows him like a bad brother, after all the seasons they worked together on *About the House*—including two final ones after I was gone, which makes her a good reality check whenever I start revising our personal history.

"You'd like Michael," I announce, picturing the way his rangy frame contrasts boldly with Jake's smallish, sinewy one. Thinking of how honorable and gentle he is, and that I'm already sure he'd protect me at all costs—not destroy me if given the chance. "He's the anti-Jake."

"That would make him like the anti-asshole."

"He is that."

"Well, sister, you can't go wrong with a good guy," she assesses knowledgably, then adds, "Just don't call Jake."

"Geez, give me some credit, okay? I do have a few ounces of self-respect left."

"Those aren't the few ounces I'm worried about when it comes to Jake," she snickers.

"My point exactly."

✧

After doing some research—in other words, asking Trevor—I located some good old-fashioned fried chicken at a place on Ventura, and I'll admit that I'm using soul food like any well-bred southern woman. As a form of flirtation. Call it pure instinct, but I'm betting Michael Warner will respond to a down-home piece of chicken like a grubby-handed child at a church picnic. Then again, maybe I'm putting too much store by that soft twang that periodically colors his dialect. But hey, if the fried chicken fails me, there's always the foil-wrapped package of buttermilk biscuits. They've transformed the interior of my Honda into the front parlor of my nana's house back in Dorian, Georgia. "Sugar," Nana always said with a sly smile, "a good supper is the key to all life's masculine mysteries."

I keep thinking that maybe Michael had a southern Nana, one who loved to cook for him like mine did, and these biscuits and chicken might take him back to that.

Driving up into their cul-de-sac, my stomach knots with nervousness. Like I'm sixteen or something, not a thirty-three-year-old woman who lost her virginity a decade and a half ago. What can I say? My dating muscles are seriously underutilized and flabby after a three-year hiatus. Somebody ought to get me a Pilates dating video, stat.

I wish I weren't the last one here; unfortunately the sight of Michael's circle of friends in the driveway tells me otherwise. He gives an easygoing grin, but my immediate thought is that he seems distant, aloof, standing there with his hands thrust deep in his jeans pockets. His coolness might have something to do with the scowl plastered across his sandy-haired friend's face. That has to be Casey, with the backwards-turned baseball cap and effortless California tan, since Marti's got her arm around a lanky man with black hair, and they're snuggling like a married couple, not mere friends.

Marti waves at me exuberantly as I shift the car into park. *Too* exuberantly, like she knows I'm about to swim in with the sharks. Her husband smiles at me, too, and Andrea bounces onto the balls of her feet, rushing my car door. Only Casey stands rooted to his few inches of driveway real estate, watching me circumspectly. And judging by the saturnine expression on his handsome face, I'd say it's a given that he's not exactly thrilled that Michael's gotten so chummy with a *woman*.

✧

At the bottom of the third inning, the Dodgers are down by two, and I'm about the same. At least I'm not completely striking out, since Andrea's next to me, a nice reminder that someone in this crowd is rooting for me, as the sun sets on the City of Angels.

Michael is on her other side, so we're too far apart to do much talking, but I can tell he's pleased to see her responding to me so strongly. The occasional smiles he transmits in my direction tell me so. And sometimes I catch him looking at me, even when Andrea's busy watching the game, and I wonder what he's thinking. It seems harder than usual to read his rich brown eyes tonight. I wonder why? Thank God he's sitting on my good side, so at least I don't have to feel self-conscious about *that*.

Andrea whispers in my ear frequently, a marked change from how quiet she normally seems to be. In fact, she's downright gregarious, commenting on the game, the players, a bizarre fat man with a painted belly several rows down from us. That guy's taking face-painting to whole new dimensions, I'm telling you. Andie keeps perching Barbie on the arm of my seat, allowing the doll to narrate her life for me. She's the one who tells me that Andrea's last day of school is on Friday. It's a parade of childlike intimacies, shared only with me. And most of the time Andrea grins and giggles shyly at just about anything I say.

If only everyone else were so easy to please. Marti's friendly enough, sitting on my other side, so that's good, but she's still kind of formal. Like maybe it's weird to her that I'm here with the rest of them. I'm not really sure. Of course paranoia's a definite possibility too.

Casey, though, maintains a churlish expression constantly, and at one point I saw him whisper something into Michael's ear that cast an angry shadow over my would-be boyfriend's face. Michael stared down at the field for a long time without talking to anyone, his jaw muscle visibly twitching. I don't think he's even looked in my direction ever since.

"He would've done this to anyone, you know." I turn to Marti, confused by her sudden remark. "Casey. He would've cold-shouldered anyone trying to step into Alex's shoes."

"Good to know," I reply. Wrapping up the remnants of my chicken and biscuit into a square of tinfoil, I remember the way he taunted me earlier. "Mike doesn't like fried chicken," he said with a harsh laugh when I retrieved the takeout package from my tote bag. "God, we all know that!"

Michael protested, explaining that he just didn't like *bad* fried chicken—as in Kentucky Fried, or heaven forbid, Popeye's—but it was too late for a save. I'd gotten Casey's none-too-subtle message: you don't belong here. My chicken gaffe merely exposed my imposterhood.

"Rebecca, I want to tell you a secret," Marti confesses, her voice hushed beside my ear. "Just listen, okay?"

I nod, watching Manny Ramirez slide into second. There's an explosion of tribal cheers and chants in every direction, but I stay still as a statue, wondering what she'll say.

She leans right up against me. "Casey Porter is the biggest teddy bear you'll ever meet. Bigger than Michael, even," she continues. "But you have to be patient. Stick with him long enough to get past his rough hide."

"I've always been a big believer in first impressions," I say, sipping from my water bottle.

"Well you've obviously made quite an impression on Casey, that's for sure."

"How do you mean?"

"He wouldn't be treating you this way unless he thought you were a serious threat." I remember the biting remarks he made in the car on the way over, the "jokes" about Michael's new "outlook" on dating. Little gibes about which team would he be cheering for tonight, what with the way he'd switched jerseys lately.

I shrug, looking sideways at both Michael and Casey, silent in their own form of détente. "I think it's because I'm a woman."

"Humph. He'd *like* you to believe that."

"That's not the problem?" Again, I glance across to where Michael glumly sits, ignoring the stony-faced Casey right beside him.

"Casey'll be loyal to Alex Richardson until his last breath," she explains patiently, leaning closer to be heard. There's a strange intimacy to being so quiet within the noisy stadium, sharing girlfriend secrets amidst the din. "So even if you were from the boys' club, he'd be acting up the same way. Hell, maybe worse, for that matter."

I nod, not sure what to say, but feeling a swell of appreciation for her analysis. "So how do you feel about Michael dating a woman?"

She laughs, loudly—a little too loudly—and it startles me, but then she leans so close against me that I feel a soft roll of flesh on her upper arm pressing against mine. She's not fat, just soft everywhere, and likes to touch constantly. "I think the better question was how did I feel when Michael first started dating *Alex.*"

My eyebrows arch upward until I actually feel my hairline lift. "Do tell," I say, hearing my soft southern accent kick in double-time. Marti reaches into her purse, retrieving a subtly disguised flask, and douses her Coke with a bit of liquid that smells like bourbon. She extends the silver container to me and I hold out my own Diet Coke for some enhancement.

"Has he told you that Alex was—" she hesitates, taking a large swallow of her drink,"—a departure? From his usual ways?"

"Yeah, he did, actually."

"Did you know Michael used to date me? That I'm the one who introduced him to Alex?"

"No way!" I exclaim like a shotgun, and she begins to laugh, shaking her head.

Now, I have to tell you that picturing my Michael Warner with this round, squat woman beside me is almost as hard as picturing him with a man. Harder, maybe, because I can't fathom a lick of chemistry between these two. Some women exude motherhood and comfort, and Marti's one of them, which in my mind doesn't exactly translate to romantic allure. Then again, looking into her luminous green eyes, wide-set within a heart-shaped face that's framed by carefree black curls, I can also see the natural beauty that would have attracted my guy. In fact, between Alex and Marti, and now disfigured me, I think I might be detecting a pattern here.

Michael Warner goes with his heart.

"It didn't last long," she says with an almost nostalgic smile. "We were much more friends than anything. We bickered constantly, like brother and sister, but we had a lot of fun too. I met Dave right after, and Michael..." she hesitates, glancing at Andrea, then stage-whispers in my ear, "...he figured out his Alex *thing* pretty much right away too."

"Was that bizarre?" I'm thinking about Trevor and our close bond of friendship. "Seeing your boyfriend hop from you to your best guy friend?"

"It might have been, but none of us knew for a long time. And when we finally did know, well, the bigger shock was how they'd hidden it from us in the first place."

"Really?" I can't imagine someone as confident and honest as Michael keeping his sexual orientation a secret from his friends. For some reason, this newfound knowledge fascinates me. "For how long?"

"Six months, can you believe it? Poor Alex, he was going crazy getting shoved back into the closet like that."

"So what happened?" I take a slow sip of bourbon-spiked Coke.

"Michael was so scared by the whole thing, so uncertain and weirded out, that apparently they almost broke up before he'd even let Alex tell us."

"But they did tell you."

"Not exactly. One Saturday morning Casey showed up at Alex's apartment, wanting to drag him off to breakfast. Michael was in the shower, and never heard him enter the apartment, and then, bam! He wandered right into the kitchen wearing only a towel and a sloppy grin on his face."

"Uh-oh."

"Oooh, Casey was pissed too," she titters in my ear, clucking her tongue. "Oh, my Lord! Warner was totally on his shit list for a long time. The Closeted One, that's what he called him every time we got together."

"Was Casey jealous, you think?"

"Protective. Possessive, maybe," she says, reflecting. "But not jealous. It was never desire with Alex; they were too much like brothers."

"How'd he handle his death?"

Her expression darkens, and she looks to the field, contemplative. "How have we *all* handled it?" she finally reflects. "We've tried like hell to be there for Michael and Andrea. Ignored our own pain, because we know it's nothing compared to..." She glances next to her at Dave, who is listening to his Walkman for the radio play-by-play. She slips a fleshy palm onto his forearm, squeezing.

"To what Michael and Andrea lost," I finish and she nods with a faint smile.

"My point, though," she says, "is that Casey put Michael through some serious hell over 'queering up' with Alex, as he called it back then. Now that you've come along, he's just as protective of Michael as he used to be of Alex."

"He's afraid I'll hurt him?"

She nods and is about to say more, but beside me, I become aware of a soft tapping on my forearm. Then a tugging on my T-shirt hem, so I turn sideways and find little Andrea staring at me. A Mona Lisa smile plays at her lips, and she asks, "Wanna go get some ice cream?"

"Now, sweetie?" I glance back to Marti, afraid of losing this confessional moment when there's so much more I want to learn. But a pair of bright blue eyes are actually crinkling with happy expectation, an auburn ponytail bobbing excitedly. Michael leans around her, extending a twenty-dollar bill and explaining, "I told her maybe just the two of you'd go?" There's apology in his expression, and I push his hand away. "My treat," I say, thinking of that first time we met in my office. There's a similar lost look in his soulful eyes now—all the more when Andrea ignores him as he tells her to have fun.

He and Casey stand so we can press past, and it's that melancholy thing in his gaze that makes me reach for his hand as I squeeze past him. For a brief moment there's the feel of fingertips brushing mine. There's electricity and nerves and a flare of desire.

Then there's just baseball and beer and a gay man glaring at me like I'm the über bitch as I worm past him into the aisle.

✧

"I'm not sure this is working, Michael." We're the last ones left in his driveway, since everyone else has pulled out and gone home. Andrea's scuttled inside to brush her teeth and put on her nightgown.

"*This?*" He blinks at me, dark eyebrows furrowing together.

"You know, the whole... whatever we're doing." I'm thinking of how little we've even talked all evening; how distant he's seemed at times. And I'm thinking of what a bust I was with Casey. I'm pretty sure I've never hit it off so poorly with anyone in my whole life.

"It's working for me," Michael protests, searching my face uncertainly, and I drop my head, feeling awkward and self-conscious. Feeling way too aware of the numb area to the left of my mouth, and how my lips tremble gracelessly into a smile.

"But what are we doing?" I ask after a moment, looking up into his eyes again. I always forget how tall he is until I'm standing close like this, and then I feel delicate as my nana's Wedgwood beside him.

"Well, I think we just had a date," he answers quietly; then, frowning, adds, "At least I think that's what it was. I told my boss I had a date. Hope that's okay?"

God, could he be anymore adorable? Could he?

"Sure. That's okay," I reply, my voice all quiet and filled with emotion. Relief washes over his face, his playful grin spreading wide.

"Scared me there for a minute, Rebecca." He reaches for my hand. "Thought maybe you were about to dump me right in my own driveway."

"I thought maybe we were only friends. You've seemed kind of strange tonight."

"Ah, strange. Yeah, guess maybe so." He stares up at the full, lazy moon that's perched right over the hillside, reflective. "Lately things with Andie have been...tough," he says, kicking at the asphalt. "Bad counseling session today. Good in theory, but it hurt."

"I'm so sorry, Michael."

"Did you really think we're only friends?" he asks again, back to his original question. I can tell it troubles him.

"I know it felt like a lot more, but I wasn't sure."

"Why not?"

"Because you're gay?" I blurt, then shake my head, wishing I could erase that statement. "No, no, because..." I try to pinpoint the insecurity that's plaguing me, and finally explain with a heavy sigh, "Because Casey didn't like me." His fingers thread through mine, solidifying our physical connection, as he steps closer. I continue, "And he's one of your very closest friends. He really, really didn't seem to like me, and I think he wants you with a guy, not a girl."

"Think I give a damn what Casey Porter wants?"

"That's the thing." I shrug, shaking my head. "I don't know."

"Well, I don't. Hey, and do you really think I'm gay, by the way?" he asks, cupping my cheek within his other palm. My face turns upward toward him, and there's unabashed desire in his golden eyes. "That it's really that simple with me?"

I have to swallow hard, and murmur, "Not gay. Not...exactly."

"I have *always* liked women, Rebecca," he rumbles, closing the distance between us. "Alex couldn't change that. Never tried to, matter of fact. He liked the way I was."

"Me too," I practically purr into his palm. I'm aware of rough skin against my cheek, of long thick eyelashes lowering sexily to half-mast as he looks at me. I'm aware, too, that I'm not beautiful—I can't be to this gorgeous man, and yet I see lust glinting in his eyes as he leans low toward me. Desire shoots to every part of my body, alarming and arousing me, and completely silencing any doubt.

My eyes close, my lips part, and I'm ready.

And oh my GOD my *cell phone* is ringing? It actually thrums right between our two hips, like an angry little vibrator. Our eyes lock and I sigh. "My phone."

"I just thought you were happy to kiss me." He grins, and I stare at him blankly, not believing that my freaking phone is interrupting this divine moment. "You gonna get that thing?"

I nod, checking the incoming number. Now, I have to tell you, I am a big believer in signs and omens. Nobody has to convince me that God speaks to us in ways both subtle and obvious. The Big Guy loves a good symbol like any great writer, and I have always known that. But Jake calling me right now? Managing to interrupt my first kiss since he dumped me? That's not a sign, that's a billboard. That's a flashing neon message that something's wrong with my life.

"My ex." I cough, still staring at the telecommunications weapon holstered at my side.

"Does he always call you at eleven-thirty at night?" Michael's clearly feeling a little possessive and it shows.

"Considering I never gave him this number, the answer to that question would be no."

The phone rings again, calling out between us into the dark, sweltering night. "What about at home?"

"Michael!"

Getting sheepish, he asks, "Okay, want me to answer it?" He's sounding protective. A bit angry, too, as he waits for my answer.

"No, let's ignore him." Finally the ringing stops, but the moment is already shattered.

We both stare at the phone like it's an alien entity, a virulent thing that burst into our pure connection.

"I still want to kiss you," Michael says after a moment, "but I'm not going to do it now."

"Why not?"

"Because when I do, it's going to be sweet and perfect. Not second best."

I laugh bitterly. "Yeah, well, don't worry, I've already had second best."

He leans close, brushing a long wild strand of hair back from my cheek with his fingertip. His skin against mine; I could *so* get used to that sensation.

"You deserve perfect," he tells me, his fingers lingering against my cheek. Near the scars, but he doesn't even seem to notice; his eyes are locked with mine. "Rebecca, you are perfect. And this *is* working."

"This?" I rasp, burning beneath his touch, his intense gaze.

"We're dating, Rebecca. That's what this is. Right here, right now, I'm saying so. No more confusion about that, okay?"

I nod, and he adds, "'Cause I know it's got to be confusing as hell to date someone... like me. So I want to be clear about what we're doing, absolutely clear. This is dating."

"This is dating," I repeat dazedly and an absolutely adorable smile fills his face, his single dimple flashing from nowhere.

"Good! We're on the same page now," he says, still grinning at me. "So when you least expect it, expect that perfect kiss."

"I'll be ready."

"How's Saturday?" He opens my car door for me.

"For the kiss?"

"For our next date."

"Uh, it's my friend Cat's birthday party," I say. "You're welcome to come. I mean, I'd *like* you to come, if you want to, but it'd be like a group thing with all my friends. And you might not want to actually do that, now that I think about it—"

"Rebecca?"

"Yeah?"

"I'd love to."

Oh, my. *This* is dating. This is dating, and it is very, very cool.

Chapter Ten: Michael

I want to kick Casey's ass in a serious way. The taillights on Rebecca's car aren't even fully vanished down the end of my palm-lined street, and I've already got him on speed dial, standing right there in the middle of my driveway. We need to have this talk now, and not where my daughter can overhear it.

I don't even let him speak when he answers his cell phone. "You were a first-class prick tonight, Porter."

"So?"

"What happened to 'you need to get back out among the living, Mike'?" I shout, not caring whether my neighbors hear. "What happened to 'you should start dating again'?" I feel hot anger burn my face, even as the next-door neighbor's dog whelps like I just kicked him.

"A *guy*, you freak," he counters bitterly. "I was talking about you dating a guy. Not some girl. Some scarred girl, by the way."

"I should come beat your face in for that."

"I'm serious, man," he says. "What's wrong with you? You are gay, Mike. Queer as hell."

"No," I answer with a forced patience that I definitely don't feel. Voice lower, I add, "I'm bisexual."

He groans into the receiver. "Huh—let's page Alex on that one."

"*Alex* is the first person who would agree with me." I stop, closing my eyes to halt my churning rage, and notice the sound of a distant siren down on Ventura. "And don't try and tell me what my own damned partner would say," I continue. "Matter of fact, you ever try that again, and I *will* come beat your fucking face in."

"He was my best friend," Casey answers evenly. "And he'd be sick to see what you're doing."

"What I'm *doing*?" I cry, pacing the length of the flagstones that lead toward the street. "What I'm doing? God, I'm hanging up on you. That's what I'm doing! I can't even fucking talk to you right now."

"You're queer, Warner. All the way, and whatever this thing is you're up to with that girl, it won't work."

"Her name is Rebecca," I say with blistering quiet. "And don't ever try and use Alex's memory against me again."

"I'm just here to tell you the truth, man. You may not like it, but that's what I'm here for."

"I *like* her, Casey," I answer bitterly. "Really like her. Is that too much for your heterophobic brain?"

"I've got no problem with straight people," he says, his voice echoing innocently through the cell. "Some of my best friends are straight."

"Right, I forgot." I stare at the roses he planted by the mailbox for my birthday four years ago. "Your only problem is with me."

He's silent a moment, until I nearly think he's gone, then says, "You can't go back, Mike. Not after this long."

"It scares you," I hiss, realization dawning. "That's it. It scares you to see me with her."

"You may not believe it, but I'm trying to look out for you."

"Know what, Case? I think I'll fall in love with her just to really piss you off!"

And with that proclamation, I hang up on one of my last remaining true friends in this world.

✧

"So Casey's disapproval of this relationship upsets you?" Dr. Weinberger probes, scribbling something on his notepad.

Lying back on his sofa, I stare at the ceiling and think about why Casey's reaction pisses me off so much. Then I get it. "He should support me. Be my friend."

"Maybe he believes he's being your friend."

"He wants me to be a certain way," I clarify, staring at the soothing upholstered wallpaper—taupe and cream-colored, intentionally neutral. No loud artwork here, no edgy prints.

"You'll agree this is a drastic change, you dating a woman."

"From what? Being alone all the time?" I ask belligerently. "Damn straight it's drastic."

"Drastic from being with Alex," he clarifies. "From being in a long-term homosexual relationship."

I shrug, settling down again, closing my eyes. Another headache's brewing, and I can tell it's gonna be a bad one. "Wouldn't it have been drastic for me to date a guy too?"

"At this point? Not quite so much."

"Thanks a lot, Dr. Weinberger," I grumble, massaging my forehead. "At least Casey's not taking my money every month."

"Michael, please."

"I'm serious, I just want someone to let me do whatever the hell I want with my love life."

"All I'm saying is that it's been how long since you dated a woman?"

Blowing out a breath, I close my eyes again because I have to think hard and do the math. Marti was my last feminine kiss. That's more than a decade, a few presidents, and some major global conflicts since I last slept with a woman.

"Thirteen years."

"Maybe that's why Casey thinks you should have a few dates with men first. To find your way back out there."

"And you think so too." I fold my arms across my chest disagreeably.

"I'm not saying that," my doctor explains. "Our sessions here are for exploration."

"I want to *explore* why my daughter calls me by my first name."

"You can't push her, Michael. You know that," he urges, but all I can hear are Andie's words from the other day. *But you're Michael. That's who you have to be.*

"I want to know, for God's sake," I mutter, frustration reaching a fever pitch. "For almost a year you've told me to wait. Not to push. To be patient."

"She is making significant headway."

"She calls me Michael."

"You know what she's been through. How traumatized she's been."

"Why do you think she won't call me Daddy?" Sitting up, I plant both feet on the floor, despite the headache that swells behind my eyes. "Really?"

Dr. Weinberger smiles at me sympathetically. He rocks in his leather armchair, fingertips forming a thoughtful pyramid beneath the bridge of his nose. "I have some theories about that, but let's keep giving Andrea time."

"No," I demand, rising to my feet. "You tell me what you think right now."

"She's trying to sort through her grief, Michael," he says in a lowered voice, staring up at me. "To make sense out of so many emotions. Guilt. *Survivor* guilt. Abandonment. Loneliness. It makes it hard to connect with anyone, even the people she loves most."

"She's connected with Rebecca."

"That's good. Very good." He nods enthusiastically. "Why do you think that is?"

Andrea and I have something in common. That's how Rebecca put it that day in her office, in her delicate sidestepping of her own obvious ordeal.

"Andie feels like Rebecca understands," I explain, collapsing onto the sofa again wearily. "Knows something the rest of us don't."

"How's that?"

"Rebecca has some scars. She's been through stuff. Heavy stuff, and Andie feels like she relates, I guess."

"And you feel that way too," he observes, eyes narrowing astutely.

"Yeah, I kinda do, actually. Only Rebecca's stronger than me. I can see that."

"Don't be so sure," he says. "People handle their grief in all kinds of ways, Michael. Some are just better at coping on the outside."

I think of her hand, the jagged rough scar in the middle of it. And I think of how ashamed she is of not being perfect. "She's lost a lot," I say, "but she keeps moving forward."

"As do you, Michael." Maybe. Or maybe not until I met her.

"I have another date with her," I confess softly.

"How does that feel?"

I'm not completely sure how to describe what being with Rebecca does for me, how it's awakening me for the first time in a year. "You ever see any of Spike Lee's movies?" I ask after a moment, and he nods. "Well, there's this weird visual effect he uses. Almost kind of a Hitchcock thing, where the people seem to move forward, but the background recedes, and it's like they're not even walking. Ever notice that?"

"I think I know what you mean, yes."

"That's how I've felt for the past year," I explain, raking my fingers through my hair. "Like I'm moving among all these people, everywhere. My family. Work. My gay friends. Straight friends. Strangers." Pausing, I gaze up at my doctor for emphasis. "Like I kind of see everyone from the end of this really dark tunnel."

"I've heard grief described precisely that way before."

"But that's just it. The other night, at the game? The tunnel was gone. The weird Spike Lee effect, all gone."

"That's great, Michael. Very healthy."

"Are you sure?" The tunnel was my comfort zone, and like a suicidal man constantly staring down the barrel of his rifle for a year, I'm wary of its sudden absence.

"You know that it is."

"I'm jazzed about the date tomorrow night." I smile. "But I feel guilty too."

"You're the one who's still here, Michael. You can't feel guilty about that."

"I haven't stopped missing Alex." That much needs to be clear:

Rebecca and Alex exist on two different planets for me. Venus and Mars, I guess. Falling for her hasn't altered an ounce of how much I long for him.

"Michael, you will probably never stop missing him," he answers firmly. "If that's your goal, it's an unrealistic one." This is news to me. I thought Weinberger wanted me to move on, to let the pain go. He continues, "Your loss is a part of you. It's organic, in a way. Your goal is to learn to live with that."

"But it can't possibly keep hurting so damn much."

"I didn't say it would always hurt. Just that it would always be a part of you." Like Rebecca's scars, or my tattoo, I realize. Same as loving Alex will always be.

"Loss is a natural part of living," my doctor continues gently. "We have to make our peace with that fact."

I nod, and we fall silent for a while; I lie back on the sofa again, watching the bend and sway of the leggy palm trees outside his office window. Dry leaves, dead leaves, still hanging in there though. A lot of crap's muddling around inside of me, a lot I probably should tell my doctor. Like the fact that lately I have this weird sense that Alex is spying on me. That I've developed a mini-obsession with wearing his old clothes, and sometimes I even swear I can still smell his scent on them too.

Maybe I should tell the good doctor that I have a midnight tendency to wander into Al's surfboard room, a small dimly lit spot at the back of our house—little more than a closet really—and just run my fingers along the fiberglass, feeling the rails and fins and concave curves of all those smooth shapes he used to love so damned much. It helps me to go in there, when I can't sleep, like I'm in some kind of Richardson temple or something. Like a little piece of him is stowed away, too, along with the twelve boards he left behind.

Sometimes I fantasize about paddling out with him, feeling the swell of icy ocean beneath my body, the foam and spray in my face. I hear him whooping beside me with pure, unadulterated joy just to be back in the water again; we're together, exactly like we're meant to be.

I wonder, too, if I shouldn't tell Weinberger that I'm thinking of taking Allie's ring off before my date with Rebecca tomorrow night. Maybe that's something he should know—or not, because maybe that should remain between Alex and me for now. Like all the other secrets we've kept between us, to the very grave.

Chapter Eleven: Rebecca

After spending all week negotiating the Julian Kingsley deal—but still not getting it closed out—I'm pretty frazzled by the time Friday night rolls around. I sure hope my overprotective mom doesn't notice; not if I don't want another round of proving how okay I am during our dinner tonight. It's not that she means to hover, but lately all the concerned phone calls and searching glances are wearing thin. I guess worrying about me has become a way of life for both my parents.

They came from Georgia to take care of me after my attack, when I was vulnerable and broken, and that's not an image easily dismissed from anyone's mind, especially not a parent's. If I'd sat by my daughter's bed, listening to the hissing click and groan of the ventilator, brushing her hair every day, praying to God that she'd wake up... well, I don't think I'd have gotten over that memory either. No wonder they hired a permanent caretaker for their farm back in Dorian, and never went home again.

For some reason, imagining my soft-spoken mother by my bedside, counting each stroke aloud as she brushed my hair, makes me think of Michael. Of how he longs to reach Andrea, but can't quite make that bridge, and I feel an answering hollow twist of pain in my chest. His anxious love for her is a vivid reflection of my own parents' worry for me—of all parents throughout the ages, I guess. Sure, sometimes I get frustrated that Judy and Benton won't go back to Georgia, and I feel smothered and fussed over. But I will be grateful until my dying day that they helped me do this on *my* terms, my way here in Los Angeles, where I could recover with self-respect. Even though acting is a shadow dream for me now, at least I'm staring at the empty canvas of possibility here in L.A.—not withering away back in Dorian, wondering what might have been.

With as long as it took me to find a parking space, my mom's already seated on the patio of the French restaurant where we're meeting for dinner. Her tapered pianist's fingers tap a rhythm on her date book as she waits, and she's unaware of my stealthy approach.

The date book is not a promising sign. Translation: I'm about to be shanghaied into something. Somebody's godson who works at Universal and is oh-so-single and oh-so-adorable, that kind of thing; my mother is a firm believer that everyone on the planet should be knit together, all by the work of her gentle, effortless hands. She doesn't know about Michael—not yet, because I'm still trying to figure out how to explain him into my picture.

"Hey, Mom." I lean down to kiss her cheek, catching a whiff of Estee Lauder, her signature fragrance for as long as I can remember. Embracing me, she holds on a few seconds too long, unwilling to let go until I make the move to pull away.

"Hey, precious. You look so pretty!" She gestures at my Ann Taylor sundress enthusiastically. "Is that new?"

"I got it a while ago." I wave off the compliment, grabbing the drinks menu; I sometimes think if I showed up in a flour sack my mom would beam about it.

"You seem shaky."

"Mom, I am fine," I assure her, nodding my head vigorously for emphasis. "Totally great. It's been a very hectic work week, that's all." Anything so she won't worry after we part ways later tonight.

Her gray eyes narrow in appraisal. "I ran into Dr. Nunnally at Vons."

I offer an unrevealing, "Really?"

"He said you aren't going to group anymore."

"He's not supposed to tell you that!" Without meaning to, my fingers trace the outline of my facial scars.

"Oh, Rebecca." She leans forward, patting my other hand in loving reassurance. "Precious, he knows how worried I stay about you, that's all. Don't blame him."

"I'm his patient," I remind her, wriggling my hand free. "He's not supposed to tell my mother what I'm doing. Actually, Mom, he's not supposed to tell anyone."

"He thinks you should get a roommate. Did you know that? He thinks living alone isn't a good fit for someone like you." She sips thoughtfully from her Perrier. "I think that's how he put it. A good fit."

"Well, so I'll get married." I watch a daddy with his toddler daughter, chasing after her in the crowd, grasping at the hem of her flowing April Cornell dress. A lifetime of pursuit captured in a single image. If Keats came back, he'd be a screenwriter.

"Please don't be sarcastic, Rebecca," she says, frowning slightly. "I would like to have a real conversation about this for once."

"All right, how's this," I say, meeting her serious gaze. "And please don't take this the wrong way, okay? But you and Daddy are like these house guests that came to stay forever."

"We came to take care of you."

"And I needed that," I agree, feeling my right hand tremble around the stem of the glass. "*Three years ago*, Mama. But I'm ready for y'all to go on back home now." God, please don't let my fingers tighten up on me now. All I need is a repeat of the pizza fiasco from the other night.

"You're not the only reason we stayed, Rebecca," she reminds me quietly, staring out at the fountain. Booming classical accompaniment begins, and she leans close so I can hear her over the crescendo. "We love it here. You know that. That's the great thing about Daddy's retirement, we can live anywhere."

"Mama, I love you and Daddy. And I love you *so* much for having stayed out here for me," I say, feeling tears burn my eyes unexpectedly. "But I've got to make it on my own now. Because if I don't, then I don't think I'll ever really get past what Ben did to me."

My mother's upper lip blanches, turning white as she bites it, and for a sliver of a moment I see pain in her eyes. Sometimes, her guard drops. It drops and that's when I know that her endless duties as my Watcher aren't nearly as joyful as she makes them out to be.

"I worry about you, Rebecca. That if we weren't here, you wouldn't be okay."

"I'm thirty-three, Mom," I remind her, my voice growing thick. "I can make it here on my own. I was fine before everything." My chest is starting to constrict; breathing's getting harder. Dang it all to hell. I can't use my inhaler in front of her, because that would undermine all that I'm saying.

"Before the accident, precious," she clarifies, and this time I feel angry at the southern propensity to euphemize blasted everything. So I clarify right back at her.

"Before the *attack*," I say, trying to calm my heart rate. "Let's call it what it was, 'cause that was no accident, Mama."

"You're right. It was no accident that Ben McAllister crossed paths with you. That evil man," she mutters, her voice trailing off as she reaches for her planner, her own hands shaking. Really shaking as she stares down at the pages, flipping through them, back and forth without looking up at me. "I wanted to talk about Labor Day weekend." A lifelong maneuver of hers: changing subjects. But funny thing is, I do want to talk about this topic for once.

"Ben's not evil, Mama."

"Of course he's evil," she says, her pale eyes widening as they meet my own. "How can you even say that he's not?"

Reaching for the basket of bread, I deflect her question with, "What's happening Labor Day?"

"Answer me, Rebecca. How can you defend that man?"

I give a noncommittal shrug, staring at the table. "How can you blame him?"

"Because he almost killed you, precious," she says, squeezing my hand so tight that her wedding ring presses hard into my skin. "He planned it for months. Followed you for weeks. He set out to end your life. That is what I call evil."

"He thought I was his girlfriend," I counter in a hushed voice, looking around to be sure we're not overhead even though it would be impossible for anyone to eavesdrop with the music. "The poor guy thought I spoke to him from the freaking television set."

"That's nonsense." She shakes her head, adamant. There is no version of reality that will allow my mother to pardon Ben. "The courts knew that defense was ludicrous, that's why they put him away." She releases my hand, patting it reassuringly, and says, "Ben McAllister was responsible for his actions."

"Mama, if you think about it," I answer, sucking in a slightly wheezing breath, "if I hadn't come out here, Ben never would've hurt me."

Color floods her fair cheeks—Irish cheeks much like my own—as she stares at me in shocked disbelief. That's when I retrieve my rescue inhaler from my purse and use it right at the table, my chest rattling, the sound of husk-like leaves brushing together as I suck in the medicine.

"Rebecca Ann O'Neill, are you saying it was your fault?" She watches me use the inhaler without commentary.

Feeling the fist-like tightness lessen its grip around my lungs, I answer, "Mama, it's just that I made my choices. They were my choices, and I knew the risks going in. World's full of Ben McAllisters, and I knew that too."

My mother bows her head, flipping through her date book without speaking. This time she's really upset. She's so different from my father, a lawyer who loves a good battle of wills; Mom only wants to make peace, to build bridges. And she can't stand it when I won't cooperate with that plan.

"Mama, you're the one who always taught me to forgive. That's what the Bible says, and that's what I always try to do. You taught me that."

"But the one person you're not forgiving, sweetheart, is *you*. Don't you hear that in what you're saying?" she asks, voice gentle. "You seem so willing to forgive everyone but yourself."

Stunned, I can only stare back at her and blink. My mother's peeled back every pretense I've been using to shelter myself for the past three years. If it's not my fault, then I lose my last element of control, because the only aspect of the attack I can manage is my own part in it.

"Well, I guess it's easier to blame myself," I answer after a moment, "than deal with the fact I'll never act again."

Weariness fills her clear gray eyes. "Rebecca, I can't tell you how sad it makes me that you've given up on your dreams, precious. You've always been my beautiful dreamer."

"I still dream, Mama," I answer, thinking of Michael and our bookstore conversation. "But nothing turned out to be real."

"Sometimes our dreams come true in ways we don't expect." She drops her voice conspiratorially, leaning close across the table. "But that doesn't mean those dreams aren't real."

Was it real that I spent a month in intensive care with a breathing tube stuffed down my throat? That I almost never sleep through the night without at least one terrible dream? That feels pretty darn real to me. But the notion of a cruel God doesn't, and that's what I'm forever wrestling with.

"Why did God let Ben do that?" I ask, not looking up. "Why'd He let him come after me?"

"I can't answer that, Rebecca. I wish that I could. All I know is that somehow, someway, everything works for the best, even the painful, terrible things." She's quoting Scripture to me, but being subtle about it. That's another lifelong maneuver of hers: to cloak God's truth in plain speaking. I'm still not sure I believe those words, about all things working together for good, but I'd like to get there eventually.

"What's happening on Labor Day?" I ask, thinking that a subject change might be smart about now.

She blinks at me, and seems caught off-guard. With her pencil, she taps the open calendar page, Labor Day weekend already circled in bright red marker. "Daddy and I are going back home."

"To visit?" I'm not certain what she's really saying.

"No." She shakes her head, staring out into the crowd of strangers, all potentially dangerous threats for her only baby girl. "We're moving back to Georgia for good, precious. That's what I was going to tell you tonight."

"Good." I nod decisively, taking a sip of wine, even though I feel anything but brave on the inside. "I think that's good, Mama."

She searches my face, trying to read me. "If you want us here, Rebecca—"

I cut her off before the regrets can begin. "Mama, I'm the one who said I'm ready for you to go back. You're right to go. I've got to stand on my own now." I picture Michael Warner's warm brown eyes, the flecks of gold flirting with hazel. Then I think of those faded T-shirts he always wears, and imagine pressing my face into one, burying myself against his chest and crying as long as I need to. He'd let me too; he'd smell like earth, his hands would be large and safe. Even the bad dreams might stay away for a while.

Then I imagine my old-fashioned Methodist mother's reaction to his postmodern sexuality, and want to rush her right on out the door.

Chapter Twelve: Michael

Stepping out the front door of my house, I'm met by Casey's landscape crew, armed with leaf blowers and lawn mowers like it's an army work detail. Casey's scrambling onto the back of their trailer, and looks up when I close the door. For a moment, neither of us smiles or says a word, until he gives me a curt nod. He climbs down, bracing a giant planter against his chest, and I meet him by the driveway.

"What's that?" I gesture toward the bright spray of purple and gold in his arms.

"Brought this for your front steps," he says, not quite meeting my gaze.

"Didn't order that, you know," I remind him, even though I realize it's one of his famous peace offerings. He moves past me, depositing the flowerpot at the foot of the front steps.

"Yeah, I know that, man."

He kneels there, tugging off a few damaged leaves with expert precision, and I ask, "So what's it gonna cost me? 'Cause I don't really have anything extra in the budget right now."

"Look, Mike, you know it's not going to cost you a dime," he explains gruffly, positioning the planter. "These are just a gift."

I only grunt in reply. Casey's the master of the wordless apology, and that's what these flowers are really about, but I'm still pissed at him about the other night. An awkward silence falls over us as he stands, brushing loose dirt off his hands. He pushes his sunglasses up the bridge of his long nose, past the bump in the middle, a memento from when he broke it back in his high-school skateboarding days.

Despite years of sunblocking, Case is one of those guys whose skin has been leathered by exposure to the elements. Years of hiking and skiing and surfing and landscaping have left him permanently freckled and wrinkled beyond his forty years of age, and right now, he's scowling at me in a way that doesn't do justice to his golden-boy good looks.

"So where you headed?" he asks after an uncomfortable moment.

"Andie's over at a birthday thing," I explain, nodding toward the YMCA at the end of our street. "At the Y. Gotta go get her."

"Huh. I thought maybe you were going to see your *girlfriend.*" I don't miss the derision in his voice, his lip curling up over the word.

"That's later," I snap, pushing past him down the walkway. To hell with him and his opinions.

"Tonight?" he calls after me, and I nod my head, refusing to continue our discussion.

"Well, don't forget the key."

I stop in my tracks and slowly turn to face him. I'm not sure he means what I *think* he means, so I repeat, "The key."

"To my beach place, man," he nods. "There's nothing like the ocean for a little romance. Girls dig that stuff, you know."

And then he smiles. One of those great, unexpected Casey Porter grins, and despite him being such a jerk lately, I have to smile too. It's like the summer sun has unexpectedly pierced a mantle of gray. "Thanks," I say, forgiveness forming inside of me.

He just waves, still grinning at me. "No problem, Straight Guy."

✧

Despite Rebecca's clear directions, I have to circle her secluded block in Beverly Hills several times to pinpoint the Malone mansion. By the time I do finally locate it, on a hill off Wilshire, my Chevy truck feels more like a maintenance vehicle than a date mobile. But I'm after the prize, my date with Rebecca O'Neill, so I shuck the working-class attitude, and motor up the vine-secluded drive toward the main house. Right past the steep, ivied walls, topped by pivoting security cameras, and right past the pool house, acting like I sure as hell belong in this part of town.

Making a last inspection in my rearview mirror, I realize that I nicked myself shaving, and rummage through the glove compartment for a tissue. All I come up with is a discarded Starbucks napkin, and I blot the mark away, feeling a scratchy protrusion of beard beneath the rustling paper. Damn dull razor—and it's a fancy party tonight, too, so I've got to look good. That's why I did something I haven't in more than a year: I pulled out my own Armani suit, a gift from Allie a few years back. He always loved to see me dress full-tilt, and thanks to him, I do like putting on the dog every now and then.

There's a sweet smell in the air. Summertime's blooming already, and like the bumblebees buzzing around the flowerbed, I've got a strange fluttering feeling of my own this evening. But then, killing the engine, I stare down at my hands. Worker's hands: calloused hands, tanned and coarse—ridiculous in contrast to this elegant suit. And then there's my silver commitment band glinting against my skin, another absurd contrast. Just couldn't leave Alex's ring totally behind. Tried, but didn't have it in me yet—so I switched hands. The sign of a widower, wedding band on the right hand. Felt so damned disloyal, I wound up adding Al's Rolex to my wardrobe mix just to compensate for the suffocating guilt.

Walking up to the garage I realize there's no obvious entryway to Rebecca's apartment. No side door, no stairs, nothing. For a moment, I stand there and scratch my eyebrow, then a throaty voice calls out, "Young man, why don't you use the intercom?" It's Mona Malone dead ahead, sipping a martini poolside, wearing an embroidered kimono bathrobe. Under the umbrella, I glimpse her silvered hair, drawn into an elegant bun. When she gives an undeniably flirty wave, I sure am glad Rebecca warned me about her landlady's identity.

I step closer, shielding my eyes against the piercing late-day sun. "Ma'am?" I call out. "I don't see an intercom."

"The castle has a secret entry," she answers coquettishly, and I get the impression this might not be her first martini of the evening. Staring back at the garage, I still don't see an entry point, and she adds more soberly, "It's around the side, covered by a patch of ivy. The intercom."

"Thanks." I smile, giving a slight, respectful bow and a big southern grin. Not sure how else to pay proper respect to someone this old and famous.

Finally, after a little recon work, I do locate the intercom. Pressing the button, there's a ringing inside, then Rebecca's sultry voice. "Yes?" she calls, drawing out the word.

"Rapunzel, Rapunzel, let down your golden hair." I flirt for all I'm worth, leaning up against the side of the building.

"It's not that long. At least not yet." She laughs, a tinny sound through the speaker, and I smile just to hear her voice.

My heart beats triple time as I try in vain to think of something clever to say. Makes me think of the first time I ever took Alex on a real date, of how dopey and awkward I felt in the car on the way over to his place. My hands have the same clammy texture right now, and I can think of nothing—absolutely nothing—witty to say at all.

"Keep growing it," I finally suggest in a husky voice. "You'll get there."

"Or I could use the stairs," she suggests, and I look up to see the curtain shift overhead, then her blonde head brushing past the window. My golden girl, lost in her Beverly Hills turret.

✧

Wow. That's the one word, almost a kind of musical note, that sings right through my brain when that garage door lifts, revealing a skimpily clad Rebecca O'Neill. Little black dress. Magic words coined by some famous designer along the way. Halston or Gucci, or maybe Coco Chanel, not even sure who said them originally. Don't really care, either. All that matters in my world is the satin material ending about halfway up her shapely, sexy thighs. She's got on a miniskirt, with a black knit halter-top affair, and it shows me what kind of curves we're really dealing with here. I've underestimated, that's for damn sure.

God, she's gorgeous. I've never seen so much of her before, and as she swings one foot out onto the pavement, I get my first real look at how leggy even a small girl can be in a pair of strappy slides.

Ah, perfection.

I stammer something nonsensical at her, something that comes out like one giant unintelligible compliment, and she giggles, blushing a little as she brushes at her hair. Taking her hand, I hope to *God* my palm's not as sweaty as this nervousness makes me feel, and we walk down the driveway together. She stops when she sees my truck, eyeing it uncertainly, and it's the first time I've thought about the logistics of wedging a five-foot-tall enchantress up into the high cab of the damned thing. "Uh, problem," she alerts me, wiggling one high-heel clad foot by way of explanation.

"Yeah, reckon so." We stand there a moment, assessing the situation together like a pair of builders out on a job site.

"Let's take my Honda," Rebecca resolves, grinning up at me. She's got such a lovely smile; it's different than all the pasted-on Hollywood veneers I usually see. It's real and complex, hinting at something much deeper than what most of the women out here possess. That it's quirky because of her scars only makes it all the more fascinating to me.

"You sure?" I ask. "I could always hoist you onto my shoulder and stuff you in there Conan-style."

"Gee, and that sounds so appealing."

"Good, let's go for it." I grab her hand like I mean business. She squeals playfully, tugging herself free.

"No, no! Honda."

"I'll drive, though," I insist, the old testosterone kicking in. See Michael date. Maybe I am capable of a Conan moment after all.

"Okay," she agrees easily. "Sure. I'll give you the directions to Cat's house."

And just like that, we're on our way. All on our own, like certified grownups, out for a night of true romance.

✧

Cat's trendy house in the Hollywood Hills is crammed full of trendy people having trendy conversations in trendy clothes, and the twenty-something crowd reminds me that *thirty-nine* feels like

Methuselah in this town. Hadn't really analyzed the age gap between Rebecca and me until tonight, but as I watch her work the party, it's hitting me that I'm practically another generation. Well, "work" the party is probably an overstatement, with her semi-reserved manner, but she kisses a load of appropriate people outfitted with store-bought suntans and The Look. I, on the other hand, try like hell to fade into the set dressing, finally fleeing to the balcony for some air, after momentarily mistaking one of Cat's younger sisters for J-Lo.

Only a few people are out here on the deck, and I stare down at the lights of Hollywood, a golden-lit roadmap spread below me. There's the rushing white noise of our city, like a scalloped seashell pressed against my ear. Listening for an awe-inspired moment, I wonder if maybe I'm getting too old for this town. Too old for a girl like Rebecca, who refers to musty clothes as "vintage" when I just think they look out of date. Thing is, she's still firmly planted on the low slope of thirty, with friends even younger still; it's less than six months until life clicks another decade past on my odometer.

That thought has me tugging at my suffocating tie when her buddy Trevor steps onto the deck. He nods politely when he sees me, withdrawing a cigarette case from his jacket pocket. His double-breasted charcoal suit is crisp and handsome on him. The wire frames look sexy, too, and I've got to admit he's the kind of guy that maybe in some alter universe would have appealed to me. Yeah, it's true; I've always gone for those brainy types.

He sidles up to me, draping one arm over the railing in a nonchalant, debonair pose, and removing a cigarette from his case, asks, "What do you make of Cat?" Guess he's referring to the way she nearly wrapped herself around me, kissing me full on the mouth when we first met by the front door tonight.

"A real piece of work."

"Yes, well that's a politic answer, isn't it?" He flips open a Zippo, and I reach for it, lighting his cigarette for him. He tosses me a very curious gaze, which I pointedly ignore. Trevor knows my score—and *I* know how to treat a fellow queer boy. Hell, Alex raised me right.

Puffing on the cigarette, he takes a long drag, staring down into the bright lights below. "Rebecca looks lovely tonight," he says after a moment, pocketing the lighter again. "Don't you think?"

"Rebecca's always gorgeous," I agree heartily, and I see a real smile appear on her best friend's face.

"I hate to admit it, but I think you might be good for her," he says quietly, staring away from me. It's obviously a problem for him, me with her.

"Hate to admit that why?"

"Look, Michael," he says, turning to face me. "Rebecca's very dear to me, and I want to be sure that you're careful. Mindful of her feelings, and all that. I mean, you can't go jumping tracks midway here. This is Rebecca, and she's not up for the confusion of that."

I cough, choking on my beer. "Jumping tracks?"

"Switching from AC to DC, if you prefer." At least he's got the balls to smile as he says it.

"Strictly a monogamous kind of guy. I just choose my team going in." Trevor needs to know my playbook rules.

"I'm more of a lifetime player. I mean, I don't quite understand how you can be satisfied without..." He pauses, then shrugs by way of explaining precisely *what* he couldn't do without.

"Yeah, well that's your deal," I say point-blank. "It's different for me."

"As I say, I don't get it, but Rebecca's the only one who matters in that regard, and obviously she does understand."

"What do I understand?" Rebecca's quiet voice interrupts, and we both turn to find her stepping out onto the balcony, champagne in hand. She's flushed from the crowded party, her golden hair spilling in a tumble down her shoulders. My first thought is that she looks like she's been doing a hell of a lot more than mingling in that party. My second thought is that I'd play for any damned team she's part of.

Trevor leans in to give her a kiss. "You're smashingly beautiful tonight, sweetie." Deft topic change, got to hand it to the guy.

"Were you flirting with my date?" she counters, kissing him back, then looks at me, offering, "He can be a terrible flirt, so watch yourself."

Trevor narrows his eyes, assessing my apparent worth, then declares, albeit with a devilish expression, "I think he's safe." Not sure if I'm safe for her, or safe from him, but either way I understand the meaning.

Rebecca swats him on the arm, giving me an apologetic look, and he adds, "But if there's a *real* queer in there, as opposed to the quasi-straight kind, I plan to chat him up."

So that's my answer, the big one I've been searching for all year. With Alex gone, I'm nothing but a quasi-queer of the somewhat straight variety.

Marti's right—I'll bet Al *is* laughing his ass off right about now.

✧

Thank God I'm in permanent possession of a key to Casey's Malibu beach home, and that he reminded me of that fact. And thank God that even though my friend can be a definite jerk, he's also from big-time money, so that he owns said beach home. The doorway is shadowed and pitch-black, and I have to fumble with my keys for what feels forever, cars whirring past us on the coastal highway. Like most of the houses on this narrow strip of coastline, Casey's abuts the road with only a thin wedge of asphalt in front. The world out here keeps washing away, one infinitesimal grain of sand at a time.

"Just take me a minute," I assure Rebecca, glancing at her sideways. She's slipped off her high heels, and they're dangling from her fingertips. I can't help imagining stripping her out of a lot more than those shoes—every last morsel of fabric, as a matter of fact. Can't help dreaming about running my hands over every inch of her svelte, feminine body. God, it's been too long. Too long since I've made love that way and now that it's close, I'm practically coming unglued.

Surely she can see how my hand trembles as it turns the key in the lock. Whose great idea was it to drive out to the beach? We could have been back to her place in half the time, but I wanted to woo her in a serious way. Wanted to take her here for that first glorious kiss, to the beach, the quintessential romantic place any two lovers can be. No accident it's where Alex and I had our commitment ceremony. No accident we're standing here at Casey's dark doorway at nearly midnight on a Saturday night.

"Got it," I assure her, my voice deeper and rougher than I mean.

"Good," she says, leaning close so that I catch the scent of her perfume, and I wonder if she realizes how dangerous I feel tonight.

Get yourself under control, Warner. She's not a guy. This is going to take time. *Slow, slow down, boy. It's just a kiss tonight.* But my darker side whispers seductively, promising of a near future I've yet to possess, *But you'll have her soon enough.*

We enter the house, my dress shoes clicking on the smooth tile floor, and I flip on the recessed lighting over the fireplace, revealing a vivid painting of Laurel's. It's Santa Fe red and burnt orange, like the fire I feel smoldering inside me right now.

"Geez," she says, brushing past me. More perfume and feminine allure that makes me go a little crazy. "This place is gorgeous."

"So are you," I whisper in a low, appreciative rumble. She turns to me, surprised. Maybe she doesn't get what she's been doing to me all night. Shyly, she brushes a loose strand away from her cheek. "I mean it, Rebecca. You are so beautiful in that little black dress."

"Every girl should own a little black dress."

"Every boy should see his girl in one."

"And you look beautiful in your suit," she tells me, tipping her face upward to really meet my gaze. Without her heels on, I'm a relative giant beside her, big and clumsy, all male to her delicate female. I'm not used to this. Not used to being so rangy and awkward when all I want to do is kiss; I'm used to reaching *upward* for my kisses, to a man nearly an inch taller than me.

Before I can sort out what to do, she slips past me, and my opportunity is missed. "Can we go out on the deck?" she asks, gesturing toward the sliding glass doors, and I swallow hard, following with a silent nod of acquiescence.

"Good," she says, dropping her shoes on the hand-woven rug, "I want to see the moon tonight."

And I want to see the moonlight in your eyes, sweet Rebecca.

✧

Rough out here this evening, the wind all kicked up and the waves rolling hard, nothing but foamy chop. We've been outside on Casey's deck a while, not talking, just quiet together. Me reclining on the lounge chair, watching her watch the sea, her knowing that I'm watching, and letting me.

"What was your first kiss with Alex like?" she asks contemplatively, staring out at the pounding waves, hands clasping the metal railing.

I notice that her shoulders are small but strong, like fine porcelain gleaming in the moonlight. Her long hair sails on the breeze, blowing around her face, and after a while, I move behind her. She glances back, wondering why I haven't answered, and I'm right there. My large hands cup her waist, because I need to feel how soft she is, how different her body is from my own. Languid green eyes track upward, meet mine, and one glance causes a sharp tightening in my groin.

Brushing a few wild strands away from her lips, I murmur my answer. "Like this," I breathe, leaning low to feel the velvet softness of her mouth beneath mine, the satin of her cheek. But kissing Allie was never like this; this is something virgin and new. This is a first kiss, what all first kisses should be, as her warm mouth opens completely to mine. She folds into me, effortless; I cup her face within my rough palms, drawing her inward. It seems to last forever, this dance of becoming one.

"I was wrong," I finally gasp against her mouth, desperate to get my bearings with her.

"About what?" She stares up at me through golden lashes, still holding onto my suit lapel.

Alex is receding behind me, like the beach, with us turned out to sea. *Forgive me, baby.*

I brush my thumb over her lower lip, absolutely aching, inside and out. For him, for her. Then I whisper, "I don't think I've ever had a kiss quite like that one."

Exactly what I thought when I shared in that first forbidden kiss out on a darkened dance floor. The first time I realized just how cunning and swift love could be.

✧

As soon as Andrea's sitter pulls out of the driveway, the remorse begins. Before I can lock the door, it descends like a wily vulture on my blissful date night. That I stayed out so late—well past midnight—that I kissed someone. The *first* someone other than Alex since his death. Oh, I feel lousy all right; so bad that I think I could be sick now that I'm here in our house. Surely he knows, right? Surely he knew the minute my heart opened up to her. I pace the length of the living room, feeling frantic and nauseous. I walk down the hall and stare through the thinly cracked doorway at our sleeping angel of a daughter, all curled up like a tiny Botticelli with her feet flung on top of the covers. She's an eight-year-old microcosm of so much that I loved in her daddy.

Closing the door, I lean my forehead against it, listening to my own breathing, waiting for something, though I have no clue what that something is. Pacing back into the living room, I notice a picture in the bookcase, of the two of us at Casey's beach house—on the same damn deck where I kissed a girl tonight.

"I'm sorry." When the words electrify the air, only then do I realize I wasn't just thinking them. That I'd given them life that way.

Sinking onto the sofa, I bury my head in my hands and wait for his answer. It's irrational, but it's what I do, like a child praying in church, expecting God to bellow down a reply. Do I think Al's going to exonerate me? Not damned likely.

Pressing my eyes shut, I feel tears burn behind the lids because I really am falling for Rebecca, and it's like I'm cheating on him. The one thing I would *never* do to him, my soul mate, I'm doing just by living on without him. It's inevitable. If not Rebecca, someone else—but the problem is the locomotive intensity of this thing with her.

There's the answering quiet of raindrops on the roof right at that moment, icy fingertips tapping out a sonorous rhythm, and it takes me back. To years ago when he and I were first getting involved, and were lying in bed together one night early on. I was staring at the ceiling. Wondering what the hell I had gotten into, all tangled up with my best friend like that.

I told him so too. That surely I'd come unglued or something, no matter how damned sexy he was. I'll never forget what he said next, or the sound of the raindrops pattering on the roof of his apartment that night. How hushed the midnight bedroom seemed when he rolled onto his side, staring at me with those honest, beautiful blue eyes.

"Michael, this doesn't have to be so hard, you know," he said, searching my face.

"Don't see how not," I answered, staring away from him—anywhere but into those eyes. "Falling for you is pretty damned hard to deal with."

"Maybe you could just open up your heart and see where it leads you," he replied with a forgiving laugh. "Instead of always fighting everything so much."

I doubt any single statement ever changed me more. Because my lover knew me well, already—I'd been fighting and running my whole life. Alex was only the latest in a lifetime of battles. And my uncertainty about things didn't fade automatically after that, but it was like I sighed. Or relaxed. Or began to trust. I'm not sure, but I stopped fighting *him* so damned much.

Open up your heart and see where it leads you...

Opening my eyes, I stare across our living room, startled that Alex isn't standing right there grinning at me, because I swear I actually heard the words. Maybe that explains why I glance toward the kitchen. I'm looking for him, expecting him to be right there. That's when I notice the message light blinking on the kitchen phone, and slowly rise to my feet.

From the first syllable, I know who it is on the recorder. I would recognize her voice anywhere, any place, because even though he was a man and she's a woman, there's something eerily similar in the timbre of their twin voices.

"...I wanted to see how you are, Michael. I've missed you," Laurel is saying, her soft, cultured voice making me shiver. "I was sorry not to see you last weekend. Like we'd planned." There's a strange pause and I can tell she's taking a quick drag on her cigarette. Still hasn't kicked that habit, not even after all these years. Then she says, "I'm coming to Los Angeles in a couple of weeks, Michael. I'd like to stay with you, if that's okay. If you'll have me."

The shivers are becoming terrified shakes. Laurel can't be coming, not here, not to my turf.

Open up your heart and see where it leads, Alex whispers in my ear again, and I want to shout at him, to tell him to leave me alone. Stop pushing me so hard; stop taking me to the edge like he always fucking has.

And then I think of how much Laurel meant to him, of the nearly frightening twin-bond they shared. That she was already crying when I called her the night of his death; that she knew he was gone.

If Alex is still roaming my world, maybe it's because he needs resolution. Not just resolution between the two of them, either—maybe he needs to know there's resolution between us all.

Reaching for the phone, my hands sweaty and trembling, I hope to God that calling her is the right thing to do.

Chapter Thirteen: Rebecca

Early summertime is downtime in the world of filmmaking. Producers leave on Friday for the beach, execs motor out to Palm Springs, television shows are on hiatus. The whole studio lot feels like a college campus during summer school, as everyone breathes a little easier and daydreams a little longer. There's no sweeter time to fall under the spell of love.

And I've been doing my part, floating from that first Michael Warner kiss for nearly two weeks now—or floating from kiss to kiss, I should say. There have been luscious handfuls of them, including a tussling session on Michael's sofa last night that reached fevered, limb-tangled proportions before we called "cut". With Andrea asleep in the next room, we both knew it was time to pull away before we wound up in a *completely* horizontal position. He sat there on the edge of the sofa, raking his hand through his disheveled hair, and I sat on my side, listening to the rush of blood in my ears. Even in the darkness, I could see the rise and fall of his chest, and I didn't miss the way he tugged at his jeans, adjusting them when he stood to help me up.

But then afterwards, as he walked me quietly to the car, I sensed him withdrawing. He offered no more kisses, not even one of his trademark flirtatious grins with "Night, Rebecca" tagged onto it for sexy measure. Just a wave and a faint smile as he opened my car door. But if he thought he'd concealed his thoughts from me, he was mistaken.

While a part of me felt insecure as I drove back over the darkened hills to my apartment—I even wondered fleetingly if he'd seen my scarred chest during the tusslefest—I also suspected the real issue. One Alex Richardson. He'd passed between us like that before, right in the middle of some intense moment of connection, changing the mood unexpectedly. Michael doesn't talk about him much, but he's often there, sometimes broad and tall, other times ghostly and whispering, *always* an eerie form of romantic competition. He's the hero, the one who got away, the first love, the soul mate. Thousands of threatening definitions could apply—and yet I'm fascinated with him. After all, he's a legend to the map of this world I'm cautiously entering, a clue to what once held them all together.

And a clue to what's keeping Michael and Andrea apart.

See, it's those secrets again. I feel them, tugging at the edges of their family like the draw and release of the tides. There's a definite rhythm to their melancholy; sometimes it's flat, and other times it swells intensely, unexpectedly lifting away. Joy is there, too, like last night when Michael chased Andrea around their patch of backyard until they both collapsed in the grass, giggling, red-faced, and breathless. But then there's the crashing wave of memory, and Andrea pulls in tight again—she's angry, features set like cold granite against her father, sulking away in her room.

I do have my questions about their relationship. Like if he's her adoptive father, then why does she call him by his first name? I know she called Alex "Daddy", but didn't she call Michael something similar—like Dad or Papa or even Father? I am curious about the reasons for that, and also about Andrea's birthmother—the agency-provided surrogate Michael told me carried her for nine months—but I know enough to wait for all the facts. Not to push Michael when he's obviously not ready to talk. I haven't gotten this far in show business without knowing when to stay quiet, that's for sure.

Still, watching their wounded dance from the outside is tough. After she stormed off last night, he sat there on the ground, looking stunned and hurt. Then he finally stood, brushing away bits of freshly mown grass from his hands and knees.

"I know that has to be hard," I said, moving to clear the dinner plates from the table on the deck. "When she opens up like that, and then closes off again."

"I keep trying to figure it out. Our counselor says to give her time."

Andrea had placed a dandelion by each of our glasses, and I sniffed mine, saying, "You don't exactly strike me as the patient type."

"Yeah? Well, I'm pretty fucking ready for a breakthrough," he said, staring at the patio door through which she'd just vanished. "I can tell you that."

"And you don't strike me as one to mince words, either." I laughed, handing him the dandelions from around our plates. Thankfully, he began to smile then, too, rolling the flower stems between his fingertips.

"She talks to you," he said after a moment, contemplative. "She tell you anything I should know?"

The hopeful expression in his brown eyes pained me, but I had to say, "Not really, but maybe she will. If we give her enough time."

He nodded seriously and bent down, kissing the top of my head. And for that moment, despite all the heat that usually stormed between us, I'm sure I became a stand-in for one closed-off, absent little girl.

✧

So here I am, poolside on Friday afternoon, playing hooky from my job before the day's even done. That earned me a standing ovation from Trevor as he watched me leave my office, armloads of scripts clutched in both hands. When I explained that Michael was dropping Andrea over to spend time with me by Mona's pool late this afternoon, his smile faded.

"Stepmother already," he observed coolly, then lowered his voice. "How convenient for Heavenly Homo."

"Shut up," I snapped, feeling unusually irritable with him.

"Just be careful, all right?" he cautioned. "Michael's a nice lad, I'll grant you that, but there's a reason his type's dangerous."

He was standing inside my office, so I plopped my skyscraper of scripts onto the chair and closed my office door. I really do need to get a Kindle. "Trevor, I appreciate you looking after me, really I do, but he's a good, *decent* guy."

He folded his arms over his chest, the muscles flexing beneath his cotton T-shirt. "Always the most dangerous type, aren't they?" he said. "Those decent-seeming ones."

"More dangerous than the naughty celebrity types?" I was referring to both our romantic histories, but he clearly mistook my remark as a personal jab.

"Touché, my dear," he said in a soft voice, and opened my door without another word.

"Trevor?" I called out, following him to his desk. "I was talking about both of us, silly. I'm the one who's spent the past two weeks avoiding Jake calls."

"I'm aware of that," he said, grabbing the phone as it rang from Ed Bardock's office. "Go. Have fun." Making a shooing motion with his hand, he urged me reluctantly out the door, and that's when I noticed his latest screensaver brilliance: *Don't mind me, I just flirt here.*

Maybe that's a sign he's ready to move on past Julian, I thought fleetingly, leaving the bungalow. Or maybe it's a sign that he's ready to move on from this job as my creative sidekick.

✧

Andrea sits on the edge of the pool by the steps, dangling her feet in the chilly water. It's still cool this early in the summer, with the ancient palms that line the backyard shading the water year-round, and Mona doesn't like to spend the money to heat her pool, either, especially since she never uses it herself.

So Andrea doesn't look entirely out of place wearing her spring suit, a short-sleeved, short-legged version of a wetsuit, which Michael whispered to me was the *only* way he'd gotten her to agree to come swimming today. Otherwise, she was too self-conscious about her scar—ironically enough. Sitting beside me now, splashing her toes around in the water, she looks the part of a true surfer girl in her sleek black suit, auburn hair pulled into a loose ponytail.

Noticing the O'Neill logo on her sleeve, I remark, "How long have you been surfing?" It's important to her, I know, as much because she loves the sport as because she loved surfing with her dead father. Michael's clued me in to that much.

At first I think she might not answer me as she stares at her feet, bobbing them up and down in the water like a pair of buoys. Then she says, "My daddy was a great surfer."

"I know, I heard."

"He won contests and stuff. His whole life." She looks up at me, intent. "Did you know that?"

"No, I didn't."

"Yeah, and he taught me how. He even let me ride on his long board with him sometimes. Except that always scared Michael a lot, when we did that." She pauses, revisiting some private memory, then adds with a dimpled smile, "But Daddy just told him not to worry so much."

"Was it dangerous?" It perplexes me that Alex would have done anything to intentionally place Andrea in harm's way.

"No, just fun," she says, serious again. "We only did it in the shallow waves."

"Then why did it scare Michael?"

She shrugs matter-of-factly. "'Cause Daddy's always worrying about stuff like that." I thought she'd just said *Alex* was the one who took her out on his board—not Michael—and am about to remark on that, but before I do, she catches her misstep. "*Michael*," she amends firmly. "Michael's always worrying about all kinds of stuff."

"About you," I add, and after a moment she nods, staring at the lapping waves of pool water.

"Yeah, especially since..." She wraps her pale arms around herself in a hug, shivering, not finishing her thought.

"Especially since the accident," I supply, knowing I may be pushing too hard. She doesn't answer, but leans forward, trailing her fingers through the water in a raking motion, leaving my question unanswered.

"Daddy liked to touch the waves when he rode. He'd just reach out and touch. Kinda like this." She combs her fingertips across the chlorinated surface, looking back over her shoulder to make sure I see, adding, "I always thought that'd be really cool. To touch my wave."

"You haven't?"

She chews on a fingernail. "I can't ride the really big ones yet."

"Maybe you will. One day."

She shrugs, utterly indifferent all of a sudden. "Yeah, whatever." She slides off the concrete lip of the pool, dropping into three feet of water, spring suit still on. Slowly, I begin unbuttoning my Polo men's shirt, the one I'm using as a poolside cover-up. I'm deliberate and slow, slipping each button through the hole, hoping she'll turn and see. See what I look like in a one-piece; that even this much material can't hide all my scars. It's why I invited her—without really explaining my plan to Michael, without telling him how it was I thought I might get through to her today.

The starched men's shirt falls open, slipping off my shoulders, and at that instant Andrea turns in the water to stare up at me.

And she sees. She definitely sees, and I see the way she nearly gawks at the long scar peeking out of the top of my suit. I know that it looks like I had open-heart surgery or something dramatic like that. Then, aware that she's staring, she drops her head.

"You can look," I encourage, popping into the pool like a heavy stone beside her. The water splashes a bit, circling us both in radiating waves, and she bends low until her ponytail floats on the surface.

She blows bubbles, then stops. "Rebecca, can I ask you something?"

"Of course." I bend my knees until I'm looking right at her, eye-level, meeting those clear blue eyes with all the reassurance I can muster. "Fire away."

Her auburn eyebrows draw together tight, freckled nose wrinkling. "What happened to you? How come you have all those scars?"

I can only wonder how to translate such a raw act of irrational violence into terms that an eight-year-old can process. I'm wrestling with that when what has to be my mother's euphemistic gene kicks in, and I hear myself say, "I had an accident."

"What kind of accident?" Andrea's small mouth purses into a hard, desperate line, and sudden blotches of color stain her face.

"Sweetie, it wasn't like what happened to you."

Her face falls. "Oh."

"But I do understand," I hasten to explain, brushing a damp lock of red hair off her cheek. She jerks away, swimming toward the steps fast, and I nearly beg, "Andrea, please listen. You can talk to me, sweetheart."

She shakes her head, climbing the steps. "You just said. It wasn't the same kind of accident."

"Andrea, I almost died." Now this gets her complete, earnest attention, and slowly she pirouettes on the steps until she's facing me. "I spent an entire month in the hospital. Getting better."

She runs her tongue over her upper lip, just watching me, and I can tell she's making quick mental calculations. Deciding if she can trust me with her own secrets or not. "How?" she asks, clutching the metal railing as if her life depends on it.

"How did I almost die?"

"No, no," she says hurriedly. "How come you didn't?"

And this is the answer I've contemplated for three years running. All I know is to give the best one I've come up with in all that time. "Because I wasn't supposed to die yet."

She nods knowingly, and I understand that she's considered these same thoughts on her own time. "But what if somebody else died, and they weren't supposed to either?"

"Like your daddy?" I supply tentatively, afraid I'll send her scurrying away for good just when we're making serious progress. I swim closer, until I'm at the foot of the steps.

"Did Michael make you do this? You know, talk to me and all," she explains with a tired sigh. "'Cause you don't have to."

"Andrea, sweetheart, I'm not doing this because of Michael. All I'm trying to say is that I understand."

Tears brim within her eyes, and she whispers, "Nobody else does."

"Well, I do."

She nods, saying in a small voice, "I think maybe I'm the one who should've died."

"Oh, sweetie, no. No, that's not true." She plops onto the top step, planting her chin in the palm of her hand thoughtfully, avoiding me, but I press her. "What even makes you think that?"

"Want to see my scar?" she murmurs, looking up at me with doleful eyes. From Michael, I know this is the touchstone, the scar that she won't show anyone; what I say next is critical to her knowing she can confide in me.

It's as if God whispers right in my ear, offering a thought. "How about I show you my scars," I offer resolutely, "and then you show me yours? That sound like a plan?"

She stares at my chest, at what she *can* see, blinking, considering, then finally nods in acquiescence. I step closer, holding the railing until I stand just in front of her. Cautiously, I gaze up at Mona's windows, but they're dark, and I don't care what she sees anyway. Peeling down the top of my suit, until only my breasts remain concealed by fabric, I reveal the longest scar of all, like a giant arrow leading right to my heart, then the second one that resides beside it. A visible reminder of my punctured left lung, the wound that caused my asthma and left me with a host of other problems, even if it's the smaller of the two.

Andrea tilts her head sideways, just looking, then reaches out a gentle, cautious finger to touch the big one, and asks what she did on that very first day: "Do they hurt?"

"Sometimes, yes. And they itch," I confess with a laugh. "A lot. Isn't that stupid?"

"Yeah, kinda," she agrees, dropping her hand away, but I catch it in my own, so that she sees the long scar through the middle of my palm. She stares at it with a mix of wonder and surprise, and asks in her breathy voice, "Does that one itch too?"

"It hurts sometimes. And it itches too," I say. "They all do. They're still healing," I explain. "Doesn't yours itch?"

"Nope. Mine just feels like..." She hesitates, examining my palm seriously. "Like nothing. Mine feels like nothing."

I'm about to ask her what she means when there's the rumbling sound of Michael's Chevy on the driveway. She glances toward his advancing truck, almost panicked, and then back at me as if she's reaching some critical decision.

"It's your dad," I explain, although she can certainly see his silver truck herself.

She nods, standing to her feet. And then with all the gracefulness of a girl raised in water, she dives off the steps, arcing into the placid surface in one fluid line.

Gone, into the depths, completely away from me.

Chapter Fourteen: Michael

I've got to figure out a way to broach the Laurel topic with Rebecca, and I'll admit that it scares the crap out of me. Not sure why, except my relationship with Laurel's so strange and complex, she often feels like a quasi-lover to me. So telling Rebecca about her, well it's like I'm revealing that there's another woman in my life, one I've kept secret up until now. Feels like I'm sharing private things that belong to just Alex and me too. I'm not sure I'm ready to let anyone else in on all that just yet, not even Rebecca.

But with one week left until the visit, I've got to come clean, and tonight's as good a time as any. Andie's asleep in Rebecca's room, on her bed, and I'm pacing around her small garage apartment trying to gather my nerve, feeling edgy and weird. She already knows me, though, and while she's cooking in the kitchen, she keeps looking my way, 'cause she realizes something's off. I'm fiddling with some of her acting awards and her pile of scripts perched on the counter. Allie always said I'm the world's worst fiddler when I'm nervous, and that's what I'm doing tonight.

"So what's going on, Michael?" she asks, leaning over a vegetable dish and tasting it. "What's wrong?"

"Nothing," I say, shoving both hands into my jean pockets.

"Humph." She goes back to cooking, reaching for a sip of her white wine.

"What?" It comes out sounding more indignant and loud than I mean, and she looks a little shocked, so I explain, "Look, yeah, I'm in a crap mood, okay?"

But I don't know her well enough yet for this kind of display, and she doesn't deserve it either. I step close saying, "I'm sorry, Rebecca." I slip my hands around her waist, drawing her back against me. She smells like suntan lotion and chlorine as I bend to kiss the top of her head. God, I want her; that hasn't stopped for a single minute in the past weeks. In fact, it's getting outrageous how much I'm thinking about making love to her. That is, when I'm not thinking guilty thoughts toward Alex about that fact.

"It really is okay," she assures me, that sexy southern accent shading her words, as she leans back into me. "I'm just wondering what's going on."

"I want to make love to you," I blurt, even though it's the smallest part of what's got me so anxious tonight. I feel her tense within my arms; hear her suck in a sudden breath. "I mean, I don't want to rush things, Becca, but I'm going crazy here."

"Crazy, huh?" She laughs nervously, slipping away from me, and I'm left standing there in her kitchen, feeling pretty damned stupid, as she works on our meal without ever looking back at me.

Never had this problem with Alex. Guys just move on a much faster timetable—straight to bed, that's the guy way. Hell, the one time in my life when things felt crystal-clear in the sex department was *with* Alex, ironically enough. No secret codes, no hidden messages, just two guys dying to do it.

"Is that all you have to say?" I demand of her. "About me wanting to make love to you?"

"Is that the *real* problem?" she asks, turning to face me. I close my eyes, and ache to tell her everything. About Laurel and how much she holds over me. How scared I am to see her again, after all this time.

I blow out a breath, and instead ask, "How'd it go with Andrea?" Funny, but she smiles up at me, that quirky half-smile of hers that I love so much, and doesn't look angry in the least.

"Michael Warner, what am I going to do with you?" she reflects tenderly, shaking her head.

"It's a simple question."

"So was mine," she observes, stepping close, and I notice that she's barefoot with her toenails painted a sexy hot pink. That one simple detail is enough to arouse me. "Tell me what's wrong," she urges, slipping her hand into mine, ignoring my cranky mood. "Other than being horny, that is." Even I have to laugh at that.

I shrug apologetically. "It's the male dilemma."

"The female too."

"Yeah? Well, we ever gonna do it, Rebecca? Or just think about it all the time?" Heat sparks in her green eyes, but then she drops her head, self-conscious, wavy blonde hair falling across her face. "'Cause right now, I'm starting to think it's never going to happen."

"It will happen." She stares at her toes, away from me, voice all quiet and unreadable.

"Rebecca, you're sexy as hell, I can't help that." She touches her face, brushing her hand over her scars. "Don't you know what you're doing to me?"

She looks up again, green eyes shining. "Michael, I've slept with exactly two people in my life. That's it, okay? It's not that there's a problem with you, it's just—" She shakes her head, walking away from me, toward the sink.

I follow after her. "Just what, Rebecca?"

She spins to face me, clutching a hand over her heart. "You don't know what you're dealing with here, okay? That's all."

"What I'm dealing with? What the hell's that supposed to mean?" I have no idea where all this blustery anger's coming from, but I don't know how to stop it, either.

"I can't talk about this right now," she says, tension visible in her features, her blonde eyebrows lifting defiantly. "I just can't."

"You asked me what was wrong."

"And it's *sex*?" she cries, placing a palm over her chest. "That's what you're telling me is wrong with you tonight? That it's because we aren't having sex yet?"

"Can you keep your voice down?" I nod toward her bedroom irritably. "I don't want Andrea to hear this."

"Fine," she says, placing her back to me again.

I wander toward her fridge and open it, searching for a beer. She's stocked it with Heineken just for me. Oh, I'm a first-class prick all right.

"So it *is* about sex," she asserts, much more quietly.

"That's an issue, but not the real one."

"Okay, then tell me."

I hesitate a moment, pacing the length of her kitchen. "It's Laurel Richardson," I say, feeling like I've just dropped a heavy pack to the floor. "Al's sister. His twin sister."

"Okay," she encourages, gentle with me, far more gentle than I deserve. "What about her?" I turn back to face her, and she's patiently waiting, nodding her head in support.

"She's coming to stay with us. Next week." I stare past her, out the window over her sink, because I just can't deal with looking into her kind green eyes. "There's a whole lot of history there, that's all. Bad shit, and I'm not sure I can deal with it, but I don't have much choice."

"Well, Michael." She pauses, biting her lip, considering. "The good thing is that at least you don't have to deal with it all alone. You've got me."

✧

We're back on the sofa again, hers this time. Mine, hers, it doesn't matter; all I want to know is when we'll finally get down to it. When I'll be deep inside her, making love like that for the first time in years— and to *her* for the first time in my life. Yeah, Queer Boy is undeniably gung-ho about his return to the straight and narrow.

Darkness shrouds her den, with only the gleaming lights from Mona's house washing over her ceiling. That and the rhythmic reflection of the pool lights playing along Rebecca's living-room wall like a lava lamp. Andie's sound asleep in the next room; there's just us, the sound of us breathing together, the feel of me hard and ready to go.

God, these jeans are killing me, I think, as I manage to lower her onto the cushions, onto her back. I slip my palm beneath her T-shirt, just exploring, edging closer to her breasts, and feel the cool of Alex's band against the warmth of her skin. I pull back, but keep on with the kisses. There's the sound of her soft breathing in my ear, quick breaths, and I feel her hands roaming my back, lower still, then stopping. My whole body spasms knowing how close she just got.

"Rebecca, Andie's in the next room, but..." I hesitate, even though I swear I'd beg her, I'd do anything to find a way for what I want tonight.

She presses her fingertips against my lips, silencing me. "Michael, we can't."

"Yeah we can, of course we can," I say, nuzzling her cheek, but she stops me, clasping my face within her strong hands.

She steadies me, until our eyes lock. "Michael, I was serious when I said there are things you don't know."

"I know everything that matters."

"No," she gasps, her breathing ragged as she shifts her hips beneath mine. "No, you really don't."

"What? You a guy in drag or something?" She doesn't laugh, just stares up at me, shocked. "Hell, that would solve some issues," I tease, leaning in to kiss her again, but she stops me, staring into my eyes hard.

"You've seen my scars, Michael," she says, her voice husky and filled with emotion. "But you haven't seen them all."

"That what this is all about?" I ask, relieved to finally understand.

"Michael, they're bad, okay. Really bad."

"Baby, I don't care about that," I whisper, brushing her hair away from her cheek. "I don't give a damn about that."

She turns away from me, and I think I see tears glint in her eyes as she whispers, "But you haven't seen the whole picture." She wipes at her eyes. "My body's not the same anymore, Michael. It's not just the scars you've seen; it's the ones you haven't. And there's my respiratory stuff: I'm sick some days, others..." One hand flutters over her chest. "There's a whole lot you don't know."

"You really think that'll change how I feel?"

"I need more time." She pulls in a nervous breath, adding, "And you still love Alex."

Now that one takes me aback, and I have to process it for a minute. "Is that a problem?" I finally ask, defiant anger edging my voice.

"No, Michael." She smiles, a sad expression that surprises me. "It's just that I think we *both* need more time."

For a long moment, I stare into her eyes, blinking. It feels like she just slapped me, pulling Alex right here between us that way. I sit up, swinging my legs onto the floor, and cover my mouth with my hands.

"Are you angry?" she asks solemnly, and I feel her shift behind me, curling her legs up so she can sit beside me. How come with me, love always has to be so damn complex?

"Nope, not angry."

"Good."

"You should know something, though," I say, turning to face her. "I'm not letting go of Alex anytime soon."

"I'm not asking you to."

"Nah, I think you just did."

She reaches for my right hand, cradling it within her own. "I'd never do that. It's just that you should at least be ready to make room for someone else first." She outlines his ring on my finger for emphasis and whispers, "Because otherwise, it might be a mistake."

"I tried taking it off. Just couldn't, not yet."

"You'll know when the time is right," she encourages me, touching the silver band with her fingertip. We fall silent a while, both of us staring down at Alex's ring. I get the feeling there's something she wants to ask of me, but can't quite get the nerve.

"What is it?" I ask, my eyes locking with hers.

"Do you ever worry about staying healthy?" She seems nervous, fidgeting with the hem of her shirt anxiously. "About AIDS or whatever?"

"No, 'cause I don't sleep around," I answer, my eyes narrowing at her. She's asked such a straight person's question. They're convinced that we—the homosexual "other"—are always sleeping around.

"I don't mean it as an insult, but it's such a big question," she rushes, "for any of us out there in the dating world, not just gay people."

"Is that why you don't want to sleep with me?" I ask, the weight of what she's saying finally hitting home.

"Oh, Michael, no," she says, shaking her head. "No, but I want to be sure that I understand."

"Al and I were completely monogamous," I answer simply, because I want her to feel comfortable about me, and about what's starting between us. "End of story, okay? Neither of us slept around. I'm clean."

She nods, staring down into her lap, seeming more fragile than anything else.

"Tell me about the two guys."

Her blonde eyebrows arch upward in surprise. "You're changing the subject."

"It's important. You're talking about my one guy. You tell me about your two."

"Well, the first—"she draws in a breath, looking oddly shy, "—was my high-school sweetheart."

"Yeah? What's his name?" I know enough about high-school sweethearts not to dismiss this guy too easily.

She laughs, glancing sideways at me. "Dr. Andrew Finkle, family dentist back in Dorian."

"A *dentist?*" I cough.

"Sexy, huh?" she agrees with a sideways smile. "I get Christmas cards every year with his whole office decked out in Santa sweaters."

"I can't believe you lost your virginity to a guy named Andrew Finkle."

"I did love him, once upon a time." A wistful expression falls over her face as she stares out toward the flickering lights of Mona's pool. "But life was a lot simpler then."

I consider telling her about Katie and being dumped at eighteen in the Greyhound bus station, but think better of it. "So who phones you all the time?"

"Jake Slater. We were on *About the House* together."

Keeping my face neutral is hard: I've met Jake actually, though I never realized he was on Rebecca's show. Certainly never realized he was her ex until now. I did some gaffer work on a cable movie of his back about eight years ago, a location gig upstate. I remember he was more interested in snorting coke on the grip truck than in doing a good job on set. A real playboy, that one.

But I keep silent as she continues. "He was one of those consummate bad boys you always hope have really changed." She sighs, rubbing her eyes. "What can I say? I was naïve and stupid. That's really all you need to know about that."

"No, I need more," I insist. "You've gotten a hell of a lot more about my past out of me."

She hesitates, folding her hands neatly into her lap. "He dumped me after I left the hospital three years ago. Maybe I'd been home for two or three weeks, I'm not even sure. I was so weak, drugged up. If my parents hadn't been there to take care of me, I don't know what I'd have done. Just walking to the toilet took everything I had." She pauses, swallowing hard. "And then Jake shows up and tells me we're through. Just like that. Over." She shakes her head, almost like she's still disbelieving. "I'd lost my career, my face, my health, and then just like that, I'd lost my boyfriend too."

"I better not run into him ever," I say, feeling the rush of adrenaline—the male need to protect. "And if he calls you again on my watch, I'm gonna explain a few things to him."

"Thanks, but I think he's just having a life crisis or something. It's weird, but I've actually forgiven him."

"How'd you manage that?" I'm thinking of Robert Bridges and how my hatred toward him for killing Alex just never dies down.

"Because me going around bitter isn't going to change the facts," she explains with remarkable calm. "Jake dumped me because my career was over, and he didn't think he could afford to be associated with that. Because, as he said, 'In this town, you can't be damaged goods.'"

"What an asshole." I scowl in disbelief. "And you loved this guy?"

"I thought so at the time, yes. He could actually be quite charming."

"Well, he was wrong, just so you know," I say, wanting to be sure she really gets how I feel, that I'm not like this creep from her past. "You're not damaged goods, Rebecca. You're all the perfect I need."

"But," she reminds me in a careful whisper, brushing a hand over her heart, "you haven't seen all the rest."

I comb my fingers through her hair, revealing the part of her disfigurement that I *have* seen. "Yeah, that's true, I haven't seen the rest." Leaning down to kiss her scarred cheek, I say, "But neither had Jake when he said that."

For a moment, she stares at me wide-eyed, surprised, as if the thought had never even crossed her mind before now, that Jake broke up with her before the bandages came off.

Then she leans close, burying her face against my chest. We hold each other like that, me stroking her silky hair, feeling her heart hammering against mine, her arms wrapped around me. For once, I don't even care what comes next.

That's what I'm thinking when she whispers against my heart, "Maybe it's just me who needs more time."

"It's okay," I whisper back. "It's okay 'cause I'll wait as long as it takes."

Chapter Fifteen: Rebecca

"Please tell me Johnny Jordan is actually smart in person," Trevor says, grilling Cat about her current leading man in the film she's shooting over at Universal. "He's always mentioning Nietzsche and Neil Gaiman in the same breath during interviews. And you know what a turn-on intelligence is for me."

Cat sips her martini, smiling slyly. "No comment." I'm not sure if she's referring to Johnny Jordan's sexual orientation or his intelligence rating—and I'm not sure Trevor actually cares about either. Like the rest of America, he just wants tidbits. We once crashed a Christmas party up in the Hills because he'd heard a rumor that Johnny would be there.

"Is he... or isn't he?" I laugh. "That is the question. Of course you have terrible taste in celebrities, so it hardly matters."

Cat high-fives me across the table. "Go girl," she says. "Preach it, now!"

Trevor blows me a sulky air-kiss. "Yes, well Jules is about to make you, darling Rebecca, so you're allowed no snarky innuendo about *my* celebrities."

He's right, of course; in fact, that's why we're doing the post-work drinks round up with Cat, a little mini-celebration of the Kingsley option.

As much as Golden Boy irks me on principle, his book *is* lyrical and brilliant and it's the first time since my attack that I can remember feeling any kind of professional excitement at all. Maybe Mom was right about God bringing us our dreams in ways we don't anticipate. All I know is I'm nearly as charged tonight as I was that day my agent phoned me with the role of Mary Agnes Hill on *About the House*. From the way Trevor and Cat keep grinning at me, I can tell that the joy of this moment must be written all across my face.

It doesn't hurt knowing that Michael Warner's in my life, either. As complicated as that relationship has the potential to be, he's the most pure, sweet love interest I've had since leaving Georgia. It's in how honest and true Michael is, something that makes him utterly unlike all the other guys I've met in this town. As the good ole boys back home would say, "he means what he says, and he says what he means." And while all that truthful energy does kind of make me a little skittish, I know that what scares me most of all is simply me.

I notice that Trevor keeps checking his watch, and I lean forward, curious. "Hot plans later?"

"Oh, some Hollywood bowling league thing." He brushes his fingers through his hair, leaning back in his seat to survey the scene. "Another fun night in the city of dreams."

"That is so not fun." I laugh. "See, that's not even close to fun."

Trevor gives my hand a sardonic pat. "Other people can appreciate a good night of sport, darling."

"Other people aren't professional hermits," Cat interjects, grinning innocently at me.

"I am not a hermit." I pop an olive from my martini. "In case you haven't noticed, I'm out right now. And I was at your birthday party a few weeks back."

Trevor leans across the table confidingly. "She does have a new beau."

"Thank you." I smile in smug satisfaction. "Exhibit A. Michael Warner, my new boyfriend."

"Oh, but you totally met him in your office, so that doesn't count." She waves me off, sipping her scotch. "I'm talking, literally right there, no?"

When I cry foul, they both just laugh at me. "Face it, Rebecca," Cat declares, leaning in to kiss my cheek, "you're the most reclusive person I know in Hollywood who actually manages to be successful. I don't even get how you make that happen."

Trevor leans back in his chair, studying me with an objective gaze, like he's an investor sizing up my worth. "She's bloody good at what she does," he concludes, "otherwise she could never get away with it."

"All right, guys," I argue, "think about it. I do lunch every day, I'm at tracking breakfasts, agent parties. You name it. Oh, and don't forget how much I read. I read absolutely everything."

A sly smile spreads across Trevor's face. "Including certain projects that I attempt to secret away in my desk. You can't get anything past our girl," he says, tipping his glass against mine with a hale salute of, "Cheers! Kudos to you on Julian's deal, sweetie."

"That's right, Trev!" Cat slugs him playfully on the shoulder. "Make her step up to the plate. Credit where credit's due."

"Okay, okay," I agree, holding my hands up in surrender. "I did the deal. I'm the master of the universe tonight."

"Brava, darling," Trev enthuses. "Brava, indeed. Soon we'll make a regular egomaniac out of you—oh look, there's Jeremy Rinzler." Trevor indicates a secluded table on the far side of the bar. Jeremy, an executive at New Line, lifts his drink in salutation and I wave back. Thankfully, Trevor agrees to do the meet and greet gig on my behalf.

Watching Trevor's easy manner, the way he laughs and leans in to make obviously clever remarks as he pumps Jeremy's hand, I envy him. Without a doubt, he's the most effortless person I know. Effortlessly funny, effortlessly smart, effortlessly handsome. From his Kenneth Cole shirt to his Alain Mikli wireframes to his meticulously tousled hair, he's the image of sophisticated perfection. And yet, I've seen behind the curtain enough to realize that's merely an impression.

"Will you *look* at him?" Cat observes appreciatively, sipping her scotch beside me. "That boy's got the gift, my friend."

"The gift of what precisely? Of being natural at everything?" I whine in a fit of momentary spitefulness toward my best friend. Maybe Jeremy Rinzler's gay.

"Don't hate him because he's beautiful," she croons, watching Trevor with an appreciative grin, then turns to me. "Hey, and speaking of beautiful, Evan Beckman was asking about you the other day."

Okay, so she lays *this* zinger on me, and then doesn't even bother to look up to gauge my reaction? Evan is the director on her current feature, one that's already generating major Oscar hype—including whispers of a nomination for Cat for her supporting role as a sexy Latin singer. All this before it's even in the can, but that's Evan's reputation. He's young and visionary and everyone in town is clawing to work with him.

"Evan Beckman? Now who's that again?"

This time, the dark feline eyes raise to meet mine, narrowing to mischievous slits. "I told Evan that you're looking great," she answers smoothly. "That you should meet."

"Is he looking for a new d-girl or something?"

Cat rolls her eyes in exaggerated agitation. "Geez, would you shut up already? I'm talking about your *acting* career!"

"Hey, you're the one egging me on with these casual side comments of, 'Evan asked about you.'"

"He did ask about you!"

"You know what I mean." Then I lean close across the table, joining her conspiracy. "But tell me everything he said!"

Cat's face lights up. "His words were, 'I think she has something very interesting. Bring her around before we wrap.'"

"He didn't really say that," I ask, incredulous. "Did he?"

"I'm serious. Apparently he's hooked on reruns of the show, and thinks you have..." She taps her forefinger against her head to dislodge some near-forgotten remark. "That you have brilliant comedic understatement. That's *exactly* what he said."

"But come on, Cat, who would hire—" I gesture at my face for emphasis, "—*this*? He's Evan Beckman, why would he even think about hiring me?"

For a long moment she inspects me, her dark gaze roaming the whole of my features, and if she weren't one of my dearest friends, I'd flinch beneath such close scrutiny of my scars. "Rebecca, you have a really remarkable look," she pronounces gently. "And you're still gorgeous. Some directors—smart ones like Evan—are looking for a distinctive look like that. I've been saying it's time you got back out to auditions."

"You do realize Bernie fired me?"

"So what?" She scowls in distaste. "He's Jake-tainted anyway, and he's not the only agent around."

"Evan Beckman." I sigh, contented just knowing he thinks I'm talented. Funny how that naive girl from Georgia, thrilled by rave reviews, can still come out to play even now.

Then my plucky optimism fades a bit. "I wonder if he wants to direct Julian's movie?" I hate being cynical, but it's the next thought popping into my head: that he's hoping to attach to the project, and will use me to get it.

"Rebecca! This was last week, before anybody even knew about Julian's deal."

I smile again, feeling radiant inside. "Then I can be excited for about five minutes, right?"

"I think you can be excited from now on, girl."

What a radical concept: I could actually act again. No agent, no job, loads of scars, but Evan Beckman is asking about me. At this rate, maybe I'll even forget all those average days eventually.

✧

While we're waiting in the valet line, braving heat that's still suffocating even this late in the day, Cat starts in with the Michael Warner survey. I notice that Trevor falls silent, and since that's such an unusual occurrence, it catches my attention.

"Have you told her the full story?" he asks after Cat waxes dreamy about Michael for a while.

"What full story?" Her black eyes widen in curiosity.

"*Trevor.*" I smile, but my silencing glare telegraphs another message entirely. I hadn't planned to let Cat in on that aspect of my new guy, at least not yet. I feel incredibly protective of Michael, and I don't want anything said that might hurt him—or Andrea—later on.

"No, no, no," Cat cries, grasping at my arm like the professional gossip-hound she can be. "I need to know. What full story?" The valet driver squeals up to the curb with her BMW, but she stands her ground, unwilling to move until she wrangles the truth out of me.

Folding his arms over his chest, Trevor sighs and looks away disinterestedly. Sometimes he's such an ornery little priss, it really ticks me off.

"Ma'am?" the young valet driver calls, holding the door of Cat's car expectantly.

"He has a daughter," I allow, hoping to throw Cat off the scent. "An eight-year-old, a really precious girl."

"Wow, so it'd be like, not just a guy, but a kid, huh?" she says. "That's interesting." Great, my little tidbit worked like a charm, and she leans in, pecking me on both cheeks. Then, as she's sliding into the seat of her car, and I'm letting loose a sigh of relief, she looks back, calling, "What about the ex? What happened to her?"

Trevor peers at me, a slight smirk on his face. I was nearly home free for a moment there. "We'll talk about that part later," I call to her, noncommittal as I wave goodbye. "It's a long story."

"Oh, oh, oh." Cat laughs through her open car window. "Girlfriend's gotten herself into a big mess, hasn't she, Trevor?"

He slips his arm around me, making peace. "Well, it's a *lovely* mess," he answers pointedly, winking at me. "We'll give our girl that."

"And it's a mess that makes me *happy,* unlike some of my other messes," I say to Trevor as we wave goodbye to Cat.

"Darling," Trevor says with a wry grin, "the happy messes are the only ones worth bothering about."

Chapter Sixteen: Michael

Waiting in baggage claim for Laurel to arrive seems to last forever, a real study in patience for a guy like me. It's damn hot for one thing: an oppressive heat wave spiked temperatures into the upper nineties by late morning, and now that the afternoon's here, the city's a regular boiler room. I only hope the weather's not some kind of omen about this visit.

Andrea keeps wandering off, too, which makes me crazy, and I have to keep following after her. "Andie!" I call to where she's flipping through some tourist brochures. She doesn't even glance my way; in fact seems to turn her back more pointedly against me as I call, "Andrea, come back over here with me."

When I reach her, she rolls her eyes. "Michael, it's not a big deal. You can see me fine from right over there."

"I don't care. Come back over now," I insist, glancing up the escalator for any sign of Laurel. "Besides, it's not polite to be over there. You need to be waiting for your aunt."

"I am waiting," she argues, and finally I just give up, wiping the sweat away from my brow, closely watching my daughter from the sidelines.

When the sign flashes that Laurel's flight has arrived from Albuquerque, my nervous anxiety spikes upward by a few notches, and I try to rein Andrea in. "Sweetie, look, her plane's here, so any minute now she's gonna be coming down that escalator. Any minute."

To my surprise, Andrea does become compliant then, standing beside me dutifully, chattering about all the things she wants to show her aunt. The art project that won the Best Overall award for third grade; Jerry's World Famous Deli down at the end of our street; her new doll, the one Laurel sent her a few weeks ago. But to my supreme mortification and anxiety, Andrea is most interested—more than absolutely anything else—in sharing my new girlfriend with her. Rebecca O'Neill and the Richardson family are on a collision-course trajectory, and while I knew it was coming, I'm still not sure what to make of it.

"There she is!" Andie scampers away from the baggage carousel to the foot of the escalator, waving exuberantly at her aunt. Laurel looks as beautiful as ever, maybe even thinner, and she's always been rail-thin to begin with. Long and willowy, that's Laurel's look, with porcelain skin. She has shiny black hair down the length of her back, gypsy style. And clear blue eyes exactly like her late twin's. That's what I notice when we first make eye contact, and it spooks me in spite of myself.

"Hello, Michael." Laurel steps off the escalator, leaning in to kiss my cheek. A delicate whisper of a kiss, practically like air brushing past, and then her full attention locks on Andrea. "Hello, my pumpkin!" she cries, folding Andrea tight in her embrace. Andie buries her face against Laurel's shoulder, holding on hard. I doubt I've gotten a hug like that out of her in more than a year. Over Andrea's head, again Laurel's translucent eyes meet mine, and I'm not sure exactly what it is I see. Affection? Guilt? An apology?

I don't keep the gaze long enough to find out. "Look, we gotta go get your bag." I gesture toward the carousel. "This is L.A., you know, not Santa Fe."

The words come out like an accusation of sorts, but Laurel gives me one of her opaque looks and nods. "Of course, Michael," she says, holding onto Andrea's hand as she rises to her feet. "Thank you for looking out for me."

"No problem."

"And thank you for inviting me." She searches my face, but this time I say nothing. After all, I *didn't* invite her here, never would have; I simply complied with her plan because I have no other choice in the matter. Not when she's made it painfully clear that when it comes to Andrea, she's the one with all the control. "I'm hoping we'll have a nice visit," she persists. The three of us walk toward the carousel, the flopping sound of her thong sandals loud on the polished floor.

"That'd be good," I agree, wondering how I'll ever make it through the next four days.

"I've missed you, Michael," she says, just like the other night on the phone. I roll my eyes at that one, and don't even care if she sees, but she's already turned toward Andrea anyway, saying, "I've brought you a present, pumpkin." I'm about to complain about the preponderance of gifts lately when she goes on to announce: "And I brought something for you, too, Michael." She holds up a large shopping bag by the handles, showing me.

I shove my hands into my pockets. "An American Girl doll's not really my style, you know."

She actually laughs. Hard to believe, but I can still joke with her a little and get a good reaction, which is as much a tribute to our former friendship as it is to the lack of it these days.

"No," she says, tossing her long, silken mane over her shoulder. "Something I made for the house."

Oh, crap. I hadn't even thought about all those damn paintings I took down after Al's death. She's going to notice that right away.

"What'd you bring me?" Andrea asks, walking backwards so she can face her aunt as we move toward the baggage carousel. "Oh, and I love my Felicity doll! *Love* her, she's so cool. I can't wait to show you my room..." And she doesn't stop, just rattles on about her life, her toys, her friends, the dangers of learning to rollerblade if you live in a hilly neighborhood.

As I stand beside them, listening, watching the same pieces of luggage go round and round, I feel like I've been here before. Been on the outside, face pressed up to the glass, trying to find a way back in. Laurel listens, just nodding and encouraging her niece, and I sense my child orbiting away from me. I haven't gotten this much out of her in a month.

It's that Richardson gift: the ability to do all the listening and make the other person feel perfectly affirmed. Alex had it—one reason he was such a good doctor, with his knack for getting his patients to open up to him. Laurel has it, uses it to "hear" her paintings, that's what she once told me. They got it from Ellen, of course, who has always had a world of patience for listening to me.

And in this particular instance, with Andrea talking to her aunt at record speed, it only points out that maybe Laurel *was* right a year ago. Maybe Andrea would have been better off living with her, instead of here in L.A. with me.

Stepping into the kitchen, the house feels cool and quiet compared to the choking L.A. traffic we just fought our way through out on the freeways. Late afternoon heat rolled like a mirage off the asphalt, and it seemed like we'd never get here, like I'd never survive all the polite chitchat volleying between us. The 405 was log-jammed with cars because of an overturned truck, and edging past that accident only made me more cranky and irritable about this whole damn visit.

Laurel shakes out her hair, dropping her shopping bag to the floor along with her funky, beaded purse. Andie slips past me, scampering to her bedroom ahead of her aunt while I lug Laurel's expensive suitcase back to the guest room. She follows me, wordless, as she sees her brother's house again for the first time since his death. Her movements are pensive as she steps through the living room toward the back hallway. I know she's wondering where all her damned paintings went, but that would require a trip to the attic for me to show her all the loving care I used in warehousing them all. Just 'cause she hurt me doesn't mean I wouldn't protect such a material reminder of my years with Allie.

Andrea and I've spent the past year steadily erasing Alex's fingerprint from this place. Bedroom shoes, eyeglasses, razor, toothbrush, these are the things that mark a home as belonging to someone distinct, and so long as that person is alive, you take every balled-up athletic sock, every discarded tissue and half-finished Coke for granted. It's only afterward, when you wander through each room, that you're spooked by the illusion that your lover might simply waltz through the ether into your bedroom, slip on those eyeglasses, and finish the novel he left cocked open bedside.

Of course Laurel doesn't understand that as she wanders through each room, admiring what I've done with the place since Allie's death—which is exactly nothing. But it's been a few years since she's visited; the last time was when Andrea was about five. So the leather sofa we bought a couple of years ago, and the thick hand-woven rug, and the mission-style entertainment center—those are all new to her. She drops to the floor, admiring the rug. "This is great," she says, tracing her fingers over the pattern.

"Al bought it up around Monterey." Shoving my hands deep into my jean pockets, I rock back on my heels. For some reason it hurts, talking about that trip we made together, like it was only yesterday.

"I never knew he liked this kind of thing."

"Sure he did."

"I guess I always thought he was a little more..." She pauses, fingering the fibers and texture. "I don't know. Classic."

"Guess it'd be hard to say, sitting two states away."

A whole damn lot she didn't know about her brother, no matter how well she thought she understood him. Especially not in death, when it came to what he would've wanted from her with his family. I think of the past year, all that's happened between Laurel and me, of how our only communication for a while consisted of angry phone calls and lawyerish e-mails. And then just silence, Laurel always trying to reach me, while I just spun farther and farther away.

Without a word, Laurel rises to her feet and continues meandering through the house, down the back hallway, until she notices our family portrait—that same one Rebecca admired on our first date. "Oh, my." She stops, studying it appreciatively with a kind of awed hush as she clasps her hands over her heart. "Oh, look at all of you."

I pace beside her, unable to stand still. Unable to tolerate the dishonest reverence she's displaying toward her brother and the family we fought so hard to weld together.

"Yeah, it's a good picture," I mumble as I move on toward the guest room, and after a moment, I hear her Birkenstocks clopping behind me on the hardwoods. "This is the guest room." I shove the door open gruffly with the palm of my hand. "Bathroom's connected. You know the drill."

"Yes, I have stayed here before, Michael," she reminds me, her clear eyes bright and teasing, but I ignore her attempt at familiar warmth. I follow her in, then hoist the suitcase onto the queen-sized bed. She enters the room cautiously, tiptoeing toward the open closet where Alex's old suits now hang. I've stockpiled a lot of his stuff in here—suits and dress slacks and the like, much of it preserved in plastic dry-cleaning bags. His winter sweaters are in the dresser, the cashmere and hand-knit stuff he loved when it got cold enough.

"You kept all this?" she asks in a choked voice, folding her arms over her chest with a protective shiver.

"Couldn't get rid of it," I explain with an offhand shrug. "Couldn't figure out what to do, exactly, so yeah, it's here for now. The stuff I don't wear."

She trails her fingertips over all his suits that aren't sealed off, sifting through each sleeve and bit of material with quiet reverence. Until she discovers his long suede jacket, that caramel-colored duster he wore from college until he died—the one he refused to give up despite juice stains from Andrea's babyhood and ink stains from his office. She presses it longingly to her face, inhaling, a lost child burying her face in a beloved blanket. I'm startled when a quiet sound escapes from her throat, a slight moan of grief, and even with all the fury I've felt toward her, tears still burn my eyes.

"Oh!" she cries out in an anguished voice, stroking her hands over the familiar worn suede. "It's so stupid, Michael, but I thought maybe, somehow, it would still smell like him."

God, don't I know that feeling? Just like me in his surfboard room, or slouching in his T-shirts, it's no different at all.

"It's been too long for that, Laurel," I answer, gruffer than I intend to be. "He's been gone more than a year." I won't tell her that sometimes I do still catch his scent now and then, like a gift right from God in heaven.

She glances at me over her shoulder, a melancholy expression on her face. "All this time, I kept thinking there was someplace he'd been hiding."

"Thought maybe it was here?"

"I know that's ridiculous."

"Well, I always think he's still over at the hospital working," I concede gently. "Keep thinking I just gotta go see him, that's all. Spooks me a little every time I drive near the place."

She turns to face me, running her fingers down the shiny length of her black hair, smoothing it. "How have you possibly done this, Michael?" she asks, searching my face. "How have you managed?"

I shrug. "You do what you gotta do."

She smiles, a beatific, forgiving expression that mirrors one I often see on her mother's face. "You've done an excellent job, Michael," she affirms, and I know what's coming next—some kind of commentary on Andrea and my single parenting skills—so I cut her off at the pass.

"Look, I'm gonna go make some coffee, okay?" I turn my back on her, walking toward the doorway, fast. "Make yourself at home—"

"I want to make peace with you, Michael." Her voice is electric-quiet, shocking me sure as if I'd reached out my hand and touched her. "That's what I want. It's why I'm here."

"It's pretty late for that, Laurel."

"Why?" she pleads, with the childlike innocence that is forever surprising me about her. "Why is it too late?"

I sigh, and turn back to find the liquid blue eyes wide and beseeching me. Softening, I say, "Look, I kind of thought I was gonna see you a few weeks ago, up in Santa Cruz, for the anniversary. Thought we were gonna do this scene then."

"Is that what you really needed?" she asks, earnest in her question. "For me to be there?"

I shake my head. "Nah, not really."

"And would it have made a difference if I'd come?" she asks, stepping toward me, hands opening. "Would you have forgiven me then, Michael?"

"Like I said, Laurel. It's pretty late for that."

Her gaze lifts, and this time there's a fragility there that I'm not sure I've ever seen before. At least not but one other time—the day we put Alex in the ground.

"Michael, I honestly didn't think you needed me there, not that day."

"No, Laurel, you're wrong about that." My voice is surprisingly quiet, but I don't feel quiet inside. "See, I *did* need you. But that was a year ago, not now."

She reaches for me. "Michael, I made a terrible mistake," she says in a rush. "I want to try to heal that."

But I jerk my arm away. "We can't bring Alex back," I blurt, staring hard into her eyes. "And we sure as hell can't undo your *mistake*, Laurel. It's as much a part of this scene as Al's death is."

"Michael," she answers carefully, "you may not believe this, but I love you. That never changed. You're the only brother I have left now."

"No, Laurel, see, I'm not your brother!" I cry, unable to stop the flow of my rage. "I ain't your brother and I ain't your friend, and I *sure* as hell ain't your lover."

"Okay," she answers numbly. "Okay, Michael, I understand that you're angry."

"Hell yeah, I'm angry," I answer with forced quiet, knowing Andie's right down the hall. "You tried to take my daughter away from me. We lost Alex and that's what you did to his memory."

She nods, pursing her lips like she's fighting hard not to cry. "You have no idea how many regrets I have. Don't you see it's why I've come?" Her voice is defeated and small; she twists a finger through the ends of her hair, and whispers, "Alex is dead, but you're still here, Michael. At least I can make that peace with you."

"Thank *God* he never knew," I say, lowering my voice when I hear a slight noise from Andie's room. "Never knew how you tried to tear his family apart like that." Her wide eyes well with tears, but she says nothing. "Yeah, so see the way I figure it, Laurel, I'm definitely not your brother." I press past her, toward the door, but then I turn back. "I'm nothing but the guy who's stuck with you from now on."

✧

"Hello?" At the first sound of Rebecca's voice on the phone, I swear I'm going to lose it completely. A vise closes around my throat and I can't speak, my whole body trembling.

"Michael? Is that you?" she asks, and that familiar accent's a salve on my open wounds.

Kicking the door of the surfboard room shut, I clear my throat. "Hey, Becca," I reply in a quiet voice.

I close my eyes and half-whisper, "Laurel's here."

"How's it going? I've been thinking about you all day."

Blowing out a breath, I lean my forehead against Allie's long board and wish that Rebecca knew it all, the whole sad, broken story of Laurel Richardson and me. "Pretty much sucks so far." Sparking pain erupts behind my eyelids, and I massage my neck, determined not to get another migraine.

"What's happened?"

"Rebecca, can you come over? Tonight?"

"If you want me to, sure. Of course," she answers. "But do you think that's a great idea? Shouldn't you have family time first?"

I want to tell her she is like family, but it's way too early for words like that.

"I can't do this alone," I answer, resolved. "I can't do this shit alone anymore, period. I miss you and I want to see you tonight, and screw Laurel if she's got a problem with that."

"Okay, Michael," she soothes, voice gentle as a feminine caress. "Okay. I'll be there in an hour."

"And Rebecca? There's something you should know." I'm thinking of *all* the things she needs to know, all the secrets hardwired into this family.

"Okay, tell me."

So much she should know, so much that might change things between us all, but I settle on the most pressing matter in my mind: what I'm feeling, hidden away in this clandestine room, safe for the moment with my girlfriend. "I think I'm falling in love with you," I confess, bracing myself for her to rebuff or laugh at me, for her to tell me it's far too soon for an admission like that.

My cell phone line only crackles with electric silence. "I just, well, just wanted you to know," I stammer, pacing the length of the small room anxiously. "I thought you *should* know, before you came over tonight and all, 'cause Laurel sure brings out my dark side these days."

"We all have a dark side, Michael," she answers evenly. "You're not unique in that."

"But you don't know what an asshole I turn into around her." And that's really what has me more upset than anything right now, the way I shouted at her in the guest room a while ago, the way I shut her out when she was trying to bridge the gap between us.

"Does she deserve it, you being an asshole?" she asks. "Does Laurel deserve that?"

"She deserves," I heave a weary sigh, "a lot of things." My love, my gratitude, my supreme hatred. Reaching out, I trace my fingers along the rails of Allie's favorite board, perched right on top of the rack, and presto, like it's a magic talisman, we're up in Santa Cruz, late July. Laurel's sprawled on the sand beside me in her bikini, telling stories on her brother while he just lazes on my other side, belly-down, listening.

They laugh, giddily remembering some near-forgotten tale from their childhood. Their voices fall into easy harmony as sentences and stories are finished, back and forth between them while the sun marks time down the length of the sand. Me, right in the middle, the cavernous loneliness that had dogged me all my life swept mystically out to deepest sea. I had a sister and a brother and a lover and a family, all wrapped up in just those two that afternoon.

"Michael," Rebecca interrupts, "don't you know by now that you can't scare me off?" Her soft voice pitches low, like maybe she's hiding out too.

"What if you don't know everything?" I press, needing to gauge what her reaction would be.

"If you were going to freak me out, that would have happened a while ago."

That one actually makes me chuckle out loud. "Yeah, good point you make there, O'Neill." I mean she's in this thing with *me*, after all— and here I am hiding in a closet from my gay lover's sister, after all these years.

"I'm in the closet."

"What?" she asks, clearly confused. "I thought Laurel knew you and Al—"

"No, no, I mean literally. I'm calling you from a closet in the back of the house. I wasn't ready for Laurel to know about...well, me."

"You being with a woman."

"Yeah, so guess I'm in the closet literally and figuratively, matter of fact. It's the bisexual dilemma, you know." An inexplicable wave of sorrow washes over me. "We're always in the closet with somebody."

"But you're ready for me to come over tonight? You're sure?"

"I can't be away from you and do this, Rebecca," I explain. "Can't keep the truth about you from Laurel, either, 'cause like I told you, I'm falling pretty hard here."

"Well, Michael," she replies, comforting as an unexpected summer rain. "At least that makes two of us that feel that way."

And before I can even answer, she hangs up the phone.

Chapter Seventeen: Rebecca

By the time I arrive at Michael's place, his house is dark except for the light over the kitchen sink, illuminating the window like a magic lantern. As I head up the flagstones to the front door, the shadowy interior reminds me of a movie soundstage with all the key players standing hushed in the wings, breath held, waiting for their cue.

There's the drifting aroma of charcoal and burgers grilling, and I realize everyone must be out back, but I ring the bell anyway. When nobody answers, I test the knob and enter. I know my way here now; I'm comfortable. It's becoming a kind of safe haven for me, I think, stepping confidently inside and walking toward the darkened sunroom that leads to the deck.

Outside, through the sliding-glass doors, I spy Andrea at the table with Laurel, their heads bent together, coloring. I mean, that has to be Laurel, even though she's nothing like I expected. She has a cascade of inky black hair, like spun silk, flowing straight down to her lower back—and she has this statuesque quality, an elegance that I've never felt I possess. Without any rational explanation, jealousy riots through every fiber of my being, based on nothing but a single look at Alex's sister.

I thought she'd have red hair and freckles and be a little gawky. I thought she'd be earthy like Marti and put me at ease. But this woman wears beauty like a mystic aura, and I know instinctively that my own broken loveliness won't ever compete.

"Didn't hear you come in," Michael says from behind me, causing me to jump.

"Oh!" I cry, spinning toward him guiltily. "I rang the bell, but—" I point toward the porch in explanation.

"You were watching her." He's staring beyond me to where Laurel inclines her head toward Andrea's, lost in some secret world. I thought this was my domain, that I was the only one who could make the sacred connection.

"She's beautiful," I admit.

Stepping behind me, he draws me near, back against his strong chest, so that we watch them together from this hidden sanctuary. We're voyeurs, lost in the shadows; their theater is ours to see.

"I used to think so," he answers cryptically, his body tensing against mine. "Is that why you were watching her? Because she's beautiful?"

I consider making excuses, but confess, "I think I'm nervous, Michael. It was easier to stand here and watch."

"Why nervous?"

"She's your family. Really," I explain, voice catching, "and so that makes me feel a little weird, I guess. And she doesn't know about me—you said so earlier on the phone—and that makes me feel weird too."

"Don't worry about that."

"But she *is* your family. Don't you care what impression this will make?"

He yields a derisive grunt. "She's not my family anymore, I can assure you of that."

"What's the problem between you two?" I'm surprised that his usual gentleness has given way to something almost savage, and it unsettles me despite his earlier warnings on the phone. He's off-balance with her here; he's hoping I'll be able to right that. "I just wonder if you shouldn't prepare her," I continue. "For the fact that you've got someone new in your life." I'm the interloper, the one trying to step into Alex's shoes, and I've never felt more inadequate to the task than standing here, tucked safely into the dark quiet of Michael's house. I feel dwarfed by his height—too fragile to meet Laurel; too delicate next to him; too feminine. The litany of inadequacies seems endless.

"Let's go outside," he answers, brusque, stepping toward the sliding-glass doors.

"Michael?" I try, but he cuts his eyes at me. There's this simmering anger there that I don't expect.

"Rebecca," he snaps, "no time like the present for Laurel Richardson to get the facts."

I follow Michael onto the deck and Laurel's eyes meet mine, mild surprise registering in their translucent depths. "Rebecca!" Andrea cries, waving at me with far more liveliness than usual. "Michael didn't say you were coming over."

"Well, sweetie," I pause, wondering if Michael's going to answer for me, but he's busy closing the door. "I guess it was kind of a last-minute plan." My mouth pulls, tight and trembling, as I work at smiling. I hope the strange, twisted expression on my face doesn't seem unfriendly.

Laurel doesn't appear to notice, standing and extending one delicate ivory hand. "Hello," she says, and the first thing I observe is how all that regal beauty echoes in her voice. Then, before I can say more, Andrea bounces in her seat, blurting, "Rebecca is Michael's new girlfriend."

"Oh," Laurel answers, her black eyebrows hitching upward. Surprise, confusion, concern—I'm not really sure how to interpret her expression, but I clasp her hand boldly. "Nice to meet you," I say, and she gives an ethereal smile. There's a jangling sound, her layered bracelets tinkle and chime with the motion of her wrist. Looking down, I notice a silver cross, larger than the other charms on her bracelet, weighing the rest down like a leaden anchor.

Michael steps beside me, gesturing between us sternly. "Laurel, Rebecca O'Neill." She nods as we shake hands, then there's this unmistakable awkwardness. She must be sizing me up, must be noticing my scars and my peculiar face. I drop my head, allowing my hair to fall across my cheek like a carefully concealing curtain.

Laurel takes her seat again, and with slow precision she sets down several crayons, two red ones in varying shades, as Andrea excitedly narrates Laurel's arrival today. "Then we went to the Farmer's Market," she tells me, all jittery with enthusiasm, "and drove right by the Chinese Theater because I wanted Aunt Laurel to see it. I mean, she's seen it before, but still."

Michael smiles at his daughter. "Never can get too much Mann's Chinese."

"Did you get out and walk around?" I ask, keeping my head positioned so the scars are concealed from her aunt.

Michael answers brusquely. "Too hot to get out today." He brushes past me and down the steps to the yard. There's something cocky to his gait, a kind of irritated swagger I've never seen before. "I've gotta check the burgers," he explains without so much as a glance at Laurel. "Be right back." Talk about body language.

And talk about me feeling vulnerable as he moves down into the yard, leaving me alone on the deck with Laurel and Andrea.

It's the first time I've ever felt exposed around him, when I've felt anything other than safe. For a moment, I stand hugging myself, wishing I hadn't worn my vintage Lily Pulitzer capri pants. Hot pink with butterflies seemed like a hip idea an hour ago. Now, compared to Laurel's fey, flower-child chic, I seem garish—cartoonish even, with my ugly scars and ridiculous clothes.

Laurel watches Michael with a wistful expression that even I, a stranger to her, can easily decipher. "I wonder if he needs any help," she says.

"He seems a little stressed," I observe, hoping that my outsider's interpretation will comfort her somewhat. In a strange way, I'm already rooting for her, wanting there to be peace between them, even though I have no idea what she did to hurt him. I trust her—like I did Michael from the beginning—on pure instinct. And despite that, I also understand that whatever she did, it warrants his pain.

"Michael's been really crabby all day," Andrea says, watching him seriously, chin in hand.

"Here," Laurel offers, drawing a chair out for me. "Come sit with us. I had no idea Michael was dating anyone."

Michael might not like it, but I decide to be honest. "I wish he'd told you."

"Yes, well, Michael likes to keep things...interesting. And we haven't exactly been talking much recently."

"Rebecca's an actress," Andrea interjects, a look of pride on her face that moves me.

"That's not exactly true anymore, sweetie."

"But you're on television all the time."

I'm opening my mouth to explain the difference between reruns and an active career when Laurel answers, "I *do* recognize you. Rebecca O'Neill—of course, now I see it."

Somehow the idea that she knows who I am, coupled with Andrea's unabashed pride in my former profession, embarrasses me. I can't look at either of them, and feeling my face burn with emotion, I glance toward the grill again to see if Michael's coming back anytime soon.

Laurel gestures to a bottle of wine, a pricey label that I've never seen around here before. "Shall I pour you a glass?"

"Yes, please."

Laurel slides the chilled glass of wine my way. "When did you and Michael begin dating?"

"A month ago. Roughly."

"Michael's not gay anymore, Aunt Laurel," Andrea interjects, laughing and scowling all at once. "Isn't that weird?"

Now my face is really burning and I'm a little ticked at Michael for abandoning me to handle this awkwardness on my own. Andrea resumes coloring. "Michael's kind of like my friend Gretchen's daddy who turned out gay all of a sudden," she explains. "All the kids in class were talking about it. Only, Michael says it probably wasn't all of a sudden." Her frown intensifies, becomes more perplexed. "It's sorta the same with Michael, I guess. Only he turned out *not* gay, huh, Rebecca?"

Great. I'm dating the *ungay*. Is that like the undead?

Laurel gives me a brief but undeniably sympathetic look. "Sweetie," I answer cautiously, "I think Michael's the one who can answer these questions."

"Relationships between grownups can be complex sometimes,"

Laurel adds.

"Oh, I understand about being gay," Andrea answers with a knowing nod. "Michael and I've talked about it a lot. And Daddy explained it to me some too. When it would come up with my friends at school."

"What did your daddy tell you?" Laurel asks, leaning forward.

"That we were a family. Even though maybe people didn't always understand that." Her expression becomes contemplative. "And Michael always says love is what counts."

Tears sting my eyes and I look again to the yard. The man of the moment seems to be lost permanently at the grill right when I need him most.

"You know, I should use the bathroom," I announce, needing to escape. "I'll be right back."

Laurel watches me as I excuse myself, an inscrutable expression on her face, but not an unfriendly one. I even think that she seems like a potential ally, as she gives another one of her ethereal smiles when I leave the table.

Inside, I feel my way through the dark house, but instead of winding down the hallway toward the kitchen, I wander into Michael's bedroom. Flicking on the overhead light, I squint beneath the hazy glare of the antique fixture. There's a cubicle-sized bathroom off the corner of the bedroom, and I walk toward it, thankful for the break from the tense scene outside. This relationship feels so hard sometimes. Michael's own daughter doesn't fully grasp his bisexuality—so what does Laurel think? That he's just walking on the *tame* side for once? I'm not even sure how well Laurel and Michael knew one another before Alex's death, much less what went wrong between them.

Applying fresh lipstick, I stare into the medicine cabinet mirror; it's a tiny bathroom, tiled black and white, circa sixty or more years ago. It's also a *man's* bathroom, in its coloring and simplicity—in fact, I'd go so far as to call it a *gay* man's bathroom, in its immaculate styling and clean, almost severe, lines. Along the taupe walls are framed black and white prints, grouped artistically, and I find myself staring right into the eyes of Alex Richardson.

Laurel has those same eyes. Beautiful like his, so clear and open and fathomless. The picture of him is exactly eye-level to me, and it's a close-up—Alex in a simple black turtleneck, leaning forward so that he stared right into the barrel of the camera lens that day. So that he's staring right into my eyes *this* day.

There are secrets here, I think, peering into Alex's wise, comprehending eyes. I don't understand how to handle them.

You are strong, he whispers near me. Strong enough for them all.

Shivering, I gaze into his cool eyes again. And yet I find such warmth there. Looking up, I discover another black and white picture, this one of Michael holding Andrea on his lap. She's only a baby, smiling and toothless, snuggling close to her lifeline. Michael's hair is disheveled, standing on end like he's just woken up; he's young and arrestingly handsome, gazing at his daughter in pure adoration, cup of coffee in hand.

Maybe it was a Saturday morning and they were relaxing together, enjoying family time; maybe Alex jumped up to grab the camera, as all new fathers are wont to do, eager to capture a priceless moment. But unlike most parents, I think Alex realized somehow that his life was fleeting—one reason this home is covered with photographs taken by him. He made sure his family was documented, archived for posterity.

He made sure of that because they *were* a family, exactly like he told their daughter. Maybe more of a family than I've realized until now: only there's this gaping, empty crater left in the middle of them where Alex used to stand.

Slipping through Michael's bedroom, something makes me hesitate, and I notice another grouping of framed pictures on his dresser. Maybe I'm searching for more clues to understanding this family's mysteries, or maybe I'm searching for more Beautiful Alex pictures, I'm not really sure. What I discover is a faded photograph of a woman, from that era when Kodak added a white border to each image, imprinted with a date stamp on the edging. But I don't need help pinpointing the time period—the woman's rayon party dress, cat-eye glasses and glamorous style clearly date the picture to the mid-1960s. She's a redhead, too, like Alex. Maybe this is his mother? She's holding a baby crooked in her arm and beaming at the camera. A new mother, obviously.

There's something in her smile that puzzles me, though, something familiar and vaguely troubling. Holding the frame within my hands, the woman begins to remind me of Andrea, I realize. So I'm right: this picture must be of Alex and Laurel's mother, what with the red hair and that same delicate smile of Andrea's. But why is she only holding one baby—and more importantly, what about this image unsettles me so?

When Andrea pops her head through the doorway, it gives me a jolt. "Hey!" she announces, grinning at me. "I came to get my Felicity doll to show Aunt Laurel."

I cover my chest with my hand, willing my heart to slow down, and she asks, "What're you doing with Grandma Warner's picture?"

Again, I stare at the haunting image of the redheaded woman. No wonder he fell in love with Alex, I think, almost laughing out loud: like all men, he went looking for his mother. "She's really pretty," Andrea says, studying the picture in my hands, leaning into me. "I have a crocheted blanket that she made in my room, but it used to scare me when I was little. It smells kinda weird and musty."

"Did she make it for you?"

"Oh, I never met her. She made it for Michael when he was a baby, right before she died."

Michael's own mother seems eerily like a member of Alex's family, almost as if, in meeting Alex, Michael were completing some lost portion of his history. I can't imagine how traumatic it must have been for him, never knowing his mother; we haven't really talked about our families much yet, so I'm still learning. But one thing this photograph makes abundantly clear: his life has always been haunted by loss. Staring at the faded photograph in my hands, I'm not sure I can ever adequately fill those empty places in his life.

Andrea vanishes into her bedroom, returning with two dolls in her arms. She introduces each of them to me. One is a fellow redhead, the doll named Felicity. The other is a brunette named Samantha, and in a low voice she explains, "Michael and Daddy gave her to me over a year ago. For Christmas." Their very last Christmas together as a family. Her voice grows confessional, feather-soft, as she hugs Samantha against her chest. "I know Daddy picked her out, 'cause I heard them talking about it."

"Can I see?" I ask, and very gingerly—as if Samantha were made of eggshell china—Andrea passes her into my arms. "You have to be really careful," she explains, sucking on her lower lip. "'Cause her leg's loose. I don't know why, but it is."

Holding the doll close, snuggling her like she were my own child, I say, "I'm good with little girls."

Andrea's face brightens. "Yeah, you are. That's how come I like you, Rebecca."

Dinner surprises me, passing easily, Andrea filling much of the conversational floor space with chatter about little-girl things. It's not lost on me how much more talkative she is around her aunt, the way her air of heavy resolve seems to vanish. After the table is cleared, Andrea produces a catalog filled with doll paraphernalia, clothing and beds and tiny trunks for storage, and they examine these together. Sometime soon I'll need to buy Andrea a gift, and I file this helpful knowledge away.

It's when they're playing there at the table on the deck, the sun nearly set and a chill falling over the Valley, that Michael reaches for my hand. It's the first time he's touched me in Laurel's presence, and without meaning to, I flinch. Yet Laurel remains unfazed—in fact, she doesn't even look at us, but I feel like I'm admitting to a horrible, guilty secret in her presence. Michael squeezes my hand harder, until I feel

Alex's band press into my skin, locking against my nana's sapphire dinner ring.

But he's not holding my hand to comfort me, or reassure me that I have a place here. That's not it. He's flaunting our relationship in front of Alex's sister. Taking my hand like that, bringing me here without warning—he's trying to provoke Laurel, and using me as the weapon.

At precisely the moment his strategy crystallizes for me, Andrea's water-blue eyes grow painfully wide. Her rosebud mouth forms a wounded shape, with only a plaintive, quiet sound seeping out as she stares down at Samantha, the doll her daddies gave her that last Christmas, clutched within her small hand. And one lonely, amputated appendage in the other—poor Samantha's loose leg, fallen off in her hand.

"Let me see," Michael says, immediately the voice of calm parental reason. I can only stare in unabashed horror, knowing how special this doll must be to her. But Andie doesn't budge, simply gapes down in horror at her wounded doll. It's like that old *Waltons* Christmas episode from when I was a child, the one where the little girl opened her present to discover that her new doll's face was shattered.

Michael is around the table before I can even move, dropping to one knee beside her. "Here, sweetheart, let Daddy see."

With a glassy-eyed, dazed look, she hands over the doll, and Michael goes to work. He prods and pokes, already walking back toward the house as he does so. "Let me take her out to the garage," he announces evenly. "To my workbench. I'll get her fixed right up. Don't you worry."

"Don't hurt her," she says, staring up at him, tears filling her eyes.

Laurel slips a comforting hand around her small shoulder. "I'm sure she'll be just fine."

But she's not just fine, and Michael returns with an ashen expression on his face. He would have loved to be the hero, the one who could make everything okay again. I know this, because I wanted him to be the hero too. "We could try New York," Laurel suggests tentatively. "I know they have a doll hospital there, at the store."

Andrea's entire demeanor changes, her eyes lifting hopefully. "I didn't know they had a place to fix them!" From Michael's sinking expression, he didn't either. "Thanks, Aunt Laurel! You're the best!"

Wrapping her small spaghetti arms around Laurel's neck, Andrea buries her face there, holding tight. Michael carefully deposits the doll on the table. "I'll call in the morning, sweet pea," he says. "I can ship the package off from work."

Andie murmurs a "Thanks, Michael," without giving him another glance.

Rubbing his eyes, he tells her, "You need to start saying goodnight, sweetie."

"Aunt Laurel, will you take me inside for bed?" Andrea asks hopefully. "And read me a story?" Of course Laurel happily acquiesces, so together they rise, Andrea slipping her hand into her aunt's as they walk past us.

Michael stands there, disbelieving as he watches them go. "I'm gonna take a walk," he finally mutters.

I'm not sure if I should follow or stay, but his face blanches as he says it, so I decide to give him some space. For a long while I sit in his yard, on the dark deck, listening to the nighttime sounds of Studio City. The freeway is in the distance, the rushing sound of cars and traffic and business. Sipping from my wine, I ache for Michael, for the burden of pain he carries. I ache so badly that the sensation grows inside my chest, like something malignant and devouring that won't let me breathe.

"Is everything okay?" It's Laurel sliding the door open, glass of wine in her hand. "Where's Michael?"

She doesn't understand the fragile balance here, how she disrupted that, stole Michael's chance to win for once.

"He left a while ago."

"Why?"

"Laurel..." I consider leaving the explanations to Michael, but something in her eyes, the love for him I see there, emboldens me. "Because he couldn't fix the doll."

She picks up the leg, holds it against her chest thoughtfully. "But he's calling tomorrow—"

"I know, but see, he couldn't fix the doll, Laurel. And *you* could," I explain, watching sadness darken her features.

Without a word, she sinks into the chair beside me, bowing her head. "I never even thought..."

"Of course you didn't."

"I love him, Rebecca. I just can't figure out how to reach him."

Nodding, I have to laugh. "I know exactly what you mean."

She tosses a wayward tendril of dark hair over her shoulder, glancing back toward the house. "Was it because she wanted me to put her to bed?"

"He's in a lot of pain." I'm voicing the thought that's been coalescing for me tonight. I've known it, of course I have, but it seems his heartache has become clearer to me this evening than before.

"I'm sure he told you that some of that's because of me."

"No, he hasn't."

We fall silent, sipping our wine together as I wonder what she'll share. But all she whispers after a long time is, "He took down every one of my paintings. Did you know that? There were so many here, and now they're all missing. I wonder if he destroyed them?"

"I can't imagine he'd do anything like that."

Digging into her beaded pocketbook, she pulls out a pack of cigarettes, her fingers tremble as she lights up. "Well, you don't know how he feels about me then. I love him and he despises me, Rebecca. You'll learn all that soon enough."

Questions burn within me, begging to be asked, but I refuse—I have to hear Michael's version first.

"I better go after him," I say. "I'm worried."

"Thank you." When she looks at me, there's such gratitude in her clear eyes that I have no doubt she's been telling the truth. She loves him, of that I'm certain—and maybe even in ways that she shouldn't.

There's no sign of Michael out in the front yard, and finally I walk to the end of his driveway and search his street in each direction. A couple of blocks up the way, I spot a rangy shadow loitering beneath the streetlamp. Quickly I cover the distance between us, and the shadow's edges fill in, become recognizable.

"She send you after me?" he asks when I come near.

"I was worried."

"I'm okay, so go back."

"Like I'd leave you out here?" I laugh, as he begins to walk, his back to me. "How could I do that?" I'm following him slowly up the sidewalk, trying to match his lengthy strides without pushing too hard.

"She's such a snobby bitch sometimes. That whole Wellesley-cum-hippie thing bugs the shit outta me."

"She loves you, Michael," I say. "That's really obvious."

He pulls up short, spinning to face me. Heat and anger are in his towering gaze as he rumbles, "Loves me? Really? You're basing that on what, Rebecca? One night around us all?"

I stay calm, staring up into his eyes. "She's upset that you're so upset, Michael."

He makes a grunting sound of denial, but says nothing.

"What happened between you two?" I ask, trying to touch him, needing to be closer, but he backs away. It hurts, him shaking me off, and it hurts that he feels like a stranger. "You're not going to answer me," I state flatly as he marches up the sidewalk, farther and farther away from where I stand rooted, waiting.

"I want to." He turns back to me. "I want to tell you everything, Rebecca." His hands open, reaching, and I rush into his embrace. Strong arms wrap around me, squeezing me close, and neither of us speaks. We stand there beneath the luminous streetlamp, holding one another, utterly safe.

"Then tell me, Michael," I say after a while, rubbing his lower back. "Tell me everything, just like you want, okay?"

"I meant what I said earlier, Rebecca. About falling so hard for you." His heartbeat quickens, speeds anxiously against my chest. I'm scared too—terrified really—as slowly I disentangle and look up into his eyes.

"You're just feeling that way because Laurel's here."

"No." He shakes his head. "No, that's not true, Becca. I meant it 'cause I feel it."

Reaching, I touch his jaw, stroking it slowly with my fingertips. "Michael," I whisper urgently, "*I* feel it too. But let's give it time."

"Is it because of Laurel?" he asks. "Is that why you're so cautious? Because she's here?"

"Of course not—why would it be?" His face darkens, becomes troubled, and it's a warning flag. "*Should* it be a problem for me?"

"Rebecca, I don't want to hurt you."

"Hurt me?"

He shakes his head, staring past me. "Things with Laurel are just damned complicated, that's all."

And then it all becomes clear—painfully, abysmally clear. "You're attracted to her," I say, stepping backwards. "That's it, isn't it? You're attracted to her; she's attracted to you. God, I am so, so dense. How could I not have seen it? There's some kind of thing between you both—except, I realize that sounds ridiculous. But I am right, aren't I? You're attracted to her—"

Michael shakes his head. "Rebecca—"

"I mean, it's not like I can blame you," I blurt. "She's tied to Alex, looks like him—"

"Rebecca, listen—"

"And she's drop-dead gorgeous, so of course you're attracted to her." I spin from him, stepping quickly in the other direction, but he captures me, turning me hard to face him. Taking both of my shoulders within his hands, he steadies me. "How could I have not caught on?" I stammer, feeling my lungs pull cordon-tight. "I must be—"

"Rebecca, she is Andrea's mother," he explains, and I dead stop, silent, wheezing painfully.

"What?" I finally manage, and slowly Michael repeats, "Laurel is Andrea's birth mother."

Rattling, my chest gives a weakened sigh, a dilapidated terrible sound accompanied by immediate vise-like tightening. I only nod, digging in my purse, which for some inexplicable reason I brought out here with me. God really does watch over me.

"Are you okay?" he asks. Fumbling past my car keys and my

wallet, my eager fingers search out my inhaler. "Just a second," I wheeze, and take in a deep breath of my medicine.

Michael watches in silence, surprised. Closing my eyes, I wait to be able to breathe again. "I didn't realize you had asthma." Raw concern is in his voice, and he rubs a strong hand down my arm, soothing me. Hadn't I mentioned this to him before? Maybe I did and he just wasn't ready to hear about my fragile side.

"It..." I struggle to breathe, feeling like my heart will explode inside me, "...hadn't really come up. I thought I'd told you, but maybe...not."

"Are you all right?" His worried gaze fixes on me, those gentle brown eyes opening wide, and for the first time it occurs to me that in loving me, he loves someone *vulnerable*. Someone who, by the wrong twist of fate, might die on him just like Alex did.

"It's because of my attack. Post-traumatic stress...stuff."

"Oh baby, I'm sorry." Bending low, he kisses the top of my head, a chaste, tender kiss that makes something strange knot low inside of me. "I didn't get it before. I'm sorry."

"I was stabbed in the chest, that night. Ben—that's his name, Ben McAllister—stabbed me nine times, actually. I was in ICU a long time, and had a lot of respiratory complications... they think maybe it contributes," I babble, nervous, clutching the inhaler in case I need it again. "Well, to the problem. But really it's anxiety. Not that you could imagine me having an anxiety problem, could you?" I laugh hysterically, feeling tears burn my eyes. What a disaster of a girlfriend I'm turning out to be. I'll be lucky if he ever wants to see me again.

"I'm sorry I brought you into this blind. Tonight." He pulls me close, right into his arms, and I wilt there, pressing my face against that strong chest. "That was unbelievably selfish of me. I'm just really sorry."

"Please don't, Michael." I can't handle his pity—his love absolutely, but never his pity. "I am still a big girl."

"Becca, this stuff with Laurel, it really is just crazy complicated," he explains, stroking my hair, winding his fingers down the length of it. "That's all I was trying to tell you. Not anything else."

"Yeah, it sure is complicated," I laugh, closing my eyes as I lean against him. "She's Andrea's mother."

"Look, but Andie has no idea, okay?" he says. "You do realize that, right? And she can never know."

"Why did you keep it from her?" I ask, feeling confused about the logistics. "If Laurel's her mother, then..."

"We had to protect her," he says. "And especially with Al gone, I had to make sure she never knew the truth. She has to believe he's her natural father, not me."

"You?"

"Yeah, I'm her real father."

Yes, if Alex isn't the father, of course it's Michael. Michael and Laurel are Andrea's parents, only she has no more idea of it than I did until now. Suddenly, I remember that photograph of Michael's mother, and realize that what unsettled me about it was how much Andrea looks like her—and like Michael at the exact same time. Andrea's a crystal-clear reflection of her natural father's bloodline, while still carrying Alex's DNA. Quite literally, they found a way to have a child that came from both their families.

"So Alex was her adoptive father?"

"He adopted her at birth, but we wanted her to think it was the other way around. That I was the one who did the adopting. She thinks we used a surrogate through one of the agencies. We never wanted her to be..." he pauses, rubbing his eyes wearily. "Confused. We just never wanted her to be confused about her family. How it all held together. We wanted to avoid questions like why her aunt was her birth mother...why her father was her uncle." He looks up at me, pain in his eyes. "See what I mean? It was too messy any other way."

"I guess discovering that your aunt is really your birth mother would be pretty confusing," I agree. "You're right."

"And that the daddy you worshipped was actually your uncle."

"But you're forgetting one thing, Michael," I remind him.

"What's that?"

"She deserves to know that her real father—"

"Alex was her real father too."

"Well, but that her *natural* father," I amend, "is alive. Andrea should know that. Don't you think?"

"No." He shakes his head vehemently. "No way. It would devastate her."

"What makes you so sure?" I'm remembering my conversation with Andrea that day in the pool, how lost she sometimes seems. "That little girl thinks her natural father died."

"I'd be taking away the last bit of Al that she's holding onto."

"But they're still blood relatives," I argue. "That wouldn't change."

For a long moment he seems to consider what I'm suggesting, growing quiet. "It's what every couple wants, you know," he finally says, smiling pensively. "A child that reflects them both. Reflects the best of what they are. That Andie popped out with a head full of auburn hair was like a gift. If she'd had my dark hair, she'd have known everything eventually."

"But maybe it's time that she did know, Michael," I suggest gently. "Don't you think Alex would've wanted that?"

"I'm not sure. I've made myself sick trying to figure all the things Allie would've wanted. For Andie, for her future, our family." He rubs a hand across his eyes, shaking his head.

Closing my own eyes, I envision Alex from the photo in the

bathroom. I envision him entrusting me with his family. "I don't believe Alex would want you in so much pain, Michael. I believe he'd want Andrea to know you're her father."

"Rebecca, you don't get it," he disagrees, voice rising irritably. "She can't know. 'Cause if she does, then she'll know who her mother is. And I can't risk losing her to Laurel like that!"

"But why does Laurel scare you so much?"

"Because she wants to take her!" he cries. "Don't you understand? She wants our daughter, Rebecca. That's it."

"She wouldn't do that, would she?"

"Oh, sure she would, you bet." His voice seethes with anger, reflected in his face. "She filed papers after Alex's death."

"But why?" I can't believe that it's true, not after spending the evening around Laurel, seeing how gentle she seems to be. After seeing her unabashed affection for Michael and Andrea.

"She backed down after a few days," he explains. "I begged her. I swear to God, I wasn't above begging. I begged her not to try and take my baby. She was crazy with grief. I know that. Told me so later, and apologized, but..." His jaw twitches as he stares back at the house, as if Laurel could hear him from this end of the street.

I finish for him, "It's hard to forget something like that."

"Yeah, it is. There's just this fear, always, that she'll come after Andie again," he says. "If her mother hadn't talked some sense into her, God knows what would've happened. So I live with it, this insane fear that one day she's gonna tell our daughter everything."

"Well, *you* could tell Andrea the truth," I suggest delicately. "That would take a lot of that fear away." I shiver, feeling the chilled hush that's fallen over the nighttime street.

He shakes his head, walking slowly up the sidewalk. "When Al and I decided we wanted a family, the one thing we both agreed on was we didn't want our kids to get hurt. That we wanted things to feel as normal as possible for them."

I'm not sure what to say, or even what he *needs* me to say. All I know is that these secrets that worked when his partner was alive now seem to be tearing their family apart. In profile, he's the picture of resolute strength—the aristocratic nose, the strong jaw and chin. Too bad I realize that on the inside of the man, the empire is crumbling.

"And now Andrea blames you for everything that's wrong in her life," I finish for him. "Even her daddy's death."

"Kind of ironic, isn't it?" Tears fill his eyes; I see them even in the darkness.

"She loves you like a daddy, Michael," I assure him, as we walk slowly back toward the house. "Anyone can see that."

"Yeah, I do know that's true," he agrees. "But she has so much anger toward me. Can't let it go no matter what."

I turn toward him and don't bother keeping a distance; I reach for his hand and pull it close against my face. He smells like the earth and everything that's natural, as his long fingers mesh together with mine. It's almost like some kind of invisible tension that's been holding him tight ruptures. He even sighs in relief as my hand closes around his.

"She has to blame someone, Michael," I whisper, pressing his hand against my cheek. "And it's a lot easier to blame you."

"Why? Why not blame Robert Bridges, that son of a bitch who was driving the SUV?"

"Oh, Michael, don't you understand?" I ask. "If she doesn't blame you, then it gets a whole lot harder."

"Why?"

"Because she has to blame Alex," I explain softly. "For dying."

Nothing prepares me for the pained, wounded cry that he makes, a keening noise that echoes down the whole street, as he pulls his hand from mine. Or for the way he bolts from me, gone before I can blink, like a deer into the night, back up the street.

Chapter Eighteen: Michael

Out in my driveway, Rebecca and I sit on the tailgate of my truck, holding hands, really quiet. She doesn't push me, doesn't ask why I bolted, and I'm thankful for that. 'Cause if she did, I'd have to admit that I'm not so different from my daughter. That all this roiling anger inside of me keeps searching out a target, and not all of it's reserved for Robert Bridges.

Alex really did a number on me—no chance for goodbye, no final kiss. No last moment to tell him how damn much he meant to me. Not even a visit in my nightly dreams, like everybody else seems to get. Oh, he's in my dreams, all right, but never to touch me or even talk to me. Forgotten memories, fragmented hopes: I have those in abundance. But never Alex Richardson himself.

Rebecca's the only woman I've ever been around who doesn't try and push me too hard. Alex understood that in me—that he could take me to the edge, but there came a point to back down. Somehow, without any need for translation, she seems to realize how to give me that same amount of room. Where Alex was all firestorm and energy and bluster, she's my calm center. She draws me inside of herself, without so much as a word.

"I still have to file his taxes," I say, after we've lingered in silence for a while. "His income tax for last year, the estate tax, it never seems to end. And it just *pisses* me off, that he left me to deal with all that shit." I turn to her, expecting her disapproval or judgment, but she smiles—an open, honest smile, nothing hidden from me. "You think he knows what a prick I am?"

She laughs. "I don't think he's worrying about that, Michael."

"You think he knows what a jerk I've been to you?" I demand, and she withdraws her hand from mine. "That was lousy, the way I set you up tonight, Rebecca. I'm really sorry."

"You used me with Laurel. To get at her." Her voice is quiet, but edged with raw emotion. She understands exactly the game I was playing; no wonder her anger has surfaced. "To shock her, I suppose."

"Yeah, some way to treat the woman I..." *Love. The woman I love?* The emerald eyes fix on me, expectant. I have to be sure, before I tell her for real—after all that she's been through, I owe her that much. "I should never have brought you here tonight without more preparation."

Her face flames hot; I can see it even by the dim street light above us. "Michael, being honest is important to me. Jake lied to me in dozens of ways, and I swore I'd never go back to that again. I need you to be truthful, even when it's not pretty."

"What you see is what you get with me. You know that." I pause, wondering how I can rationalize the secrets about Andrea. "Protecting my daughter, though, you got to know how tough that is."

"I understand that," she says, nodding her head adamantly. "I do. I just wish you'd told me about Laurel before, that's all."

"Me too." I run my hand down the length of her hair, wanting her to know how damn much she means to me. None of this is about her. I want her to know that too.

"And it makes me uncomfortable, when people figure out who I am," she continues, her voice trembling slightly with emotion. "Figure out what happened. I mean, of course people know. The world knows, but when I go into something like this, and then someone remembers or recognizes me—well, Andie told her, but you get my point."

She's rambling like she does when she's nervous and self-conscious, and I hate that I made her feel this way. "Baby, it's just that people find you interesting, your acting career and all," I try, knowing it sounds lame. "That's good."

"But when people figure out my *story*," she presses, winded again, like earlier. "About Ben and—and my attack, you know. I hate that."

She touches her cheek, reflexively going to the scars, and for once I catch her hand in mine, stopping her. "I love what you are," I insist. "Exactly what you are."

"Michael, stop." She wriggles her hand out of mine, but this time I capture her face within my palms, turning it upward until I stare into her eyes, glittering with emotion.

"You are beautiful, Rebecca. Hear me when I say it." She searches my face, her eyes shifting. I know she wishes I'd stop, that I'd let her hide, but damn it, I don't feel like it tonight. "I *like* the scars, Rebecca," I repeat, still holding her firmly under the spotlight of my full gaze. "I like that you're different and *real*. Hell, I love everything about how you look, baby."

She winces visibly, but I won't back down. I'm fueled by all the emotion of this night. "Don't you get how proud I was to introduce you to Laurel? It wasn't just about shocking her or pissing her off. I wanted her to meet my girl." The mask of pain vanishes, replaced by her quirky, lopsided grin. "And for what it's worth," I add, "you're the only woman in forever who's managed to light my fire. That alone is some kind of major accomplishment."

And then, we're kissing. I don't even know who moves closer, who breaks through the veil separating us, but suddenly her lips are meeting mine. Her breasts press against me, her long hair brushes soft as silk against my cheek, and I'm touching her everywhere, all the curves and softness. I find her hips, feel the buds of her nipples, hard through the cotton material of her blouse. And I feel her exploring me. Whatever's *not* been working between us physically—whatever's held us back—has been unstopped, that desire and heat always shimmering between us has rushed to the surface. We've broken free, found our way to sunlight and air and life, right here in my truck.

"Here." Reaching behind us with one hand, still holding her with my other, I quickly spread out a tarp, a work cloth left here in the bed of my truck. "Here, Becca," I urge her into the back of my pick up. Like two good southerners, we're ready to lose it all in the bed of a 4x4.

Together we curl there, obscured from all my neighbors, wrapped in one another's arms. Her hands seem so small as they explore my chest, my back, as they trail up beneath my T-shirt, her warm flesh pressed against my own. It seems we can't stop touching one another, that we each need to know that the other is real.

"Michael," she moans in my ear as I begin toying with the button of her capri pants, working frantically to open them. "Michael, we're in your truck."

"I know." I laugh breathlessly, pressing her onto her back, being gentle as I can be under the circumstances. Feeling hard metal against my knees, even through the thick material of the tarp.

She laughs with me, clasping my face in her hands, steadying me until I'm staring hard into those warm eyes of hers. "Michael, this is a truck," she enunciates clearly. "I am a good girl. I do not *do it* in a truck." See Conan Strike Out. *Here we go again*, I think, and bury my face against her neck with an anguished groan of sexual frustration. I can almost hear the sound of Chuck Barris's giant gong.

"Michael," she whispers in my ear, a soft panting sound that's all girl. "I want our first time to be really special."

"Me too." I nearly beg, "But soon, baby."

"Maybe in Malibu?" she suggests, running her fingers through my hair, reminding me of our Fourth of July plans for next weekend at Casey's house.

"Yeah, maybe in Malibu," I mumble, feeling the crash of sexual hope. "Maybe Marti'll take Andrea out one night or something."

And I want our first time to be special too. Sure as hell don't want it in the back of my truck in the driveway. Of course she's right; I'm just a little out of my head lately. Rolling off her, I collapse with a sigh.

One of these days, this queer boy is going to figure out how to get a damn girl in bed.

"Just for the record, I don't think Alex is worrying about what's happening here," she says, snuggling close in the crook of my arm. We're still lying together under the dark, open sky, cuddling like a pair of lovers, even though I've barely even touched her breasts. I feel like we're lovers already, though. That's the weird thing about being with Rebecca.

"You don't know, though." Stroking her hair, I nestle closer. "Maybe it goes both ways. Maybe Al knows how mad I've been at him. Maybe he's watching everything." I glance back at the house, lowering my voice self-consciously. "And maybe he's pissed at *me*."

Her green eyes narrow, but I see warmth glinting in their depths. "Michael, Alex isn't worried with the things of this world."

"Yeah? How do you know that?" I ask, voicing the question that perpetually stays on my mind.

"He's gone on," she says quietly. "To someplace else. Someplace *better*."

"I'm not sure I buy the whole afterlife idea."

She stares at the sky, considering. "Then where do you think he is?"

"I don't honestly know. Maybe he's right here with you and me." I snort with ironic laughter. "Now there's a thought." I look around and imagine what he'd say about the deep, toe-curling kiss we shared a while ago. Oddly, I have the sense he'd approve. Especially of Rebecca.

"Was Alex a spiritual person?" she asks, the blonde eyebrows drawing together in an expression of intense concentration that I find adorable.

"What do you mean, exactly?"

"Well, did he believe in God? Have faith in something bigger?" she explains, choosing her words carefully. "Someone guiding us beyond *this* world."

"Oh, absolutely, yeah. I was his pet heathen," I laugh, feeling a surge of love for him. "He never gave up on converting me. He believed in God. Jesus. All that stuff."

She loops one arm around my neck. "But you don't?"

It's impossible to hold back the derision I feel. "According to the Christians, Jesus isn't interested in my kind." According to my *father*, I want to say, but keep those words inside myself. "Not a *hom-o-sexual*." I imbue the word with all the southern gusto of a tent-revival preacher.

She shakes her head in denial. "Jesus came to the world. The whole world."

Dropping my charade, I become serious again. "Alex always believed. Truly. He was passionate about his faith." I feel something strange catch fire inside of me. "So yeah, maybe Al's in heaven. I'd like to believe that."

I wonder if all those kids he loved and lost at the hospital were waiting for him, when he made it there. Sometimes I even picture them forming a joyful knot around him, like a garland of flowers to crown his good deeds, all their tiny bodies pressing in. I've pictured him with his father, too, the man he worshipped as a child but lost too soon; I've pictured them together, catching up on years' worth of lost time. That's a lot more comforting than the notion that all his fire and vigor were simply extinguished in the blink of an eye.

"When you were in the hospital, did you think about death?" I ask her, since after all, she came close to the other side.

She stares up at the sky, contemplating. The lights of our city have created a hazy halo overhead, pressing down on our darkness. "I did have a near-death experience. Not when I was in the hospital, but..." Beside me, I feel her whole body quiver with emotion.

"Becca, tell me," I urge, brushing my fingers through her hair, combing it back from her cheek so I can stare into her eyes.

"There was a moment, after Ben left me—he thought I was dead, you know. He left me there on the sidewalk of my apartment and I remember seeing myself from above and thinking, *That is so much blood. Who is that poor girl?*" She gives me a bittersweet smile. "It was like being on a Ferris wheel, where I kept going higher and higher and the world on the ground got smaller and smaller, and I couldn't take my eyes off this tiny little woman on the ground. I felt so bad for her, losing all that blood. And then this warmth began to overtake me." She places her palm over her chest, rubbing it. "Like nothing I'd ever felt before, and then I didn't care about the woman anymore. All I wanted was more of the warm feeling, wrapping all around me. I heard singing, all these voices praising God and Jesus. Like millions of voices, all at once."

She stops, swallowing, and I notice that she's begun to breathe heavily, sucking in big gulps of air. I don't want her asthma to kick in again. "Becca, it's okay. We don't have to talk about this," I soothe, pulling her closer. She forms against me like a reedy little flower, and I feel the strong muscles in her arm—the powerful biceps that betray how hard she trains her body—as she nestles close.

Gazing up into my eyes, she whispers, "Michael, I didn't want to come back. The feeling of love and goodness there, it was that strong." She searches my face, and I realize that she's never told anybody this much. "Do you understand?" she asks, and I nod mutely. "Where Alex is, it's not like this world."

"But you *did* come back."

"I guess the whale kind of spit me back out," she laughs, overly loud. Her near-death experience is a much bigger part of her internal

179

world than she might have wanted me to know.

"You never told anybody about this, did you?"

"Michael, ever since I came back, it's like something inside of me has been frozen. It's been hard and cold and dead feeling. But since meeting you and Andrea, all of that has begun to thaw out. I'm not sure I wanted to talk about how it felt until now. I mean, where I went, it's real. God is there, but I'm stuck here." Then she laughs, one of those golden, joyful giggles of hers that makes me laugh too. "Besides, my mother would *so* freak if she knew I went to heaven!"

I nod, grinning, "Yeah, that's kind of a freaky statement there, Rebecca. By most anyone's standards."

Her expression grows serious again. "But Michael, I also wanted you to know because of Alex. I want you to understand that where he went, it's not like here. All the suffering and inconsequential stuff, it's all gone. He's happy there."

I can't find my voice. I try, but it just flat eludes me. What I want to tell her is how much I've worried about his last moments. Whether he hurt or suffered. Whether he knew he was going to die. That one gets me most: the thought that he saw that car coming and comprehended what was happening to him. It keeps me awake at night, wondering if at the moment of impact an explosion of pain rocketed through his whole six-foot-four frame; if it sounded in his brain like rifle fire.

And it keeps me awake, questioning whether he simply vanished into ether and nothingness.

Reaching for her right hand, I touch her scar, the jagged flame through her center palm where she tried to stop the knife. "How bad did it hurt, Rebecca?" I need to know. More than anything else I've ever asked of her, I need this. "When he stabbed you?"

"I—I don't really know," she answers. "I can remember trying to breathe, how hard it was. I can remember the feeling of the knife cutting me, the cold sensation of it. How unreal it all seemed. I couldn't believe it was happening—that's what I kept thinking, that it wasn't real. And I remember the fear, but I'm not sure about the pain."

"Why not?"

She pulls my hand close beneath her chin, settling it there before she speaks. I know that what she's about to say is important just by the way she's staring into my eyes.

"Because, Michael, I don't remember the pain. Afterwards, in the hospital, sure, it was unbearable," she answers in a hushed, almost reverent voice. "But nothing of how it felt while Ben was stabbing me, or even right after he left me for dead."

"Rebecca, I'm not sure I understand what you're saying—"

"Michael, when I went to that place? When I left here and started there?" she says, her voice filled with wonder. "Well, it was so perfect, I think God took all that pain away."

✧

Rounding the hallway, back toward my bedroom, I see that Laurel's still on the deck. The glowing ember of her cigarette flares in the inky darkness as she takes a drag. I suppose she's waiting for me, hoping to talk before bed. Then again, this is her ritual, smoking late like this. If she were home, back in Santa Fe, she might paint until the middle of the night, or morning even, if the muse were whispering to her just right.

I want to tell her how sorry I am—sorry that we can't ever seem to get things right. We should be able to, with as much as we both loved him, with as close as we once have been. But then I think of that day last summer, just a month after he died. The papers being served to me at work; I think of sitting in my truck without the air-conditioning on, calling Marti, my hands shaking so bad I could barely dial the numbers on my cell phone. "Michael, calm down," she urged. "Calm down and tell me what's going on." Marti's own voice was shaking—it was too soon after losing him; too soon for another shocking phone call *not* to unsettle her.

"It's Laurel," I managed to grind out. "She's trying to take Andie away from me."

Marti had known Laurel her whole life, wouldn't believe it, insisted there must be some misunderstanding. After a few tense moments, I phoned Laurel directly, there at her gallery. Her voice was tight, distraught as she told me that I shouldn't be talking to her. Only to her attorney.

"Are you fucking kidding me?" I shouted into the phone. "Laurel, you gotta be kidding, 'cause you'd never tell me to talk to you through a damn attorney!"

"Michael, there's not an easy way to handle this," she answered, and seemed eerily calm. "But we must think about Andrea's well-being."

"No way in hell you're taking my child from me. No way!" I shouted, and then, without even waiting to hear the lame explanation she'd begun to offer, I hung up the phone on her. After that, I lawyered up—fast, just like her—and prepared for an ugly battle. Only when Ellen phoned me the next night did I finally lose it, bawling like a baby into the phone, crying so hard that my whole body shook with it.

Her words, in classic Ellen Richardson style, touched the surface of much deeper veins of emotion. "Laurel has spoken with her attorney," she said, "and everything is now resolved, darling. She's so sorry, Michael, you must understand."

"You fixed it," I said numbly, realizing that once Ellen had figured out what Laurel was up to, she'd intervened.

"Laurel never wanted to hurt you," she explained gently. "She is very sorry for what she's done."

"Sorry?" I cried, wiping at my eyes. "Like that settles it?"

"Michael, darling, you are hurting so badly. I know that. But try to understand, if you can, that Laurel is too."

I do believe Ellen was telling the truth that night—that Laurel never would've tried a trick like that unless she'd been blinded by grief. But it doesn't make it any easier to believe her now. And Rebecca thinks I could let Andie know the facts?

Watching Laurel sitting there on the deck, feet tucked up beneath her, hoping I'll come back, I know that trust, once lost, isn't easily found.

Slowly, without taking my eyes off her, I back away.

Entering my bedroom, I discover Laurel's shopping bag placed neatly in the center of my quilt. She must've snuck it in here while I was outside with Rebecca. The bedside lamp's been turned on too, creating a warm, inviting mood for the whole room. She's nurturing me, or at least trying to, by leaving a gift here for me to discover.

Standing in the center of the room, I stare at the bag and imagine its contents. It's a painting; I know that. I knew that earlier today, when she told me she had a present for me, for the house. The question is, what would Laurel have painted for me now? What did she *hear* when she sat down to create this mysterious, faceless work specifically for me?

Turning Al's band on my finger, I swear I hear him tell me to loosen up. "You over-think this stuff, Michael," he'd laugh. "Just see what it is." Alex loved surprises, gifts, and he especially loved it when Laurel bestowed a new painting on us. There was no greater fan of Laurel's lyrical work than her own brother.

Reaching into the brown paper bag, I feel around, and can tell it's a small canvas, maybe a couple feet wide, no bigger. Carefully I retrieve it, the crumpled tissue paper rustling within my hands. I peel back the layers until the painting opens to me like an exotic flower. Dramatic splash of fiery red cresting over a mass of succulent green and blue, and there's the familiar coppery amber—unbelievably, she managed to capture the exact shade of his hair.

She's painted Alex. Alex on a beach, an abstraction, his pale arms extended upward to the sky as he holds the sun, the light literally radiating into his whole body like powerful cosmic energy. He's rejoicing, the way it looks to me. Sweet Alex in the afterlife, right on the beach, exactly like in Andrea's dreams. Exactly like Rebecca just told me outside.

She's made him beautiful, filled with all that spirit and kinetic *energy* that defined each day of his life. Somehow, miraculously, she's detailed my lover's very essence, and I know this small painting is Laurel's love poem to me, to what I had with her brother—and it's her visual sonnet begging me for forgiveness.

Problem is, I'm not sure I'm capable of that kind of forgiveness. Not with the truth out there, the truth of Andrea's parentage, waiting to destroy me like it always is—because a whole lot of my bitterness isn't even about what Laurel did. It's about all the power she still holds, and what she might do with it one day. It's about how Alex dying changed the delicate balance of things, here in *this* world. Why didn't we work this stuff out before he died?

Dropping heavily onto the bed, staring at the image of him I hold within my hands, I know exactly why we didn't settle so many issues—because we always thought we had another day.

Allie, you left me in a mess of trouble, I whisper to him in my head. Why aren't you here to help me figure it all out, baby?

That's the real source of my anger, not the taxes. It's that Alex should've realized he might die. He left a will, a planned estate, money for Andie's college—he just didn't tell me what to do with the truth about our daughter.

Setting the painting on the dresser, I lie back on our bed and lose myself in the swirling colors, the powerful brush strokes. I nearly fall asleep like that, bedroom lights on, staring at Alex, arms reached high to God in heaven. I'm not even sure how late it is when I finally strip out of my jeans and turn out the light.

I enter the glass atrium by a maze of other rooms. First through a hatch-like portal, then a narrow hallway; finally coming into the bright, airy openness of the butterfly house. At the far end of the palm-lined path, squatting down to Andrea's six-year-old level is Alex, patiently explaining something to her. Metallic purple and ginseng-brown wings flit past her eyes as she reaches a timid hand to try and catch just one of the dozens of butterflies.

"Don't touch, doll," he cautions, capturing her tiny hand in his much larger one. "We can only look, okay? This is their home, not ours."

"But I *want* to touch them so they'll know how pretty I think they are."

"They know, precious girl," he assures her, smiling at her fleeting innocence. "They know."

Then, Alex looks up at the sky, squinting as if he expects what comes next. As if he's commanded it in some way. From above, a cascade of spectacular butterflies comes pouring through an opening in the ceiling, a river of iridescence floating right down to Alex and Andrea. Nothing stops them, all these pulsating, beating wings, descending from the sky overhead.

Alex sees me and waves, smiling broad as life, his strong hand clasping Andrea's shoulder.

"Daddy!" she cries out loud, reaching with both hands toward the butterflies. But he seems oblivious, keeps waving at me, smiling. Again Andrea cries out, and this time her voice surprises me in its despair: she's forgotten the butterflies and instead focuses on him, hopping beside him, hungry for him to notice her.

Then again, even more plaintive, "*Daddy!*"

Abruptly I wake to find the covers tangled around my legs and Andie wedged beside me beneath the sheets. She must've walked here in her sleep—either that, or made her way silently while I slept on, oblivious. Her small frame has formed against my much bigger one, and she's tucked up against my ribs like a warm, lumpy pillow. Over and over in her sleep she's moaning, "Daddy...Daddy."

"Sweet pea, wake up." Slipping a tentative hand onto her back, I nudge her. "You're dreaming." She doesn't move, only cries out again, and it seems nothing will rouse her. I keep at it, becoming more insistent, and finally she jerks awake, staring up at me in the darkness.

"You're okay," I assure her, remembering Weinberger's strategies for coping with these nightmares. "I'm right here. You're okay."

"I'm scared," she mumbles, blinking back the sleep, her delicate mouth turning downward in a disturbed expression.

"You're right here with me," I promise, nestling down in bed again and pulling her close. "You're okay. Nothing to be scared of."

For a while, we're silent except for the soft sound of her childlike breathing, until she whispers, "The accident was scary."

I sort through a strategy. "But that's just a dream now, precious. You know that. You understand the difference."

"But it could happen again, though. What if it happens again?" She looks up at me with a lost expression, beseeching me to be more than mortal. Less vulnerable than her other daddy proved to be. I can't promise that I won't die: it's not a promise that's mine to give.

"I'm right here," I whisper back, willing her to feel reassured. "I am not going anywhere."

Nuzzling close, she exhales, a drained kind of sigh, and without another word she drifts back into sleep. But not me. For hours it seems I lie there, staring at the ceiling, listening to my daughter's downy-headed sleep sounds, praying that God will always protect me. Until the first purple light cracks the sky, I beg the One in whom I barely believe to keep me safe and alive and whole for the sake of this one precious girl who needs me so much.

I beg Him to help me believe like Alex did—at least just a little.

✧

I wake to find the covers peeled back and Andrea gone. From the kitchen, I hear cheery-voiced laughter and giggling. The nightmare's forgotten, left in the flotsam of darkness, and now she's back in the embrace of Laurel's tender care. Good. For once I actually welcome it because Andie needs a mother in her life. Not that I *want* it to be Laurel, of course, but if she can get some nurturing from her aunt, then I think that's a good thing. Especially after last night.

I wonder how often she dreams about the accident? I thought that ended a while ago, but from what she said in the middle of the night, I've gotten to wondering. Maybe Rebecca was right, maybe I shouldn't spend so much time fighting Laurel. I think of the painting she left on the bed, our conversation in the guest room yesterday: maybe I can trust her, like she wants me to believe.

Wandering into the living room, I discover Andie and Laurel on the floor, pasting together a collage. When Andrea spies me, she leaps to her feet, hiding the work behind her back. "Don't look!" she cries and I frown, confused until she explains with a grin, "It's a surprise, Michael."

"Oh, I see." I touch the top of her auburn head, giving it a love pat. "A *surprise*."

"It was Aunt Laurel's idea."

Laurel won't meet my gaze, and I guess she's uncomfortable about last night. Strange, but I've woken feeling different this morning, a little more ready to let her back in.

They go back to their collage, and I head to the kitchen to pour a cup of coffee. "You know," I call to them across the bar, into the living room where they're spread on the floor, "I was thinking about phoning into work. My boss said if I wanted, I could take today off since I've got... family here."

"Yea!" Andrea cries, and her glee at the prospect of me kicking around with them warms me on the inside.

Laurel smiles at me cautiously. "I'd love that, Michael," she agrees. "I'd love to have you with us all day."

"And who's up for some waffles?" I ask.

This one really gets a reaction out of Andrea, because she loves to pour the batter into the iron. "Can I help?" she asks, already scrambling to her feet.

"We'll make them together," I say, and she beams with delight. I'm not sure we've made waffles like that since Allie died. Which leads me to believe that Laurel's visit may actually be a good thing.

After breakfast, Laurel, Andrea and I bike around Studio City. It's so damned hot I swear I might expire by the time we peddle past the public golf course. So we stop for a small lunchtime picnic that Laurel has prepared for us, spread out on a park bench right along the roadside, beneath leafy palms that provide us some reprieve.

Laurel's got her long black hair swept up into a neat ponytail, looking more athlete than hippie today. I can relax around her more this way, because she reminds me of Alex in her Nikes and running shorts, fixing me with that clear blue gaze. Not sure if it was my long talk with Rebecca, or maybe the painting, but some of my bile seems to have dissipated. I've even had fun, biking around like a family.

Andrea seems to catch onto that vibe. "People probably think you're my parents," she says, taking a bite of her turkey sandwich. Poking through her lunch sack, she inspects the rest of what Laurel's packed.

I slip my arm around her. "Well, I *am* your father," I remind her with a forced laugh. There seems no other way to respond. Thankfully, Laurel avoids us both.

"Michael. You *know* what I mean." Andie sighs in exasperation. "That you're my *father* and Aunt Laurel's my mother. That's probably what people think, seeing us here."

"The assumptions people make," I reply numbly, and Laurel looks away, out at the passing traffic.

"We could pretend that it's true," Andie suggests. "That you're my parents, just for today. That would be cool. Aunt Laurel, I'll call you Mommy all day and you have to answer." She turns to me, excited, but then her expression becomes perturbed—what will she call me?

"I could be Daddy," I suggest gently. "Just for today."

"If I'm Mommy, then Michael definitely gets to be Daddy," Laurel agrees, her eyes meeting mine for a fleeting moment. "That's only fair."

"Okay," Andrea agrees reluctantly as she thinks on it a little more, taking another bite of her sandwich. "But only for today." Then she spies a cat nosing around in the bushes behind us, and goes to offer it a tiny bit of turkey, leaving me alone for the first time all morning with Laurel.

Neither of us knows what to say, but then I break that silence. "Loved the painting, Laurel. It's gorgeous. I've gotta figure out where to put it, though."

"Maybe with all the rest of them?" she suggests with a wry smile. *Busted.*

"I kinda figured you'd notice that." I nod, staring out at traffic, avoiding her. "That I took the others down."

"If you don't want them—"

I silence her with my upraised hand. "I want them, Laurel. I want them and you're not getting them back."

"Well, it's just, they're like my children, Michael. Do you understand?" Her right eyebrow migrates upward toward her hairline as she talks, a physical trait of Alex's. The more excited or agitated he got, the more his eyebrow did the exact same thing. "They're connected to me, part of me. It hurts, not knowing where they are."

I ignore the comment about her children. I ignore all that she's just managed to cram into those few short sentences. Gently, I lift my hand and touch her eyebrow, tracing the outline of it with my forefinger. "They're in the attic," I almost whisper. "Wrapped in paper, boxed really careful." The silky shape of that eyebrow, so familiar beneath my finger, the brush of the hairs, the dramatic lift...it's so like his that it almost breaks me.

Laurel blushes, dropping her head. But she doesn't ask why I'm touching her, thank God. Maybe she understands. "Oh. Good," she says, nodding as I drop my hand away. "That's good."

"I have always loved your work, Laurel," I say, even more softly. "That never changed."

Tears fill her eyes. "I dreamed the one of Alex. The one I gave you last night," she explains. "It sang to me, in a dream."

"That's kind of weird."

"No, it's not," she insists seriously. "It sang for you, Michael."

Andrea returns, interrupting my thoughts. "*Mommy,*" she announces, jarring me, "look what I found!" She's carrying a smooth, flat rock, held like treasure in her small open palm. "You can paint on it."

"Thank you, sweetie." Laurel leans forward, kissing Andrea's cheek. "This is a great find. Maybe we can paint on it together, before I go home."

Andie agrees, bobbing her head excitedly. "That's exactly what I thought."

"Hey, maybe the rock'll sing too," I quip as Andie plops between us again.

"Michael, that painting has life," Laurel insists in a firm voice. Something in her words makes me shiver despite the midday heat. "It will speak to you, but you have to listen." I think of falling asleep last night, staring at it, of the sway it already held over me. I think of Alex, gone from this world, but maybe having life inside that canvas.

"Laurel, it's a beautiful painting," I say. "I love it, seriously. I was just teasing you."

She smiles, her eyes crinkling at the edges. It's hard to believe that we started out so young together, and now we're getting older. "I do know you, Michael Warner." She reaches for me, touching my hand very gently. "I know you well and love you much."

"Yeah, yeah," I grumble, even though she's moved me with her words. "You're just trying to get those paintings back out of storage."

"No, they're yours," she disagrees, turning the smooth stone in the palm of her hand. "They may be my children, but they belong to you now. Not me." I get her pointed meaning, the reassurance that she's offering.

"You've been very generous." I slip my arm around Andrea's shoulder. "With Alex and me. Those are some amazing paintings."

"So, Daddy," Andie interrupts, "this mean we can hang some of Mommy's stuff up again?"

"Only if you stop calling Aunt Laurel *Mommy* like that."

"Why?" she asks, her auburn eyebrows knitting together in innocent confusion.

"Because it's freaking weird, that's why." And then we all laugh together, sitting there on our little park bench along the golf course, enjoying the shade of the palm trees as a family in our own strange, imperfect way.

After a quiet dinner and probably too many bedtime stories, Laurel kisses Andie goodnight, stroking her hair back from her cheek, then leaves me there in the dark, only the hall light spilling into her room.

"I had fun today," Andrea says, her small fingers curling around the edge of the blanket as I tuck Felicity in beside her. "It made me think of when Daddy was still alive. We used to do fun stuff, back then. Family stuff," she adds. "I miss all that."

I never noticed when the family times stopped—have I been that wrapped in a haze of grief for the past year?

"Maybe we could do that kind of stuff with Rebecca some time?" she continues, licking her lips thoughtfully. "Go on picnics, or to the zoo. You think maybe we could?"

"I'd love that." I press a kiss to her forehead, inhaling her fresh little-girl scent of shampoo and Ivory soap. "And I bet Rebecca would too."

"Okay, well, goodnight," she says, and I squeeze her hand.

"I love you." Turning on the CD player by her bed—her nightly ritual for falling asleep, to Sarah McLachlan—I move toward the doorway.

"Sleep tight," she calls out to me.

"Sleep tight, precious girl."

"Don't let the bed bugs bite." I flick on her nightlight, and am about to answer, when that soft, breathy voice adds in a whisper, "*Daddy.*"

Chapter Nineteen: Rebecca

"Someone's on the phone for you from Foglight Productions," Trevor speakerphones me. "Says she's putting together an *About the House* fan gathering."

"Oh, geez." I groan, continuing to type an e-mail to a producer. "Tell her no."

"It's a fundraiser, she says."

"No."

"The fans would go crazy if you agreed." Trevor has decided that me participating in this fan gathering is a good thing, and has therefore become this woman's co-conspirator.

I reach for my coffee—my fourth cup and it's not even noontime yet. "Put her on," I grumble, adjusting my headset.

We talk and it turns out the fan thing is in late August; if I would be willing to come and sign publicity stills and glad-hand with the fans at a celebrity auction, it would truly crown the event a success. "I mean, you're the ungettable get," the coordinator tells me, none-too-tactfully. "*Book Rebecca O'Neill*, that's what I was told. You're my mandate."

"I've never done one of these before. Never," I explain, feeling overwhelmed already. "I just don't do fan events, not after what happened to me."

"Well, Ms. O'Neill, I completely empathize with that," she placates, handling me with all the careful acumen of a celebrity organizer. "But this is a fundraiser, to help children with leukemia. And that's such a worthy purpose for participating."

"Kids with cancer?" I'm thinking of Alex, of course, and of how strange that this benefits his very cause. Well, not so strange—cancer is common enough. But then she adds, "All proceeds are to go to the children's hospital at UCLA."

"I'll do it." Who said that? Me?

"Oh, my gosh!" the coordinator squeals. "Wow, thank you, Ms. O'Neill. Thank you so much for agreeing. You've really made my week."

I'm betting this coordinator gets a bonus if she can fulfill her "mandate".

"Please just make sure security is tight," I caution, feeling my stomach flutter with unsettled anxiety. "I may bring my own bodyguard with me. Hire someone for the event myself. I know that may seem like overkill, but—"

"You have my guarantee," she promises. "And I completely understand."

I check the August date in my calendar. It's a little less than two months from today. I wonder if Michael would like to go? I could introduce him firsthand to the crazed fans of *About the House*. The weirdness of the subculture, of long-limbed tall girls masquerading in blonde wigs as five-foot-two-inch tiny me. Of people auctioning off scarves or sweaters for a thousand bucks all because I happened to wear one of them in a single episode. Michael needs to know about this facet of my life, I think, and make a note to mention the event.

The phone calls keep coming all morning long, and I'm about to dart out for a quick bite at the commissary when Trev steps into my office, his face ashen. "Line two," he says, closing the door behind him. He leans there, slightly breathless and disconcerted. "It's Jake. He absolutely insisted that I put him through. That's bloody wrong, don't you think?"

Jake hasn't relented, not since the calls began; I think he's left a total of eight messages in the past month. "I'll talk to him." I'm perversely calm at the prospect of speaking to my ex-boyfriend after all this time. *Three whole years.* "It's really no big deal." I shoo Trevor out of my office, and although Jake can't see me, I freshen my lipstick, blotting my lips together before I pick up the phone.

"Hello, Jake Slater." I manage to sound sexy and composed, thanks to Michael. A few months ago, and his call would have meant the world to me. Even a month ago, right before I met Michael. Now I'm only looking for some closure on a bad chapter in my life.

"Rebecca. Hey." He sounds marginally stunned, like he didn't believe I'd actually answer. "How are you?"

"Oh, you know, Jake," I laugh, sipping my coffee. "Just peachy. Things are going great for me."

"That's what I hear. You've got a load of heat, Rebecca." He's still got that sleepy-sounding, stayed-out-until-four-doing-coke kind of voice. "The Kingsley deal is buzzing all over town."

"Good timing, that's all it takes." I'm thinking of how *off* his timing has been ever since the show was cancelled. The time-cop pilot, the spate of poor choices. The gossip that he's still coking around way too much.

"I want to see you, Rebecca. It's why I've been calling." He doesn't sound so sleepy-voiced now—he sounds focused and direct.

I count out five seconds of distinct silence, then say, "Jake, that's nice. But the thing is? I don't want to see you."

"You're not still pissed, are you?" How petty of me, being angry with him for such a trivial thing as abandoning me after I nearly died.

"No, Jake, I am *not* pissed, but I have a boyfriend, someone pretty steady and serious—"

"God, Rebecca, I only meant as friends!"

"Oh really, Jake?" I ask blithely. "Because I heard Darcy dumped you, so naturally I assumed you were sniffing your way back to home port."

"All I want is to check up on an old friend," he replies, tittering softly, and I think he's amused to even talk about being dumped. "Figured you'd dig that. Shooting the shit together, like the old days. Get a couple of glasses of wine, you know."

Intentionally, I call out to Trevor through the door, instructing him to phone CAA to talk about deal points on a contract. Then, counting in my head I allow ten seconds of silence to pass. "Jake?"

"Uh, huh."

"I don't want to get together, okay?" I answer, smiling to myself. Feeling healthy and whole and triumphant, even if I'm gloating a tad.

"Just a thought," he says. "Just a thought."

"Not ever, Jake. I'm over you, and besides, I'd rather spend that time with people I actually like."

And without so much as saying goodbye, I hit the disconnect button on my phone.

That's when I realize he's probably going to be at that same dang fan gathering I just committed to attending, and I bury my face in my hands with a groan. Except, I'll have Michael at my side. Strapping, gorgeous Michael, of the deep voice and the towering six-foot-three-inch frame. That should be enough to intimidate Jake, who at five foot eight has a serious short guy's complex. Grabbing my purse, I head out for a quick lunch, and decide that a walk past Michael's workplace isn't actually out of my way.

There's a deer head mounted over the doorway to electrical construction, a true testimony to the macho creed behind the place. As I poke my head inside, I hear the sounds of drills buzzing, overlaid by The Who. Roger Daltrey's rousing "yeeeeaaaaaaah" of "Won't Get Fooled Again" echoes through the soundstage that serves as home to their department.

Across the vast space, I spy Michael working, unaware of me. He's tinkering with a piece of equipment on a workbench, and I'm not sure if I should simply walk over to him—call out—or what the right protocol here would be. We've met at the commissary a few times, gone off the lot for lunch. But I've never dared enter Macho Town, especially not without an invitation.

"Can I help you, ma'am?" a voice calls out, and I turn to see a grizzly old guy, the sort of fellow we used to call an old-timer on the set, wearing his threadbare T-shirt for a show cancelled some twelve seasons back. Most of these old guys know the skinny on a studio like this one; they know where all the bodies are buried, as it were.

When I explain my mission there, the man whistles loudly, "Eh! Warner!" Michael looks up, and instantly his face brightens when he spots me. "There you go." The gray-haired man moves past me with a conspiratorial smile.

"Hey," Michael says, beaming at me as he approaches. He rubs off his hands on the hem of his T-shirt, sliding something into the tool belt slung low around his hips. A guy with a tool belt—every girl's dream. Well, and undoubtedly many guys' dreams too.

"I hope this is okay—" I glance at the man, who seems a lot like his boss, but Michael waves me off before I can finish.

"Of course it's okay."

"Because I don't want to get you in trouble at work or anything," I explain.

His gaze roves the petite length of me, particularly lingering on my expensive suit. "You're the studio shit, so of course it's okay."

"I am not the studio shit." I smile, shoving my hands in my slacks' pockets self-consciously.

"Yeah, you're our consumer, you know," he explains, bobbing his head amicably. "It's our job to keep your lights on." He gives me a wicked, suggestive grin.

"I'm going to pretend I didn't hear that."

"An old electrician's joke." Echoing from a tinny radio in the back, The Who becomes the Stones, and I wonder if they listen to anything around here that was released after 1980. We chitchat a while, and then I bring up the real reason for my visit, the fan gathering at the end of August.

"Yes, unbelievably, it's true. I still have fans, even after all this time," I explain, then add with a laugh, "I mean, apart from you and my parents."

I notice that a couple of young guys are watching from the back, whispering and chuckling at our expense. "Looks like we're generating some gossip," I warn, cutting my eyes in their direction, and he glances over his shoulder.

"Ah, Lorenzo and Gordon. Ignore 'em. They can give me hell after you go."

I think of his long past here, working in the electrical department.

I wonder if they ever knew about Alex, and if so, what they'll make of me. "You've worked here seven years, right?" He nods, his dark eyebrows furrowing together, as he tries to follow my thinking.

I look over toward his co-workers again, dropping my voice. "What did they think about—"

"Never met him." His mouth forms a hard line; the humor and warmth between us vanishes.

Comprehension dawns for me. "They didn't just not know him," I press quietly, "they never knew he existed *at all*, did they?"

He takes off his baseball cap, mopping his brow with the back of his hand, and laughs sadly. "In this place?" He glances over his shoulder again, to the land of classic rock and heavy testosterone. "What do *you* think, Rebecca?"

"Oh-kay. I'm tracking right with you on that one."

But what about when Alex died? Did anyone here have a clue what Michael went through, his grief and heartbreak? I imagine not, I think, as a loud drill drones over our conversation. He was forced to put on a pretense as to how he lived his life, to wrestle through his sorrow in utter silence. A wave of loneliness washes over me at the thought of being so closeted.

"Tell me more about this fan thing," he encourages, glancing sideways at his friends in the back. They seem to have moved on, but we both know the workplace gossip will begin as soon as I go. Interestingly enough, he seems unconcerned about that.

"They call it a gathering," I explain, rubbing my scarred palm, which aches some today for no apparent reason. "For *About The House* fans. There's an auction, a dinner, a bunch of socializing. I'll have to sign pictures and mix. That kind of thing."

"Jake'll be there?" The golden brown eyes seem not threatened, but rather intensely possessive.

"He doesn't miss a moment to grandstand." I almost tell him about the phone call, but something makes me keep quiet about that fact.

"I might have to beat his face in," he grouses, that jealous streak flashing hot. "Good chance for me to do that. At this event." He folds his arms over his chest resolutely, tipping his chin upward with a defiant slant. I'm glad my name isn't Jake Slater right at the moment.

"Oh, you wouldn't."

"You're right, I wouldn't." He grins, shifting his weight. "But I could definitely protect you from him. So count me in."

Relief washes over me, knowing I'll have Michael with me, because although I didn't realize it, I'd felt on edge about the gathering until this moment. Not just about Jake, but all those potential Bens that could be there, waiting, without me knowing it.

"Good," I sigh aloud, "because I definitely need you with me." As soon as the word "need" passes my lips, I regret it—regret seeming clingy. Regret trying to put too much onto our relationship. Regret defining him into the role of my protector, which seems too serious a step, despite how intense we're becoming. "Not *need*, exactly," I stammer, trying to retract my verbal misfire, "but you know. It would be cool, to have you there. I mean, Jake's such a jerk, and he's short too. Did you know that? Well, he's not exactly short, but he's way shorter than you, so no, I don't need—"

A slow, sexy smile spreads across Michael's face, as he says, "Baby."

"I'd love to have you come, that's all," I continue chattering, looking toward his friends again.

Michael just keeps smiling. "Of course."

"Cat will probably go, so that will be fun," I continue. "We can laugh together, I mean—"

He takes me by the shoulders, staring hard into my eyes. "*Becca*, I love it," he insists warmly. "I'll go. I can't wait."

I'm doing it again, the neurotic rambling thing that only seems to emerge around Michael Warner. For whatever reason, he gets me so worked up that the superfluous word problem simply *unleashes* upon him. "Just tell me to shut up next time," I caution him, laughing. He touches my hand, reassuring me in a brief, explosive moment of his skin brushing against mine that makes all my nervousness wash away.

"I wanted to thank you," he says, voice becoming quiet. "For the other night." The walkie-talkie holstered on his hip erupts in a crackle of communication. He listens, and with a flick of his wrist, silences the noise, then continues, "You really helped me about...well, everything."

Looking up into his eyes, I say, "I'm glad I could help."

"Laurel really liked you. I could tell," he says. "She's a little shy, you know. Real shy, actually, but she warmed right up to you."

"How's it been going? With her?"

"Better since you worked your magic," he replies. "I took yesterday off, we went out together, all three of us, biking and stuff. She goes home tomorrow."

"You're feeling better."

"I've been angry a long time, Rebecca," he answers, leading me out the doorway onto the sunny sidewalk. Away from his co-workers, so he can talk openly. Once we're in the bright sunlight, standing in the walkway that runs the length of the soundstage front, he continues, "Been carrying all that crap around inside of me. I'm tired. I'm tired of feeling bitter toward her. Toward—" he pauses, adjusting his tool belt, "—a lot of people." *Alex.* He means Alex, and I understand that it's hard to talk about that.

"It was really easy to see how much she loves you, Michael," I tell him, thinking of the look on her face the other night when she realized he'd left the house. Her realization that she'd overstepped, trying to help with the doll.

"But it's still hard to trust," he admits. "I can't help that. It's just true."

"Of course it is."

His demeanor brightens. "So, hey, Casey's stoked that you want to learn to surf," he announces, his dark eyebrows hitching upward in excitement. "He's told me to pick out a board for you."

"Casey," I repeat, wondering how Casey got involved in our big surfing plan.

"Yeah, he teaches loads of people," he explains. "Me included, way more than Al ever did." My stomach knots nervously, thinking of Casey and his disapproval of me, imagining having to learn anything from him, especially anything scary. "So, I'm bringing a long board for you, next weekend," Michael continues. "Okay?"

Even though I don't feel it inside, I smile and tell him, "That sounds fine." I'm thinking of everything that we have planned for next weekend in Malibu, and my anxiety intensifies when Michael adds softly, "We're still on, right? For next weekend?" He searches my face, and I know he sure as heck doesn't mean about the surfing. He means Malibu; our first time together, like I promised the other night.

"Still on," I assure him, with a thin smile.

"Good, because I've kinda been thinking about that a lot," he says, squeezing my hand tight.

I'm smiling on the outside, but thoroughly freaking out on the inside. There's no positive spin for this, the truth about my naked body, all those hideous scars. Right now, hunky Michael Warner is grinning at me, a shy blush creeping into his face, and he's clueless. He has absolutely no idea that his girlfriend's body doesn't look sexy or appealing once her clothes are stripped away. He has no idea that my naked body is just plain dreadful, with the searing scars across my chest and abdomen.

My only hope is that we can make love in the pitch-black dark. Or that someone can rush in a body double at that critical moment. I mean, where's Hollywood when you really need it?

Chapter Twenty: Michael

Rebecca stands on the curb in front of my house, laughing with Marti, the setting sun catching highlights of honey gold in her hair. She's worn it loose this last night of Laurel's visit, and it seems richer than usual, wavier and thicker, as it cascades across her shoulders. In fact, everything about her appearance seems more dramatic tonight. Then again, maybe that's only my feelings for her that I'm keying in on.

"I'm thinking that dress was designed by a straight guy," Casey observes, studying her thoughtfully as he takes a swig of his beer. She's just arrived and hasn't spotted us yet, sitting here on the front steps tucked back behind two tall flowering planters.

"What makes you say that?" Although I know exactly what that aquamarine sundress is doing to me. All vintage and Melrose-looking, it's a damned sexy wisp of a thing. Barely a dress at all, I'm telling you.

"Well," he answers, pushing his mirrored sunglasses low down the bridge of his nose so he can see better, "'cause if I had a straight bone in my body, then that wouldn't be the *only* bone in my body. That's all I'm saying."

I elbow him in the ribs and tell him to shut up, though my eyes never leave Rebecca.

"I'm serious," he says, still studying her appreciatively in that strappy dress, cut well above her knees, "she's hot, Mike."

Planting my chin in my hand, I sigh. "Welcome to my world."

"What was she wearing that night at the ballgame?" he asks, considering. I could easily answer: khaki pants, with a clingy little T-shirt that emphasized her well-developed biceps. I'm lost in that thought, rubbing my chin, when Casey bursts into laughter beside me. I turn to him, surprised. "Ah, man," he chuckles softly, shaking his head in apparent amazement.

"Something funny, Case?" I'm thinking he's going to make a disparaging comment, something cutting about me turning into Straight Guy.

"You've got the look, that's all," he explains, studying my face closely. "I don't believe it, but you do." He gives me an affectionate slap on the knee. "Gotta hand it to the girl. She obviously does quick work."

"I have no idea what in hell you even mean." I feel my face flame hot at his remark.

"Just that last time around," he says, "it took about a year for you to get The Look. The one you had when you and Alex got together." He shakes his head again, chuckling in appreciation, as Rebecca turns our way. He lifts his hand, greeting her with friendly vigor. "Hell yeah she's hot," he concedes in a low voice. "If she's given you *that* look."

Hot, he thinks? And he doesn't even know the half of what she does to me.

But maybe Casey *does* get what Rebecca's all about. He coaxed her into joining him there on the front step and proceeded to be a nice guy for a while; unbelievably, considering what a grump he can be, he's actually capable of charming the pants off anyone when he tries. And I do know he's trying with her, if only because of me.

Right now, he's actually cornered her back in Al's surfboard room, offering to help fix her up with the right board for next weekend, talking rocker and tail kick, and a bunch of crap she doesn't understand. Poor Rebecca, she looks anxious as he leads the way to the back of the house, but when you get Casey Porter on surfboards, it's hard to shut him up. I trail behind them, trying to give an appropriate amount of space, and I spy Laurel in the guest room, packing her suitcase.

I lean in through the doorway, holding onto the frame. "Packing up?"

She gives me a quiet smile. "Almost done."

I'm going to miss the familiarity in those blue eyes, the chance to stare into them like I've done for the past four days. I walk into the bedroom, and she digs inside her suitcase, retrieving something.

"I'm wondering what to do about this." She extends a flat stone toward me, the one Andrea found on our bike ride. "We were going to paint it," she reminds me, "but maybe you'll help her?" The stone rests in her open palm, an invitation to me—an opportunity for us to parent our child together, for once.

"Yeah, Laurel," I agree, nodding thoughtfully. "Yeah, I'd like to paint that with her. What kind of stuff you think we need?"

"Oh, you have it," she replies. "It's there, in the living room. I brought her some paints, you know. A whole set."

I can't help smiling, thinking of how talented our daughter is. "She really loves art."

"I know," she agrees, "and she's really gifted already."

"I'm not so good with that stuff, you know," I admit reluctantly.

"Alex could sit with her for hours and create all these intricate things, but mine always come out like big globs."

Laurel takes my hand, and delicately slides the rock from her palm to my own, closing my fingers around it. "Michael, you are very exceptional. In many ways."

"I know enough to appreciate your work, Laurel," I say, and from the surfboard room I hear Casey laughing with Rebecca. Sounds like Marti's in there too. That's got to be a good sign that they're all yukking it up together.

I know it's now or never—the things I want to tell Laurel, just us. We won't be alone like this again before she goes; first thing tomorrow, Andie will attach to her like a barnacle until we've deposited her curbside at the airport. So I close the bedroom door, turning to face her.

"Let's talk a minute," I say, and she nods, sitting down on the bed. Her bare feet dangle over the edge, and unlike Rebecca, I notice that she doesn't paint her toenails. She's all natural, including the shell ankle bracelet she's wearing, something woven and handmade.

"I wanted to thank you, again," I begin, tentative as I close the distance separating us, "for that painting of Alex."

"I'm glad you liked it."

"But what you said about it speaking to me?" Her clear eyes narrow, though she says nothing. "I don't think I get what you mean."

"Maybe it's something you need to think about," she suggests softly. "Some more. Maybe?"

"No, Laurel see, I want to know what you meant by that. How can a painting sing?" Despite myself, I feel my anger rising. "Got enough shit I'm always thinking about." All the mysteries; all the thoughts about where Alex went, where he might not be.

Laurel stares at her hands, toying with her charm bracelet. She rubs the cross between her thumb and forefinger, quiet.

I think of Andrea and her dreams. "Why'd you paint him on the beach?" I press, and she only smiles. One of those inside-out kind of Laurel smiles that begin somewhere deep inside of her.

"Michael, art comes from the soul of the creator," she explains quietly, "and reaches out to touch *your* soul. That's what art does."

I'm still perplexed by her mystery. "You telling me that Allie will talk to me?" I demand, stepping closer. "Is that it?"

She only continues smiling, a warm, tender expression—not closed off to me, like a few days ago.

"Michael, I'm going to pray that you hear what you're supposed to hear."

"Pray." I snort at that one. God seems to have me trapped by a posse of believers. "Sure, Laurel, you pray about that. Knock your socks off." My words come out bitter, and that's not really what I wanted, so I add, "I appreciate all the help I can get, you know."

"We all need help, Michael," she agrees, swinging her bare feet as they dangle off the side of the bed. Her eyes never leave me, serious and intense, the thick black lashes opening wide around the quiet blue. Alex had a way of watching me like that when he was trying to talk to me about important stuff. It always made me squirm, and I feel pegged in the exact same way now by her; just change those lashes to a dusty red, and it could be my lover looking right through me.

So I wrestle the conversation in a different direction, a more comfortable one. "Hard to believe it's already time for you to go." I turn away from her, walk toward the closet and thumb through his clothes. My hand lingers on his suede jacket.

"It's been a quick few days," she agrees, a melancholy sound that she can't hide filling her voice.

"So maybe we'll do this again, huh?" I suggest, turning toward her hesitantly. "Not wait so long."

A glorious smile spreads across her face: relief, joy, it's all there. "I'd love that, Michael," she agrees, giving her long hair a casual toss.

"Maybe next time you could bring Bruce?" Bruce is her live-in boyfriend of about ten years.

She laughs. "Well, now *that* I'm not so sure about."

"Is Bruce still struggling with commitment, Laurel?" I tease.

"No, not really. I just like...spending time with you." That old feeling falls over me—the familiar one where she's like my secret lover or something. Just 'cause we share Andie between us. "Laurel," I stare down at the floor, "I'm still not over what you did."

"I know that."

"I think it's going to take some time," I say, turning back to the closet again. The clothes seem like an accusation, hanging there, a disembodied part of Alex's life still left on planet Earth.

"I understand," she answers quietly from behind me.

Reaching for his faded suede duster, I gather it within my hands and pull it off the hanger to hold it against my chest. One last time, I inhale the scent, try and find him in there, lost somewhere in the clouds of memory.

Then I turn, and extend it toward his sister. "Here, Laurel," I say, not quite meeting her surprised gaze. "You should have this."

"Michael?" She shakes her head, adamant. "No, it's yours." His shirts I can wear, his watch. His ring. Even his damned boxers. But not this suede jacket that he wore so often and long.

"I know it's big, but you'd use it, wouldn't you?" I ask, still extending it toward her like an ungainly appendage. "In the winter? Maybe you could even have it resized?"

"Of course." She tries to blink back the tears that well in her eyes.

"Then you should definitely have it," I insist, dropping it on the bed beside her. "Your brother would want it that way."

"Thank you." She pulls it close, like she's not sure what to do. I'm not sure what to do either, standing there in the middle of the room—there's a sudden awkwardness between us that I don't fully understand.

"Yeah, so..." I blow out a breath, stepping closer to her. "Maybe I'll come see you some time. With Andie. Maybe we'll drive out later this summer." It's been growing in my mind over the past day, this plan, but I haven't been sure how to broach it until now.

When she looks up, her tears begin to fall in earnest, tracking silently down her cheeks. I see her swallow hard, wrestling to find her voice, but she says nothing, simply nods at me with a fragile smile.

I speak for her, understanding that her emotions are too strong. "So okay," I say, "maybe we will." Then bending low, I press a fleeting kiss against the top of her head, the kind I reserve for Andie most of the time. Then I turn and walk fast out the door.

✧

At the airport, I pull up curbside to let Laurel out, parking temporarily. The police keep blowing whistles to keep traffic flowing, but we won't be here long. It's better for Andrea—for all three of us—to keep this farewell pretty quick.

"I wish you weren't going," my daughter says, gazing up at her aunt with doleful eyes. Laurel strokes her auburn hair away from her cheek.

"I know, but you'll see me again soon."

"Are you sure?" Glancing in my direction, Andrea seems worried that I might get in the way of that promise.

I've been giving them room, but I step a little closer. "Yeah, we'll see Aunt Laurel real soon," I reassure her. "We might even drive out in a few weeks." Her blue eyes grow wide, her mouth forming a delicate, hopeful smile. "That would be so cool!"

"I would love that," Laurel agrees. "We could even do some art. In my studio."

"And don't forget," Andie tells her cryptically. For a moment, Laurel seems unclear, then she breaks into a broad smile. "Oh, *right*," she says, "I won't forget." Both of them bob their heads in agreement over this shared secret. Seeing the playful, happy smile on my daughter's face, I don't really mind being left out this time.

Laurel drops low to the ground; opening her arms, she draws Andrea close for a hug. "Pumpkin, I'll be praying for you," she promises quietly, stroking the silky red hair beneath her fingertips. "I'll e-mail you every night, too, okay?"

"Okay." Andrea wraps her thin arms around Laurel's neck,

holding on tight.

Kneeling there, not worried at all about dirtying her jeans, Laurel loses herself in this one, final moment. And I envy everything about her ability to do that.

Andrea buries her face against her chest, nestling close—closer than she usually lets me hold her.

Laurel's eyes drift shut, and she simply holds Andrea. She's drinking in the very scent of our child. Memorizing her, before she has to leave her behind again. Watching them together, I find myself thinking of the hospital—of the first time I held Andrea, and the look on Laurel's weary face. Joy, heartbreak, amazement; it was all there. Many times—long before Alex died—I've thought of what that cost her.

I know she wants to take her back today. She aches with it, deep in her bones because Andrea is her child, same as she's mine. And leaving her behind now, when she knows what a hole she has in her life—that's got to be killing her. I know, because living with that hole, that giant crater Alex's absence has left, well it's killing me too. Every day I stare into it, like a mirror; every day I know what my baby girl's got missing in her life.

But watching them there at curbside, Andie's cheek resting against her birth mother's shoulder, I think of someone else that's missing. And it isn't Alex, oddly enough. For some unexpected reason, I remember the other baby Laurel carried briefly, of Andrea's lost fraternal twin. The tiny second baby that appeared on the first sonogram, but had vanished by the next, before we could even find out if it was a boy or a girl. It was in the bloodline, they told us. Twins could be expected with in vitro fertilization. Still, that soaring feeling when I saw those two tiny sacks on the screen was the most unexpected miracle of my life.

And then one simply disappeared.

Of course we focused our joy on Andrea, but sometimes I do think about her—

I say *her* because I've always felt the other baby was a girl, just like her sister. Maybe one day, when Andie's old enough, I'll tell her about her vanished twin.

It seems to me that life is an accumulation of losses. All these lives brush past our own, impacting us, changing us. Sometimes their mark is as fleeting as a tiny thumbprint. As insubstantial. Like a tiny, ghostly ship down in the murky depths that vanishes before we even see it again.

I would have liked to call that child Ruth. After my mother.

Laurel and Andrea step apart, Andie backing closer to me. I slip my hands on her shoulders. Laurel stands there, suitcase clutched in her hand, smiling at me—and I realize she's waiting. Waiting for me to hug her too. So I lean close, bending to give her a quick peck on the cheek. But she takes hold of me now, and doesn't let go. Against my face, I feel her warm, familiar breath as she kisses me. "I love you, Michael," she whispers softly, touching my jaw with her fingertips. "I love you. And don't forget that you will *always* be my brother."

I try to think of something to say, but there's nothing. I have no words at all. So I just wave as she steps backwards from me, tears shining in her eyes despite her beautiful smile. Then in one graceful move she disappears through the opening glass doors to the airport into the throngs of people. With that one pirouette she's gone from our lives again.

When Andie tugs on my hand, I realize I've been standing, staring after her aunt. Staring at nothing for a while.

"It will be okay," my brave daughter says, smiling up at me. God, she's so much stronger than I've ever managed to be. I miss Laurel. I miss her a hell of a lot, something I never could figure out how to explain over the past four days; how so much anger and resentment can cohabitate easily with love.

I nod and squeeze Andrea's small hand in mine. "It will be okay," I agree.

It will be okay, because it has to be. With everyone I've lost, all the lives that have brushed against mine then faded away, I can't afford to lose anyone else.

Chapter Twenty-One: Rebecca

Andrea and I stand in Mona's driveway, watching Michael recheck the surfboards on his truck rack before we leave my place for Malibu. He adjusts the straps, giving them quick tugs; Andrea balances on the low brick wall beside Mona's flower garden, hopping along as she walks. She's definitely excited about this three-day trip, even though she's quiet. And I notice the way she steals furtive glances at the shopping bag in my hand, one that's filled with little girl beachy things I couldn't resist buying. I figure I'll keep the contents a surprise unless she asks.

Michael gives the surfboards a final, reassuring pat. Like he's getting their agreement to cooperate in our travel plans. "Everything okay up there?" I call out with a smile.

"Want to be sure they're really down tight," Michael explains, vaulting over the side of the truck bed. It's one of those fluid, all-guy maneuvers—truck to driveway in a single motion. That same masculine gracefulness must be breathtaking on a surfboard.

Brushing off his hands, he says, "Last thing we need is a board flying off and hitting somebody."

"That happened to Daddy once," Andrea explains, climbing down off the garden wall. "When he was in high school. Somebody's board broke his windshield. That's what he said."

Michael takes the tote bag from my hand, giving me a gallant, flirty smile. Out here in the late morning sunshine, the gold flecks in his eyes almost assume a hazel hue.

Andrea turns to me. "Hey, Rebecca? Are you really going to surf?"

"I think so. Maybe." I fight a sudden attack of nervousness at the thought. "What about you?'

Her expression grows thoughtful as she stares up at her much smaller surfboard perched atop the other two. "Michael brought my board," she says, chewing on her lip, "but... I don't know."

"Why not?" I think of how she's talked about surfing, of how much I can tell she loves it. But she doesn't answer, only shrugs and walks toward the truck, shoulders slumped forward.

It's hard to get a fix on her this morning—one minute she seems aflutter with excitement and now she's suddenly subdued. I follow after her. "Andrea, did you know we're sharing a room?" She climbs up inside the cab of her father's truck. "Marti and Dave's kids are sleeping on the pullout sofa and you're with me."

Her face brightens. "No, Michael hadn't told me that."

"We can make it like a slumber party," I say.

"Cool." She bobs her head enthusiastically. "And tell stories each night!"

"That sounds like fun," I agree.

"Rebecca?" Her expression grows serious again. "I'm not sure I want to go surfing."

"That's okay, sweetheart." I brush an errant lock of auburn hair out of her eyes. "You don't have to perform for anybody."

"No?" She searches my face.

"This trip is going to be fun. But you don't have to work at that. Okay?" She nods, chewing on her lip as I slide in beside her. "We girls will stick together," I promise.

Michael slips behind the wheel, grinning like a kid. "Everybody ready?"

In his eyes, I see expectation. That over the course of the next three days our relationship will deepen; that his daughter will heal; that we'll all make new memories together. That some of our innocence might be restored.

As we pull down Mona's driveway, I realize his warm eyes mirror everything I'm feeling inside about the next few days.

✧

"Okay, suit up! It's totally going off out there. Double overhead!" Casey shouts as he slams the door to the beach house behind him. While Marti and I were buying groceries for the next few days, he drove down to the point to scout the current wave conditions.

Malibu is a decent place for a beginner like me to get their toes wet. Although there's always a crowd, in Michael's words, "it's a pretty mellow wave in Malibu."

"Double overhead," Michael snorts, winking at me playfully from where he sits at the kitchen bar watching a Dodgers game. "You are so full of it, man."

Casey ignores him, turning to me. "You still game, Rebecca?" The wind has kicked up since our arrival, and it's become grayer, overcast. It's slightly chilly, and I know that even in July, the Pacific won't be overly warm.

"Sure." I give a resolute nod, my stomach tightening with nervousness.

Casey seems to read my mood. "We're not going to start you way out, Rebecca. You'll be on the small waves. Close up on shore."

Michael swivels his barstool, glancing out through the living room windows at the wide expanse of ocean. "It's getting a little choppy out there, Case. Sure it's okay?"

"She'll be fine," he says. "We'll stick to the shore break and just kind of practice getting the feel of the board."

Michael laughs. "Yeah, man, I notice you're a lot nicer about her first time than you were on me."

"Maybe that's 'cause *she's* a lot nicer than you."

"Sure, Porter, whatever," Michael chuckles, rising from his seat. "Let me see if Andrea wants to come." He walks down the hall toward the bedroom his daughter and I will share for the next few days.

Casey turns to me. "Rebecca, there's nothing to be intimidated about, you know."

Marti enters the kitchen tailed by her oldest daughter, Olivia. "Sure there is," she announces with a laugh. "Sharks and locals, in no particular territorial order."

Olivia makes a face; she's about Andrea's age and has a head full of black curls just like her mother. Her damp flip-flops squeak on the tiled floor like squeegees on a windshield.

"Great. Sounds like so much fun." I twirl my finger in the air for emphasis. "Woo freaking hoo."

Michael enters the kitchen, his expression troubled. "Andie won't come," he announces under his breath—loud enough for the group of us in the kitchen to hear, but not so loud as to be overheard by his daughter. He glances back toward the bedroom. "She's just watching TV. Says she doesn't want to surf."

"What do you think the problem is?" Marti asks.

"She's never fun anymore," Olivia whines, but Marti shushes her.

Remembering our conversation in the driveway, I wonder again what Andrea's hesitation must be. We all huddle close, like an offensive football team around the quarterback.

Michael answers, "I think surfing's too...familiar." *Too Alex.* We all know that's what he meant.

"She needs to start making new memories," Marti sighs heavily. "Maybe I'll go talk to her?"

Michael looks to me. I know he thinks I can accomplish this job. "I'll try," I volunteer quietly. "But I don't think we should push her."

"Thanks, baby," he says, touching my arm as I step away. I only hope that when it comes to Andrea this time, I won't let him down.

Flopping onto the queen-sized bed I kick off my sandals and sit Indian-style beside Andrea. Bunkmates for three days—when was it exactly Michael had thought we'd have our intimate rendezvous? Maybe Marti will give us a night on our own at some point, like Michael mentioned. Otherwise, after all the kissing and touching and looking I've done these past few weeks I might go crazy having to wait much longer.

Sprawled on her stomach, Andrea plants her chin in her hand, her eyes never leaving the television. "Whatcha watching?" I ask, though I can see it's some kind of Disney program.

"Don't know."

"I was going to head down to the beach for a while," I say. "I brought a kite. Did you see it? Actually, I brought three and you can pick the one you want. Would you like that?"

She shrugs, but remains silent. I found the kites at a shop in Santa Monica, a place where my dad loves to buy them. I made a point of stopping in there two nights ago, because I wanted us to have something special we could do together, and one thing I definitely remember from my childhood summers in Jacksonville is flying kites with my father. I bought a butterfly, a dragonfly, and a prism; I figure Andie can pick the one she likes best. I also tucked my mother's red velvet cake recipe into my suitcase, because I want to bake her a luscious red, white and blue cake for Fourth of July.

"Well, okay," I say, launching purposefully off the bed. "I guess I'm going to try surfing with Casey and your dad, then. I'll see you later!" This time she does glance my way, and I almost sense that she's torn. "Unless...you want to come?" I ask, hopeful.

She shakes her head. "See you when you get back." She fixes her eyes on the television again.

Grabbing my oversized beach bag, the one with my one-piece and my cover up in it, I leave the room, wondering if the best strategy might not be simply to give her some room for a while.

In the car on the way over to the point, I begin to have second thoughts about this surfing plan. Staring out the open window, the wind tangling my hair, I wonder what on earth I'm doing. Trying to hold my own in a Man's World, is that it?

Then we round a bend in the road, and I catch a glimpse of a few rogue surfers, splashes of color against profound depths of sea, and I'm reminded of the mystery, that transcendental *thing* that always seems to surround the sport like a holy penumbra. For years I watched the surfers down at my parents' beach condo in Jacksonville; I watched and wondered, but I never tried it. That's the problem with nearly dying—it brings into relief all those things you've never attempted, but always meant to do.

Casey's radio plays an old Elvis Costello tune, one I haven't heard in forever, and Michael starts to hum familiarly.

"The point's packed," Casey observes, slowing as we pass some parked cars on the shoulder. "Skeeter and Dobro are here, and that's a sure sign that all the kooks are out."

I'm sitting in the backseat, right behind Michael; I notice how the dark hair along his neck is trimmed close, how it spikes a little, and my fingertips burn with the urge to touch the prickling hairs. To lean forward in the seat and kiss him right there, on the nape of his neck.

But my appreciative reverie is broken when he launches into a crash course on surfing safety. "Just remember," he cautions, "if you get caught under a wave, don't fight it." Slinging his arm over the back of the seat, he turns to me with a serious expression. "'Cause if you do, you're spending energy. And that can cost you your life."

My eyes train on a tiny fleck of a scar right at his hairline—how could I not have noticed it before? A silver crescent of a moon, as if someone took their fingernail and drew the line. "Gotta save all the energy you've got, Becca. Okay?" His eyebrows draw together like he's wondering if I'm listening—or maybe just what I'm thinking.

"Oh, sure," I reassure him, but my chest tightens reflexively. "No problem."

"Just curl up into a ball, like this," he continues, demonstrating a kind of ducking maneuver, protecting his face behind his hands. "You can be under those waves as long as a minute so you want to conserve." A whole freaking minute without air? *Asthma, anyone?*

Casey edges the Explorer over onto the shoulder of the road, where several other sand-encrusted vehicles line the pavement, most of them plastered with salty stickers for companies like Sex Wax, Roxy, Counter Culture. The list goes on. Of course, how counter culture can something really be, if it has to advertise the fact that it is?

Casey picks up the education course. "Just remember, those board fins are sharp, man." He thrusts the vehicle into park, turning to face me. "Whatever you do, don't let one catch you in the face or the arm. They'll cut you right open. Buddy of mine went down to Baja last month and had to get a bunch of stitches in his leg."

Just what I need: more bleeding, more surgery, more scars. "Maybe this isn't for me," I say, running my fingertips along my face. Feeling the bands of scar tissue. Why did I think this was a good idea again? Something to do with Keanu Reeves? Wait, or was it Alex Richardson?

Michael's golden brown eyes narrow in concern, as he dangles his hand over the seatback, reaching for my own. "You don't have to do this, you know."

"I know," I agree, feeling like this is my Big Chance to fit into a testosterone-driven club that was formed several decades ago. Like this is a rite of passage and I have to nail it perfectly or I'll never live up to Alex's memory. "But I really want to try," I say, thinking of those surfers in Jacksonville. "I've always wanted to."

"She'll be fine," Casey insists. And he's the one who grew up surfing, after all, so he should know. This causes the rush of blood in my ears to quiet a bit. "I mean, hell, you aren't even gonna get up on that board today," he continues. "You may never get up."

"Thanks for the vote of confidence," I laugh, drawing my hair up into a haphazard ponytail.

"Nothing to do with confidence." Casey opens his door. "Just the facts of the sport, Rebecca."

I swallow hard, nodding, but for some unexpected reason it's not even the surfing I'm afraid of. It's the thought of stripping out of my long-sleeved Polo shirt, of Michael seeing the scars on my chest for the very first time. That's much scarier than the thought of dancing with the sharks on a thin slice of board.

Michael drops his surfboard onto the sand, staring out into the waves like a mystic. "Lot of chop," he observes stoically. "Rough for a first-timer."

"Maybe I should just watch," I volunteer, dropping my own board beside me. It was an ungainly and awkward journey down to the beach with the thing—I can't even imagine trying to balance on it.

Casey snorts, shaking his head. "You can't tell a newbie all that shit about not panicking," he scolds Michael. "All it does is make them panic. You can't do that—they just gotta get out there and go for it."

"It's fine," I say, studying the slab of fiberglass that's supposed to somehow support my hundred and nine pounds across roiling fists of sea. "I'll be fine." *Or, alternatively, I'll be dead.* In that case, maybe Alex can teach me how to surf.

"It's not a big deal." Michael clasps my shoulders within his reassuring hands. "You can stay here."

"That's a great idea!" I bounce onto the balls of my feet, feeling relief wash over me. "I'll sit here on the beach and watch you guys. Maybe tomorrow the waves will be calmer."

"Okay," Michael says, but he doesn't seem convinced that it's okay to leave me on shore. Reluctantly, he strips off his surf shop T-shirt, revealing a clingy wet suit. It's more like a satiny second skin, and my breath hitches in my throat to see the way it outlines more muscles across his shoulders and chest than I ever imagined he possessed.

Casey grins a little wickedly, watching Michael draw his forearm over his chest to stretch his triceps. "Wet suit?" Casey snorts. "It's

July, for crap's sake."

"I'm cold natured," he huffs, tossing me a self-conscious glance. I work to ignore the way his shoulder muscles ripple beneath the tight material of that short-sleeved suit.

"You're showing off." Casey drops to the sand and begins waxing his board, his hand moving in brisk circular motions.

"Shut up. I am not."

"Uh, yeah, I think you are," he says, then winks at me with a sly smile that catches me by surprise.

Well, if Michael Warner is showing off, he has good reason because that wet suit is absolutely delicious on his well-toned body. Broad shoulders, defined triceps—how could I have not fully realized the beautiful body he's been hiding beneath those faded T-shirts and Armani suits?

He slides out of his long swim trunks to reveal the lower half of his "spring suit," a kind of short version of a wet suit. When he stands there, Adonis of the Beach studying the waves, feet planted solidly apart, I realize that I simply cannot breathe. *Deep breaths, girl. You don't want to literally die of desire.* That would be just a little too embarrassing.

But I can't help noticing that even a certain...bulge proves impossible for that slick material to hide. My gaze wanders there, and when he turns back toward me, I pull my shirt tight around my body, feeling self-conscious to realize that he's *this* luscious while still half-dressed. What if he were undressed? What if he can tell I'm undressing him with my eyes?

Casey glances between us. "Oh, wait. I get it," he gibes good-naturedly, his jaw falling slack. "You're not showing off, Mike, that's not it. You're *hiding!*"

"Hiding what?" Michael grumbles, and by now I swear that a faint blush has crept into his olive complexion.

"*You* know," Casey says and makes a little fluttering gesture with his fingers, then touches his own shoulder. "The ole army memento." Again, he forms a fist, but waggles his fingers like some kind of...creature.

"Ah, geez," Michael groans, rolling his eyes as he focuses intently on the task of waxing his board. "Please, Becca, just ignore this idiot, okay?"

"I'm right." Casey grins at me, and I wonder what this joke is that he's trying to let me in on.

"What's he talking about?" I ask, curious, but also interested at how shy Michael unexpectedly seems.

"It's nothing," he says and now I'm certain that I spy splotches of color staining his cheeks. Pulling my knees close to my chest, I watch him, see the way his sinewy shoulders ripple and pull beneath the wetsuit. Absolutely beautiful. *Ridiculously* beautiful, as a matter of fact—no wonder he's been gay. That's not a straight guy's body. It's a masculine body that's been honed and sculpted to perfection for another *man*. Or, maybe it's just the body of a guy who works for a living, of a guy who plays hard in the ocean during his spare time.

He stops waxing and turns to me, the golden brown eyes flaring with something I don't quite recognize. "It's a tattoo, all right," he barks. "That's all. A damn tattoo." Then, he looks at his friend. "Happy now?"

I wonder why a tattoo would be the source of such embarrassment, especially with a guy's guy like Michael Warner. Unless...

"What kind of tattoo?" I ask gently.

Poor Michael, I feel bad when he thrusts an anxious hand through his disheveled hair. I think Casey regrets his own teasing. "I bet our girl loves tattoos," he says.

Michael mumbles, "It's a butterfly," and Casey's exaggerated hand gestures suddenly make a lot of sense.

"A...butterfly?" I scrunch my nose in surprise. I could have guessed a million things, but never that.

"Yeah, yeah, go ahead and laugh." He glares at Casey. "Both of you just laugh your damned asses off."

"I'm not laughing, it's just—" I search for the right word, "—kind of surprising."

He looks at me. "An old army joke. Papillon, that's what they called me. Got the tattoo on a drunken dare and I've lived with it ever since."

"Uh, huh. So you *were* hiding it," Casey says.

Michael points at the ocean. "It is fucking cold out there, man!" he shouts, surprising me with his volatility. He grabs his surfboard and stomps out into the waves without looking back at either of us.

Casey and I watch him step out into the ocean that pools eagerly around his legs, then sail onto his board, chest first. Neither of us speaks until finally Casey sighs. "How can someone that beautiful be so damned touchy about a tattoo?"

"Well," I suggest, "maybe it makes him feel a little...gay. Having a butterfly?" Then to cover myself I add, "No offense."

Casey frowns, watching Michael paddle into the waves. "Then why'd he get the damn thing when he was still straight? Huh?"

"Sometimes images gain more meaning after the fact." I think of Michael with Alex, of how an innocent army joke must have become an emblem, an ambiguous definition in itself. I wonder if it held special significance between the two of them, and if maybe that's why Michael's so protective about it.

"Nah, sometimes people are just afraid to be vulnerable," Casey looks meaningfully at the way I'm huddled on the sand, arms wrapped protectively across my chest. "You weren't scared to go out there, not really. I don't think you're scared of anything."

"Are you kidding?" I laugh, watching Michael sail awkwardly over the face of a breaking wave. "I'm scared of everything."

"You were ready to do this until we got down to the beach."

"Duh. You heard all the things Michael warned me about."

His blonde eyebrows shoot upward, curious. "Has Mike seen you in your bathing suit yet?"

For some reason, I feel close to Casey. Like I can be real with him. "That really isn't an image I'm thrilled about," I admit. "Any more than he's thrilled with his tattoo."

"You're gorgeous, Rebecca. Absolutely gorgeous. You know that's what he thinks, don't you?"

"Casey, please..."

"Not an image that squares with your reality?"

"Not at this point."

"Try this on for an image, then." He removes his T-shirt, tossing it onto the sand beside me. "*He's* even more gorgeous out of that wet suit than he is in it."

Studying Casey's own sculpted, fit physique, it's not hard to fill in what I couldn't see of Michael moments ago. "Oh, my." I blow out a slow, dreamy sigh. Surfer boys sure do age gracefully.

"Yeah, thought you'd like that one." Grabbing his board, he warns, "I'll get you out there yet, O'Neill."

Back at Casey's, I find Andrea lazing on the sofa with a book—not outside with Olivia on the beach where she belongs. So I implement a plan of action, and explain that I'm going out to fly one or two of my kites. That I'd love for her to tag along. With Michael in the shower, I figure now is a good time to make headway with her. She declines politely, but I give an upbeat smile.

Walking down the steps to the beach, I find an open area right in front of the house with plenty of good room to launch a kite. My choice is an easy one—the butterfly.

After a stuttering start, the kite zigzags into the open sky, flapping like a piece of paper caught in a floor fan. Holding the string tightly within my hand, I unfurl another few feet. The butterfly nosedives sharply, but then catches air and sails high again. Carefully, I ease down, sitting on my towel.

Behind me, I hear muffled footsteps on the sand—small steps— and I know that like my own tiny minnow, Andrea has answered the pull of my lure. It's only a matter of time until she's hooked completely.

"How come you brought kites?" she asks, standing behind me.

Never taking my eyes off my airborne creature, I answer, "Because kites are fun."

"But they're for kids."

"Who says?" The kite ascends even higher. Pressing my hand to my forehead, I shield my eyes against the hazy, late afternoon sun.

"They just are," she answers, settling beside me on the warm sand. She's wearing a giant straw hat that's sunk low down her forehead. I can barely see her eyes.

"Want to help me?" I ask, offering the ball of string to her, but she shakes her head. I've learned enough about precious Andrea, how she opens to me on her own terms.

For a long while, we sit together in silence, the gulls overhead competing with our kite's peaceful performance. I envy both, watching them fly free, unencumbered. Beside me, Andrea digs her toes around, dislodging dark sand from below; it's cooler underneath, she tells me after a while. Not like the sand we're sitting on.

"I don't want to surf," she says, reaching for the string still held tight within my hands.

"Be careful," I caution gently, "or it will get away from us." She takes the twine from me with confidence, gripping it like an expert. The kite lurches slightly overhead as we make the pass off, but then sails boldly again.

"Michael wants me to surf," she continues, pushing her hat back so she can see over the low brim. "It's a big deal to him. But I don't want to."

"Then don't."

"But he *wants* me to."

"Well, he can surf," I say. "Casey can surf. I can even surf, maybe. But I don't see why you should, not if you don't want to."

"It's something we did with Daddy," she explains, auburn eyebrows furrowing sharply together. "It was always Daddy's thing. That's why he's making such a big deal out of it. He's trying to make it like it's something we do together, but it isn't."

"You know, could be he just likes to surf," I suggest, trying not to push too hard. Trying not to remind her that even she has told me how the three of them surfed together; that it was *never* only something she did with Alex. Memory serves the mind in many ways: sometimes self-deception furthers the healing.

"No, he definitely likes it," she agrees with surprising ease. "But mostly it makes him think of Daddy. That's why he's always in the surfboard room." I shake my head, not sure what she means. "He goes in there all the time, when I'm in bed. I think he even sleeps in there sometimes. He really misses Daddy."

My heartbeat quickens, but I remain on track for her. This moment isn't about me, or my sense of competition with a dead man.

It's about a lost little girl, one who needs me desperately. "So, if it's something y'all used to do as a family," I try, "then why not help him out with that? You know? He does miss your daddy. You miss him, too, so you could maybe just give it a go?"

"You *know* I can't." She begins to tug the kite back in, slowly winding the string around the ball.

"I don't understand, sweetie."

"But you know why." She stares at the sky, away from me. "I told you."

Noticing the long shorts she's wearing now, I remember that day at Mona's pool and her scar. "You could wear your spring suit," I suggest, understanding the real issue finally—or at least one of them.

"But that's geeky. It's summer."

"That's not one bit geeky. It's cold out there." Father and daughter are both hiding, each for their own reasons.

"I just don't know if I want to surf without Daddy, that's all," she admits, thrusting the kite string back at me. I take it, nodding in understanding.

We sit quiet for a while, me slowly winding it back in—and then I take a bold risk. "You know, I showed you my scars, but you never did show me yours. That day at the pool."

"You didn't show me *all* of yours." She challenges me with her clear blue eyes. Somehow, she knows it wasn't the full truth.

"Well, sweetheart," I draw in a strengthening breath, "I showed you the ones I could."

She pulls her knees close up to her chest, protecting herself. "You'll think mine's stupid," she half-whispers into the wind. So quiet, I have to lean my ear down low toward her, to be sure I hear. "That it's stupid," she repeats, wanting to be sure I understand her meaning.

I shake my head in sharp disagreement. "I would never think anything important to you is stupid."

She looks up at me, the pain she's been battling to conceal since we met vividly apparent. "Promise?" she asks, and I hear tears in her small voice.

"Andrea, of course, sweetheart," I assure her. "Deep down, you know you're safe with me."

She stares at the ocean, thinking on that statement. "Yeah," she agrees after a time, "I guess that's why Michael likes you too."

"I'm going to try surfing again," I offer. "Want to go out with me?"

Her dimples pop into view. "You're just really cool, Rebecca. And you're tough too." God made me durable, I want to say, but I'm not sure she'd understand what I mean.

"You could wear your spring suit," I continue, "but I hope you'll show me that scar some day."

The smile fades. "Yeah, maybe." Then, "Rebecca? Do your scars make you think of what happened? Every time you see them?"

"Not every time, sweetheart," I reply. "But a lot of times they do."

Memory. I read once that every cell in our body warehouses our memories on a microscopic level. Maybe scars have memory too. Maybe that's why they're so powerful, because they contain all that happened to us in that one explosive event, branded onto our bodies organically.

Watching the memory and pain dancing across young Andrea's beautiful face, I wish that I could wipe her scar away. The one on the inside, that she lives with, that reminds her of such a violent loss. The one that she runs from, pushing her other daddy perpetually away.

"You know, surfing late is the best," she answers knowingly, rising to her feet. "'Cause you get to paddle into the sunset. Sometimes you can even surf until dark."

"Maybe we'll try tomorrow," I agree. She brushes sand off her hands and knees, walking back toward the house.

"Rebecca?" She turns back to me like an afterthought.

"Yes, sweetie?"

She shoves her hands into her pockets, a shy smile forming on her face. "Thanks for bringing those kites for me."

✧

As the sun begins to set, Michael seems quieter than usual, and I wonder at first if my time with Andrea troubled him somehow. When we have a moment alone on the deck, I ask him if he's okay.

"I just wish I were getting more time with you," he says, dropping into one of the lounge chairs. "Alone, I mean."

"I thought maybe you were mad I didn't try surfing earlier."

"You kidding me? I don't care if you never go out there." I consider filling him in on the details of my conversation with Andrea, then think better of it.

"But it's your thing."

"I like it. Hell, I love it," he says. "But I don't need you to love it. Not really."

"I'm still trying to picture your butterfly," I confess.

He looks up, daring me a little with his eyes. "We can arrange for a viewing," he says. "Sort of a 'you show me yours, I'll show mine' kind of thing."

"You flirt!" I laugh, feeling my face burn hot. And it's not because of the hazy late-day sun.

He clasps my waist with both of his large hands, dragging me closer toward him. I feel so small comparatively, and think of his assessment that day on the lot: that I'm delicate and feminine. With an easy flick of his wrist, he unfastens the bottom button of my shirt. "I could peek right now," he cautions, but I catch his hand.

"Or not," I say.

The stormy eyes narrow like a cat's. "I've waited long enough."

"Then strip, Warner." I command, taking a step back from him. "Out of that T-shirt."

"Okay," he answers easily. Too easily and in one swift move to his feet, he's shirtless. Out here on Casey's deck—the rest of our friends scattered down on the beach right below us—he's half-naked.

I find myself eye-level with his strong, dark chest. No butterfly. But then he pivots, slowly, until I find myself staring at a bright, colorful monarch on his left shoulder. Without hesitating, I reach my fingertips and touch it; like I might lure it nearer, or capture it as my own. But it's Michael's warm, soft skin I'm feeling beneath my hand, not an exotic, winged creature.

"Beautiful," I whisper, tracing my finger over the detailed design, not caring who sees. "You are so beautiful, Michael."

I lean close, up onto my tiptoes. Until my lips press against his back and I kiss him, right on that shoulder, burning hot beneath the butterfly tattoo.

"I want to make love to you," he says, the words spoken out into the ocean wind. "I'm crazy with it, Rebecca."

"Me too," I agree, slipping my arms around his waist.

He turns, until he's holding me close against his bare chest. "Everyone's going out tonight," he tells me. "Did you realize that?"

I swallow hard. "No. No I didn't."

"This could be the night we stay in," he says. "Let's ask Marti to take Andrea with them to dinner, but you and me, let's stick around here." He brushes my hair beneath his fingertips, and there's something different in his eyes. Something I first noticed the other night at his dinner party.

Below us a tinny radio overlays the lulling sounds of the ocean and crying gulls. In the distance, there's laughter.

This is freer than I've felt in such a long time.

"Michael," I remind him quietly, "you should know that...I don't look like I did. Before."

"You've said that."

"I want to be sure that, well, that you *know*." I press my eyes shut, feeling the muscles of his arms, closed tight around me. Secure. "You know, just how it looks with the scars and all. I mean, it wasn't *just* Ben—there were the surgeries to save my life."

"Thank God," I hear him whisper under his breath.

"It's just not as simple as you think." There, now I've explained the situation, I think. Still, it's easier to keep my eyes shut than to see his obvious disappointment.

I feel him cup my face, tilting it upward, until slowly I have to open my eyes. "Rebecca," he says, his voice quieter than usual. Like he's trying to still all my raging doubts. "It *is* simple because I love you," he says. "And it doesn't get any simpler than that."

Chapter Twenty-Two: Michael

Rebecca and I stand together at the large window of Casey's bedroom, quiet, staring out at the dark ocean. The full moon reaches silver fingers across the surface of the water, reflecting all the churning emotions inside of me.

"Moon's almost full," I breathe, kissing her exposed shoulder. It's warm beneath my mouth, silver beneath the moonlight. Delicate and soft, and I have to bend low even to kiss her there. "Yes." She shivers at my kiss. "No wonder we're crazy."

I run my fingers down the length of her bare arm. "Nope, been crazy for months now," I murmur, feeling my groin tighten. "Moon's no excuse. I'd say it's all you, Rebecca O'Neill."

That lacy little camisole she's wearing with blue jeans isn't hurting things, either. Thank God everyone is gone for a few hours.

Slowly she pivots until she's facing me, pressed up against my chest. Her breasts are luscious and round, her nipples already jutting out with her arousal. I dip my fingers beneath the strap of her camisole, exposing a long scar along her breastbone. With a quiet gasp, she covers her heart with her hand, stepping backward from me.

"Rebecca, it's okay." Being naked with me is a safe place to be; she should know that.

She nods, swallowing, and cautiously drops her hand away. There's a second scar, smaller beside the first, like an unequal twin.

Taking my fingertip, I trace the biggest one, following the thick length of it like a map to her heart. "Becca, I love you," I reassure her. "*You.* Not some perfect Hollywood chick."

She stares at me, her mouth open in shock, then begins to laugh. I frown, puzzled. "I'm serious," I say.

"I know." She touches my cheek, still giggling happily. "It's just that everyone in Hollywood wanted me to be perfect," she says with a gorgeous, sideways smile. "Until you."

"I'm not everybody."

She kisses me slowly, whispering, "I'm starting to figure that out."

For a brief moment, I remember my first kiss with Allie out on that dance floor, lights and sound and heat drumming through my body as his lips touched mine.

I have that exact same forbidden, upended feeling with Rebecca right now.

In an explosive flurry, we back toward the bed; I tug at my T-shirt, yanking it over my head. Together, we collapse in a heap of warm flesh, exploring every inch of one another.

"Show me that butterfly," she groans in my ear, as I roll her onto her back.

I growl, "Later," toying in frustration with the fly of her jeans.

"Let me help," she whispers, and snakes out of them easily. Some more wrangling, then I'm down to nothing but my boxers and an achy hard-on, those lacy little panties of hers making me half-crazy. So I begin to kiss her...low.

Then lower even still.

Arching her small hips up against me, she tangles her hand in my hair. "Michael, no!" she cries out.

I've been kissing her navel, licking it—now I'm confused. See, I have plans in mind, and staring up at her in the darkness I wonder if she doesn't *like* those plans. She reaches, tugging at the top edge of her bikini underwear where two very long scars are visible. But I don't give a shit about that.

She needs to understand that my male self is focused on only one thing—my dark, warm prize, only slightly farther down from where I've been showering her with these kisses. One thought pounds hard through my body: *God, men are so much easier to figure out.*

"You don't want this?" I ask, swallowing hard. Blood rushes in my ears, loud. Hell, it rushes through my whole damn body.

She runs a shaky hand through her disheveled blonde hair, sinking into the pillows without another word. She's given so much damn thought to these irrelevant scars; maybe now she's realizing how insignificant they really are between us.

"Relax, baby," I whisper, bending low and pressing a sweet kiss against her abdomen—against the largest scar of all. Very slowly, I trail kisses down the length of it, peeling back her panties until there's only her. Letting her know I want to love every inch of her.

Once the lingerie is stripped away, and there's only my mouth against her warm skin, she releases an aroused, happy sigh of feminine pleasure.

And with that one very girlish sound, I nearly lose it completely.

I go lower still, licking my tongue along that one long scar, pressing her thighs open a little wider so she's ready for what I'm going to do next. Oh, man, it's been a long time since I've tasted honey this sweet.

She lifts her hips the moment my tongue gives her a first stroke, her hands digging into my scalp, twining in my hair.

"Oh, Michael." She's tensed in reaction to what I'm doing, and moans a little. But I want to be sure she's not uncomfortable, so I stop, looking up the line of her body as if I'm a sailor staring across a ship's bow. "You good with this, baby?"

Slowly she lets her hips drop to the mattress, leaning back into the pillows. With an audible swallow, she nods, eyes shining bright.

"So you liked that?" I can't help but feel a little wicked, and with my hands wrapped about her thighs, and my mouth just inches away from my gleaming prize, I feel powerful too. I bend low, flicking my tongue. "You like this?"

She releases a kitten-like moan of pleasure, blinking, but her thighs tense again. Maybe it's just been too long since I've been with a woman, but am I getting the right reaction here? I'm not sure. "You're not uncomfortable?"

She gives a little shake of her head. "It's...Jake never did this." She swallows, hard. "I've never done this before."

Oh, now I get it. Wow. I'm going to be the first to pleasure her like this? A flare of fiery heat chases down my spine at the thought of being special like that. And with a possessive growl, I realize I don't ever want another man to touch her again. No one else besides me.

"Your dentist lover back in Georgia? No?"

She swats me on the shoulder and I dip my head low again, working my hands over her hips, down her thighs—while my mouth works a sweeter, warmer place. With every flick and motion of my tongue, Rebecca makes the most erotic little cries and it's like they shoot into me, driving me harder. Making me want her even more.

Then her hips jackknife upward, and I feel the pulse of her pleasure against my tongue. I take firm hold of her buttocks, squeezing, urging her to ride out her release.

"Yeah, baby, that's it," I murmur, and slowly her hips drop back down to the mattress. "Oh, sweetness, that's it."

She's breathing heavy, and I crawl up her body like a prowling bobcat until I'm positioned atop her, heavy and totally male. And my erection is also heavy and totally male as I push it greedily between her thighs.

My heart is pounding like it might explode as I settle my hips against hers, feeling the soft, curving shape of her against me. It's hard not to feel like I could shatter her, she's that small and delicate. But it's part of what turns me on, too, that she's feminine...different from me.

I prop my elbows around her on the pillows, and simply stare into those eyes of hers. That's when it happens. This strange, hushed

219

moment. As if the ocean just beyond the patio stops roaring; as if Rebecca herself stops breathing; as if I am caught in a timeless spell, captive to this woman.

I never thought I'd get here again, but I am. I'm in love with this woman, and at an almost desperate, fevered level.

"I'm in love with you," I murmur softly, brushing my lips against hers. She wraps her small, muscular arms about my neck. "God help you and me both, but I am so damn in love with you."

She takes hold of my face, breaking our kiss and forcing me away. Then our eyes meet, and that sacred, beautiful stillness descends upon us again. Over our moment, over this joining. It's as if all separation or the possibility of it vanishes, and even though I'm not inside her yet— even though my whole body is trembling—we're one. We're already one.

"I want you, Michael," she whispers on a heartbeat. "I really, really want you."

I move my lips against the column of her throat, teasing my tongue along her fast-beating pulse. "Good thing, baby. 'Cause I'm dying to get inside of you."

Her hands roam and move across my shoulders, fingers spread wide over the exact spot where I have my tattoo. I flash on the image I had before, of her mouth trailing over it, licking my shoulder, body grinding up against mine.

"Kiss it," I groan, and her hands stop their exploration.

"I don't..."

I lift off of her in a push up, knowing we'll have to change positions. With eyes narrowed and my hard cock jutting toward her, I fight the urge to beg. "My tattoo, baby. Kiss my tattoo."

I move onto my stomach, a position that could be achingly familiar, but I send those memories out to the horizon at the first flick of her warm tongue against my skin. She slides atop me, the lightest slip of a thing. Damn, she's like a butterfly herself, I think. My miraculous, healing creature. My Rebecca.

But then she's straddling me, and I can feel that warm dampness between her thighs as it touches my lower back, as she bends again and slowly kisses the stretched wings of my tattoo.

"Like this?" Her voice is thick and husky, lost to what's happening.

"Yeah, baby. Good. That's good."

Warm hands move along my nape, slide across my hips, and I keep thinking I should take control here. But I feel more confidence and seduction in these strokes of Rebecca's than any other time we've been together.

She feels so bold because she knows I can't see her or the scars. I realize it then, my heart slamming, and I don't know if I should flip her onto her back and *make* her accept my love—or if I should go with this current, very sexy groove, this power that's starting up between us. A power that is intimately linked with my own past, not just Rebecca's, I think, as I lay spread face-first beneath her body.

But what happens between us now, it's got to be about the present—about who we are in each other's arms, not the embrace of the past.

"Becca?" I ask softly, arching my back and lifting my head so I can look over my shoulder at her. The glimpse I get in return tightens my throat. Her blonde hair is disheveled and wild, her lips swollen from my earlier kisses, and a flush has hit her Irish cheeks that makes me want to claim her now.

"Becca, now it's my turn."

"For what?" Her hair falls over one shoulder, another heavy lock over her eyes.

I smile, moving up onto my knees and reach for her. "To shatter every one of your defenses."

I'm the one who's shattered, I think, snuggling Rebecca a little closer. We're both sweaty and sticky, but definitely very satisfied. I've got a smile on my face that just won't fade. How could I have forgotten what it feels like to be inside a woman? Lying here afterwards with Rebecca, staring at Casey's ceiling, I can't believe I ever forgot. The softness. The warmth, all close around me. It's like I just lost my virginity all over again; I'm seventeen, all dewy-eyed and invincible. Like my very first time with Katie back in high school, I'm filled with innocent wonder. Amazement. Rebecca is tiny and curvy and soft; she's everything Alex *never* was. I guess somewhere along the way I forgot the difference.

Beside me, she's nestled close within the crook of my arm. The bathroom light spills over our bed, and I can't stop watching her, even though I'm sleepy as hell. Between surfing today, and now sex, I'm flattened.

She's so beautiful, the gold in her hair shimmering in the near dark; I swear I could get going all over again. She rolls closer, splaying her palm across my chest. She rubs me there, running her hand over the curling dark hairs.

"That was really incredible," she says, a sweet, tender smile forming on her lips.

I stroke her hair, holding her close. "Definitely incredible." Worth the thirteen-year wait, I want to say, but figure I'd better keep *that* to myself. Closing my eyes, I wait for her to say something about how she's falling in love with me, something dopey to satisfy the seventeen-year-old she's brought out to play tonight.

But she's silent beside me, for a long while. Alex was way more talkative than this, and he was a *guy*.

So getting nervous, I finally ask her, "You okay?" Maybe I've lost my touch, too long out of the saddle and all that. My heartbeat becomes wild and unsteady inside my chest when she turns to me. Her face is clouded with uncertainty.

"Mm...can I ask you something?"

I nod my encouragement. "Sure, baby. Anything, you know that."

She rolls onto her side, staring hard into my eyes. "Don't get mad, okay?" Those words almost always preface something that will make me *furious*—I know that much from twelve years in a committed relationship.

"Sure." I swallow, clearing my throat. "Go on."

"Okay, this is going to sound lame, but I still need to ask...or I'm afraid that if I don't ask, that I'm being naive."

My stomach knots hard because I suddenly have a feeling I know what's coming; I brace for it like a swerving, oncoming car. "Go on."

She sighs. "I realize I asked this before..." Her voice trails into nothing.

"Oh, I get it," I say. "You're still worried if I'm healthy." I try to laugh it off, but this moment was all about the romance for me, all about committing myself to her—now it's all about the Dark Gay Cloud. "A little late for that, Becca, don't you think?" I ask, feeling sad. "But yeah, sure. I'm healthy." I try to hide how damned much she's hurt me.

She told me she was on the pill last week, so I didn't worry about other forms of contraception. Never even crossed my mind that she would.

"I know this is stupid," she stammers. "It must *seem* really stupid, but given your lifestyle..."

"Lifestyle," I repeat dully, watching the ceiling fan whir soundlessly overhead. "Good euphemism."

"Okay, I mean that you were *gay*. For a long time."

"Baby, if I were *gay*," I bark, turning to face her, "then I sure wouldn't be here in bed with you right now." I can't believe that something so sweet—our very first time together—has taken such a lonely turn. I feel defensive too, like she's become an outsider pointing the finger at me and my past choices.

"But you are bi," she continues, reaching to stroke my hair, but I deflect her touch. Her voice gets really quiet and gentle. "Please don't be mad that I'm asking."

"Rebecca, I am perfectly healthy. I told you that before." I roll out of her reach. "Alex was it for me. I've told you that. We've talked about this." My anger grows more powerful. "And he sure as hell wasn't a promiscuous kind of guy. You do realize that a *monogamous* gay guy is a lot safer than a promiscuous straight one?"

"Still, I worry about all this stuff sometimes," she continues, drawing in an uneasy breath. "No. No, that's not it. I don't worry about you, Michael, because I know you and Alex were fully committed." She lifts her gaze to mine. "No, what I worry about is that I won't be...enough. That I won't be...enough. That I can't ever be enough, long term."

I sit up in bed, truly angry for the first time. "Are you shitting me?"

"No, I'm totally serious, Michael," she says. "I'm a woman and pretty much, historically speaking, it was boys who turned your crank."

"*Alex.* I loved Alex." I blow out a breath, staring at the ceiling. She never knew Alex, can't know the way he was, his charisma. Can't know how we were together. "That's what this is really about, isn't it? You think I can't stay straight or something?"

She stares at me, her mouth slightly open. "You're still in love with him." *What did she think? That I'd let him go?*

"I think I'll always love him," I answer. "But that doesn't mean I can't love you."

She's still nestled beside me, naked, but I sense her closing down. "Being with me means you don't betray him," she says, frowning. It's like a realization is forming for her. I'm not sure I follow—and I'm not sure I like it.

"Rebecca, he has nothing to do with this."

She turns to me, a melancholy expression on her face. "He has everything to do with us," she says. "I'm safe, because I'm not a threat to *him.* I'm a woman, not another man."

"You know, I loved a girl once. I mean, other than you. I lost my virginity to her, back up in Virginia. It's not like I've never loved a woman before now. I'm hardly some kid, baby. I'm way older than you, don't forget."

"You're *thirty-nine.*" The right side of her mouth turns up at the corner with tender amusement. "You're only six years older than me."

"Hey now, I'm old enough." I smile back at her. "Enough that I know exactly what I'm doing here."

"I guess it's just weird to me, thinking of you with a guy. I mean, we've made love now, and then I think about your past." She looks away from me with a slight shiver, and somehow rather than feeling judged or exposed, I understand. She loves me. I know it, even if she hasn't said as much. It's not an easy place for either of us to be, standing squarely between this moment and my sexual history.

It's interesting to me that this conversation is only coming up now—after she's made herself so vulnerable to me, physically and emotionally.

I trace my finger across the long scar on her breastbone, thoughtful. "I think what you're trying to get at," I answer quietly, "is whether or not I'm capable of staying straight."

"Yes, exactly." I see relief in her eyes.

"But, see, it doesn't work like that for me," I explain, bending low to kiss the jagged arrow-shaped scar across her chest. "I'm just me. I'm me, and I'm in love with you, Rebecca. That isn't gonna go away."

"Then why am I so scared?" She searches my face; I draw her closer.

"Because you're in love," I explain. "And that's always a scary place to be."

She pulls back, staring up at me intently. "I do love you, Michael. I hope you know that."

"I'm beginning to get that idea," I tease, all my anger dissolving with one look into those liquid-green eyes. I notice that she's shaking a little, naked there beside me, so I pull the sheet up over her shoulder.

"I love you very much, Michael," she whispers, closing her eyes. "I don't want to do anything to hurt you. But loving you like this, it's terrifying, you're right." Her eyes flutter open again, filled with tears. They're not tears of pain or heartache—just tears of deep emotion.

Those tears remind me of my sheer panic when Alex and I first got together—and then I realize that for some blessed reason, I'm *not* frightened with her. That nothing about Rebecca O'Neill ever makes me want to hide or run the other way at all.

Pressing my lips softly against hers, I repeat powerful words from a rainy night long ago. The words that changed my life and my heart.

"Baby," I whisper, "instead of fighting everything so much, you could just open up your heart and see where it leads you."

And I swear somewhere in the mystic universe, I hear Alex cheering me on.

Chapter Twenty-Three: Rebecca

"Rebecca, wake up."

"Hmm?" I blink back sleep to find Andrea staring into my eyes, her auburn hair a disheveled morning mess. Beyond the bedroom windows July Fourth has broken bright and sunny over the Pacific, all the overcast clouds burned off from yesterday.

Andie nudges me in the ribs again. "Rebecca, let's go surfing." Her clear eyes have a conspiratorial twinkle.

I smile. "I thought late day was best."

"Oh, but early morning's great too—lots of colors." Beyond her, the orange-red of daybreak refracts off the waves.

"Okay," I say. "But you're sure about this?" I'm thinking of how hesitant she's been until now.

Sitting up in bed, she stares out at the glittering morning light, her expression growing somber. "Yeah, I want to do it," she says, scrunching up her nose. "Is that okay?"

"That's great," I enthuse. "Let's go tell your dad." I flinch at my wording choice, but she doesn't seem to mind for once.

"It would be fun if you got into surfing," she tells me. "If it were something you liked to do too."

Reaching to the bedside for my hairbrush, I gesture her closer. "I love the beach, sweetie," I warn with a laugh, "but I may not be very good at surfing." Michael's litany of scary surfing tips from yesterday nearly chased me away from the sport for good.

She scoots near, turning her back toward me, and I begin brushing her shiny hair.

"Silly," Andrea laughs, glancing over her shoulder at me, "who cares about that? Just surf 'cause it's fun, okay?"

I think of that little girl who sat beside me on the edge of Mona's pool only a month or so ago. Who talked about a hidden scar, one that kept her from wearing a bathing suit—a scar that evoked powerful and ambivalent feelings, even toward the sport she clearly loved. She seemed an ancient woman in a child's body at Mona's that day.

But today, with all her quivery excitement about going out into the ocean, she finally seems eight years old to me.

When I finish with her hair, I hand her the brush. She hops from the bed, then with a quick glance my way, slips out of her nightgown and Barbie panties, her small little-girl body naked before me. Reaching into her suitcase, she retrieves her bathing suit, wiggling into it. She stands in front of the large windows, staring out at the ocean like she's gathering her nerve.

Then pivoting slowly toward me, she announces in a hushed voice, "This is it." She takes her index finger and points to a longish silver line on her upper thigh, tapping it significantly. "This is my scar."

Mentally, I scroll through my options. I could tell her that it's nothing, hardly noticeable at all—which would be the truth. Or I could say that I'm sorry; after all, she's haunted by the same demons that are so familiar to me. But staring into her trusting blue eyes, neither choice seems right.

"Come closer," I encourage her. "So I can see."

Beside the bed, she stands so that I'm nearly eye-level with it. Her scar's different from mine, pale against her freckled skin. Like someone zigzagged along her leg with a silver-tipped felt marker.

Scowling, she touches it with her small finger. "They couldn't get me out of the car," she explains in a solemn voice. "That's how I got it."

"I'm sure that was very painful."

She shrugs but remains silent, eyes downcast.

An inspiration comes to me, one that I'm uncertain about. "Andrea, sweetheart," I begin tentatively, touching her on the arm, "I have a thought." She glances up, meeting my gaze. "You want me to tell you what it is?"

"Sure." Her eyebrows furrow with sharp concentration.

"I know your scar makes you sad. That it makes you think of unhappy things, like your accident," I say. "And your daddy's death."

She nods her silent agreement, still listening. Once I'm sure I haven't pushed her away, I continue. "Well, what if we had a plan? What if we decided your scar would remind you of his *life*?"

Her expression becomes troubled. "But I got it in the accident."

"I know, but it could remind you of the good stuff," I say. "You could touch it, and think of your daddy, even though he's far away."

She runs her thumb over the scar, tracing the length of it. "It used to hurt. But then that stopped," she tells me. "I didn't want it to stop. I *liked* to feel it." I recall her words that day at Mona's: *Mine feels like nothing.* My own scars are always itching and aching, causing terrible complications, yet I have an idea of what she's trying to say.

"When it hurt, it felt real."

She nods. "Daddy still felt real."

"That's why maybe using your scar to remember him is a good thing," I reply, lifting my fingers to her cheek. She lets me stroke her face, closing her eyes. "Better than feeling the pain. He's always with you this way."

A slow smile spreads across her face, until her dimples appear and her eyes open again. "Oh, he's always with me," she answers with a determined nod. "I know that. He told me so in a dream. But don't tell Michael," she rushes to add, leaning closer. "It upsets him when I dream about Daddy."

I drop my hand away, curious. "Why would it upset him?"

"'Cause I think Michael wishes he'd get a dream too," she explains, biting her lower lip. "I heard him say something to Aunt Marti about it once."

Do you still dream? That very first question we posed to one another. He turned from me then, troubled. At the time I thought it was just his happily-ever-after that was no longer intact. Now I'm thinking it might have been the literal dreams too.

"Dreams are important," I half-whisper. Andie looks up at me.

"You dream," she observes. "You dream a lot, don't you, Rebecca?"

I give an intentionally opaque answer. "Sometimes." All of the nightmares, the ones that won't entirely go away, they've abated these past two months since Michael and Andrea came into my life. But she doesn't need to know all that.

"I dreamed about Daddy last night," she continues in a quiet voice. "That he was talking to me. He does that sometimes, tells me stuff I should know and all." She grows serious, focused. "That's how come I want to go surfing now. 'Cause he told me I should."

"He did?"

She settles on the bed, staring into my eyes. "He told me to surf again—" she pauses, getting a mischievous smile, "—because of you, Rebecca."

"Me?" My eyes widen in disbelief.

"Daddy told me it wasn't just for Michael," she explains. "He said *you* need surfing too."

✦

I've been riding my surfboard on my stomach for what seems hours, to the point that I feel worn out. Not Michael, though. He grins from ear to ear, riding sluggish little waves and showing off like a teenager performing for the Y-camp girls on the other side of the lake. He showboats, walking out the length of his board—something they explained is part of longboarding style. Casey floats on his own board beside me, coaching me.

"Rebecca, you can get a wave and ride on your knees," he tells me.

227

"That's your next step."

Sitting back on my board, I observe the scene around me. "I'm not sure." I watch Michael paddling back toward me with Andrea. They caught the last wave together, having fun and giggling as they rode it to shore side by side on their boards.

"Rebecca." Casey splashes me with water, demanding my serious attention. "You should try."

My heart pounds within my chest, fear and adrenalin blending together. Trailing my fingers through the water, I say softly, "Casey, I don't want to die."

He laughs, edging closer in the water. "You're not going to die, you freak."

I look around us at the breaking waves and the teeming pack of surfers in the lineup. "But all that stuff Michael said yesterday—"

"—He said because he *loves* you." He gives me a meaningful look. "All right? And the last person he loved *did* die. Think about that for a while."

I stare down at my board, my mouth tugging into an awkward smile. "Well, when you put it that way..."

"Surfing saved my life, Rebecca," he continues, gesturing around us. "There's no greater peace than being out here in the water, riding the waves. I want to give that to you."

"Why?" I ask, surprised by his seriousness.

"Because of what you've done for Mike." He nods toward Andrea, paddling in our direction on her small board. "And her."

I shrug off his compliment, not sure what to say. "Casey, that really wasn't my doing." I don't feel responsible for these positive changes in Michael and Andrea's lives; I hardly feel right taking credit for them.

"No?" he asks, staring into my eyes meaningfully. "Were you around this time last year? Mike was barely hanging on. He stayed depressed and drunk a whole lot of the time. It wasn't pretty."

My throat tightens. "I hate thinking of him in that much pain."

"He tried to pull it together..." He shakes his head. "He kept trying, but I don't think he got better—not *truly* better—until you came along. Everything seemed to change then."

I smile. "You didn't like me at first."

"Screw that." He rolls his eyes in mock irritation. "I liked you enough."

"You liar." I splash him, giggling. "You thought he belonged with a guy."

He gives a grudging laugh, and I know that I've hit the truth. "But I changed my mind, O'Neill," he says. "You did notice that, right?"

"When exactly?" I tease, tossing my wet hair back over my shoulder. "Last week or yesterday?"

"Shut up. You're good for them—both of them. Course I can see that," he admits. "Sure, I thought Warner should've stuck with the boys, but..." He shrugs, squinting at the shore thoughtfully. "But you brought them back to life, and I can't argue with that."

"They were ready to find healing, that's all."

"They needed *you*, O'Neill."

"I needed them too," I admit quietly, but he doesn't hear me. His focus is trained behind us, at a mounting wave.

"Okay, look, that one's got your name on it." I follow his gaze as the wave burgeons upward. It will break somewhere in my proximity. "Go for it, Rebecca!" he shouts, glancing back hurriedly at me. "It's yours! Paddle, Rebecca, *go*! Paddle! Paddle!"

He makes motions with his hands, demonstrating, and, lacking a better plan, I begin paddling like crazy. Feeling the wave burst forth under me, I rise upward in answering instinct onto my knees, clutching hard to the board as it takes off toward shore.

Charging forward, the wave vibrating and thundering beneath me, I begin to laugh—a cleansing, liberating, wild laugh of freedom that won't stop.

Off to my side, I'm aware of passing Michael and Andrea heading out on their boards, conscious that they're cheering me on. Michael whoops with pride. Behind me I hear Casey shouting me onward too.

I can do this, I think, grinning like a little girl, like I did the first time my dad helped me canter on my horse. I can do this: I can be free again.

✧

Sitting on the beach, swaddled in a towel beside Michael and Andrea, the day is ending the way it began, down by the ocean, and it's as if all the hard years have washed out to deepest sea. Like the undertow reached up from that one wave I rode and snatched all the black things away, dragging them out to the distant horizon. To a place you only imagine as a child, the edge of nothing.

"I'm so proud of you," Michael whispers in my ear, kissing me there. The three of us are sitting together, watching the waves and laughing. A full day behind us, our bodies tired and saturated with sun.

Kissing his jaw, I long for more of him—for as much as he gave me last night. "Proud of what?"

He grins. "'Cause you're my surfer girl." He draws me close, against his side. "I'm proud of you for going out there. That's a big freaking deal."

Beside him, Andrea bobs her head in agreement. "You're gonna be on your feet soon, I bet," she says.

Up the shore, I hear the staccato sound of firecrackers popping. In a little while, the sun will sink below the horizon and the sky will begin to light up. It seems a celebration choreographed just for me. I've lived with fear for so long, it's become like breathing—not always easy, but impossible to shake.

But today—if only for today—I know that it's gone because I can breathe. Easy, effortless, exactly like it should be.

Hours later, and everyone's gone to their respective rooms, collapsing in bed after a full day in the sun. Beside me Andrea's nestled close, her body warm in contrast to the chilly air conditioning in Casey's house. But unlike Andie, I can't sleep despite my exhaustion; I keep replaying the events of the past twenty-four hours in my mind.

A muffled sound from the living room startles me: the television set. Glancing at the clock, I see that it's after midnight; seems someone else is battling insomnia tonight. Crawling out of bed, careful not to wake Andrea, I decide to investigate. Maybe I'll get a glass of water while I'm up.

Stepping into the hallway, there's the sound of laughter and familiar voices, all coming from the TV. I stop and listen. I hear Michael and Casey and someone else's—a man's voice that I don't immediately recognize. Then Marti's laughter. Moving stealthily, I peer around the corner, and see them all on the television screen: it's a home video playing. Michael sits on the floor in front of the TV, remote in hand, rapt. He reminds me of Andrea watching cartoons or Disney, he's that absorbed.

I discovered a mound of these home videos earlier today while trying to locate *The Princess Diaries* for Andrea. They were stacked beside the VCR, with labels like *Huntington* and *July Fourth* and various dates from the past few years. At the time, I burned with curiosity, knowing Alex must be on several of the tapes.

Although he has plenty of videos at home, ones populated with Alex and their shared memories, I think I understand what propelled him to watch these particular videos right now, in secret while the rest of us are asleep. Because he betrayed Alex last night. By making love to me, he betrayed his *real* partner.

In the video, Alex stands on the beach, laughing with Marti. It's unsettling to see him "live". I'm accustomed to his pictures, to his arresting blue eyes, but seeing him on screen, watching his movements and facial expressions, my mental portrait of him becomes more complex. I get a better fix on his lanky size—that he's even taller than Michael, and simply towers over small Marti.

He would have towered over me too. It's an unsettling thought, imagining him alive and beside me. Steadying myself against the wall, I begin to shake: if Alex had lived, there'd be no right now. I wouldn't be here at all because he and Michael would be together.

They stand on the beach, blabbering about something indistinct, something I can't hear. Watching the way the group circles together I understand another thing I could never have fathomed from a simple photograph. Alex drew attention and energy from everyone near him. Like their sun, the others orbited around him. But what he took, he obviously gave back unselfishly; there's an electricity in their group interactions that I haven't noticed in his absence. A fire.

"Hey, Michael," Alex calls out, pointing at something on his tall surfboard, clutched within his hands. "Check this out." I hadn't thought his voice would sound so deep. The warmth I had anticipated, but not the deep fullness of its resonance.

Michael enters the frame and their voices grow quieter; he frowns about something, touching the board as they discuss it. The camera cuts away to a group of surfers down the beach, and I see that there's some kind of amateur surf contest going on. Camera cuts back to Alex; for the first time I notice a number on his forearm, grease-penciled onto it. He must have been competing.

Alex touches Michael on the arm, and I shiver in reaction, as if he'd just touched me. It isn't a sexual or provocative touch. His hand has simply brushed unselfconsciously against Michael's arm as they were talking. It's the relaxed familiarity of longtime lovers. As they step apart, Alex gives him a warm smile, a smile that speaks endless volumes about what they shared.

My chest tightens painfully, the familiar swell of anxiety rushing through my body. What a fool I've been. I can't possibly compete with that, I think, retreating into the dark hallway. Obscured in the darkness, I listen to the voices on the tape, to the laughter and camaraderie they all shared back then. I hear Michael's voice. *Alex, baby, you're gonna win out there today.*

Michael's voice echoes down the hallway. *Knock 'em dead, baby!*

Baby. The word burns my mind like an after-image from gazing at the sun, blotting out everything else.

Quietly, I vanish into the bedroom without a sound. Michael hasn't seen me hidden here in the shadows, and yet *I've* seen so much.

Chapter Twenty-Four: Michael

Sitting in a ramshackle seafood restaurant overlooking the Pacific, it's just Rebecca, Andrea, and me. Everyone else shoved off for home late this Sunday afternoon. I'm excited we've got a few days to ourselves, a few days when we can keep forming this tentative family we're making together.

Packing up his Explorer, blond hair askew with wind and sun block, Casey seemed sad to go. He lingered a long time, particularly with Rebecca, which made me smile. I think they're becoming regular buddies; I could tell he was proud of her for nearly making it up on that surfboard.

"Next time, I'll get you onto your feet," he told her with an awkward hug.

"I can't wait," she said, smiling at me. Marti and Dave were easy, but winning over crusty Casey Porter is a true accomplishment. She should feel good about it.

Marti hugged her too, kissing her cheek and promising to phone her this week about a "girl's day out". Rebecca is weaving easily into the fabric of my world, which both pleases and ultimately unsettles me, for reasons I don't entirely understand.

Drumming my fingers on the tabletop, I stare out at the beach. I've been to this same restaurant with Alex dozens of times. We came here even before we were together, when we were just friends hanging out down at Casey's place. Alex whispered, "Gay friendly," in my ear that first time, and I stared at him, kind of surprised. He explained, "Owner's a gay guy. Lots of gay staff." I got from his explanation that it wasn't like a gay bar or restaurant, just a place where he and his crew could feel comfortable. Later I understood it was a place where the two of us could feel comfortable too.

So it's unsettling to sit here now with this woman who I'm beginning to imagine as my wife. Been a long damn time since I thought of spending my life with anyone other than Allie, and glancing around at the familiar surroundings, I feel a little guilty. Like I'm

Butterfly Tattoo

stepping out on Alex or something. If the owner—a guy named Vince Peters who was always friends with us—spots me, I'll feel busted for sure.

"You okay?" Rebecca studies me closely from the other side of the table. Maybe my expression was more transparent than I realized. Andrea inserts pegs in an IQ test game, lost in concentration.

I give her a weak smile. "Yeah, baby. Fine. Totally fine." I don't feel fine inside: I feel guilty, coming here with her. Without *him*.

That emotion is already gaining life within me, when our waiter appears—and spooks me completely. A redheaded young kid, he looks a hell of a lot like Alex. Glancing at Andrea, I wonder if she notices too, but she's caught up in the game she's playing. She looks up with marginal interest, the same level of curiosity she'd grant a seashell discovered on the sand.

I wonder why she can't see it, this eerie resemblance the waiter bears to Allie? Am I the only one feeling spelled here?

He can't be thirty yet, maybe only twenty-seven or so. Roughly the age Alex was when we first met, with the same coppery hair cropped close along the nape of his neck, like wiregrass to the touch. Of course, Alex's style was more disheveled and rowdy despite the close cut— never completely a doctor's look. And of course Allie certainly never had a twangy Texas accent, all range and open prairie, not like this wild-eyed cowboy kid does when he greets us.

Still, it's irrelevant what he's wearing or how old or how tall he is—or even what he sounds like. From the moment he grins at me, a broad winsome expression filling his thoroughly freckled face, my heart leaps right out of my chest.

I bump into Alex all the time: in shopping malls, at the grocery store, on the studio lot. He's in a thousand crowds of people, in a thousand different faces, no matter which way I look. But this time is different. This fresh-faced kid reminds me more of Alex Richardson than any single man I've encountered since the day he died. Only when he asks again if we want to hear the dinner specials do I realize I'm gawking—not listening—and stare down at my hands to hide my intense emotions.

"Sure," Rebecca interjects, helping. I look to her, lost, wondering if she realizes, and there's an unexpected, sad expression on her face even as there's something tender there. God, please don't let all my careful little pieces come undone, not here in front of them all.

I mumble something incoherent without looking up, placing my order for fried shrimp by memory.

"Sir?" the stranger prompts me, and I gaze up into his clear blue eyes again, shaken completely. That wholesome smile, the sun-drenched freckles; I know I'm staring hard when he asks gently, "Your menu, sir?"

233

Under my breath I mutter an apology, relinquishing it into those freckled hands, dusted with auburn hair. Allie's hands were freckled like that, I think, as our fingers brush, ever so slightly, and I nearly burn with the physical connection. And then he turns. He turns and he's gone, back to the kitchen, and my sense of loss at that moment is so acute I almost forget that my girlfriend is there, at the table, watching me fall for Alex all over again.

Noticing Rebecca, I find all the color washed right out of her face. She saw it too, exactly what I saw. And if she hadn't seen it in the waiter's face, she saw it all reflected right on mine.

Back at the house, Andrea goes straight to her room to take a bath and get ready for bed. It's my first real chance to talk to Rebecca after the dinner fiasco.

But I don't talk. Instead, I sink onto the sofa, flipping on the television. Rebecca stands in the kitchen, distant from me. She's barely said a word since the restaurant.

"I figure we might drive up the coast some tomorrow morning," I say, avoiding her probing gaze. "I know Andie'd love that. We can be back on the beach by afternoon."

Rebecca doesn't answer me, only walks across the room, staring out the window. I can't see her face, can't gauge her emotions, though I have a pretty good idea what she's feeling. Through the glass, she watches the dark ocean, silent, her face inscrutable.

"I got up last night," she says, staring out the windows. "While you were watching videos."

"Oh." *Oh shit.* I couldn't sleep, felt on edge thinking about how we'd made love. I guess I needed a connection with Alex after that—and after riding all those waves without him. I just missed him: nothing terribly complex.

She eyes me warily. "You seemed fine on your own, so I went back to bed."

"I wish you'd told me you were up."

She shrugs, turning her back to me again. "I wasn't sure what to say."

"You could've said you were awake," I try gently. "Just like me. I'd like to show you tapes of Al some time. If you want to see 'em."

She sighs, a heavy, defeated sound. "Did you have to flirt with him, Michael?" For a moment, I blink in confusion, thinking she means Alex. But then I understand who she means.

She finally turns to look at me. "I mean, staring I understand. Pretending he was Alex, I get that too. But did you really have to flirt so much?"

I don't answer right away, truly considering her comment. I've fucked up big time; I know it. I just don't know how to rescue the situation. "Didn't think I actually flirted," I finally say, trying to smile. "I do draw the line at some point."

"And that's supposed to make me feel better?" She folds her arms over her chest. "About you hitting on a guy right in front of me?"

"I wasn't hitting on anybody." And I wasn't—I would never do that in front of Rebecca *or* Andrea, but I don't add that lame argument. "I was just chatting with the guy."

"You flirted." She shakes her head in disbelief. "I haven't spent ten years in the entertainment business without learning to recognize some major flirtation when I see it."

I drop the denials, feeling a little like Bill Clinton in his Lewinsky days. "It didn't mean anything, Rebecca." And it didn't. I guess I did flirt a little, even though I knew I shouldn't, but some dark part of myself couldn't seem to hold back. Not because I wanted Nick the Waiter—but rather because I wanted him to be Alex. "Becca, I'm never gonna see that guy again. It didn't *mean* anything."

She pushes past me, toward the bedroom she's sharing with Andrea. "See, that's where you're wrong, Michael," she says, voice quivering. "Because it meant everything to me."

✧

I wake to an empty bed with ruthless morning sunlight forcing its way through the billowing curtains. The bedroom door is slightly ajar, and I hear the television and Katie Couric's overly optimistic voice from down the hall.

I spent the night unable to sleep, restless and aching for Rebecca—wishing she were in my bed, not sleeping in my daughter's room. I wanted to make love last night, but she worried about Andrea waking up. Deep down, I know her hesitation was far more complex.

Passing through the living room, I hear the shower running. It must be Andie in the bathroom because through the crack in the door, I glimpse Rebecca, blonde hair drawn into a neat braid down her back. She's cradling her cell phone against her ear, zipping her suitcase. In blue jeans and a white T-shirt, she's dressed for the road. I'm a peeping Tom, staring in at her, listening to what she's planning.

She glances at her watch. "I can be there by two. Set the meeting for three." There's a pause, and she gives her suitcase zipper a purposeful tug. "Trevor, look, I'm positive about this. I'm coming home." With that, she snaps the phone shut and stands still as a statue. That's when I make my move.

"You leaving?" I ask, aware that we may have approximately five minutes to do this alone before Andrea emerges from the shower.

Rebecca tucks her phone into her purse, heaving the large

suitcase onto the floor. "Ed wants me to produce Julian's movie." She tosses her braid back confidently, exposing the scars on her face without hesitation. "It's a really wonderful opportunity for me."

I gesture around the room. "But we've got this place for two more days."

"Michael, look—" she begins with a weary sigh, but then says nothing else, staring past me toward the hallway.

"You could wait," I suggest. "Drive back with Andie and me still."

"It can't wait and we both know I'm finished here. That *we're* finished, Michael."

"No, that's not true," I disagree, stepping toward her. As I reach for her arm, she jerks it from my grasp, like she's been scalded.

"Michael, please. You haven't been honest with anyone else, but at least be honest with me."

"I've never been dishonest with you," I answer evenly. "You know exactly how I feel." Green eyes search my face, my heart, and I ache to put eloquent words to my feelings, to make her understand that the waiter meant nothing to me. That the videotapes meant nothing to *us.*

"Yes, well..." She tips her chin upward in proud defiance. "I know a lot more than I did a few months ago."

"You should know that I love you," I answer forcefully, determined that she understand the truth.

Her demeanor becomes resigned. "What I *know* is that this isn't working, Michael. I guess it never was."

"Last night doesn't mean we can't make this work, Becca. Please," I beg, desperate, stepping toward her, but she turns away in the face of my pitiful excuses.

"What about the fact that you're still wearing his ring?" she asks in a soft voice. In shock, I stare down at my hand, though of course she's right. I hadn't thought about it, had meant to remove it before we made love. But somehow, I just didn't.

While I wish I had an explanation, there's nothing I can say. She turns to me, bright tears shining in her eyes, the careful façade crumbling. "A cab is waiting outside," she says, rolling her suitcase toward the door. "I've already told Andrea goodbye."

She hesitates, turning back one last time, and I can't believe the melancholy in her expression. "Michael, the thing I've finally realized is that I'm not who you're looking for." Her tears begin to flow in earnest. "And if you're going to keep searching for him, you might as well look in the right place."

I reach for her, and this time she doesn't fight me. "Rebecca, God, I love you," I insist, desperate to keep her from going.

I stroke her cheek tenderly, tracing the outline of her jaw. She doesn't flinch, but drops her gaze to the floor. "Please tell me you're okay," I say, voice catching. "Because I love you, baby."

"I love you too, Michael," she whispers. "But it's not enough." She sucks in a gasping breath, resting her cheek against my shoulder with a shattered sigh. "I finally understand that *I'm* not enough. I won't ever be enough to make you forget."

✧

I'm not even sure how long I've been here in Casey's room, just lolling in the bed, unable to get up. Andrea thinks I'm sick. Food poisoning, that's what I told her, and she's been watching videos and reading books all day. Bored out of her mind, I can tell, but I'm stuck here, at the bottom of my ocean, struggling to find my way back to the air. Where's Alex when I need him to help me sort out all this emotional shit?

I'm not good at being straight, I'm not good at being gay: I was only ever good at being with Alex Richardson. And for a little while— the most pristine perfect moment—I sure as hell was good at being with Rebecca O'Neill.

Lucky me, as early evening falls I find a marathon of *About the House* reruns on TNT. This minister's son might even say that kind of "luck" has an air of the divine to it. Never did watch the show before, not with Rebecca begging me not to. But since she's dumped me on my queer ass here in Malibu, I think it's only fair that I view her past as openly as she's always gazed at mine. God, she was breathtaking then, with a ballsy confidence like she had the whole world by the tail— Alex's style of confidence, not the fractured eggshell kind I've always seen in her.

Sipping my sixth beer of the evening, I lean back in bed and study my girl, all sassy and funny and shoving Jake Slater right in his place—my girl, just a different version of her, back once upon a time before life played havoc with her. Closing my eyes, I imagine kissing *that* Rebecca, her lips meeting mine, her delicate hands threading through my hair, her cheek soft and porcelain beneath my fingertips.

And I blow out a grief-stricken sigh of remorse, because whether we're talking *that* Rebecca or *my* Rebecca, there's not one iota of difference for me. They're both like shooting for the moon because I'm nothing but a common electrician sitting in a rich friend's beach home aching for an unattainable celebrity actress.

Andrea appears in the doorway, watching me. Sharp light from the living room makes me squint.

"What, doll?" I slur at her and she looks worried, her auburn eyebrows furrowing. Entering my room cautiously, she stares at the television, then glances at me sprawled gracelessly on the bed. "You're watching Rebecca's show."

"There's a marathon."

"Cool," she answers, settling on the end of the bed, spreading her hands neatly in her lap. The more outrageous and stupid I've become, the more adult she seems. "Can I watch too?" It's less a question and more a statement of her intentions as she sits by my feet, back ramrod straight.

"Guess it's 'cause of the holiday weekend," I explain thickly. "This marathon."

Jake is chasing Rebecca around the living room; she's swatting at him, then Cat opens the front door. Laugh track. Rebecca gives Jake a saucy stare and she has never looked more gorgeous to me. Except the night we made love in this same bed. Except the night we kissed the first time. Except this morning, walking out of that damn bedroom without me...

"Michael, are you okay?" Andrea stares at me over her shoulder, translucent blue eyes wide and worried.

"Yeah, Andie, sick. That's all, just sick." She looks at the bottle of Heineken clutched in my hand, then back at my face. "It'll get better," I promise, the soundtrack of *About the House* overlaying our conversation.

Turning back to the television, she responds quietly, "You miss Daddy, don't you?" The room spins, and I close my eyes, murmuring, "Yeah, I sure do miss Daddy."

"And Rebecca. You miss her too."

"I definitely miss her too."

"Is she coming back?" I know she doesn't mean to Malibu, but back into our lives at all.

My head hurts like a mother, and I rub the bridge of my nose, still not looking up at my daughter.

"Michael? *Is* she?" There's fear in her voice that I don't like, and my eyes snap open. She's standing at the foot of my bed now, Rebecca on the screen behind her, beyond her small shoulders.

"I hope so, sweet pea." I reach for her with my hand. "I sure hope so." I fear she might flee from me as she stands there just chewing her lip, staring at my hand. I'm cursing myself for being such a terrible parent, for not having it more together than this. She knows how out of control I am—she can see it plain as day, and an eight-year-old needs her father to be okay.

"Don't worry, Michael." She lifts her chin resolutely, brave to the core as always. "It *will* get better, you're right. It always gets better," she says, and then leaves me alone in my misery.

✧

Casey answers his cell phone on the second ring. I have no clue what time it is; I'm suspended, hanging somewhere out in the drunken

ether, a timeless void of being in-between. I know it's nighttime; I know that Andrea's in bed asleep. I know that slowly I am sobering up, having made some coffee for myself a while ago.

"I've screwed up," I announce without even saying hello. He hesitates on his end, and I reckon he knows something's wrong from the cotton-mouthed sound of my voice. He's heard me in this place before: back months ago when I used to call him at dark, off-kilter moments like this one. "Totally screwed up. I'm dishonest about everything."

I gulp down a few swigs of black coffee. "That's what my girlfriend told me. Right before she dumped me on my fucking ass."

"Well," he asks seriously, sucking in a breath, "so what're you going to do about that?"

"Don't know. Go pink triangle again, reckon."

"That's not the answer, man," he chides me gently. "You're in love with Rebecca O'Neill."

"She agrees with you about me," I grudgingly admit. "About me being a fag, like you said." It's not the full truth, but at the moment it's enough for me to share. "That I should be with a guy, not her."

"Yeah, well people say all manner of shit when they're upset." Clearly he realizes how hurt she must've been to tell me something like that, but thank God he doesn't ask for details.

"I love her, Case."

"So what's the problem?"

My mind spins with all my stupid mistakes. I'm not sure which one to choose from. I rub my eyes, trying to bring the room back into clear focus.

"There was this waiter," I begin, and I hear him groan on the other end of the line. "Yeah, this waiter and he looked like Alex—it wasn't just me, Rebecca saw it too, and..." I stare at the opening credits of the next episode of *About the House*. Rebecca smiles out at me, tempts me with a coy toss of her hair. "Kind of freaked me out, the way he looked like Al, red hair and all that. Guess I sort of unraveled."

"*Unraveled?*" he coughs. "What the hell does that mean?"

"I flirted."

"You idiot." He sounds genuinely angry. "You're a total idiot, you know that?" His voice rises with irritation.

"Thanks for the sympathy."

"I've been sympathetic for a long time, but that's the stupidest thing I've ever heard," he says. "Why would you flirt with some guy in front of her?"

"Because I miss him," I snap, sitting up in bed. "What do you think?"

"You either love *her* or you miss him. You're gonna have to choose, man. You can't hang in between like that. She's been through

a lot of heavy shit. She doesn't need that. She doesn't need you flirting with some guy right under her nose."

"That wasn't all," I confess, swallowing hard.

"What the hell else?" he thunders. Casey's nothing if not capable of tough love. If I'd called Marti, I'd have gotten exasperation, but definitely more compassion. Maybe deep down I needed my gay friend to knock me into line.

"She found me watching that Huntington tape. The one by your TV," I remind him. "Alex's last contest."

It was made about two weeks before he died, and I'd *needed* to watch it after my first time surfing again since that day, but I didn't try explaining that to Rebecca when she was so upset.

"How'd she react to that?"

"She didn't tell me..." I blow out a heavy breath. "Until after I flirted with the waiter."

"Oh, Michael." He only calls me Michael when he's either very upset or extremely frustrated with me. "You're right. You *have* screwed up, pal."

"Thanks a lot. I called for your help."

"And here it is." His voice grows serious again. "Alex is gone. He's *been* gone. You've found someone you love, someone who loves you. But you gotta decide what you want. Right now, I'm not sure you know."

"I want *her.*"

"But you're still holding on to what you had. It's gone. Alex is back on the riverbank somewhere, but the river kept on flowing. With all of us." His voice becomes thick with emotion, and he clears his throat before continuing. "I loved him too, you know. Seriously. But he's dead, Mike, and he isn't coming back. It's time to accept that fact."

It's like staring in the mirror. Like staring right into Alex's eyes. I sense him, gazing back *through* me. Quietly I admit, "I can't figure out how to let go."

"And she figures that's her fault," he says, startling me back to the moment.

"It's not her fault."

"But it's hard to see past all those scars, man. They pack a load of power. No wonder she figures you're not telling the truth."

I'm reminded of my conversations with her about Andrea's parenthood—how the secrets upset her—erosions in her perception of me as a straightforward honest guy. Especially when I'm flirting with the damned waiter right beneath her nose. Secretly watching videos of Alex. "She doesn't believe I'm really attracted to her."

He sighs into the phone. "She believes the mirror, Mike, not you."

"You're right." My voice is hushed with the reality of what I've done to her—to us. "God, you're right."

"So what're you going to do about it?" he asks.

Staring at her on the television, a plan begins to take form in my hazy, semi-sober mind, and despite the booze, the plan is very clear.

"Simple, Case," I say. "I'm gonna get her to believe."

Chapter Twenty-Five: Michael

I park on the side street that runs beside Ellen's house, and let the truck idle a while. Andie's sound asleep, slumped against the window, her mouth slack and making sleepy wheezing sounds. When I woke her before daybreak this morning, explaining that we were going to leave Casey's place and make a trip up the coast to Grandma Richardson's house, she didn't even question me. All the things she's had to endure from me in the past year—the instability that's come with my shaky mental state—it amazes me how smoothly she's handled most of them.

So I'm letting her rest while she can, especially since I've got to be back at my job in the morning. Besides, it's easier to stare at the palm trees lining this road than deal with the reality of facing what I'm about to do today. But it's part of my plan for making Rebecca truly believe my intentions; in order to win her back, I've got to come clean. Not just with Laurel, but in a lot of aspects of my life.

And Laurel—along with our secrets—are first on my agenda. She's here in Santa Cruz, home visiting her mother for the week. I know this because she told me she'd be flying in from Santa Fe for a long Fourth of July weekend here with Ellen. Makes it perfect timing for this conversation we need to have, but my stomach still swashes nervously. I kill the truck's engine and try gathering my nerve.

A background headache pulsates behind my eyes, begging to become a full-blown migraine. Leaning back in the seat, I rub the bridge of my nose, and watch a pack of surfer boys walk by, salty boards in hand and cocky grins spread across their faces. My mind wanders to Al's childhood here, how he was nurtured on the ocean life, even as he was inspired to be something far more—to use his brilliant mind to help those kids of his. It was a strange blend, so many aspects in one man. I'll never meet another guy like him, that's for damn sure.

For the first time that thought isn't automatically chased by stifling pain. It's more an objective realization; an appreciation of his uniqueness, and that even though he had a twin, there will never be

another human being precisely like him. There's just the realization that life is a gift, and Alex was part of life's gift to me.

Watching a gaggle of young kids speed down the sidewalk on their skateboards, sun-bleached hair flying, laughing and being crazy, they could be Alex and Casey and Marti, back twenty-five years ago, they're that familiar. The wheel keeps on turning, another season upon us.

Smiling as they pass my open truck window, I have a thought. Maybe the thing is, the gift means more precisely because it *is* always passing away, like the waves or the sand or the sun tracking across the open sky.

Maybe that's what Alex has wanted me to know.

Laurel pops out the backdoor of the house, tracking right toward me. Bustling purposefully down the sidewalk with a box in her arms, she doesn't see me at first, but then something makes her glance my way. The cool clear eyes widen, the delicate mouth opens.

She steps around the front of my truck, half-smiling and half-staring at me. "Michael? What's going on?" she asks in an uncertain voice, as my Nikes hit the pavement. "Is everything okay?" She looks past me, toward the truck, and seeing Andrea she visibly panics.

"Andrea's fine," I rush to assure her. "Don't worry, nothing's wrong."

"Oh. Good." Her smile opens up, the restraint fading away. Her joy that we're here begins to fill her eyes. Looking from me to our daughter, again she asks, "What's going on?"

"I need to talk to you." I glance back at Andie, still asleep. "Later, after Andrea wakes up."

"Of course, Michael." She nods her head, as if this is the most ordinary situation in the world, me appearing here without so much as a warning call. "You're sure you're okay, though?"

Leaning up against the truck, my shoulders slump and I feel all the strength drain right out of my body. In one quick moment I'm finally done in, deflated of energy like the week after Alex's death, all the exhaustion of the past year overtaking me at once.

"Nah, Laurel, I'm not okay. I haven't been okay for a long damn time." Tears burn my eyes, and I stare at my shoes. "But that's why I've come here," I explain, feeling as naked here on the sidewalk as I did the other night with Rebecca in bed. "Because it's time I squared away my mess."

✧

It's dusk, the sun poised low on the Pacific horizon. Laurel and I are strolling together on the sidewalk near Lighthouse Point, having left Andrea in Ellen's attentive care. At this time of day, everyone is

243

out: the joggers, the walkers, the surfers, the skateboarders. Santa Cruz's ocean-side culture is always an amalgam.

As we approach the lighthouse, she indicates the strip of rocks stretching like gnarled fingers out into the ocean. "Let's walk out there." She points to a cordon that's meant to keep visitors off the rocks. A large sign warns of possible drowning or death should one slip into the angry churning waters below. The surfers aren't worried about that—we're overlooking world-famous Steamer Lane, a spot I surfed with Alex plenty of times.

She swings a long leg over the chain. "Come on," she beckons me.

Holding up my hands, I laugh off her invitation. "Maybe not."

"Michael, come on," she urges, tugging at my hand. "I want to show you something. I promise we'll be careful."

I follow her over the barrier, out onto the point, carefully watching my steps on the slippery surface. As a single parent, I can't be cavalier about this kind of thing. Laurel has a lifetime of confidence with this place, while I have a year's worth of tragedy and oppressive doubts.

Out toward the tip of the point, tourists stand taking photographs of the sunset. Laurel holds my large hand, firm in her smallish one, appreciating the view. With a sweeping ocean vista surrounding us, I understand what she wanted me to see: the raw beauty of her brother's world, the world that nurtured and raised him, almost as surely as his own family did. Further out in the water, sea lions are gathered on a slip of black rock, and they bark, splashing in and out of the water.

The high tide causes wave upon wave to slam the point, ocean spraying upward on the rocks and onto us. A chill settles over me, even now in July.

"This is his world," I say, my words almost lost in the briny wind.

She smiles, a wistful, appreciative expression. "He certainly loved it here."

"Does it hurt you?" While it was his world, it was also *theirs*. "To come back here? To see it again and know he's gone?"

"Oh, no. It always makes me feel close to him," she answers without hesitation, staring out at the horizon. "I can think of all our memories, the happy times. I feel young again here."

I laugh. "Laurel, you are young."

"I'm young enough, but life marches on." She gets a faraway look in her eyes. "We were born the same day, the same hour, he and I...yet he will never grow old. That's very odd to me."

My mind fills with her painted image of Alex, arms outstretched to the sun, standing on the beach. "Like in the painting," I say. "He never ages."

She searches my face, then answers softly, "Yes."

"Still haven't figured that painting out, Laurel. Been thinking on it, turning it over in my head," I explain, and she listens, settling on the rocks at my feet. "But maybe I just don't get what you mean about it singing for me."

"When the time is right," she answers, taking my hand. "You will." She draws me down to the ground beside her. I find myself facing her, both of us sitting like a pair of teenagers at a bonfire, knee-to-knee and cross-legged. Smiling at me in that soothing, almost-beatific manner she possesses—the way that used to always make me feel strange and warm inside when I needed comforting—she waits for me to speak.

I draw in a steadying breath. "I want Andrea to know the truth." She stares back at me, one hand frozen by her face, tucking the wayward strands behind her ear.

Her lips part, a soft "Oh" sound escaping, but nothing else.

"I think she needs the truth," I continue. She only blinks at me, silent until finally I begin to laugh. "Look, Laurel, I wasn't trying to totally blindside you or anything. I figured this would be good news—or whatever—in your mind..."

She interrupts me, still looking stunned. "I only want what's best for you both." She sounds numb and mechanical, like those words are rehearsed.

I pose a question that's been growing inside of me during the drive here, a question that's forever bobbed just below the surface between us. "What about what's best for you, Laurel?"

"I didn't do this for me." She gives me a fragile smile. "I did it for Alex and for you."

I remind her of the obvious. "Yeah, but Al's gone now. Maybe it's not the best thing anymore. Not best for any of us."

She bows her head. "I'm not sure Andrea ever needs to know the truth," she says in a soft voice. "I was wrong a year ago. I've told you that."

"You also told me it would be my decision to make," I say, thinking of her words last fall. Words she sent in a letter, words included with one of her apologies. "That I was her father, and I'd be the one to make the choice. Remember that, Laurel?"

She says nothing; only stares back at me with an unsettling blankness in her expression.

"I've had to think pretty hard about what your brother would've wanted," I continue. "How he'd have wanted things to play out with our daughter. We had no contingency plan, no strategy in case one of us died." I pause, staring at her meaningfully. "Which leaves this shit up to me."

She gazes out at the vast ocean. "I think Andrea is doing better," she says, then looks back to me. "She's involved, interested in things again. Michael, you've done such a great job with her. I don't see why you need to—" She hesitates and then with a sudden gasp, covers her mouth and begins to cry. Not faint tears, or delicate ones, but a loud, horsy sob escapes her throat.

Finally, she manages to continue. "I don't see why you need to take Alex from her that way," she whispers in a hoarse voice. "All her memories of him as her father." Her tears fall freely, and she wraps her arms around herself protectively.

"He'd always be her uncle," I say, voicing Rebecca's very words to me from a few weeks ago. "They'd always have that bond. And he would always be her adoptive father. That was legal and nothing's gonna change the way that was."

"I don't want her to lose him," she tells me, a resolute strength falling over her like a mantle.

"I can't believe you're arguing to keep this secret," I say, my voice sharp.

"She should know you're her mother," I insist. "She *needs* to know that, Laurel. Not so you can...change the shape of our family—"

"I wouldn't want to."

"But so she can understand how it all fits together. Her *place* in this family. That's the only way she can ever be completely okay. The only way we all can, I think," I say. "She can't keep this up, going around calling me Michael, feeling like an orphan. She's got both of us. She should know the truth."

"I don't want to be her mother," she says, staring over at the lighthouse. "I can't be her mother, Michael. In a strange way, I don't think I really *am* her mother. She had you and she had Alex...that didn't leave a place for me."

"But there's a place now," I suggest gently, touching her face. "A big place is left in her life."

"For Rebecca," she whispers, the tears fresh in her eyes. "You're making a life with Rebecca."

"That's part of why I'm here," I answer softly.

"You plan to marry her."

"I hope so." I hesitate, laughing ruefully since before we can marry, we'd have to actually be a couple again. "But well, we've got some problems."

"Because of me?" Laurel asks.

"Nah, Laurel," I say. "Because of your brother."

She smiles—a gentle, sympathetic smile. "Rebecca is special," she says. "Very special."

"She's definitely that. It takes a special person to walk into a mess like the one we've all managed to make, to enter it and embrace us with an open heart."

"You'll marry her," she predicts, her expression serious. Something about her words feel prophetic—beyond this moment even.

I give a silent nod of agreement.

"And if you marry her, Michael, there's no real place for me," she continues matter-of-factly. "Not as Andrea's mother. Not if we really want Andrea to be happy and adjusted and to have the family she deserves."

"That shouldn't be how we reach this decision, Laurel."

"I decided it a while ago, Michael. I know that with all the confusion she's had, all that she's lost, she doesn't need me to be her mother. I need to be *Aunt* Laurel," she explains. "I need to be a constant. A given. Someone she can rely on."

"Oh, Laurel. You're already that." Without hesitating, I draw her close into my embrace. And we hold each other, there on the rocky point, feeling the spray of salty ocean, hearing the cries of gulls and surfers and wind.

Pulling away from me, she makes an agitated gesture, twisting a lock of her hair in her fist. "When?" she asks, swallowing. "When do you plan to tell her?"

"Soon. Not yet, but soon," I explain. "I want to talk to her counselor first. But I need to know you're okay with it."

Wiping at her eyes, she gives me a bittersweet smile. "I'm afraid," she admits. "So afraid, Michael. But somehow...my heart tells me it's safe."

I give her hand a quick squeeze. "It's never safe to love."

The most vulnerable feeling in the world is to be a parent. She knows it and so do I. The only comparable emotion is giving your heart away, like I've done with Rebecca, and like I once did with Alex. Love is all about the risk, and very rarely about the guarantees.

I stare out at the waves, hearing the familiar shouts of the surfers from down below us, charging their boards across sunset-dappled ocean beneath the fading sky.

"It's never safe to love, Laurel," I say, "but I've come to think it's always worth it." And I can almost feel Alex right beside us.

Chapter Twenty-Six: Rebecca

I'm late for a three p.m. production meeting, hurrying between bungalows when I hear a familiar voice. "That Armani suit still looks killer on you." I turn to find Michael Warner behind the wheel of a golf cart, grinning up at me.

I keep walking. "Hi, Michael."

He slows the cart to match my pace. "Of course, you know how much I like you in black," he continues, his voice upbeat, flirtatious. He's pretending nothing's changed between us—that I haven't spent the past weeks since we broke up in Malibu avoiding all of his phone calls.

I counter with my Cool Girl attitude, giving my hair a sassy toss over my shoulder. "What's going on, Michael?"

He rakes a hand over his short, spiky hair—shorter than when we were together. "Other than me checking out that suit?"

"No," I correct him. "What are you doing around *here*?" I gesture toward my office.

"Oh, I reckon it's just the usual repairs and whatnot," he reflects softly, staring past me at my building. "Same old stuff I'm always doing round here, Ms. O'Neill."

Ms. O'Neill? I'm not sure whether he's being sarcastic, or trying to put a professional distance between us, but I don't wait to find out. I begin walking quickly away from him, but he follows behind me in the cart, still chatting.

"Been thinking of a job change, actually. Maybe getting back into production work."

I stop, turning toward him. "Leaving the studio?" If he changes jobs, I'll probably never see him again.

"Actually, one of the shows that's crewing up for the fall, right here on the lot," he explains, tapping his fingers on the wheel. "I'm on a short list. I figured it was time I got a better-paying job. Made a little more of myself, you know."

"What about Andrea? Aren't those long hours?" I'm wondering

about his motivation, and it occurs to me that I'm no longer privy to these thoughts of his. To what drives and motivates him, to the nuances of his world.

"Hours are pretty good, except on taping days. I can get Inez to stay then," he explains with an off-handed shrug. "And I need a change. Trying to make a lot of changes in my world right now, Becca. I think it's time for that. And I wanted you to know that...well, that I'm trying to overhaul myself."

He's pressing in too close, trying to work me back against an emotional wall—open up the silence that's barricaded between us. "I better go." I give my watch a nervous glance, backing away from him. "I've got a meeting in five minutes."

"I'm changing that dark crap inside of me...the stuff that drove you away. I know why you couldn't see how I feel, Rebecca. I understand. And I'm working to change that in myself."

I feel tears burn my eyes. He's looking at a new job to...impress me? Making big life transformations so I'll, what, feel wooed?

I shiver a little, angry at myself that I do feel wooed. That's exactly what I feel, dang it.

"How's Andrea?" I ask. I've been worrying about her quite a lot over the past month; I've been concerned that she didn't handle my sudden departure very well.

He thrusts the cart into park, turning to face me. "She misses you. Talks about you all the time."

I step much closer. "But she's doing okay?" The words come out more urgent than I intend, filled with genuine love for his daughter.

"She's doing good," he assures me. "Really good."

I finger my meeting notes nervously. "I'm glad. Tell her I send my love, okay?"

"I love you, Rebecca." He swings his long legs out of the cart, rising to his full lanky stature right in front of me. "You won't take any of my calls, so I'll just say it here. Right now. I love you."

"Michael, we've talked about this," I explain, feeling my face flush. Looking down, I wave my folder. "I've got a *meeting*."

He studies me, smiling incongruously in the face of my rebuff: how is it possible that he seems more handsome now than any other time previously? It's almost like some tension, always there around his eyes before, has vanished.

"You do realize it's the third of August," he tells me, kicking at the tire of his golf cart. "You know what that means, don't you?"

Folding my arms across my chest, I say, "No, Michael. I don't know what that means." I keep my voice cool—as ordered and controlled as the small group of extras being wrangled by some assistant director over in Chaplin Park.

"We have plans on August twentieth," he reminds me softly. "That fan gathering of yours."

"Oh, no." I laugh. "No, we don't, Michael. You're relentlessly determined."

"You're uninviting me?"

"We're not dating anymore!" I cry, shaking my head at his unbelievable chutzpah.

"Know what I think would be great?" he says. Stepping into my space—closer than I can endure without squirming—he lowers his voice. "If you and I kept that date. If you put on that little black dress of yours, the one you wore to Cat's party. And I put on something cool. Like my Armani or Kenneth Cole. Whatever."

He smiles at me, his golden-brown eyes locking with mine. Seemingly unaware of all the hurt and pain I've stockpiled against him these past weeks, he continues. "And then if we went to that gathering and we showed Jake how happy you are. How happy *we* are together."

I stare back at him, incredulous. "Are you nuts?"

"Yeah, Becca." His eyes begin to sparkle. "Probably am. But see, after you left me in Malibu, I decided something really important." He grows very intense in the way he watches me, amber eyes narrowing. "That I would get you to believe me."

"About what?"

"About how I feel for you. That it's real, and it won't die just because you're a woman and Alex was a guy...my love for you won't die, ever, just like it hasn't for him. But you're it for me now, Becca. You are the one. He's gone and much as I'll always love him, I'm alive and here. And so are you." He steps much closer, lifting a palm to my cheek, and I don't duck away. "And so are you, Rebecca O'Neill. It's not just me that's been in the dark for far too long."

My eyes drift shut and I savor the feel of his hand against my cheek; I lean into his palm, wanting to cry in relief at being touched by him again. But then my chest grows tight, and the fear surfaces again. The fear that if I take this chance on this unusual, risky man, that I'll wind up slashed and dying—not physically, not like before—but that my heart and soul will be destroyed.

"I want to take you to that fan event and show Jake and all your friends that we're happy together. That you're alive again and so am I."

Slowly, I move his hand away from my face, opening my eyes. "We're not happy. We're not even a couple." Backing away from him, I shake my head decisively. "You're not coming with me to that gathering, Michael. I am going alone."

His voice drops low, becomes serious. "Alone's a bad way to be, baby. Believe me, I've tried it."

"Don't call me that anymore." My rebuff sounds weak and unconvincing, even to my own ears.

"What do you want from me, Rebecca? You really want me to let you go? To let you out of my life?" he asks. "I have so much to tell you, so much I want you to know. Things I've realized since Malibu...things I've realized about you, Becca—you and me—that I want to talk about."

I stop in my tracks, my throat raw. "Michael, we did talk about this. The last time I saw you. We agreed you needed to get back out there. That it's time to start dating again. Not me, but the right kind of...people. You know I'm not what you need."

"Only one person ever said that, and it was you."

"Michael, I will always be a woman, and you—"

"Do you want me queer?" he asks, and it strikes me that he's not looking around, not worried about his boss or his electrician pals. "Is that it, Becca? Does that make it easier for you?"

"Than what?"

He seems to gaze right through me. "Than feeling vulnerable because you love me."

My mouth opens, but nothing—absolutely nothing—springs to mind for me to overcome what he's just said. "That's exactly what I thought," he answers boldly, giving me a challenging look as he climbs back into the cart. "It's a whole lot easier for you if I'm gay. The only problem? I love you. I love you, Rebecca, and I'm not giving up."

✧

Several days after running into Michael on the lot, I'm at Whole Foods. It's a Sunday night and I'm totally depressed because I can't decide if I'm being foolish to shut down my heart and life to Michael, or if I'm being a smart girl who knows how to look after herself. Seeing the array of fresh spices takes me back to the first night when I went to his bungalow and cooked for them, the first night I found out the truth about his sexuality.

Is it possible that I really misunderstood everything between us so badly? He says he loves me; he keeps saying it. He called me last night, too late for friends—just late enough to create a familiar intimacy as I lay in bed, trying to tell myself to chastise him for ringing me after midnight on a Saturday night.

"So, you just in from a big night out?" I asked him, trying not to sound like he'd just woken me up. After all, a hot single woman should have plans, not be stretching her legs and struggling to sit up in bed so early on a Saturday night.

He blew out a heavy breath. "I should be with you. You should be with me, Rebecca. That's what should be going down tonight, so no, I didn't have a hot date."

"I told you what I think."

"Tell me again."

"You need to have a few dates with some men. See how that feels."

"If I do that, give it a test run on your behalf, then would you believe that I love you?"

Tears filled my eyes. "I've gotta...got to run."

"Wait!" He stopped me right as I was about to click the end button on my cell. "Just hold up, Becca, please."

I waited, but said nothing. He stayed silent too, the only sound his breathing for a long moment. "You tell me what it will take. Tell me how I can make you believe how real this is for me, and I'll do it."

The tears burned my eyes in earnest then. There's just too much pain in my own past, my own life, for me to ever believe in his love. Not now. And I knew it right then.

Coughing for a moment to clear my throat I said, "You want to prove how you feel for me? Then don't call me anymore, Michael. Don't call me or try and see me. Let this one go."

And with that, I flipped my phone shut and wondered if I hadn't just thrown away something truly precious and rare.

"Hey, surfer girl." The husky voice jolts me back to the moment, and I whirl around to find Casey Porter studying me. For a moment, I'm so caught off-guard that I'm rendered speechless, my hand going protectively to the scars along the side of my face.

He tilts his head sideways. "Thought we'd made friends after Malibu."

"Of course. How are you, Casey?" I manage to rescue my common sense and behave more smoothly in his presence. Never mind that this is one of Michael's two best friends and that bumping into him unexpectedly terrifies me. I'm likely to get a lecture or unsolicited advice, or something else—not even sure what. All I know is that bumping into Casey has my heart thundering painfully inside my chest.

But Casey's a direct guy, I learned that the hard way, so he doesn't waste time and goes right for my jugular. "You ever going to let him make it up to you, Rebecca?" He steps closer, dropping a bag of avocados into his cart. "Mike needs you right now. You know that."

I shake my head slowly. "Needing me and loving me are two different things, Casey. We both know that. You called it right in the first place. He belongs with a guy, not me."

"You're wrong." He takes hold of my arm with gentle force. "Rebecca, *I* was wrong. He's crazy gone for you. I saw it in his eyes from almost the beginning. He's in love with you, and it's real, and if you don't fight to make it work, you're not nearly as strong and smart as I thought you were."

My mouth gapes open. Literally. This man was my major opponent, the one who would seemingly never buy into the possibility that a relationship could work between Michael and me.

"Damn, I hope I'm not that much of a shock."

"You were the one who said he couldn't be with a woman. You were the one who said he was gay, that we were a mistake." I poke him in the arm pointedly. "*You* said those things. *You* put them in my mind."

"No, I didn't. They were already there. Hell, they've been living there ever since you met Mike, of course they have."

"Don't tell me what I think or what I feel."

"All right, then try this on, Rebecca O'Neill. Is love enough?"

"Enough for what?"

"Enough to cover a multitude of sins...enough to work when you find the right person to spend your life with. No matter who they are? No matter what's in their past?"

I open my mouth, ready to give a snappy, self-protective comeback, but Casey lifts a hand. "Don't answer that question."

"But you asked—"

Suddenly he smiles at me, a huge, radiant grin that reaches his eyes. "Answer it for you, Rebecca. Answer it for yourself, not for me." Then his expression grows more somber. "But I can tell you that Mike doesn't have it in him to keep calling forever. Not if you keep making it clear you don't want him. His heart's been too broken for that. So you better decide what you want pretty soon."

I tilt my chin upward. "I want him to find a man who will make him happy."

Casey's eyes narrow on me. "You sure about that, surfer girl?" He stares at me a long moment and then turns and pushes his cart away.

✧

When the night of the fan gathering rolls around, I find myself towing Trevor there, my best friend fitting neatly into the date proviso slot. While I'm not thrilled with Jake seeing me dateless, it's still better than attending the party alone. Outside the hotel where the event is happening, we sit in the car. I'm shaking. My whole body quivers, especially my hands which I can't seem to rein back in, and I'll never be able to mix confidently with the fans if I can't compose myself now.

Then again, maybe it's just being here in Studio City, only a few blocks from Michael's home that has me so unsettled.

"I can't do this, Trevor." Fighting to breathe, I pat my chest; as if perhaps I might discover some unexpected air somewhere inside my lungs.

"You can."

"Take me home," I wheeze, praying I won't need my inhaler tonight. Thinking about my nerve pills, back on my dresser in my everyday purse.

"If that's what you want, Rebecca, I'll do it." He eyes the back door through which we're supposed to enter. There's a bouncer-type guy—brawny and intimidating—watching us from the doorway. Perhaps he already recognizes me.

"I'll make a fool out of myself here," I rasp.

"No, darling, you won't. You're adored here. You're fawned over." He laughs, glancing around the parking lot jammed with cars and people filing into the hotel. "If you ever have a bad day, you need only log onto any fan site and vicariously worship yourself."

"You make me sound like such an egomaniac."

He winks at me. "A little self-adoration is often a good thing."

Pulling down the visor, I stare into the makeup mirror—at who I truly am now, with the quivering smile and the perfectly flawed face. "They're expecting someone else."

"They're expecting Rebecca O'Neill," he counters. "And perhaps Mary Agnes Hill—who never even existed, so no worries there."

"It's Jake." I shake my head. "I can't stand the thought of his gloating."

He corkscrews his eyebrows upward. "About bloody what?"

"My no-longer-existent love life." I release a defeated little sigh.

"Ah, we can handle that." He dismisses my concern with a wave of his hand, leaning across from the driver's seat to kiss me. Our chariot is his vintage Porsche Roadster tonight, which trumps my Honda in a paper-rock-scissors contest any day of the week.

"You have your inhaler?" he asks me, handing me my hot-pink Coach bag. I nod, feeling much like a little girl as he carefully guides me out of the car and toward the party entrance.

"Don't worry, Rebecca," he whispers in my ear. "I'll take good care of you tonight."

Trevor's calming hand never leaves the small of my back, as he steers me through the throngs of people, protecting me. I'd told the coordinator I would bring some kind of security guard—which I never really intended to do—but Trevor makes the perfect substitute. He so completely doesn't look the part of a security guard that maybe any would-be stalker will think he's the ultimate real deal—like a Secret Service guy. He directs me toward my table, never allowing anyone to hold onto or touch me for too long. Then next thing I know, I'm positioned in my assigned seat, a bevy of fans crushing close—but not frighteningly so because of the ease with which Trevor controls the scene. At the table I sign headshots and fan art until my hand grows numb; yet whenever the crowd makes me anxious, it seems Trevor simply snaps his fingers, and then I can breathe again.

He also manages to keep me positioned well apart from Jake—who in classic form was painfully late for this event. We knew Cat wouldn't arrive until night's end since she's wrapping her Evan Beckman picture, but unemployed Jake has no excuse.

I'm starting to breathe easier, lost in the glow of fan appreciation, when from behind me I hear, "So they booked Blondie." The same lazy manner of talking, the same cocky tone. The same belief that my whole world must be rocked by his attention. "Blondie looks hot too."

I never even turn around. "I'm busy, Jake," I say, taking a young girl's hand, clasping it across the table. She fiddles with a photograph—never meeting my eyes—and tells me that she discovered the show in reruns. Behind me, I sense Jake still standing; feel it in the way the small hairs on the back of my neck bristle; sense heat coming off his body.

His hand brushes my shoulder. "Too busy for a drink, Rebecca?" he whispers against the back of my neck.

"Too busy for you," I say dismissively, and continue signing pictures. As he brushes on past me, I hear him say under his breath, "You'll come around, Rebecca. You always do."

Shaking out a cramp in my hand, I steal a glance in his direction—long enough to see his profile. Unfortunately, even viewed from the side, he's still heartstoppingly handsome.

It sure would be nice to prove him wrong about me—just for once.

✧

Outside by the hotel pool, Trevor and I find a quiet sanctuary toward night's end, sipping margaritas and kicking back on lounge chairs covered in a dewy sheen. He grabbed a towel and wiped my seat dry before I sat down, ever the perfect Gentleman Date.

Twirling the paper umbrella in my drink, the world feels fuzzy— and I feel free out here beneath the moon, away from the stifling crowd back inside the hotel. Only a few people mingle here; presumably the fans are inside the hotel itself, semi-stalking the other actors and writers. When the Beach Boys come on, "God Only Knows" playing over the poolside speakers, Trevor stands gallantly, offering me his hand.

"Come dance." He tugs me unsteadily to my feet.

"Whoa!" I laugh, catching his arm.

"I've got you," he assures me softly, clasping me with both hands. He's not an overly tall man, but even with my strappy slides, he's a good six or seven inches taller than me. We fall into a slow dance together, oddly hushed.

After a time of us quiet together in one another's arms, he says, "You really should talk to him, you know."

"Jake?" I look up into his warm eyes. "No way."

"No, darling," he answers softly. "*Michael.*"

I stiffen in his arms. "I'm surprised to hear you say that."

"You love him, and I worry that perhaps I put you off him, with some of my silly warnings and all that."

"They weren't silly," I say, pulling away. "You were right."

But he holds me fast, steadying me close to him. His black eyes never leave me. "When I saved your life, Rebecca, it wasn't for *this*. For constantly protecting yourself, perpetually running, never taking a chance," he continues in a rush, his accent growing thick and more difficult to decipher. "I was wrong about Michael, but I thought you'd have known it for yourself by now."

I pry his hands from around me, pulling away.

"Don't run from me," he cautions sharply. "Save that maneuver for Michael Warner." And for the first time in several years, my best friend sounds genuinely angry with me.

I turn back, planting a hand on my hip. "You warned me to be careful about his bisexuality. About his *kind*!" I say in an irate tone. "Those were your very words!"

"Before I knew what kind of man he is."

I shake my head with a snort, backing away from him. "What kind of man is he, Trevor?"

"I'm getting back with Julian," he blurts, closing the distance that separates us. "You should know that. He's coming in next month, before our story meeting. We're going to give it a go together."

"I see." I set my jaw.

"Yes well, love, that's it. I've realized that as much as he's hurt me, I do love him. I never stopped loving him."

"Good for you."

"He has changed. People are capable of it, you know," he insists. "He's spent the past year in counseling. He's been sober for eight months now. He's a different person." His voice grows quiet. "All the best is there, and the worst seems finally gone, now that he's off the booze."

I nod, keeping my voice even. "Okay."

"Is that all you're going to give me?" he cries sharply. "*I see? Okay?* Bloody hell, Rebecca, when did you become so frosty and controlled?"

"When I was stabbed nine times in the chest, face and abdomen," I cry back at him. "When you got the stupid paramedics to come and bring me back." I shake my head, stepping closer. "When I realized Michael Warner still loved someone else..."

The tears begin then, spilling hot across my cheeks, and for once Trevor doesn't rush to make it better. I stand there by the pool, feeling a distance settle between my best friend and me.

"Michael Warner loves you," he insists. "You're only too scared to see it."

I wipe at my eyes. "I don't want Julian to hurt you."

"And I don't want you to let Michael get away."

I close my eyes and try to blot out the white-hot pain that shoots through me at his words. Because what I realize—and Trevor doesn't— is that I think I've already made that decisive mistake.

Perhaps it's my weakened emotional state after my confrontation with Trevor, but somehow when I see Jake inside the hotel lobby— truly see him—for the first time all night, I capitulate on the drinks invitation. He sidles up next to me by the hotel bar, wearing a goatee and an expensive T-shirt, a pulsating crowd of blonde girls circling him.

Tonight he's cultivating a kind of grunge-Hollywood fashion statement, and while it should make him look like the cokehead he clearly still is, he manages to affect me. He is a sexy man, always has been—from his steel-gray eyes to his sinewy body—and under the murky-fingered influence of my margaritas it occurs to me that I could sleep with him tonight.

"Rebecca. Hey." He tosses his shaggy, longish brown hair out of his eyes, giving me that familiar bad-boy smile. Staring back, I think of all the times I made love gazing right into those same stormy eyes.

"Hi, Jake."

His gaze roves the length of me, hesitating significantly on my hips, next, my chest; finally my face.

"Looking good, Rebecca." Something warm catches fire in me at his praise, burning like whiskey. We always did have chemistry.

"Thanks, Jake."

"So, hey. Rebecca? Out for drinks after?" He nods toward the exit door. "Skip this scene in a few?"

I give him a guarded smile. "Sure, Jake."

Jake sits in the corner of Mia Mia, a stylish bar on Sunset, wearing sunglasses even though it's almost midnight. He's all about cluing everyone in to his celebrity status. He's my bad drug, the one I've always returned to. Especially at emotionally broken moments like this one, he's my recurring obsession, ready to trip me up.

I slide into the seat opposite him; my defenses are up even though I did agree to come out with him. I glance around us. "I'm not really sure why I came."

Jake makes me feel more vulnerable, more exposed simply because I'm more recognizable paired up with him out in public like this. Even though I felt triumphant at the gathering, this is different: this is a trendy hotspot in West Hollywood, where the see-and-be-seen quotient is high.

I loved that about being with Michael: I felt normal everywhere we went together.

"No kiss? I'm hurt, Rebecca."

I toy with the menu. "We'll see how you behave."

He laughs easily. "You know I'm *always* good."

I laugh along with him, trying to think of something clever, and that's when I glance toward the door. Entering the bar I spy Cat, who looks like she's searching for someone in particular.

"You told Cat we were going to be here?" I ask, disappointed despite myself that we won't be alone for this mini-reunion.

"Mentioned it, yeah." He glances in her direction. "Oh, holy shit, man. That's Evan Beckman with her! She brought Evan Beckman." Quickly Jake runs a hand over his hair, smoothing it out.

"Oh, God," I groan quietly because Cat is glancing all around Mia Mia like she's looking for *me*. Her hand shoots upward when she sees me, and she gives a dramatically cheerful wave. I give a subdued one in response.

Don't get me wrong: I am totally into meeting Evan Beckman. And I am totally into the possibility that he's interested in me for a part. What I'm not totally into is having his path and Jake's collide at this precise moment in my personal history.

They weave their way through the late night crowd, finally reaching our table. We stand, and introductions are made, with Jake salivating way too much over Evan for any of us to feel comfortable.

"Evan and I were coming out for a drink," Cat explains. "Jake told me you'd be here later, so I thought I could bring him by. So you two could meet."

"Hi, Rebecca," Evan says, grinning at me in that trademark boyish way of his. The one *People* magazine and *Entertainment Weekly* capture so regularly. He has wide-set, earnest brown eyes that seem to be forever smiling, always a hint of amusement around the edges, as if he's working hard to suppress a good chuckle.

We settle back at the table, and then Jake, in a flurry of overdone excitement, excuses himself. I know exactly where he's going: to the bathroom to snort a few lines. Like all people with addiction problems, Jake tends to think that if he gets high, then the moment will be even *more* spectacular. I guess the idea of cocaine and Evan Beckman at the same experiential moment is magnificent enough to warrant his quick retreat.

"Evan is casting his next film," Cat begins, and I can tell she's thankful for Jake's vanishing act. For a moment, I even wonder if she paid Jake to leave.

Evan continues, leaning closer across the table so I can hear him over the din of noise. "Rebecca, there's a part I've been thinking could be just right for you."

Evan is known for picking people who've been a little down on their game and reviving them. Tonight at the gathering Cat told me, "He wants to Tarantino you." When I gave her a semi-confused look, she explained impatiently, "He wants to resurrect your career, girlfriend."

"What kind of part is it?" I ask, and then rather pointedly toss my hair over my shoulder. Evan needs to see the damage close-up to realize exactly what he'd be dealing with. Still, even as I confront him with the truth, my heart begins to beat with expectation. I feel wanted.

Evan gives me a gentle smile. "I don't mind the way you look, Rebecca," he tells me honestly.

"Why not?"

He leans back and takes a thoughtful sip of his wine. "I guess you could say you have the right...appearance. For this part."

"I see," I answer evenly. Nagging doubt begins to penetrate my thoughts. Evan studies me carefully, taking off his baseball cap to reveal a large bald spot I wasn't quite expecting. You never see him without a hat of some kind, and now I know why. "So," I say, "this character is scarred."

"Yes, Rebecca," he answers. "The character I have in mind for you is a lot like you."

I laugh. "An unemployed actress?" Too many margaritas and too much crowd-exposure tonight have left me feeling blank and fuzzy.

"Rebecca," Cat interjects, cautioning me with her eyes not to do anything stupid.

Evan is clearly unaffected by my sarcasm. "I could use anybody, Rebecca," he reminds me. "Makeup can create anything, you know that."

"But you're interested in..." I pause, thinking of how to frame it. "Well, making my actual scars a sort of *presence* on the screen. That's what you're after?"

"The authenticity of it, yes," he says, clearly pleased that I get his vision for the character. "Her scars are a kind of character unto themselves. They're part of the canvas."

"So, the lighting, the camera work, it would all be to overstate them, definitely not *understate* them?"

His gaze never leaves my face. "Would that make you uncomfortable?"

I imagine my smile spread across a gigantic Cineplex screen, every flaw in my appearance magnified many times over. "It scares me," I answer honestly.

"And I respect that." He gives a firm nod. "I totally respect that." He looks to Cat, then back at me. "We just thought it might be a great role for you."

"We?" Cat's been behind this introduction? What happened to my great sense of comedic understatement? To him being a fan of the reruns?

"Cat and I have been talking about it, yes."

"He's been watching the show," Cat interjects, and from the anxious look on her face, I can tell she knows the game may be up.

Evan grins. "I love your work, Rebecca." His smile is genuine, reaching his eyes. "You are so terrific with comedy. Brilliant."

"So is this a comedic role, then?"

His expression becomes guarded. "Not really."

"Oh, I get it," I say with a slight laugh. "The only thing that *really* qualifies me for this part is my facial disfigurement."

Evan stares back at me, his face growing ashen, and I actually feel bad for him. He's only trying to do a good deed here for me. Charity, celebrity style.

He watches me. "I wouldn't be offering the role if I didn't think you were one terrific actress," he tells me seriously. "You could bring an amazing depth of feeling to the part."

"Evan, thank you," I say sincerely, reaching to take his hand. "You're awesome to think of me. I am so incredibly honored, but I just don't think I can make myself that vulnerable at this stage of the game."

I remember Jake off in the bathroom and in that single moment my destiny feels encapsulated. I can never get away from myself. My scars, my past: I own them now. There will never be a day when a part for a normal person, a normal character with a boringly normal life floats my way. There will only be my ruined face.

Cat leans toward me. "Rebecca, you should at least let Evan tell you about the movie," she almost begs.

But Evan doesn't say another word. He just smiles at me. A sympathetic, gentle look that tells me he understands how I can let this opportunity slide past me.

"Thanks," I say, giving them both a little wave as I turn to go. "But I better go find Jake."

I grab Jake by the arm as he exits the bathroom; those familiar gray eyes now distinctly red around the edges. One look at him tells me my suspicions were correct.

Guiding him by the elbow, I redirect him from his path toward Evan's table. "Let's go over here." I indicate a pair of bar stools on the far side of the place.

"What about Evan Beckman?" he asks, incredulous. "We're having drinks with Evan Beckman."

"Not anymore we're not."

A quizzical frown comes over his face. "Why not?"

"We just had a fight."

"Oh." He gives a shrug and that, as they say, becomes the end of that. Sometimes it can actually be convenient when your ex is Coke Boy. "Really?"

"No, Jake, not really."

"Oh." He gives his head a stunned little shake, trying to compute why Evan has vanished during his trek to the bathroom.

We slide up onto the bar stools, and he plops his large briefcase duffel between us. He's clearly trying to cultivate a kind of director or writer look, though I guess that's where he keeps his stash. We order drinks and I wonder why I really came out with him tonight. What it is I'm always searching for when I come back to him.

"You miss me?" He chuckles.

"No, Jake. Not really." I keep my voice even, but beneath the table, my hands begin to tremble.

"How's the new boyfriend?"

"What makes you think he's new?"

"Because last I asked around, you weren't seeing anybody," he says. "That's what I heard a few months back, and then kapow, you mention a boyfriend."

"Well, he's fine, actually," I lie. "He's wonderful. He loves me. He treats me well. It's a nice departure from being with you."

"I hear you," he mutters, acting suitably subdued. "I hear you, Rebecca."

"Why am I here, Jake?" I pose the question that's in my own mind. "Why are we doing this? Can we just cut to the chase? We're not really here to relive the bad times. Are we?"

Beside him, he retrieves a script from inside his satchel. He slides it across the table toward me reverently. "Will you look at this?"

"A screenplay." I stare down at the binding, confused.

"Yeah, something I wrote. I was hoping you'd take it to your boss."

"You were hoping I'd take it to Ed," I repeat in disbelief. *A Guy Like That*, Jake's script is called. Well, at least it's not *Beautiful, But Me*.

"Yeah, Becca, that's what I'm hoping. Will you do that for me?"

"That's why you've spent the whole summer pursuing me? For a *screenplay?*"

He rakes his fingers through his shaggy bangs, obscured from me behind the dark lenses. "You make it sound so mercenary." He laughs.

"You do have an agent," I remind him irritably.

"He doesn't do stuff like this." He gestures at the script, tapping it with his fingers. "He's only handling my acting gigs."

"Of which there are so many."

He chuckles softly. "You probably think I deserve that, don't you, Rebecca?"

I lean forward, thumping the script with my hand. "I thought you missed me, Jake," I explain in a low, fevered voice. "That you wanted to see how I'm doing."

"I did," he answers with a casual shrug. "I do."

I shake my head, thinking of dear Trevor earlier by the hotel swimming pool—of him dancing with me and holding me and trying to convince me that Michael still loves me, devoted and believing the best in me when I least deserved it. And I think of Michael in his golf cart, desperate to get me to listen, while all the time I kept pushing him away. And I think of Evan Beckman, offering me a second shot at my career, and me backpedaling as fast as I could away from him.

"I've been a fool," I say and stand to leave without taking his script.

Chapter Twenty-Seven: Michael

It's sweltering hot when Andrea's wrapping up her first week of school. Man, when I was a kid, you didn't start back when it was one hundred degrees. But here it is, not quite the end of August, Andie's back in her routine—and I'm feeling like a successful parent. So far, I'm managing to remember all major homework assignments, and I've even gotten her enrolled in ballet and Girl Scouts. I'm Super Dad, clear-headed and together about this stuff for the first time since Alex's death.

The key seems to be maintaining a constant mental checklist, which I'm silently running through right now while we sit in the carpool line outside her school. That's when I remember her lunchbox and, glancing between us on the seat, I find it right there—but only after the momentary seizure of panic.

As I nudge my truck closer to the front door of her school, she turns to me. "Don't forget tomorrow's a teacher workday," she reminds me with a well-earned look of suspicion.

"Already on the calendar."

"So you called Ms. Inez?" She stares at me in wide-mouthed surprise at my efficiency.

I give her a smile. "Already on it, sweetie."

She smiles too, holding her backpack close to her chest as we pull up in front of the school's main doors. "Have a good day," I tell her. "Be careful and be safe."

I know the drill here: it's my job as the parent to be as inconspicuous as possible, not to make a fuss. No big hugs or sloppy kisses—just her scrambling onto the curb, and me giving an aloof wave goodbye. I'm doing just that, but then she surprises me, leaning across the seat to give me a quick kiss on the cheek.

"Bye, Daddy," she says, then pops out of the truck without ever looking back. I stare after her, stunned, and wonder what's gotten into her this morning: I haven't told her the truth yet, even after talking to Laurel. Not sure *when* I'm going to tell her, but I figure I'll know when the time's just right.

Maybe I'm becoming Daddy in her eyes again—earning the name—now that I'm not such a shoddy, heartbroken mess. I'm even doing a pretty damn good job of concealing my pain over losing Rebecca, keeping it together much better than I did after Alex died.

Of course with Rebecca, it's different than with Allie. I know in my heart that I'll eventually figure a way to get her back.

✧

The next morning, I'm up before Andrea, showered and dressed for work. It's Friday and I've put a lot of thought into how I want things to go today. Her birthday's next week, eight days away, and although she's having a big bash at the ice-skating rink, what I'm doing today is my biggest gift for her.

Staring at myself in the mirror, I'm momentarily startled by the man who stares back at me, at his dark curling hair, neatly trimmed. At his clear eyes—unlined by dark circles of exhaustion for the first time in about a year. He even looks like he's putting some healthy muscled weight back on, thanks to his time at the gym.

Touching my bare chest, I think of Rebecca—of her small warm hand stroking me in that very spot. Then, my hand wanders to my shoulder, and I remember her kissing my tattoo, her mouth against my sun-warmed skin, and I burn with the fleeting memory of it.

I've tried calling her a few times, but she never answers the phone or returns my messages. Still, I have an inexplicable peace when it comes to my relationship with her. Technically we're broken up, but I still feel connected, like we're only spending time apart right now.

Tugging a crisp white T-shirt over my head, I give myself a final once-over in the mirror. I'm a handsome guy still, at least on my good days—but lately I make sure I look my *best* every workday for one reason. Just in case I bump into her.

Walking into Andie's room, I sit on the edge of her bed. "Hey, sweetpea," I whisper in her ear. "Time to get up." Her eyes slowly open, a sleepy, confused look on her face. "I have a birthday surprise for you," I explain with a grin. "Time to get dressed."

She squints at me. "But Ms. Inez is coming today."

I only smile back at her, walking toward the closet. "What about this?" I ask, pulling out a sundress. "You want to wear this one?"

"For what?"

"We're going on a little field trip."

At the studio, we hurry down an alley between two sound stages. So far, Andrea hasn't figured my surprise out—or if she has, she's keeping quiet. She holds my hand dutifully, the yellow ribbon I used to tie her hair in a ponytail flapping in the breeze as she works to keep pace with my long strides. I'm walking fast because the AD told me to be on the set no later than 8:30, and we've only got five minutes to make that deadline.

We duck between another set of buildings, and then just ahead the giant placard for *Evermore* looms, huge—at least half the height of the building. Andrea squeals when she spots it, hopping beside me. "You got me a pass! Didn't you? You got me a pass!"

I shove my hands into the pockets of my jeans, feeling peculiarly shy with my own child. "Yeah, sure did."

She flings her arms around my waist, holding tight. "Michael, that's so cool. So, so cool!"

"You know, it's kinda hard to get on that list," I explain—not exactly apologizing for that day last spring, but at least clarifying the situation. "I had to put in for these passes over a month ago."

"I am so, so, so excited!" she cries, lifting up onto the balls of her feet and doing a ballerina pirouette. And then she stops, smiling up at me, her voice becoming serious. "Thank you, Michael."

She suddenly seems at least seventeen, and in her eyes I glimpse the woman she will one day become. A lump comes into my throat. "Happy birthday, sweetie. Early birthday."

"Can we see Rebecca after? Maybe?"

I anticipated this question, but it still makes my stomach tighten with nervous anxiety.

I scratch my eyebrow, searching for a solid excuse to explain the improbability of such an event. "Andie, she's working, you know."

"But couldn't I go say hi?" she asks, gazing up at me hopefully. "Just for a minute?"

She probably doesn't want to see me, I ache to tell her, but from somewhere else I hear, "Sure, I'll give her a call."

While Andie sits on the set happily watching them film her favorite show—a scene involving her most favorite character, Gabriel—I sneak away. When the buzzer sounds, signaling that cameras are no longer rolling, I step out onto the bright street behind the sound stage. Nearby, there's the rumbling motor of a honey wagon, and I poke a finger in my ear so I can hear as I dial the phone.

Trevor answers, his distinctive British accent immediately recognizable. For a moment, I think I'll simply hang up. As much as I love Rebecca, my heart tells me she's still not ready for this—and that she's especially not ready to see my daughter. But I mumble something into the phone, identifying myself and asking if Becca's there. Trevor's voice brightens, becomes much more upbeat. He's pleased I'm phoning her; I can hear it in his tone.

Although he promises that she'll be right with me, I wait a long damned time out here on the street. Finally, the buzzer sounds again, warning that the cameras are rolling once more and that it's no longer safe to enter the stage.

I'm about to give up when she comes on the line, greeting me in her sexy, southern-accented voice. She sounds familiar, yet formal, but just the sound of her voice makes my chest clinch.

"Hey, Becca," I say, feeling unexpectedly quiet. "How are you?"

"I'm doing great, Michael. Really great, thanks." She's talking down to me—talking to me from the end of a great tunnel. She's talking to me like she would Jake. Damn it, I ain't Jake, and something about her talking to me that way kind of pisses me off. So I get pretty direct and forceful, sidestepping the need for delicate formality. "I need to see you," I tell her simply.

She hesitates. "Michael, we're not a couple any more."

"I need to see you, Rebecca," I repeat, wondering if I could leave Andrea in the capable hands of the AD while I jog over to Rebecca's offices. "Andie's here today, and she's asking about you, and I thought maybe we could all go to lunch later"

"That's not *you* needing to see me," she answers softly. "That's *Andrea* needing to see me, and you needing to provide some kind of resolution for that."

"I need you too," I half-whisper into the phone, aching for her. "You've known that for a long time."

"Michael, I love Andrea. She is so incredibly precious to me, but—"

"Please, Rebecca," I beg. "It's been tough on her, you coming into her life then vanishing like this."

"I know that it has, but I can't be in your life just for her sake." She sounds crushed; the distance and order replaced by obvious pain. "That's not enough for me, and it's not fair to her, either."

"That's not fair. You know it's not just for her. You know how much I love you. How much I miss you."

Silence fills the line between us, the sound of blood rushing in my ears my only answer. "Rebecca?" I prompt her.

"I miss you too," comes her quiet, emotion-filled answer.

"Then see us," I answer hopefully. "For lunch, today. I'll come get you."

"I-I'm not ready yet, Michael."

"When will you be ready?"

"I'm not sure."

I open my mouth to tell her I love her; that I want to talk to her, for God's sake. That I want to spend forever with her; that I can handle anything but this wall of silence—but the phone goes dead before I can reply.

✧

My daughter has a perfect, glorious birthday outing, all except for not seeing her favorite celebrity on the lot, Rebecca O'Neill. I mumble a flimsy excuse about Rebecca's work schedule, and Andrea nods, frowning slightly. But the day's too fantastic for her to stay down long. We finish off at the commissary, eating together at the cafeteria table.

While we sit together, she keeps looking around, like she's searching for someone. Hoping to spot Rebecca, perhaps. Finally, I ask, "Who you looking for?"

She stares down at her plate of food, picking at it. I'm pretty sure she won't answer, but she surprises me.

"Daddy brought me here. Remember?" She looks up at me, her clear eyes shining bright. "That last day before he died."

With all that happened the next day—with all that's happened since—I never even thought about it. "No, I didn't... I didn't remember that."

She nods, looking around again. "It was last day of school, remember?" she prompts me, cocking her head sideways as she studies me. "You both came to my party, and we were gonna have lunch here, but you had a job to do."

"So Daddy brought you by himself," I finish.

She nods her head, glancing around the cafeteria. "I kinda kept thinking about it. Later," she admits. "That it was the last thing he ever did with *just* me. The last really special thing." Her mood grows serious, and she glances around the commissary again. "We played a game together. We kept trying to see how many people we could find in weird costumes. He said he wanted to be an extra and play an alien one day."

"That sounds like Daddy," I agree and we both laugh.

"How come Rebecca didn't want to see me?" she asks with a slight frown. "Is she mad at me? 'Cause if I did something to make her not like me..."

"Andrea, sweetie, no." My voice becomes firm. "It's not *you*. Rebecca's got some issues with *me*."

"Is she mad at you?"

I blow out a breath. "It's kind of complicated."

She takes a drink from her milk, sipping through her straw, and then asks, "Complicated for her? Or for us?" The amazing wisdom of my almost nine-year-old.

"You know how we've been through some hard stuff?" I begin, choosing my words carefully. "In the past year? Losing Daddy and learning to be on our own, all that stuff?" She nods, taking another sip of milk, her eyes never leaving me. "Well, Rebecca's been through some tough times too. Some really hard stuff."

She leans close across the table, dropping her voice. "At the beach, I heard Aunt Marti talking to Casey. She said somebody tried to kill Rebecca. That's how come she's got all those scars." She searches my face. "Is that really true?"

I don't want to upset her, but she deserves to understand the facts. "I think we're probably all very lucky we still have Rebecca."

"You mean 'cause she could've died," she clarifies. "'Cause that's what Rebecca told me. She said she understood about what happened to me. That she almost died and all that."

"She understood about you being in the accident?" I'm not sure what Andie's saying precisely, and at first she doesn't elaborate further. But then, without looking up, she whispers, "I told her maybe I should've died."

My mouth goes dry. She's offering my first real glimpse into what has haunted her since the accident, and I know that what I say next is crucial. Like that first night she met Rebecca, she's trying in her own nine-year-old way to communicate with me.

I clear my throat. "What did...Rebecca say about that?"

She shrugs, glancing around the commissary again, as if she's searching for Alex here among all the other crazily clad actors and extras. As if he might have been hiding here, ever since that last day they were here together. "So what are we gonna do now?" she asks, directing the subject away from this topic that I desperately want to explore.

I can't hold back any longer. "Andrea, you don't really believe you should have died?" I blurt.

She shakes her head. "No, I don't," she answers easily, taking her sandwich apart. "Not anymore. I did, though...for a while." Then she glances up into my eyes. "Michael, can we stop going to counseling now? I hate it there."

"Nobody loves seeing the doctor, but we all need to go sometimes."

She blinks back at me. "Only if we get sick."

"Or if we're hurt," I remind her. "Doctors help us then, too, remember? Like Daddy used to do over at the hospital? He'd help the kids who were sick?"

Her head pops up, and she opens her mouth, drawing in a breath. There's something she wants to say, something monumental; I know it like I know the hairs prickling on my arms.

But then her expression changes and she tugs her hand out of mine, becoming melancholy as she stares out the tall bank of windows beside us.

I've pushed too far. "What is it, sweetheart? What's wrong?" No answer, just a slight shaking of her head. "Tell me." My voice rises slightly with panic that I've broken our connection. "What are you thinking?"

She looks back at me, pain shadowing her blue eyes. "Daddy was hurt, and they didn't help him."

Panicked, I stare at her, blinking. All the people surrounding us, the din of noise and clatter of silverware intensifies around me, until I can hear nothing else, only the rushing void humming between us.

This is what I've been waiting for, hoping for. But now that I'm here, I'm terrified. From another dimension I hear a voice that sounds a lot like mine. "Sweetheart, Daddy couldn't be helped. They had to save you. It was too late for Daddy, you know that."

"No," she whispers, tears filling her eyes. "No, they could've *tried* with Daddy. But they took so long helping me."

"Is that what you think?" Tentatively, like reaching for a feral child, I touch her arm and she flinches. But she allows my hand to stay, as I ask fiercely, "That his death was your fault?"

She says nothing, doesn't answer at all. "Andrea, please," I beseech her. "Tell me. Do you really think his death was your fault?"

"I just wish they hadn't worked on me for such a long time." The paramedics told me that for more than an hour they carved and welded and worked the bent Mercedes door while she remained unconscious, unaware that her little leg was caught in the mangled wreckage. "I wish they'd helped Daddy too," she says, wiping at her eyes.

"Andrea, this might be hard to understand, but Daddy was already gone by then. The paramedics who arrived on the scene *knew* that. You know it too."

She gets a strange, distant look in her eyes, staring out the windows again. I'm not sure why, but it spooks me a little. "But he talked to me. In the car."

I'm supernaturally calm. Relaxed even, as if her comment doesn't fly in the face of everything we've been told about the accident: that my partner died immediately on impact.

"What did he say?"

"Not to be scared." She glances up at me, tears shimmering in her soft blue eyes. "That the men would help me."

I get an idea, and ask, "Like in the dreams? When he tells you he's okay?"

She nods, and I wonder when hot tears began rolling down my own face. "Sweetie, he was just looking after you," I say. "Like he always did."

"But it felt real. Like he was *alive*."

Sucking in a breath, I conjure up the lost faith of my childhood. The faith Alex was forever working to resurrect within me. I remember what Rebecca told me about the night she nearly died.

"I think he *is* alive. Just not here, not with us."

"That's how come I can't call you Daddy anymore." It's so quiet I almost miss it, this whisper-thin admission—the key to my existence. "You can't be Daddy too," she explains, "'cause then he won't be real anymore." Looking up at me, it's as if she's begging permission—maybe permission to stick with this thread of reasoning, or then again, maybe permission to finally let him go.

Or maybe she's seeking permission to truly be my daughter once again after such a broken journey together.

"Letting me be Daddy doesn't change what he was to you."

"They'll see you, and..." She looks away, hesitating. "They'll think you're my only daddy."

"You know that wasn't true."

"But you are my only daddy," she whispers, staring up at me. Beseeching me to help her through this moment. "My only *real* daddy," she finishes. I wonder if she's saying what I think, right here in the commissary. My heart races in my chest, my mouth goes dry.

I find myself yearning for the lie, wanting to rush to that default. *But I adopted you. Daddy Alex was your natural father.* Only, this time I don't. "Sweetheart, you know, our family's never come easy. For you, Daddy, and me. It was always kind of different."

She nods. And that's when I'm sure she *knows.* That perhaps she's always known—seen through our carefully constructed illusions for a long time now with the God-driven intuition of a child.

"Aunt Laurel's my mother, right?" she asks uncertainly.

"That's right, sweet pea. Aunt Laurel's your birthmother."

"And you're my father?"

I nod. "Yes, Andrea, I'm your daddy."

"That's what I thought," she answers, sucking in her lower lip. I swear there's relief on her face, as if something painful has been washed away at last.

"But you will always have a connection with Daddy," I tell her fiercely. "You do realize that, right? He adopted you, and he will always be your other father."

She nods, looking around the busy cafeteria. Like she's still searching for him. "But you still have to be Michael," she says softly. "'Cause they'll call him my uncle or... Or they just won't know he was my daddy at all."

"Well, then you tell people," I suggest. "Can't you do that?"

She considers my question, tears still shining in her eyes. "Do you really think he stayed there in the car with me? That he talked to me?"

"I think he's with you lots of times. With all of us." I remember a lost Bible verse from childhood, something about the "great cloud of witnesses". When I was a kid, I thought my mother was in that crowd, staring down at me from heaven on a riser of baseball bleachers. "I think he watches over us from heaven. That's why he's always talking to you in your dreams."

Despite the tears, a small smile forms on her lips. "Maybe that day? In the car?" she asks, the smile growing. "Maybe he just hadn't gotten to the beach yet!"

"He hadn't had time," I agree.

Then we're laughing together, uncontrollably, joyous fits of it, just like at the cemetery months ago, and I hold her hand tight, not ever wanting to let go.

"But he's always at the beach now," she says.

This time, I finish for her. "And the waves are always good!"

Chapter Twenty-Eight: Rebecca

A few days after Michael called me when Andrea was on the lot, an invitation arrives on my desk, a small white envelope printed with neat handwriting. Absentmindedly I open it while chatting with Trevor about Julian's arrival next week. As the visit draws near, Trevor is already becoming somewhat useless in the assistant department, unable to focus and prone to long gab sessions in my office. Still, he's a perfect best friend, having forgiven me easily for our poolside spat at the party.

"Oh my goodness." I stare down at the invitation clutched in my hand.

In bright rainbow colors it announces: *Andrea Richardson's Turning Nine!* Pressing it against my lips, a wave of loss washes over me. Apparently she's having a party at the ice skating rink over in Studio City, right near her house. No note is on the inside—just this invitation.

"A rocking ice skating party," I explain to Trevor, tracing the outline of the white-booted skate on the front, the blade sparkling with silver glitter. Closing my eyes, I imagine dear Andrea choosing this invitation herself. Of course she'd love the sparkles and the colors; she loves anything bright like this.

"Good, so you're going."

"You hardly seem surprised about this invite," I reflect, noting that he seemed well aware of this upcoming party. My eyes meet his. "You didn't read this, did you?"

He shrugs, polishing his eyeglass lenses. "It's my job to open your mail."

"I guess that's how this one envelope landed," I pause, shuffling through a huge pile of other mail on my desk to illustrate my point, "on the very top of the stack. Huh?"

With a slow, deliberate gesture he slips his wire frames back up the bridge of his nose. "It's what you pay me for."

"I'm not even sure I can go," I say, but I'm already flipping open my calendar. It's next Saturday afternoon, and I don't have any plans. Trevor steps around the desk until he's right beside me.

"Rebecca, don't look back at this in ten years and regret anything." My eyes lock with his. "Don't waste time wishing or thinking you might have played this hand differently. You love him."

"I spent long enough regretting things with Jake," I whisper softly.

"You shouldn't let something this precious go so easily."

I draw in a strengthening breath. "I'll think about it."

"You know, Cat phoned me last night," he says with a quizzical expression. "Told me that Evan Beckman's been asking about you."

"She told me that before."

"Cat seems to be under a misguided impression," he says with a soft laugh. "She seems to think that although Evan has indicated a desire to," he pauses, clearly searching for the right word, "*Tarantino* you, I believe she said, that he believes you're not interested in the part." He tilts his chin upward. "I wonder where he'd get a peculiar idea like that?"

Leaning back in my desk chair, I begin to laugh. "What kind of silly girl would pass on a part in an Evan Beckman film?"

He studies me in a way that says he knows me too well for me to put anything over on him. "Perhaps a silly girl who worries far too much about what the world will see."

"Perhaps," I offer, wondering how fast I can shoo him out the door and call Evan to apologize for my hasty departure the other night at Mia Mia. "Or perhaps she's a silly girl who still wants to read for that part."

"Now *that*," he says with a wink, "is my girl."

✧

My mother stands knee-deep in boxes, tape gun held expertly in her hands, when I arrive around lunchtime to help. Their moving van is due at seven a.m. the next day, and although there's still much to pack—of course they're boxing it all up themselves—she's serene. Completely unruffled. When she opens her arms and embraces me, I know that this single personality trait is the one I'll miss the most in the coming months: her ability to make the stormiest of situations feel placid. To bring tranquility to the chaos in my life, just like she has to this moving scene.

"Your father is playing golf," she announces, shaking her head with a smile. "Can you believe that?"

"I still say it's the real reason he stayed in L.A.," I tease, and she settles atop a large sealed box.

With a wave around at the sea of packing materials and brown boxes, she laughs, "Welcome to my parlor, precious. Want some tea?"

"*Sweet* tea?"

She doesn't always add the sugar and mint that makes her iced tea taste like home. This time she grins. "Of course."

With our matching chilled glasses, we settle into a lunchtime visit; my mom regaling me with details about the move home—and me listening, a bittersweet smile pasted across my face. It will never feel the same in this town without my parents here in Santa Monica, yet I know I can never complete my healing if they stay. Why must growing up—finding freedom—always be so bittersweet?

While we talk, I catch my mother watching me occasionally, stealing sideways glances to assure herself that her only child really is all right.

"I'm fine, Mama," I say finally, with a soft laugh to play off my words.

"What?" she denies, sipping her tea innocently. "I didn't say a word!"

"You can go home without worrying," I promise, smiling at her. "I am doing really great, Mom."

"But see, until you're a mother, you won't truly understand," she says tenderly. "You're my baby girl. You'll be my baby girl, even when you're thirty-five. When you're forty. When I'm eighty and on my deathbed, you will still be my baby. That's my prerogative as the mama."

My thoughts go to dear Andrea and how protective I felt of her—still feel of her, even now. She stirred some place inside me, a concealed chamber of my heart I hadn't known I possessed until I met her. She unlocked motherhood within me.

My mother leans closer toward me. "What is it, Rebecca?" she asks, sensing my thoughts with the laser-keen accuracy of the one who carried me inside her womb for nine months.

"I'm just thinking of someone," I explain, smiling. With all that Michael and Andrea have meant to me, I can't believe I've never uttered a word about them to her.

"And?" she prompts.

"Oh, Mama, you're going to get it out of me, aren't you?" Somehow, with her leaving tomorrow, I need her to know everything about Michael. "Can we go sit on the patio?" I ask, knowing how much I'll miss our Sunday afternoons out there, sipping her iced tea and playing gin. "I think I need some advice, Mom."

✧

My mother listens to the whole painful tale, from that first day at the studio to our courtship over the summer, then winding up in Malibu. I pour out my heart, crying some as I tell her about finding love and then losing it. What I had with Michael was as gorgeous and fickle as those roses my nana always grew, requiring an expert's touch—and I am clearly no expert on love.

She asks few questions, raising her blonde eyebrows only a couple of times, especially when I explain that Michael's dead lover Alex was a man.

"Oh, goodness," she titters gently at that point in the story. "We won't let *that* get out back home."

I cut my eyes at her, laughing. "Mama!"

She continues. "Imagine Darnelle Bogart if she heard that one," she breathes, leaning close to me with a conspiratorial smile. "Can you think how fast that would travel around town? Like lightning, I guarantee you!"

I smile. "Mom, we're talking about someone I love."

"Of course, Rebecca," she says, remembering herself. She continues smiling in slight amusement though, and while I wish she had reacted more seriously, I'll admit I'm relieved she's not chiding me about his lifestyle—or my own choices.

I explain about the break-up, about how he couldn't seem to let go of Alex, and her expression grows much more serious as she listens quietly.

"That only means he's loyal," she observes gently.

"But not to me."

"No," she disagrees. "It means he's loyal to anyone he loves. And you say he loves you?"

I stare at her hardwood floor, tears threatening to fill my eyes. "He did. But it's been almost two months."

"Well, of course he still loves you then, Rebecca," she says. "Because he is loyal, you can count on it. Just like he's loyal to this Alex."

"Mama, I think he's waiting for me."

"He probably is," she agrees.

"That scares me."

"Rebecca, love is never without its risks or doubts, precious," she begins thoughtfully, an appreciative expression filling her face. "Love is patient; love is kind. Love bears all things. Hopes all things." She's doing it again: wrapping life's plain truths in Scripture; she always makes it seem that the one can't be separated from the other.

Love bears all things. Of her words, those are the ones that reverberate right through me. I love Michael. I loved him before, and I still love him now. Couldn't I have borne his grief long enough, until he found his way through to the other side of it? Was my own love so tentative and fragile that it wasn't strong enough to bear the weight of his sorrow?

I bow my head, tears filling my eyes, and my dear mother simply sits beside me, wordless. She slips her arm around my shoulder, squeezing. After a time I look up, wiping at my eyes.

"You don't care that he's been with a man?" I ask, trying to picture Michael assimilating into my hometown culture, a world where Darnelle Bogart could slingshot the risqué news of our romance down Main Street in a single afternoon. "You don't worry about the gossip back home?"

"Oh, honey, I was joking," she assures me. "How will they ever know?"

"They could find out." There's always the *National Enquirer*, but I don't remind her of that.

She swats her hand at me. "Like we care!" she laughs. "Daddy and I have weathered all kinds of gossip and survived." That's true enough: with a hometown celebrity for a daughter—one with a TV expose devoted to her—they've been through it all.

"Well, this may come as a surprise to you, Rebecca Ann," she laughs. "But I *have* lived a little. And in my experience, there's nothing more important than the loyal love of a good man."

Inside her house right then, the phone rings: it's the moving company calling for directions. Our conversation is interrupted; long enough for me sit in her garden surrounded by her wind chimes and small pavement stones and sculptures, and think of how I'll miss my mother once she moves tomorrow. As long as she was here I could always run home and be safe.

I'm safe right now, but life—to be truly lived—involves risk. And I know that it's time I started living again.

Chapter Twenty-Nine: Michael

I've done my best to make a lot of things right in the past few months. To establish more credibility in my life, to get more honest. Coming clean with Andie about our family was the biggest of those steps. Sitting here on the back deck, deliberating about trying to call Rebecca one more time, I know that there's another call I should make. That I *need* to make, but I've been putting it off for more than a year now.

I pick up my cell, turning it in my palm, and know that I need to tell my father that Alex died. That we had a daughter together, years before that. And that he's a grandfather.

Truth is, ole George has tried calling me plenty of times in the past few years; I just never take the calls. I think about Ellen's words that day up in Santa Cruz. That I'm a dad, too, and I know how that kind of estrangement must be killing him.

I stand up and walk to the sliding doors that lead inside. I lean in through the open door and call out to Andie. "Sweetpea, there's somebody I'm going to want you to talk to in a little while. I think. So when I call you, come on out here, okay?"

She makes a sharp cry and tells me that she just beat her high score on Super Mario Cart. I listen for a moment, smiling as she talks to herself, and know that she's starting to come alive again. That she's healing.

And more than ever, I know I have to go make that call to my father because I'm healing too.

✧

So maybe I finally have added stalking to my list of failings because for the past seven days I've made a point of driving by Rebecca's place. I just keep thinking that if she's outside somehow, maybe going for a jog, that I can pull over and lay everything on the line. I could talk to her about Andrea's party, find out if she plans to come.

In my mind, that party is my last real shot with her. If that moment passes us by, she'll be like a sundial with me the shadow. Our point of intersection will pass like a lengthening shadow—permanently.

But the drive-bys don't yield any reward, so I'm forced to do what I'm so very terrible at: be patient. I have to let her come to me on her terms now. That's what Marti told me last night over Mexican food. "You've done the pursuing, wooing thing," she told me after I admitted to having sent her flowers last week. And owned up to the party invitation. And the late night calls.

"Rebecca has to find her way out of her darkness and back to you, Michael. You can't find that path for her."

I growled, shaking my head. "I suck at the waiting game."

Marti swatted me on the arm. "Too bad, lover boy. This one's not as easy as Alex."

"And that sucks too."

"Lord, Warner, did you forget what you're dealing with?"

I gave her a blank look, so she finished the statement. "A woman! Rebecca is a woman. Alex was easier to figure out because he was a guy, and Rebecca's not exactly opaque, but the stuff she's been through...yeah, it's gonna take a whole lot more patience than you naturally possess, old friend."

I sank down in that booth and decided I could man up on her account, become stronger and more resilient than I'd acted since we broke up. I could do the army drill and dig into the trenches for the very long haul.

Chapter Thirty: Rebecca

The ice skating rink in Studio City is teeming with cars, even at two o'clock on a Saturday afternoon. I never RSVP'd for Andrea's party; I knew if I talked to Michael on the phone, I would cave completely. That I'd be little more than a mushy puddle of regret, and I wanted time to think about my decision.

Even today, I'm still frightened and uncertain, but I know I need to be here for Andrea. I adore her, and I'm fairly certain she asked Michael to invite me. I won't let her down by not coming. More than that, though, I know what I want. *Who* I want. I've been running from him long enough.

Entering the rink, a blast of cool air contrasts to the hot September day I left outside. Boppy teenage music blares over the speakers, a nameless tune that all the little girls gathered here undoubtedly love, transforming the large dank interior into something of a disco cave. Just past the entryway, I glimpse rows of tables with balloons. There's a small lettered sign on one of the long tables with Andrea's name on it. Nobody is at the table, though—there's only the stack of birthday presents and a pink cake with a sparkling silver ice skate drawn on top in icing.

I'm glancing around, looking for a familiar face, when Michael calls out my name.

I turn. He's leaving the concession stand, juggling a container of soft drinks and popcorn between his hands, grinning at me. "I knew you'd come," he says, his throaty voice electrifying me. "You wouldn't miss her birthday."

I return the smile. "Can I help you with those?" I ask, reaching for the popcorn.

"Yeah, that'd be great," he says, relief showing on his face. "I was afraid I might drop something. Pretty damn expensive, buying all this stuff." He nods toward the stand. "But the kids have to get it, you know."

"Or it wouldn't be a party," I laugh, and he nods in agreement.

Together we walk toward the table, and I deposit my wrapped present with all the others. I'm quivering on the inside, fighting hard to keep my composure on the outside, just from being this near him again. Just from knowing what I really want for the first time in three years.

We sit down on a pair of benches facing one another. Neither of us seems to know what to say, and an awkward silence falls over us. He points toward the ice. "The girls are out there. Marti and Casey are watching them for me. Well, and a few of the parents."

"That's good." I offer him a warm smile. I want to transmit all the love I feel for him; all the emotion that I've tried to stifle these past weeks.

"Just so you know that it's okay," he explains, sounding nervous. "Us being over here, you know. Not watching and all that." He rubs his open palm over his hair. It's shorter than I've seen it before, cropped super-close, which is an incredibly appealing look on him.

You're so beautiful, I think on the inside. Outside I have no idea what to do.

I nod, and again there's silence, just the two of us sitting together at the long empty tables, wishing so much we knew what to say to one another.

"Is Andrea having a good time?" I try, gazing out at the ice.

"Oh, yeah," he grins, nodding. "A real blast. She loves ice skating. Always has."

"That's good." I stare down at my shoes. "I want it to be special for her."

Silence comes between us, the sense that each of us has so much more we long to say. But framing all those things into words is the problem and for one long moment, we simply stare into one another's eyes.

He clears his throat. "I've been wanting to apologize to you, Rebecca." He blows out a ragged breath. "For a lot of things."

I hold up my hands. "Michael, please. You don't owe me an apology."

He scratches his eyebrow thoughtfully. "Nah, see I think I do. I just careened into things with you, and didn't explain much. I wasn't fair to you at all. You'd been through a lot of stuff too, and I should've thought about that more—"

"Michael, *please* don't," I whisper, reaching out and closing my hand over his. He stares down at it, like it's a curious, unexpected find. "You have nothing to apologize for, okay?"

Without looking up at me, he says, "I promised myself that if you came—if I ever saw you again, really—I'd apologize."

"For what?" I squeeze his hand. "For letting me into your life? Into your pain? For being honest with me about all that, and about how you felt? If anything, I should be apologizing to you."

"I hurt you," he says. "I know how much I hurt you."

"But I'm strong, Michael. Stronger than you *still* think."

His fingers thread together with mine. I don't flinch; I don't fight him. I hold my breath as he slowly strokes my hand, touching the jagged scar that flames through the center of my palm.

"Your lifeline," he whispers, outlining my mark.

Tears fill my eyes. "Only you could help me see it that way."

"Andrea knows everything," he says. "About Laurel and me..." He stares out at the ice.

My chest clenches tight. "That must have been hard to do."

"No. Actually it wasn't." He glances back at me. "You were right about that, of course. The truth was what she needed."

"What changed your mind?" My lungs draw tight, the air getting tougher to draw inside. His answer matters more than I even want to admit.

"I wanted you to believe me. That I love you. If I ever saw you again, ever really got to talk to you, not some lame-ass late night call, I wanted you to know exactly how I feel. That I've loved you from the beginning," he rushes, squeezing my hand. "I needed you to know that I'm a truthful guy. That it's not all bullshit. I needed you to know that I want to make a family with you. It's real, what I want. I want you, but it's more. I want a life with you. A full, whole life."

Bowing my head, tears blur everything. In the background I hear laughter, the sound of kids approaching. The sound of my future—my potential future—I think as my tears begin to fall.

"Michael, you didn't have to tell her for me," I manage to say, though my throat is closed tight.

"Actually, I did. But I needed it for Andrea too. And for me." He draws in a breath, and gazes beyond me, out at the ice, contemplative. "You know, Alex wanted to take Andrea to New York for her birthday last fall. He wanted to take her to Rockefeller Center for ice skating. And that never happened 'cause he died." He looks back to me significantly. "That taught me something, Becca. That we only have today. That's our only guarantee. Not even the whole day. Just this hour. This minute."

"That's why you had the party for her, isn't it?" I ask, realization forming.

"We couldn't take her to New York together, so yeah." He glances around the rink. "This seemed like a good substitute."

"*You* can still take her to New York."

"And one day I will," he agrees. "Maybe you'll go with us." He gazes into my eyes for a long moment. Hope, promise, love; everything he's spent these months yearning for flickers in his golden eyes.

My cheeks flush warm, something fluttering wild inside my stomach. "I'd love that," I answer, and he breaks into a gorgeous smile, his dimple showing.

"I'd love it too," he answers softly. "For us to go as a family, all three of us."

"A family?" My voice catches and he unfolds my fingers, revealing the center of my palm. Very slowly he traces his thumb across my scar.

"Your lifeline tells me you've got a bold future, Rebecca O'Neill." He studies the jagged mark left by Ben's knife in the center of my hand. "I see children, a husband. Maybe three children of your own... and one adopted daughter who worships every piece of ground you walk on."

With an intense expression, he scrutinizes the scar that I've detested for so long.

"Do you see anything else?" I ask in a shaky voice, realizing he's just proposed marriage here in the rink. "An alternative future?"

"*Is* there an alternative?" His expression grows intensely serious. "'Cause I can't see any future for you that doesn't include Andrea and me."

Leaning close, I gaze with him into my palm, open there on his knee. "That's funny," I say. "Neither can I."

Wordlessly, he clasps my face within his large hands, drawing my lips to his for a kiss. "I love you, Rebecca. It's deep and scary and intense. But it's right. God, I know that it's right."

Covering his hands with mine, I notice something. "You took off his ring," I say, feeling tears sting my eyes.

"It was tough, but it was time." He nods. "Time for the future."

"I'm still frightened, Michael." I close my eyes, feeling his lips brush against mine. "But I'm determined to run free this time."

"And I'll run right with you, wherever you take me," he promises with a kiss. "As far as you want to go."

For some reason, kissing him there in that chilly ice-skating rink, I recall surfing. Riding high and charging the waves on my knees, free like the wind, like the unhindered little girl I used to be. Alex wanted me to surf so I'd understand that feeling, I think, because he lived that way. And so I'd recognize it when it came again for me, like it has today.

Free, free like the wind, I think, as I kiss my fiancé one more time.

Epilogue: Michael

Fall in Monterey Bay brings crisp hues of blue and gold against an azure sky—nothing like the hazy scrim holding fast over Los Angeles, with the Santa Ana winds kicking fire and smoke and moodiness down our way. No wonder October's always been my favorite time to escape to Santa Cruz; and no wonder Alex made such a point of bringing me here that first fall we were together, walking me out the length of the pier until we leaned over the railing and listened to the sea otters barking. We stood there, feeling the fresh wind and brine in our faces, and I knew I'd found my lost home.

No wonder I made such a point of bringing Rebecca here today. 'Cause she needs to know this world—his world—because it's more a part of me than any of the countless towns where my father's lived and ministered. It's *my* world now too.

We came up yesterday to spend the night and go to church with Ellen this morning. Surprisingly, I managed to sit through the service without squirming too much; I liked Father Roberto's style. I should've known that anyone Allie loved would have been someone I'd relate to. Now that the service is over, everyone's filing out of the small historic church.

My dead partner's childhood priest is standing in the portico of St. Anthony's, greeting his parishioners as they move into the dappled sunlight. I've heard so much about Father Roberto over the years that it's almost weird to think I only met him one other time before—Alex's funeral. He sure knows a hell of a lot about me.

Alex often confided in him about my spiritual standoff, and from what I've heard, Father Roberto often counseled patience to my partner. Yeah, boy, the good father's sure gonna be surprised to see me here today. He catches sight of Andrea first, and his weathered face lights up. "Hey, Father Berto!" She bounds up to him, slipping her pale arms around his rotund, robed body.

"Why, Andrea Richardson!" He laughs jovially, reaching deep into the sleeve of his robe for a handkerchief to wipe his perspiring brow.

"Nobody told me you were here visiting."

"We kind of snuck in," she says, looking between Rebecca and me. That's a good way to put our last minute visit to Santa Cruz this weekend, so that Ellen could finally meet Rebecca before we begin planning our upcoming wedding in earnest. I needed to tell her in person, and like I expected, she cried. But she looked very pleased too, fussing over Rebecca and our engagement—to the point of embarrassing both of us. Maybe it's easier for Ellen this way somehow, me winding up with someone so completely different from her son.

Father Roberto glances at me, clearly surprised to see me in church for once. Extending my hand boldly, I remind him of my identity, not that he'd have any doubts. "Michael Warner," I announce. "Good to see you again, sir."

Then remembering myself, I indicate Rebecca, knowing this one's gonna shock him for sure. "Uh, Father, this is my fiancée. Rebecca O'Neill." But he doesn't seem nearly as surprised as I expect him to be. Maybe Ellen debriefed him ahead of time? Then again maybe not, since he asks with twinkling eyes, "Irish Catholic?"

Becca smiles and shakes her head. "Southern Methodist, sorry."

"We're happy to greet all kinds in the house of the Lord," he affirms, then turning back to me, "Where are you going to be married? Do you know yet?"

"Back in Georgia," Rebecca answers. "At my home church that I grew up in."

"Ah, lovely. That will be just lovely. A southern wedding."

"Next spring," I explain awkwardly.

"I'm going to be the flower girl," Andrea pipes up with an angelic smile. "I get to pick my dress too."

Ellen breaks away from a group of women nearby to join us. "I see you found Michael." Ellen reaches up and pats my cheek, bestowing a radiant smile on me. "I'm very proud of my adopted son." Then, she turns to Rebecca, extending her arm around her inclusively. "*And* of my daughter-to-be. Isn't she beautiful, Father?" she asks, reaching to brush a long strand of blonde hair away from Rebecca's cheek. It's her scarred one, and for a moment I wonder why Ellen would be so thoughtless, but as she stares at sweet Rebecca admiringly, I get it. She's just working her Richardson magic on my chosen one. And while Becca blushes a little, and seems embarrassed at the compliment, I also see how pleased she is at the way Ellen dotes on her in front of all her friends.

On the outside steps, I turn back to look at the church. I wonder why I always fought passing through these doors for such a long time. The Lion of Judah, I've heard God called, and growing up I always thought that lion wanted to devour all of me. Before I could crawl he took my mother, and then when I found sweet Allie—my first true love, my soul mate—that lion and my father turned both their backs right on me.

But lately, you know, with all the good in my life—all the perfect gifts I have—I'm starting to think the one who did that turning away was actually me.

✧

Back at the house, we wind our way up a curving staircase to the third floor, an area I haven't seen since my earliest days with Alex, not since a building inspector told Ellen that it wasn't safe to climb up to the cupola anymore without serious renovation. Now, with the recent restoration work she's had done, that majestic perch is finally open again so Andie can see it for the very first time, something she's always wanted to do.

Laurel leads the way, her clogs echoing like thunderclaps on the antique hardwood steps with Andrea following close behind. The stairs are steep, creaky, and my daughter measures out each one, taking giant steps behind her birthmother. For a moment she nearly stumbles and I place a steadying palm on her back.

"Thanks, Daddy," she says, and as usual I grin just to hear her call me that again.

Rebecca is our rearguard: solid, strong, confidently taking each unknown step as if they've always been a part of her. It's eerie how much she belongs in this house, and not for the first time I think of how much Alex would have loved her. And she would have definitely loved him—not like I did, no, but there would have been a soul connection, I'm certain of it.

"Oh, wow!" Andrea proclaims before we even reach the top of the stairs that end in one windowed circular room overlooking the Pacific. Clear blue sky rushes out to a horizon line of dark, mysterious ocean.

"It's something, isn't it?" Laurel halts at the top, stepping sideways so we can all fit along the railing. She stands, hand on her hip, admiring the towering view of the rocks and ocean down below.

I remember the first time Alex unveiled this secret room to me, his favorite in the whole house. Right at sunset he snagged two glasses of wine for both of us, and led me up the narrow, spiraling staircase, whispering like it was a conspiracy. We slid down to the floor together, hidden from his family, and nestled right up against the windows until the burning daylight melted into night. Like a pair of renegade pirates sequestered away together.

Laurel glances around the area, her eyes taking in all the timeless relics, the driftwood and paperbacks. A few of her oil paintings lie propped against the windows, early crude works from when she was just a girl.

"When Alex and I were little," she says, "we used to come up here and play for hours." Although she smiles, I glimpse sadness in her expression. "We'd pretend we were sea captains or royalty."

"It's amazing!" Andrea agrees, slipping past Laurel to the cushioned window seat that offers the best view through the huge pane of windows. Across the road and far below us, foamy waves break on the rocks. Rebecca steps onto the landing beside me, and I reach for her, needing to feel her. Cupping her shoulder, I draw her close, and we stand together beside Laurel that way, staring out the window. For long moments, none of us speaks because we're awestruck by the mysticism of the view, the memories, of the knowledge that Alex Richardson left some part of himself here years ago. And of the knowledge that in a very elemental way he lives because he lives between us.

"I want to show you something, Andrea," Laurel says, dropping to her knees. "It's in the window seat." Lifting the cushion up, then tugging on a rope handle, the bottom gives way to reveal a cubbyhole. "It's something your daddy and I put in here, a long, long time ago. Come look."

"What is it?" Andrea asks, lifting onto her tiptoes to stare over Laurel's shoulder.

"You have to see."

Delicately, Laurel removes a fragile bird's nest from inside. "It's a robin's nest. We found it over in Lighthouse Field one day," she explains. "Our treasure, we called it. Of course everything was treasure back then."

Andrea peers at the downy husk of a nest, her blue eyes sparkling. "It's really old, then."

"Yeah, it is," Laurel agrees quietly, and her voice fills with a wistful tone I understand completely. Alex should be here. But Laurel shakes the mood, her clear blue eyes widening mischievously. "I want to tell you a story about your daddy," she says and Andrea kneels in front of her, nodding encouragingly. "Did you know that he always knew you were coming one day?"

"How?"

"I don't know. But he did. Whenever we played games up here, and imagined that we were a prince and a princess in the turret, he would say, 'let's remember this and bring our kids up here one day.'" I'm not sure where Laurel's going, but I listen intently, feeling Becca's heartbeat beneath my hand. She's wearing this soft, oversized sweater that lets me nestle her right up against me, be as brazen as I want.

Laurel goes on: "'Let's play like it's later,' he'd say."

"What do you mean?" Andrea asks.

"He always wanted to pretend that we had grown up and that there was another little princess. He was the daddy and she was the little girl."

"Is that true?" Andrea asks, her voice breathy and quiet. Frankly, I'm thinking Laurel must've made this story up, until she reaches into the window seat and retrieves something else, something that must be fragile and precious from the way she holds it in the palm of her hand. Then I see it, and it's unbelievable. Three tiny sculpted figures. "I made these for his Christmas present," she explains, revealing two little red-haired children, a boy and a girl. "When we were ten. Look, this is the other princess," she says, showing a redheaded little girl.

"Wow! He knew I was coming," Andrea says in wonder, and whether it's even precisely true or not doesn't really matter as she cradles the little figurine in her palm. She feels known, wanted. She feels as if she were destined in some way to be linked to the man she will always remember as father.

"You have no idea how much he wanted us to have you," I assure her.

She nods, pressing the little child doll to her lips, and just stares out at the ocean. Pensive, as she often gets, and none of us push her. After a while, she quietly asks, "Aunt Laurel?"

"Yes, sweetheart?"

"He really was my daddy, wasn't he? Even though he was my uncle, he really was my daddy, right? In the ways that count?"

"Oh, yes, pumpkin. Absolutely."

Andie cradles the little figure in her hand for a moment, then delicately, almost prayerfully, places it back into the bottom of the window seat. Like she's offering a benediction.

Then she turns back to us, focusing on Laurel. "Aunt Laurel, can I ask you something else?"

"Anything."

"What do I call you now? Now that I know you're my mother?"

Laurel kneels there, right down on Andrea's level. "Whatever feels right, pumpkin," she says. "You can call me Aunt Laurel, like you always have."

"Or Mom?" Andie suggests, her blue eyes hopeful.

"If that feels right, that's okay too," she answers with a gentle smile. "I carried you for nine months, Andrea, and there's a place inside of me that will always belong to you. I will always be your mother, no matter what you decide to call me."

"When Daddy and Rebecca get married, I might call Rebecca Mom too," Andrea says softly. "That won't make you mad, will it?"

I feel Rebecca's body tense against mine; know that she's holding her breath. This is the first either of us has heard of this request.

Laurel nods her encouragement. "Of course that's okay."

"You know, I'm lucky," Andrea says with a shy smile, glancing back at Rebecca for a moment. "'Cause I've had two daddies. And I get to have two mothers too. Not everybody gets that."

Laurel whispers, "And I'm lucky, because I have you."

Andrea hurls herself into Laurel's arms, burying her face against her birthmother's chest. For endless moments, they hold one another, Laurel stroking her long shiny hair, Andie snuggling even closer. "I love you, Andrea," Laurel says, and I see tears glint in her eyes. "Very much, sweetheart."

"I love you too," says Andrea, her voice muffled. Then she leans back and stares right up at me. Fixing me with that unnerving, blue-eyed look that sometimes reminds me so much of Alex, she asks, "Daddy? I'm glad I know the truth." I can't help the tears that instantly mist my eyes. "That you really are my daddy."

"Me too, sweetheart." I hold her tight and close, afraid of so much as breathing. "Me too."

"Know what else?" she asks, eyes sparkling. "I'm gonna teach Rebecca how to *really* surf next summer. She's gonna rip! And I'm not even gonna think about my scar again 'cause it doesn't matter anymore," she says. "That scar's just a tiny part of me."

Pure wisdom, from the mouth of a nine-year-old, and the thing is, I know that she's right. I know that of all the perfect, beautiful memories that Alex and I once shared, of all the new memories I'm forging with Rebecca and Andrea—and of all the most tragic times in my life—one thing is true.

For better or worse, they're all a part of me.

About the Author

To learn more about Deidre Knight, please visit www.DeidreKnight.com. Send an email to Deidre Knight at Deidre@DeidreKnight.com or join her Yahoo! group to join in the fun with other readers as well as Deidre Knight! http://groups.yahoo.com/group/DeidreKnightgroup

An injured horse. A wary woman. Healing them could cost his heart.

Second Hope
© 2009 JB McDonald

Nat Jackson knows what she's good at: healing horses. Relationships? She learned about the price of those from her mother. When Cole Masterson shows up at her Second Hope ranch with a bad shoulder and a lame horse, she's more than willing to treat the animal. But his money comes with a catch—he insists on staying at the ranch while his horse undergoes treatment.

The horse, she can handle. Resisting the man...that's a complication she doesn't need.

Money is no object when it comes to his horses, and Cole knows Second Hope offers the best in equine rehab. He hadn't counted on Nat's fractured heart awakening his desire to mend it. Her skills have his horse on the fast track to health, though. There's not much time to work his way through her defenses before it's time to leave.

Nat has no intention of getting her hopes up only to have them dashed. Cole's already thrown his heart over the fence—and he has no choice but to follow it in pursuit of the woman of his dreams.

Warning: This book contains hunky cowboys, gorgeous horses, awesome cowgirls, lots of tight Levi's, and heartbreaking injuries. Oh, yeah, and m/f sex.

Available now in ebook and print from Samhain Publishing.

Enjoy the following excerpt from Second Hope..

Cole's gaze landed on her. She was looking about as if seeing a treasured friend, gaze light with joy. The filtered sunshine poured over her, making sweat-damp skin glow, creating soft shadows in the curves of her body, the planes of her stomach. Her tank top was snug, outlining the heavy curve of her breasts and the long lines of muscle down her torso. Jeans hung low on her waist, a leather belt with a silver buckle accentuating the swell of her hips.

Streaks of dirt smeared one arm and shavings pooled near her ankles, in the folds of her jeans. Her scuffed boots had mud caked on the heels. Her nails were dirty, and her black hair had escaped from its braid, clinging to the long line of her neck.

"It's beautiful." Cole smiled softly.

Nat glanced at him. The moment of realization when she knew he'd been watching her was plain. She laughed quietly and looked away, wandering off toward the nearest oak. "I've always liked this place. When I first started the ranch I'd come out here just to get away. Clear my head. See something alive and growing, rather than the horses that needed so much help. Out here, nothing needed me like that." She glanced back, one hand spread on the trunk. "We got a lot of wrecks, in those days. We couldn't afford the best of anything yet, and a lot of the horses were rescues. A lot of them couldn't be saved."

He didn't know what to say, so he simply remained quiet.

She looked at the tree, head tipping back as she gazed upward into its branches, chin tucking as she lowered her face, tracing the line of the trunk back down to her hand. Her thumb rubbed over a scar in the bark, and she smiled faintly. "This was the first horse we managed to pull through. Just Aaron and I then—he was a snot-nosed little punk trying to get as far from his family as he could without leaving the horse world. Blue mohawk and stoned every night. And then we healed King, and something about that healed Aaron." Her smile grew, blooming across her face. "He called his parents that night. He'd run away when he was sixteen, and it was the first time he'd spoken to them in five years."

"Maybe he just needed to know he could do something good without them." Cole could remember the first time he'd succeeded at a job without standing on his father's or brother's shoulders. It had been liberating. For the first time, he'd felt grown up.

He wondered, suddenly, if Nat had ever been a child in that way. If she'd ever had shoulders to stand on. "Your grandmother helped you with this place, didn't she?"

Nat shrugged. "She gave me the money. When she died, she left me the rest. I think she was trying to keep my mother from having it. They never spoke. My grandmother didn't approve of my father, whether or not he was a doctor." Her smile was bitter. "She had more sense than my mother did."

Cole wandered closer, lifting his good hand to brush it over the wooden scar she kept fingering. The bark was paler here, and there was a line of smaller scratches, a few inked lines from a marker, some dates. "Are these all the horses you've helped?"

"The ones we saved, that first year." Nat pointed to one of the red lines. "These are the ones we lost."

There were more than a few, but they didn't outnumber the scars. "You did well."

Nat chuckled, shifting to lean against the tree, shoulder pressed to wood. "Considering what we had? We did all right. The cases got tougher as time went on, but we got a lot more rich people too."

"Like me." He grinned.

Her mouth tipped, echoing his expression. "Like you. Only most people just send their horses. Not sure how good I'm gonna be at mending rotator cuffs."

He laughed at her teasing. "Well, you have to start somewhere, Doctor Nat."

She just shook her head and chuckled in return, but her eyes were lighter now, the sadness gone. "Does it hurt much?"

"Not much. I think it's healing pretty well." He stretched his neck, rubbing at where the sling dug into his shoulder. "I think this is giving me more pain than the tendon, anymore."

"You could adjust it?" She stepped closer and he went still, turning his head slightly so she could get a better look.

Her touch was featherlight, her scent intoxicating. Like blueberries and cream, rich and sweet without being sickly.

"Is this any better?"

He couldn't tell any difference, but he could feel her body heat. His gaze caught hers, and fire rippled between them. "Yeah." His voice dropped into its deepest registers, coming out husky.

Nat's tongue flicked out, dampening her lips. Dark pupils dilated to spill black across her irises. "You didn't even pay attention."

Cole smiled. It stretched over his face, slow and seductive. "No. I didn't." He didn't think she cared, from the way her eyes flickered to his mouth, following his lips as he spoke. His hand rose as if of its own volition, rubbing away a smear of dust along her jawbone. She had a delicate jaw, for all that she was strong. Like a razorblade, sharp and fine. It narrowed down to a perfect little chin under a full mouth. He remembered that mouth from the night before. Remembered how her lips had parted under his, the tiny exhale he doubted she'd been aware of. The way her tongue had stroked his, the way she'd tasted, felt, smelled.

He wanted to taste her again, feel her under him, smell arousal and sex build. Moving slowly, remembering how she'd taken the lead before, he slid his fingers around the nape of her neck. Her skin was chilled despite the warm weather. When he fitted his mouth to hers she shivered, the finest tremble of skin and muscle, so faint he almost didn't feel it.

She wavered, seemingly caught between stepping closer and stepping away. He kept the kiss light, gentle, fingertips and soft brushes of his mouth, nothing more. He didn't want to push.

She stepped closer, fitting her body to his. He nearly groaned with relief, pressing tightly against her. One slender hand wrapped around his neck and her mouth opened, deepening the kiss. Her tongue slid against his and he responded, exploring her mouth, the way she tasted. His pulse beat thick and heavy under his skin, in his groin. He shifted his thigh to press between her legs. She caught her balance, opening for him slightly, pressing back.

The temptation was to push harder, to pin her against the tree and keep things moving along fast until they both came. He fought it, keeping his movements slow and gentle. Once you'd won over a skittish horse, you didn't mess it up by asking for too much, too soon. Still, his good hand skimmed over her jaw, under it, tipping her head up so he could duck his face into her neck, nibble on the slim line of her throat. Her skin was warm, a little salty, and he could feel the beat of her heart in her jugular.

She exhaled, breath soft and shivering. Cole did it again, teeth scraping gently over flesh, pulling that exact little tremble from her that was so thoroughly intoxicating. His fingertips slid over her skin, down one of the slim tendons that framed her throat, and lit on her collarbones. He brushed over them, marveling over how tiny the bones were, like bird wings arcing in from the points of her shoulders.

Her hands moved firmly over his rib cage, over the heavy pads of muscle, pulling him closer. His fingertips glided downward, touch featherlight against the edge of a perfect breast clothed in the thin material of a tank top and bra. A shiver crept through her, her hand stuttering on his ribs.

Cole smiled against her before placing a careful kiss on her neck, another on her throat, opening his mouth and flicking his tongue across her flesh. Her hands tightened in his shirt, curling into small, demanding fists. With his good hand he grazed her arm, trailing down, feeling the tiny soft hairs and the firmness of muscle under skin. Then he found her waist, kept moving down until he felt the edge of her jeans. He tugged at her tank top, pulling it free to find warm, elastic flesh.

His kissed her again as his fingertips skimmed over abdomen muscle, teasing at the edge of her rib cage. Her mouth opened, tongue brushing against his lips. She tasted like warm summer sunshine and lazy mornings, long rides and slow laughter. Tongues tangled and slid together, tasting, exploring, growing bolder and more heated. He slid his hand up under her shirt, following the line of her rib cage to the edge of her bra. There he hesitated, giving her a moment to pull back, to slow things down. Instead, she pressed into him with a tiny sound almost caught in her throat.